"Dianne Sylvan ... ability to bring h ... pound with action, re ... for the next install-ment of the Shadow World series . . . Sylvan presents readers with yet another compellingly compelling story."

—*Nocturne Romance Reads*

"The third Shadow World urban fantasy is a great, exhilarating entry with several stunning twists, including a fabulous, shocking cliff-hanging climax. Fans will believe in the Sylvan mythos thriving in a modern technological world . . . Fast-paced with backstabbing and betrayal, *Shadow's Fall* is superb."

—*Alternative Worlds*

"*Shadow's Fall* is an exciting, well-executed third installment to Ms. Sylvan's wonderful Shadow World, and I now wait impatiently for the fourth installment."

—*Smexy Books*

"It's the true talent of a writer who can have her readers feeling the same things as her characters along with them, and Sylvan's highly developed characters do just that."

—*SF Site*

PRAISE FOR

SHADOWFLAME

"I absolutely loved this book! . . . Fans of vampire books everywhere, I have found the next big thing, and it is the Shadow World series by Dianne Sylvan. The twists and turns that Sylvan placed in this book kept me flying through the pages . . . Queen Miranda is one of the strongest female characters I have come across, and hands down this series is going to be sensational! I cannot rave enough over this one."

—*Fresh Fiction*

continued . . .

"Dianne Sylvan's writing is captivating. She creates a world that will suck you in from the get-go. Her writing style is fluid and unrelenting. *Shadowflame* follows the same near-flawless writing style that book one did . . . I enjoyed the suspense and Dianne Sylvan's creative way of keeping readers on their toes."   —*Nocturne Romance Reads*

"If you thought *Queen of Shadows* was fantastic, you are going to be blown away by *Shadowflame* . . . Dianne really knows how to rip your heart out and get you feeling everything the characters are feeling as you read. Go out and buy it now; if you have not read *Queen of Shadows* yet, go out and buy that one, too, because you won't want to miss them."
—*Urban Fantasy Investigations*

"*Shadowflame* succeeds the previous *Queen of Shadows* in so many ways, and you are left wondering if it is even possible to turn the pages fast enough. Dianne Sylvan has truly created a vampire world that I would want to be a part of for years to come . . . A phenomenal book from beginning to end."   —*Mystifying Paranormal Reviews*

"Dianne Sylvan is the queen of emotional storytelling . . . I loved it. Even the gritty, hard parts. Sylvan goes where other authors don't dare. And I praise her for it."
—*The Spinecracker*

PRAISE FOR
QUEEN OF SHADOWS

"Sylvan's powerful debut is packed with startling action, sensual romance, and delightfully nerdy vampires . . . [Her] compelling take on vampirism, her endearing characters, and a complex, unabashedly feminist plot will have readers hungry for a sequel."   —*Publishers Weekly* (starred review)

Ace Books by Dianne Sylvan

QUEEN OF SHADOWS
SHADOWFLAME
SHADOW'S FALL
OF SHADOW BORN

OF SHADOW BORN

DIANNE SYLVAN

ACE BOOKS, NEW YORK

THE BERKLEY PUBLISHING GROUP
Published by the Penguin Group
Penguin Group (USA) Inc.
375 Hudson Street, New York, New York 10014, USA

USA / Canada / UK / Ireland / Australia / New Zealand / India / South Africa / China

Penguin Books Ltd., Registered Offices: 80 Strand, London WC2R 0RL, England
For more information about the Penguin Group, visit penguin.com.

OF SHADOW BORN

An Ace Book / published by arrangement with the author

Ace Books are published by The Berkley Publishing Group.
ACE and the "A" design are trademarks of Penguin Group (USA) Inc.

For information, address: The Berkley Publishing Group,
a division of Penguin Group (USA) Inc.,
375 Hudson Street, New York, New York 10014.

ISBN: 978-0-425-25980-1

PUBLISHING HISTORY
Ace mass-market edition / April 2013

PRINTED IN THE UNITED STATES OF AMERICA

10 9 8 7 6 5 4 3 2 1

Cover art by Gene Mollica.
Cover design by Annette Fiore DeFex.

To Mom and Dad,
who gave me a home, love, and room in which to dream

PART ONE

On Dark Wings

One

"Brave new world, friends! Brave new world!"

Bill raised his glass to the entire bar, or at least the half-dozen vampires that were out tonight. This was the only place he'd found open, but tonight was a night for a party.

The bartender looked nervous at his toast. "Keep it down, Bill . . . Somebody might hear you."

"Screw 'em," Bill replied with a laugh. "We're free, man. No more rules, no more looking over your shoulder." He turned back to the bar, but nobody was making eye contact; in fact, they looked scared. "Oh, come on—eighteen years we've been too afraid to piss in this territory without permission. Now it's back to the good old days—the Auren days. Remember when we could eat whoever we wanted and live like real vampires, not some pussy-whipped hippies?"

He looked over at the guy two stools down. "How about you, friend? Have a drink with me to celebrate."

Eyes a strange shade of lavender fixed on his. "Why not?"

Bill motioned to the bartender, who let out an exasperated breath and poured out two shots. The other vampire, a slender, sort of girly-looking fellow with pierced eyebrows and a black leather coat buttoned up to his neck, clinked glasses with him, then knocked back the shot smoothly.

"Are you a native of this territory?" the pale-eyed vampire asked over the rim of his shot glass. He looked at Bill as if he were studying him in a zoo, and if Bill hadn't already had most of a bottle, he might have been uneasy.

"Ninety-eight years," Bill said. "Long enough to have seen Primes come and go and know we're better off without this one."

"And what about the next one?" he asked. "What if he's as bad as Solomon?"

Bill laughed again. "Nobody's as bad as Solomon. Bastard was tracking all of us like criminals, making us live like slaves."

"Oh? I heard that the population here nearly doubled in his tenure—why would that happen if everyone was so miserable?"

"Beats the shit out of me. All I know is, I'm gonna go out there and rip a few throats, and there isn't a damned soul who can stop me."

He set down the glass and smiled. "I can think of at least one damned soul who can."

Before Bill could reply, there was a sword pointed at his throat.

Bill's shot glass clunked down onto the bar, spilling the last few drops of whiskey, but the bartender was standing there gaping and didn't make a move toward it. "I—I—"

With his free hand, the pale-eyed vampire opened the collar of his coat, revealing the glowing emerald that hung from his neck. Bill swallowed hard, terror gripping him in a cold fist.

"Tell all your friends," the vampire said in a quiet, calm voice that everyone in the bar could still hear. "This territory is still protected by a Signet. The law stands as before. Put one fang out of line and I will gut you, take your head, and sow your corpse with salt."

Bill was panting. "Who . . . who the hell are you?"

An icy smile. "Just a temp." He lowered the sword, casting his gaze around the bar. No one was looking, but everyone was listening. "Spread the word," he said.

Then he tossed a folded bill onto the bar, nodded to the bartender, and walked out into the darkness.

There's a vampire on my couch.

"Lark, seriously, this is the fifth message I've left you. I've been trying to reach you since last night—I need you to come over, okay? I'll explain when you get here."

The living room was as dark as she could get it, with blankets hung over the one window, but Stella had a candle burning on her altar and its light flickered in the jewel-toned hair of the unconscious woman who hadn't so much as twitched in nearly thirty hours. Once in a while Stella could see her chest rise and fall, but it was the only sign Miranda Grey was even alive. Her skin was ashen, and the aura of power that had surrounded her when they'd met seemed to have evaporated into the night as Stella half led, half carried her to the car and across Austin to Stella's apartment.

Even the light in her Signet was dull. It still shone, but through a glass darkly. Stella would have called it a coma if Miranda were human. Did vampires have comas?

There's a vampire on my couch. This is not my life.

She wanted desperately to call her father. He might have some idea what the hell was going on . . . but her intuition told her to wait, and it was intuition that had led her to the building downtown just before the front of it blew out and turned the whole world into hell. She somehow didn't think the human police would know anything more about the whole thing than she did.

Miranda hadn't spoken or even acknowledged Stella's presence once they were in the car. She just fell against the window and passed out.

Stella stood in the doorway between the living room and the tiny kitchen, chewing on her fingernail, wondering what she was supposed to do now.

She'd done the best she could to make Miranda comfortable, whatever that meant in this situation—she'd pulled her boots off, unbuckled the sword from her waist and laid it on the coffee table, wiped the soot off her face and swabbed at the wounds all over her torso . . . but by then the gashes were already healing, leaving only angry pink scabs in their wake. Stella had debated with herself on whether to do anything else, but the sight of all those bloody holes in Miranda's shirt was too creepy, so she wrestled the singer out of her clothes and into a set of Stella's pajamas. They were about three sizes too big but would have to do for now. She doubted Miranda would care at this point.

Long about noon, there was a knock.

Stella jumped about a mile and squeaked. Warily, she checked the peephole, then let out a massive sigh of relief. She darted over to the couch and yanked a throw blanket down over Miranda's exposed skin, just in case—the front door opened into a short hallway, but she had no idea how much sunlight was too much.

Lark was just about to pound on the door again when Stella opened it.

"Jesus Fancy Dancing Christ, Stell! What is all this?" Lark, who looked more worried than Stella had ever seen her, held up her phone and the list of missed calls and texts.

"Where the hell have you been?" Stella demanded, hauling her inside and locking the door again.

"Hung over, of course," Lark replied. "I had my phone off. What's the big emergency?"

Stella ushered her into the living room and gestured helplessly at the couch.

Lark gave her a dubious look. "Um . . . you know how I always said I'd help you bury a body? That was a metaphor, sweetie."

Stella sighed again. "No . . . look."

She lifted the blanket.

Lark's mouth dropped open. "Is that . . . ?"

"Yeah."

"What the . . . ?"

"I have no idea."

"How did . . . ?"

Stella pointed at her altar, where the tarot cards were still spread as she'd left them. "I was doing a reading, and I had a vision. I followed it downtown to this building that was on fire, and found her in the street."

Lark, eyes still huge, sank down in the rickety armchair they'd scavenged from behind a furniture store. "There's a famous person on your couch."

Stella nodded.

"And . . . she's wearing your Hello Kitty pajamas."

Wordlessly, Stella picked up the remains of Miranda's shirt from the table and held it up so Lark could see the dozen holes in it. "She was shot," Stella said. "With a bunch of arrows."

"Arrows." Lark lowered her eyes from the shirt to Miranda, then seemed to notice what was on the coffee table. "And the sword . . . ?"

"Hers."

Stella and Lark stared at each other for a moment. Stella took a deep breath. "Remember that night we went to the fetish club and you blacked out? Well . . . you didn't black out. We were attacked. By vampires. Miranda wiped our memories, or she tried to, but it didn't work on me because of my gift. I bet if you concentrated hard enough on that night, it would come back to you, too. I don't think they're used to messing around with Witches' memories."

There was no immediate reply, so Stella went on hurriedly. "I was right—she's a vampire. She's a really important vampire, it turns out, and so's her husband. There's a whole freaking society of them out there. And I don't know what went down last night, but someone tried to kill her, and I brought her here. She hasn't woken up. She hasn't even moved. I didn't know what to do, so I called you."

Lark just stared at her for a minute.

"Okay," she finally said, very carefully, as if speaking to a psychotic who might go off at any second. "Are you sure she's a vampire?"

Rolling her eyes, Stella bent over Miranda and gently took hold of her face; she pried the singer's mouth open slightly, exposing her upper teeth, and poked at a canine.

Lark sucked in an astonished breath as the tooth slid downward, then back. "Okay. I believe you. Okay. What do we do?"

"I don't know. I just . . . I have this feeling she's in danger and we have to keep her safe."

"Why in hell would you want to protect a vampire? She could kill us!"

"It's not like that," Stella insisted. "She's one of the good guys. I think. They rescued us from the ones that attacked us and took us to some kind of clinic. I heard her husband talking to my dad—they've got some kind of law enforcement that keeps other vampires from hurting people."

"Your *dad* knows?"

"He knows about them. He doesn't know I remember what happened."

"Then we should call your dad, Stella! Whatever this is, it's way past our pay grade!"

"Not yet. After she wakes up, maybe. But not yet. Please, Lark . . . you've got to trust me on this."

Lark looked like she wanted to be anywhere but in that chair at that exact moment, but she just shook her head. "Then what? Does she need . . . blood? Like, people blood? Would that wake her up?"

Stella bit her lip, then said, "I think it might. That's one reason I wanted you here. I was kind of scared to give her any without someone else with me, in case . . ."

"In case she tries to suck you dry. Because she's a good guy."

"Basically."

Again, Lark shook her head in disbelief. "You are certifiably nuts. What am I supposed to do? Got any wooden stakes?"

"No—look. I'm going to cut my finger and see if she'll drink it. If she starts trying to hurt me, you grab that blanket and pull it off the window. I don't know much about them, but I know they can't do sunlight."

Lark got up from the chair and went to the window, obviously not convinced Stella's plan was anything approaching a good one. Stella took the sword from the coffee table and slid it out of its sheath.

"Holy crap," Stella murmured, examining the blade. It was beautiful, sort of Japanese looking but shorter than the ones in movies, and had carving along half its length. "I think this is Gaelic. I wonder what it means . . ."

"It means we're both total morons," Lark grumbled. "Would you get on with it, please?"

Stella assumed quite rightly that the blade would be sharp; she barely touched it to her finger and berry-bright blood welled up along a cut. The edge was so keen it almost didn't hurt.

Holding her finger up so it wouldn't drip, Stella opened Miranda's mouth again and touched the cut finger to her tongue.

"You washed your hands, right?" Lark asked.

Stella ignored her, watching Miranda's face for some response as several drops of blood oozed out of the cut. For several minutes there was nothing; then, she thought she saw Miranda's lower lip tremble the tiniest bit—

It happened so fast Stella couldn't react. Miranda's eyes flew open, her irises gone silver and almost glowing in the candlelit darkness; her lips drew back in a hiss, her canines growing long and flashing—

She struck like a cobra. Stella cried out at the pain of teeth in her throat, and she tried feebly to fight the vampire off.

Suddenly light blazed into the room, and Stella heard a faint sizzling sound, then a scream of terror and agony. The body holding her down flung itself backward, scrambling into the corner, and Miranda curled up on herself, arms over her head, her screams splitting the air.

"Cover it! Cover it!" Stella yelled.

Lark, ghostly white with fear, did as she was told, casting the room back into darkness.

The air was hazy with smoke and the stench of burning

meat . . . skin. Burning skin. Stella fought not to gag, seizing the blanket from the couch and pressing it to her throat.

"Are you okay?" Lark asked in a tremulous voice.

"I'm fine," Stella said. "She barely got me. Just stay where you are."

Stella half crawled to the side of the couch, peering around it into the corner between a bookshelf and the seventies-style storage end table where Stella kept the cat box.

Miranda seemed so small, just then, shrinking into the corner, a child in too-big clothes, shaking violently and hiding her face. She made soft noises that sounded eerily like an animal dying slowly in a trap. It looked like the burns had already healed.

"It's okay," Stella said softly. "You're safe."

No answer. Stella tried again.

"Um . . . I don't know if you remember me, but . . . I'm Stella Maguire. Detective Maguire's daughter? I was at that clinic the other night and you sang for me. This is my apartment. I brought you here . . . you were hurt."

Miranda lowered one arm, barely exposing her eyes, which lit on Stella without recognition. Stella nearly cried out again—there was so much pain in her eyes, such immense grief, it threatened to swallow everything . . . she was falling . . . the world was burning . . . *no, no . . . please . . . make it stop . . .*

"Oh, God," Stella heard Lark whisper, and then she started weeping.

Stella realized what was happening just in time to keep herself from falling over the edge; she shielded as hard as she could, putting up as many mental barriers as she knew how to craft between herself and Miranda. "Lark, shield!" she commanded. "Do it now!"

A moment later Lark stopped crying, her breath coming in shallow gasps. "What the fuck . . ."

"She's an empath," Stella said. "I think she's projecting."

Waves of sorrow and pain hit Stella, but she held on, reaching out toward Miranda with careful psychic "hands."

Stella wasn't a pro at dealing with other people's gifts, but she took a deep breath and switched to her Sight to try to figure out what Miranda needed.

"Holy mother of shit," Stella managed, followed by a number of other profanities born out of pure amazement.

The last time she'd seen Miranda, the vampire had been in control of herself, strong, healthy. Stella had been under a haze of drugs, but she'd still been able to sense that Miranda had sophisticated, powerful shields to regulate her gift and make herself appear, at least on the surface, more human.

It looked like those shields had been blasted open. Her aura was raw, full of gaping holes like her shirt had been, especially around her heart center; it was as if something had been torn from her . . . no, not something. *Someone.*

Stella understood what she was Seeing even before she knew what to call it.

"Oh, Miranda," she whispered. "I'm so sorry."

Miranda was still staring at her, not seeming to recognize her or even her own name, and Stella could see why; her energy was a tattered wreck, under barely any control. She was a powerful projector, but her sensing ability was way stronger; right now she was probably feeling the emotions of everyone within a mile radius. Add that to the trauma of what Stella sensed had happened . . .

"I'm going to help you," Stella told her. "I promise. Just . . . close your eyes and relax, okay? I might be able to help you get your shields back up."

She turned to Lark. "Come here . . . I need all the power I can get."

Lark didn't move. "She just tried to eat you, Stella! Not to mention, you've never done anything like this before. She might just drag you down with her."

Even without Miranda's empathy affecting her, Stella felt tears start to burn her eyes. "We have to help her. Didn't you feel it? She's dying on the inside. She's lost. It might be too late to save her, but . . . if we can help it not hurt so much, we have to, Lark. She just . . . she has to know she's not alone."

With a sigh, Lark came over to them, sinking down onto the carpet and holding out her hand to Stella wordlessly. Stella offered her a shaky grin and took it.

"Okay, lady," Stella said to the broken, immortal woman in front of her. "Let's see what we can do."

* * *

The Southern territory is still reeling from the sudden disappearance and presumed death of its Prime and Queen, David and Miranda Solomon.

Sources claim to have witnessed the Prime's assassination on the roof of a building in downtown Austin, but there is no confirming evidence at this time. The exact fate of the Queen is unknown. At the moment of the Prime's alleged death, the Texas Geological Survey recorded a tremor of 2.7 on the Richter scale centered in Austin, the first such seismic event in the area since the death of Prime Auren 18 years ago.

Reports of widespread violence in the first night following the assassination have given way two days later to reports of near total shutdown of the entire Austin Shadow District. Even with the Second in Command and most of the Elite unaccounted for, the vampire population of the city is staying off the streets, apparently intimidated by the possibility of a new power rising to take the Signet.

The identity of the assassin is still unknown. SignetPulse will continue to update as new information is verified.

Jonathan scrolled back up to the website's header. There had always been newspapers in the Shadow World, but nowadays everything was digital, making their existence even harder to prove; the news blog was password protected, catering primarily to the Courts and the Elite, but it wouldn't be impossible for a human to get in. It would, however, be damn near impossible to believe anything he or she read.

Jonathan still wasn't sure he believed it himself.

He glanced over at his Prime, who was sitting cross-legged in one of the hotel chairs, staring with narrowed eyes down at a phone. "Any luck?"

Deven made an irritated noise. "Bastard didn't keep his passwords anywhere. They were all in his head. So was whatever code he used to lock down the Haven and the network. Even if I could get into his phone, all it would let me do is make calls."

"What about Eagle Eye? You said she's the best."

"Second best. She tried to break in and her system nearly fried."

"She hacked the Department of Defense database but she can't get into David's e-mail?"

Deven shook his head. "If we want to recall the Elite, we're going to have to do it the old-fashioned way, by word of mouth."

"Dev . . ."

"I've got our people out trying to find them, but apparently they had protocols in place for this kind of thing and are all hiding out pending further orders or a new Signet claim. Good policy, since one of the first things new Primes tend to do is kill off the competition."

"Dev . . ."

"I've got eyes on the Haven, but it would be stupid of them to use it as a rendezvous, so right now there's not a soul there except the humans who come to tend the grounds. Even the horses have vanished. The whole place is powered down. The doors are bolted shut with steel that would take C-4 to open."

Jonathan started to say his name one more time, but Deven's head snapped up and he said, "Don't say it, Jonathan."

"We can't stay here forever," Jonathan told him gently. "We have our own territory to look after."

"Everything's fine there. We're getting reports on the hour."

"Deven . . . I know you're upset. We're both feeling guilty—"

"Are we?" Deven asked harshly. "I'm sorry, did I miss the part where *you* killed twenty-eight people for nothing? Was it your idea to get Faith to steal the Stone? Or were you the one who wanted us to be honest when it could have made a difference? I don't need you to shoulder my guilt, Jonathan. I can handle it."

Jonathan regarded him silently: the way his eyes had gone dark, the way his hands clenched the arms of the chair. There was an edge in his voice Jonathan had never heard before, not in more than sixty years of knowing him. If Jonathan had heard it from anyone else, he would have thought that person was about to break. He wasn't sure if Deven was capable of breaking . . . and if he was, God help them all.

"I'm sorry," Jonathan said softly, "but you can't have this one, baby. You and I are a team, and we both fucked up utterly. We were arrogant, believing ourselves infallible, and David and Miranda . . . and Faith . . . and Eladra, and the Order . . . paid the price. If it's your fault, it's mine, too."

They were still staring at each other when Deven's phone chimed. The Prime gave it a look of loathing but tapped the screen anyway. He sighed.

"What is it?"

Deven dropped the phone on the bed. "Incoming data from 8.4 Carmine. Eagle Eye had more luck cracking into Monroe's files than the South's network. Monroe had detailed notes from his time undercover in Hart's Haven. She's sending everything she found on Jeremy Hayes."

"What happens now?" Jonathan asked. When Deven's face foretold an angry retort, the Consort clarified, "I mean . . . in the natural order of things a new Prime would come forth and claim the Signet, the same way it happens every time, everywhere. But the Signet is broken, and no one knows where the Queen's is. Even if someone strong enough shows up—Hayes, for example—what is there for him to claim?"

Deven sat back in the chair, eyes on the ceiling. "I don't know. I don't know if a Signet has ever been destroyed before. It would fall on the Order to make a new one, I suppose."

"So much for that."

Deven sighed. "The metalsmiths are still alive, Jonathan. So are the warriors. And there are other branches of the priesthood out there—Cloisters all over the world. They won't have access to the original books of Mysteries, but they'll have copies of some of the texts. The Order as a whole isn't dead." He lifted his head and met Jonathan's eyes again. "If two thousand years of persecution couldn't end the worship of the goddess, I certainly couldn't. There are even humans who revere Her. Wiccans and the like." Now he smiled slightly, though there was no real humor in the expression. "In the grand scheme of history, my actions are of little consequence."

Jonathan raised an eyebrow. "Oh? What about the Awakening? Do you think it worked?"

"There would have to be something to awaken, love."

"You really don't believe in any kind of god—even though Eladra believed you were destined to take her place as High Priest of the Order?"

"Eladra believed a lot of stupid things." Deven pushed himself up out of the chair, suddenly impatient. "I'm going out. I want to do a round of the District to make sure everyone's behaving."

Jonathan didn't mention the change of subject. He knew when he'd pushed it too far. "What would you like me to do?"

The Prime pulled on his coat and reached for Ghostlight. "Check on the intel from 8.4 Carmine. See if any of it is useful. At this point Jeremy Hayes can choke on a dick and die, but I still want to know how he got involved in all of this."

"Deven . . ."

He paused, hand on the door. "Yes?"

"I love you. Remember that, all right?"

Jonathan heard him sigh. "I love you, too. Don't wait up." Then he was gone.

The building was slated to be torn down starting that Thursday. The fire had left it structurally unsound enough that there was no way to renovate it without spending more money than it would cost to raze it and start from scratch. Still, the destruction had been neatly contained to that one building and the area immediately in front of it, and neither the fire nor the tremor that came after had done any serious damage to the neighborhood. One thing was sure: Hayes had known what he was doing with the explosives.

On the roof, the night was strangely quiet; perhaps it was Deven's imagination, but sound seemed dampened there, as if held still by the city's restless spirits.

During the day workmen had been here, a few brave souls taking measurements and angles, but once the yellow tape was up and the demolition paperwork on its way for approval by the city council, the place was abandoned again, an empty, burned-out husk with little left behind of all that had died there.

The first night after, Deven and Jonathan had both come back to try to track Miranda, and while poking through the wreckage out front, Deven found what he knew to be the hilt of Faith's sword. He'd had Volundr craft it for her when she left California, a symbol of the changing of the guard. Faith and David had risen as high as they could in Deven's Elite, and when David fled Deven's side to seek out his fate in Texas, Faith had followed him, the way she always followed him, even into death.

"I hope for the devil's sake he keeps Guinness around, girl," Deven murmured, "or you might just stage a revolt and take over hell."

Deven stood on the roof unmoving for a while. His eyes picked out the spot where they had left David's body, but nothing was there now; whatever ashes had remained had scattered in the three-stories-up wind.

Perhaps the workers who had come up here had walked through the ashes and now the Prime of the Southern United States, the most remarkable being Deven had ever known, was now being tromped all over Austin on the soles of their boots.

Slowly, Deven knelt where he had knelt that night, aching in a way he had thought he was no longer capable of aching.

After seven hundred years he should have been immune to this. People died; beloved people died even sooner, most of the time. Everyone he had ever known had left him, one by one, and everyone who was left would, too, except for Jonathan, who was supposed to go when he did . . .

. . . but where, then, was Miranda?

They all knew how it happened. Most of them had seen it once or twice in their tenures: One Signet fell, and moments later the other, sometimes screaming, sometimes in shocked silence as the power imbalance simply burned them out from the inside. That was how their bonding worked: Having a soul mate might not be like the romance novels, but there was one promise they all counted on . . . not having to die alone . . . or outlive their partners. After hundreds of years of existence, there was precious little that could comfort a Prime, but that promise, the knowledge that they didn't die alone, had been enough.

But now . . .

Whatever had happened here was not how it was supposed to go. Whatever the Awakening ritual entailed, somehow it had bypassed the rules. If Miranda had died when David did, she would have been found by someone; the scene was crawling with police and firefighters for hours, and Deven's Elite had searched every building in a five-block radius. No footprints, no blood trail, no sign of her.

She couldn't have gone far in her condition—what reports Deven had claimed she was badly wounded and had been caught partly in the explosion, so she was probably only semi-conscious, assuming she could even hold her mind together enough to run. Anyone who knew the Queen would have taken her to the Hausmann, and anyone who didn't would have taken her to a hospital. There should have been a body . . .

. . . there should have been a Signet left behind.

Deven reached into his coat pocket and closed his fingers around the shattered remains of David's Signet. In the nights that followed David's death, he had been back to this roof over and over and had found many of the ruby's shards; they were all in a box at the hotel. He had no idea what to do with it, but he knew he had to keep it, at least for now.

He sat down on the concrete roof, knees to his chest. His mind was full of the memory of David's closed eyes, that feeling of profound absence where there had been such vibrant life . . . why did anyone ever think the dead were merely sleeping? Anyone could tell when a body was empty.

Even vampires, who had already died once, had life in their flesh until it had burned . . .

. . . away . . .

Deven frowned.

There was something missing here. Something *he* was missing. *What was it?*

Something about ashes . . .

When a vampire burned, the fire consumed flesh, bone, organs, even clothing; all that was left behind was metal, and even then not always. Cheaper jewelry and belt buckles and such tended to melt from the intense heat.

Signets, however, always survived the sunlight, which was why they should have found Miranda's wherever she had fallen. There weren't many people who would make off with a Signet they found on the ground; vampire or human alike would feel its power and sense that it was not to be touched unless it woke for him. It was possible it had been taken, of course, but unlikely. Most of their kind still feared the Signets.

He had David's Signet; he had David's phone; he had David's wedding ring. As far as he knew, the Prime didn't wear any other jewelry unless Miranda had given him something. David hadn't been much for embellishment; he went for fine hand tailoring when it was required, but when he wasn't "on duty" he usually slobbed around in jeans and one of his silly T-shirts from *Star Wars* or *Firefly* or whatever. Deven remembered very clearly what David had been wearing in death: standard vampire black, leather coat, boots, the kind of thing he would have fought in.

Fought . . .

Wait . . .

Deven twisted back up onto his knees, staring around the roof, peering into the shadows.

There *was* something missing.

David had died with a sword.

Deven had thought of it only later—he should have taken it along with the phone and ring. They had left David's wrist com, too, he realized, but he assumed the alloy they were made of had a low melting point—otherwise it should still be here. The com was really no great loss; David's was no different from any of the others except for its programming, and it would take the Pentagon to hack into the com network—literally, since David had created it with their cooperation. Not even David Solomon could launch a satellite into space without help.

But his sword . . .

David's sword was another of the Order's creations, and though David pretended not to believe in the superstition Deven clung to and insisted Deven not name it, she had indeed been forged with a name, the letters carved in among the ornaments Deven had commissioned so that it wouldn't look like there was anything written on her at all . . . but Deven could see the script and knew what it said.

Deven's sword was Ghostlight, for the way he moved, a will-o'-the-wisp, barely seen but deadly to follow. Miranda's was Shadowflame, for the Queen's bloodred hair and the fire in her heart. David's . . .

Deven and Jonathan had laughed about it, because if David didn't want to know, there was no reason not to name the blade something they believed would suit the Prime—both by reputation and by enthusiasm. Deven had it christened "The Oncoming Storm."

It was one of the names given to the Time Lord in *Doctor Who*, who never died, but regenerated into a new form over and over, and whose power and brilliance were known and feared throughout the universe. Deven liked to imagine how hard David would roll his eyes if he knew the sword's name, even if he would appreciate the nerdy reference.

And David Solomon, Prime of the Southern United States, had died here, in this place, with The Oncoming Storm at his side . . .

. . . but where was it now?

It would not have burned or melted. It would have been left on the ground amid the piles of ashes.

Someone had taken it.

That someone might even have been Miranda.

His heart was in his throat . . . but all this meant was that someone had taken the sword from the roof after David's body had burned. It could have been anyone, from one of Hayes's henchmen to a human worker. And if someone out there had it . . . Deven's hands clenched with anger. No mere mortal, or vampire trash, had the right to lay hands on such a thing.

He called one of the Red Shadow operatives he had in town, 2.2 Alizarin. "I need to divert you from your current objective."

"What is your command, my Lord?"

"Start making inquiries about a stolen sword. It will look very similar to my own, but the grip is larger in diameter, the blade about two inches longer; it's balanced for a left hand and, last I saw it, was carried in a black scabbard. I doubt anyone in the District will have it, since they'll know it's hot, but try pawnshops and dealers in the area. The second you find it, bring it to me."

"Yes, my Lord. Consider it done."

Deven rose smoothly, straightening his coat. He should get back to the Ambassador and read Monroe's files on Jeremy Hayes. There were simply too many questions that continued to go unanswered . . . and he made it his business to hunt down answers. He collected knowledge like he collected weapons, and there was no question which was deadlier in the right hands. If they had known what the Awakening ritual was really for . . . if they knew now . . .

Deep down, however, he had a feeling he *did* know.

He took the remains of David's Signet from his pocket and held it up by the chain, concentrating on it; then he let it go.

It hung in midair, suspended, the way the entire Shadow World seemed suspended to him right now, between one reality and another, one set of impossibilities and another.

Lifetimes ago, Eladra had been fond of saying there was meaning in everything. She had seen omens in the stars and heard whispers in the trees. The world, she said, was a holy instant, a thousand thousand possibilities merging into one reality. Every action was fraught with consequence. Nothing happened by chance.

Meaning . . . meaning in a sudden connection among a handful of Signets when for centuries they had all been sundered. Meaning in David's death. Meaning in all their lives colliding. Meaning in the slaughter of twenty-eight innocents.

Meaning in a missing sword.

Deven sighed. The Signet fell back down into his outstretched hand.

Eladra would have been amused by his thoughts. Worse yet, she might have found hope in them that he was at long last coming around to her way of thinking. She had tried for so long to help him believe again . . . in God, in miracles, in love.

She had failed on all counts . . . but a hundred years later, David had made him believe in love, and that, in itself, was a miracle.

And now David was gone.

As much as he wished he could find meaning in any of it, Deven knew that there was none. This was how their lives went. Signets died all the time. At least one went down per decade, and he was replaced, and the world carried on without him, uncaring. If there was a god's hand pulling the strings, he—or she—was a clumsy puppeteer indeed.

Deven knew that Jonathan was right; they should leave, let nature take its course and go back to the way things had always been. David and Miranda had caused tremors in their world, but in the end, the earth would grow still again, and they would be another Pair of names in a long list, footnotes in vampire history. There was no reason to stay here and prolong the inevitable. It wasn't Deven and Jonathan's problem. Perhaps they'd be allies with the new Prime, perhaps not. Same shit, different decade.

He spoke quietly, wondering if David's soul—assuming such a thing existed—was anywhere it could hear him, or if the Prime had moved on to whatever torment or oblivion awaited vampires after death.

"Tell me how to let you go," he said. "Tell me how, after all this time, I should say good-bye to you."

A light wind picked up, catching a handful of litter and scattering it across the rooftop. Deven heard a rustling, fluttering noise and lifted his eyes to a power line about fifty feet from where he stood.

An enormous raven perched there, watching him, its glittering gaze steady and unblinking.

Deven rolled his eyes. "I wasn't talking to you," he said, and turned away, intending to Mist off the roof and head deeper into downtown for a late-night hunt before returning to the hotel.

Just before he reached into himself for the power, however, he glanced back over his shoulder at the bird, inexplicably uneasy under its watchful eye.

It was gone.

TWO

For a while, Miranda wanted nothing more than to die.

Her dreams were full of fear and grief, the pain of so many others leaking into her head like rain through a rotting ceiling. Each drop eroded a tiny bit more of her, until there was nothing left but a raw, exposed emptiness, a void where there had once been warmth.

Please don't leave me here alone. Please.

Finally, she felt herself shutting down. Her heart simply couldn't take any more. She had nothing left—no power, no love, no strength, no will to continue. There was no reason to fight her way back from the abyss. The agony of the world was all she had; perhaps it was all she had ever truly had. In the end all her power had changed nothing. She was dying alone in the dark the same way she almost had in that alley so long ago. The circle was at last complete.

She could sense something at the edge of her being: something trying desperately to reach her, to catch her. Something kept trying to wrap itself around her and draw a veil of peace over the gaping wounds.

She turned away from it. She couldn't fight anymore.

"... *trying, Lark. But this isn't really my area. She's too strong for me—even both of us together aren't enough.*"

A familiar voice, a thousand miles away on the other side of the flood, tight with fear and exertion:

"*Come on, Miranda. Don't give up. You can do this.*"

The thought of letting go and sliding down into the black was so inviting, promising silence . . . yet she was curious . . .

"*Damn it, Stella, you're going to kill yourself—*"

It was true. The first voice was growing weaker, the energy that was attempting to hold on to Miranda failing. That power was considerable, and the talent was there, but confronted with the enormity of the damage to Miranda's shields and psyche, it simply couldn't succeed. A mortal hand wasn't strong enough for this, but the Witch had thrown herself into it recklessly and fully, not realizing that it was too late, that Miranda was too far gone . . .

And now Stella was, too. The young human was willing to give her life to save someone she didn't even know, purely out of love.

"*Stella! Stell, stay with me, goddamn it, don't you fucking leave me—*"

Please don't leave me here alone. Please.

So much fear, and so much pain in the world she wanted to leave behind . . . but so much love, and courage . . . and no matter what she had lost, no matter how much she was bleeding and screaming inside, she had taken up the responsibility . . . she wore it around her neck.

She had chosen once to return from the edge and claim the Signet for her own. She had fought her way up through freezing cold water, lungs burning, and hauled herself onto the riverbank to save those she loved.

It was who she was. She had told Cora—what felt like a thousand years ago—that nothing could take that away from them . . . and nothing could . . .

. . . not even death.

She wouldn't allow it. Not in that alley, not in the black water, and not now.

She came back to herself in a roar, a surge of strength filling her and spilling over into the frail young creature who lay unconscious beside her.

Miranda sucked in a deep, hard breath and sat bolt upright, her fingers clenched in Stella's. She poured energy into the Witch—and through her into her friend—replenishing what Stella had so selflessly given her. Then she kept pulling, drawing more and more power into herself from a seemingly inexhaustible source somewhere beyond any place she could name, until her entire being sang with it.

She drew her shields back around her like a raven settling its wings.

The room came into focus. A small apartment, shabby but comfortable, with the smell of night in the air. In one corner a gray tabby cat poked its head out from behind a pile of books, its eyes huge and frightened as it stared at her.

Slowly, Miranda turned to face the Witches.

Lark had dived forward to rouse Stella, who was sitting up, the two girls holding on to each other for dear life, their eyes as wide as the cat's. They were both pale with shock, but Stella was otherwise unharmed.

Miranda looked down at her hands. Her flesh seemed to be glowing for a second as if it were white-hot, but it was returning to normal as the energy she had channeled finished healing her wounds and restoring her sanity. The stone in her Signet was glowing, too, as if a miniature star had woken in its depths, and as her mind began to clear from the haze of power, the light dimmed to its usual level.

She looked down at herself and blinked.

Hello Kitty pajamas?

"Where am I?" she asked softly, startled by the sound of her own voice. It was hoarse, scratchy, as if it had been dragged over broken glass.

Stella's voice, however, was tremulous. "In . . . in my apartment."

"What day is this?"

"Wednesday . . . Wednesday night." Stella took a deep

breath, and when she went on she sounded a little more steady. "You woke up on Monday for a minute . . . I've been trying to help you shield."

"She almost died," Lark said suddenly, anger sparking in the words.

"Lark, I'm fine," Stella said. "I knew what I was doing."

"No, you didn't! Either that or you're suicidal. I don't know which is worse. You've spent the last two days barely sleeping or eating—"

Miranda lifted her gaze to Stella's. "You've been doing this for two days?"

Stella blushed. "I didn't want you to die." She fiddled with a lock of her hair, suddenly seeming to remember whom she was talking to. "I mean . . . you haven't even done your second album."

Miranda smiled in spite of everything. It made her face hurt. "I take it the memory wipe didn't work."

Now the Witch snorted. "Not so much. Sorry."

Lark, however, was not ready to back down. "So are you going to tell us what the hell we've gotten into here, or what?"

Miranda looked into the girl's eyes, and Lark turned bright red and lowered her gaze, her hand tightening on Stella's arm.

"How much do you know?" Miranda asked.

Stella replied, "I know what you are, and a little about *who* you are, but nothing really specific."

"How did you find me?"

The Witch gestured vaguely toward a small altar set up on the other side of the room. "I was doing a reading," she said. "Trying to figure out what to do about all of this. I got this vision that told me you were in trouble, and all of a sudden I had to go find you. I can't explain it—I just had to. I drove downtown and there was this building . . . it blew up. There was a fire, and I found you out front."

Miranda drew her knees up to her chest, putting her head in her hands. Flashes of memory came to her: chaos on the city streets. The Stone of Awakening. Faith bound to a drum full of explosives . . .

"Oh, God," she said, shutting her eyes tightly. "Oh, God . . . Faith . . ."

The look on her Second's face, so full of pain, her body wracked with poison and her heart torn with guilt . . . that last smile before the world burned . . .

Her mind was slowly cycling through the events of that night, the memory returning, each moment more wrenching than the last.

Arrows . . . the guards dragging her up the stairs, leaving a trail of her blood . . .

An altar . . .

"No," Miranda moaned softly. "No . . . no . . ."

She heard Stella speak, but the words were meaningless in the face of the horror unfolding in Miranda's mind.

She had fought with every last inch of her will to free herself from their grasp and run back to the roof, but she was too weak, too weak from blood loss . . . she couldn't remember what she had felt first, the explosion or . . .

"No . . ."

She remembered. She had felt it. She had felt the life draining out of her, out of them both, felt the hammer fall . . . the impact of her body with the cold ground, her soul being torn from her, ripped in half, that kiss of warmth she had felt in her mind for the past four years violently torn away, the wound ragged, bleeding, bleeding . . .

She felt a hand on her shoulder. "Miranda, are you okay? What—"

All around her she could hear things falling off shelves. Her shields were starting to crumble. One of the girls cried out.

She pulled the energy back in, forced the barriers back up, but the fall continued in her mind, a hammer falling, shards of scarlet thrown in all directions, one last breath, she felt it . . . she felt it . . .

The world grew very still. Everything went completely

silent, allowing her words to be heard, to make the impossible, the desolation, real.

"He's dead," she whispered. "David is dead."

Grief took her body in great racking sobs, and all she had to grab on to were the arms that wrapped around her, one pair, then two . . . human and fragile, perhaps, but strong enough to hold the broken heart of a Queen.

Jonathan woke with a start, his eyes on fire with tears, and struggled to straighten himself from the position he had slouched into in the armchair.

He had to fight with all his strength not to break down weeping—the sorrow was overwhelming, so deep it felt like his soul had been rent in two.

The book on his lap fell onto the floor. The noise was jarring enough to throw him out of the trance . . . and trance it had to be, because he felt almost exactly the same way when he came out of a precog episode. But this . . . this was different . . . this was something happening *now*.

The door of the suite flew open, and Deven stumbled in, ghostly pale. He fell back against the door as it shut, and Jonathan saw he was shaking, breath coming in tortured gasps.

He felt it, too.

Just like that night, by the car, when they—and across the ocean, Jacob and Cora—felt David die.

Only this time . . .

Prime and Consort's eyes met, shared pain yielding to shared realization, and they both spoke at the same time:

"Miranda."

Stella had never seen the look on Lark's face before, and she didn't say anything about it until they had helped get Miranda into Stella's bed and the Queen had collapsed into an exhausted sleep. Stella pulled the bedroom door shut, confident that even with the sun up outside the bedroom was in near-total darkness.

Lark sank onto the couch. She was staring off into nothing.

"Is it too early for tequila?" Stella asked, attempting a smile.

After a moment Lark reached into her bag and pulled out an Altoids tin; inside was a lighter and half a joint. She shot Stella a questioning look.

For once, Stella just nodded. Now was not the time to argue with her.

Stella went into the apartment's microscopic galley kitchen and put on a pot of coffee, ignoring the stink coming from the living room. She'd never been a big fan of marijuana, mostly because of the smell; it reminded her of dirty gym socks, which was why she didn't usually let Lark smoke at her place. The only time she'd ever enjoyed it was in brownies, but she and Lark had gotten the munchies and ended up eating half the pan, so she was sick as a dog for days. After that she'd lost her appetite for the stuff.

She stuck her favorite mug directly under the coffeemaker's spigot to catch the first strong cup. Foxglove had given it to her last Halloween; it was painted to look like a cauldron and said *Witches' Brew* on the side.

In here, everything was so normal. Stove, fridge, microwave, pictures of her and Lark stuck to the fridge door, an empty can from the wet food she'd fed Pywacket last night as a treat. Poor cat . . . he wasn't too keen on having a houseguest.

The sense of normalcy vanished.

Miranda had cried until she lost consciousness, utterly wrung out. By the time she was too tired to go on, it was morning, and Stella and Lark were both frayed to the nerves from trying in vain to comfort her.

There was nothing they could do but be there. Still, it seemed to be enough; Miranda's shields held except for that one tense moment when things started falling over, and even once she had fallen asleep she maintained control. She was suffering, yes, more than Stella could imagine—but that was the amazing thing. Stella could only *imagine* it. Miranda wasn't projecting it onto her. The amount of strength it must have taken to hold that much together was almost inconceivable.

She dumped sugar into her cup and mindlessly drank the entire thing in a couple of swallows, then filled it back up.

By the time she returned to the living room Lark had put her joint away and looked, if not better, at least less like she was going to have a nervous breakdown.

"Thanks for your help," Stella said, sitting down. "I mean it . . . thank you for staying with me through all that."

Lark shook her head. At first she didn't speak, but then she said, "I always used to be so jealous of you."

"Why?"

"You're psychic," Lark replied with a shrug. "You have a bona fide gift. Most people can do magic if they get the training—it's natural energy. We're part of nature. You just have to learn how to tap into it. But you . . . you have the Sight, and that's different. It always seemed so . . . special. Kind of romantic, you know? But if that's what happens . . . if being that powerful means you fall apart like that and take half the world down with you . . . no thanks. I'll stick to being a regular old Witch."

"It's not always like that. When I was younger, before I got training, I had some . . . bad things happen. I couldn't control what I Saw, and sometimes I found out stuff I didn't want to know. But what she has . . . it's not the same."

"Well, I know that—it's empathy, not Sight. Feeling, not Seeing. But still—"

"No, I mean it's *different*. She's not human. She's got the gift, yeah, but there's way more going on than just empathy. She was pulling power from something . . . I don't even know what to call it. She's hooked up to some kind of battery bigger than any one person should be able to control. I don't think she even realizes it yet. Whatever happened to her out there . . . I don't know how she's even coherent."

"She's not, at the moment."

"But she will be. She's freaked, understandably so, but she's got the power under control. Nobody can do that, Lark."

"Like you said . . . she's not human."

Stella's eyes fell on the bedroom door. "To tell you the truth I'm not really sure *what* she is."

* * *

The hunger saved her.

She barely moved until Friday; it wasn't so much that she was too mired in mourning to go on as that she simply didn't know what else to do. She had fought her way back to her body, chosen to live . . . but she didn't know how to live. She didn't know how to take that first step into a life alone.

Miranda had never thought of herself as the kind of woman who would fall apart without her man, but then, she had never expected to be a vampire with a mystical bond to her soul mate, either. For three years David had been her partner, her friend, her lover—but more than that, he had been her balance, and now she was tilted precariously off axis, staring down into that endless darkness and trying to regain some sort of equilibrium.

In the end she didn't have to decide . . . she had to feed.

Vaguely, she heard Stella say that she had to go to work, and she was leaving a key in case Miranda needed to go out. The thought occurred that Stella was an extraordinary human—the trust she had placed in Miranda would have seemed foolish to most people, but Miranda and Stella were not most people. Miranda didn't know much about Stella's gift, but she knew that it had a similar flavor to her own, and that meant Stella could read the truth of someone and judge whether that person was worthy of her trust very quickly, if not instantly.

Slowly Miranda became aware of her body: her upper jaw hurt, her mouth was dry, her stomach wrapped around her spine and cried out against its ill treatment. She felt like her entire body was coated with dust on the inside . . . and that dust was rapidly forming sandpaper in her veins.

When had she last fed? It must have been Monday, when she first woke and bit Stella.

One thing was certain. Whatever she had suffered, whatever pain the future still held, she was still a vampire.

Her joints felt stiff and achy as she stretched and climbed out of Stella's bed. Her legs were weak and shaky . . . no, this would never do. She would not waste away like a Victorian widow. Not today.

Cautiously, she poked her head out the bedroom door, sniffing the air to discern the time of day. Late evening. The sun would be down in half an hour.

The blanket was still pinned up over the window, and though the watery edges of waning daylight wouldn't burn her skin, just looking at the window made her head begin to pound.

Miranda tottered around the apartment for a while, distracting herself with the novelty of Stella's home. It was clean but cluttered, shabby salvaged furniture draped in Indian print bedspreads and fabric remnants. The scent of incense hung heavy in the air, and it was oddly comforting. There were a lot of books.

She felt eyes on her back and turned in time to see a bushy tail vanishing into the bedroom.

She ventured into the kitchen and found herself staring at the fridge door, where Stella had hung snapshots of herself, Lark, and other people Miranda didn't know, all caught in various stages of laughter or affection. In one, Stella posed with an older woman in some kind of shop; in another she and Lark were dressed as Halloween witches, each with a plastic pumpkin full of candy in one hand, middle finger of the other extended toward the camera. Miranda smiled.

It occurred to Miranda she was going to need clothes, unless she wanted to hunt in Hello Kitty pajamas. She returned to the living room and found where Stella had piled her belongings. The Witch had thoughtfully laundered Miranda's clothes, even the shirt full of rips and tears, and everything was folded almost reverently.

She thought about taking a shower but decided to wait until after her hunt; she would return sweaty and possibly bloodstained, so she might as well wait.

Even with her body commanding her to hurry, Miranda took her time getting dressed, trying not to think about why her shirt was ripped or what had happened the last time she'd worn that pair of pants. Finally she picked up Shadowflame and, with shaking hands, buckled the sword onto her belt before wrapping her coat around her.

By the time she was ready, the sun was well set. She found the key where Stella had said it was and, with a deep breath, took a step outside.

The world spun around her. Groaning, she bolstered her shields and tried to breathe, leaning back against the door for a minute until she felt strong enough to take another step.

She concentrated on figuring out where she was. She pinpointed the neighborhood easily enough and decided to head for a small park she knew was nearby where there would most likely be joggers at this hour. People in Austin learned to be comfortable going out in the dark; the summers were so hellishly hot that some activities, like working out, were simply not possible at midday.

The world was so quiet. Her boots were unnaturally loud on the sidewalk, and she started at every noise. The urge to run back to the safety of the apartment was overwhelming at times, but she gave in to the older, more pressing urge and followed her senses toward the park, concentrating only on putting one foot in front of the other. She didn't have to make sense of the world right now. She didn't have to think about anything. She just had to hunt.

In the end she didn't make it to the park. She heard footsteps approaching, rubber soles striking the ground rhythmically. Miranda stepped back off the sidewalk into the shadows and waited.

The young woman who crossed the Queen's path had expertly highlighted hair pulled back into a swinging ponytail. She was a seasoned runner, judging by her muscle tone. The earbuds she wore, blasting techno, kept her from hearing the soft step up beside her.

She squeaked faintly as Miranda's hands closed around her neck and hauled her off the sidewalk. In a single fluid motion Miranda spun her back into the vine-covered fence, pinning her, and as the hunger swept up over her, she snapped forward, her teeth striking the girl's flesh so quickly the pain wouldn't even register for a few seconds.

The girl struggled fitfully, but Miranda was stronger; she seized the human's mind and held her still, pressing against the girl as if they were lovers, hot, coppery blood filling her mouth and, swallow by swallow, easing the burning inside her, calming the tremors.

Don't fight. I won't hurt you if you don't make me.

When she was sated, she lifted her mouth from the girl's neck. She stared at the wounds for a moment, tempted . . . so tempted . . . to dive back in, to take the rest, to fill herself so completely that all thought and emotion drowned in the fever . . . but only beasts lost control. She was of a higher breed.

The girl ran on, remembering nothing.

Miranda stood there for a while, leaning on the fence, breathing in the night around her while her body healed itself from the effects of five days of deprivation.

By the time it was done she was hungry again.

She reached out in her mind, looking for signs of life, and found another human walking along the opposite side of the street, her energy full of purpose and anger. The woman had just left a fight with her boyfriend and needed a walk "to clear her head." It was the same old thing—he swore he wasn't interested in that slut in the marketing department, but she didn't believe him . . . not the way he checked out her ass every time she walked by his desk . . . it was only a matter of time, men always had to fuck everything they could get their hands on, they were like dogs . . .

Miranda slipped across the street and stood on the leeward side of a tree, waiting, her eyes going silver with hunger.

Moments later, the woman stumbled, eyes dazed and hand to her throat.

"Are you all right?" Miranda asked, taking her arm to steady her.

"Yeah, I . . ." She looked around. "I guess I got a little lost there for a minute. Thanks."

"Be careful," Miranda told her. "This is not a good world to be lost in."

The woman's blood was flavored with anger and Vietnamese food, and it was enough to satisfy her. Miranda carefully wiped her mouth with her sleeve in case her lips were stained and turned back the way she had come.

Was all of Austin this quiet? It was so strange that these humans were going on about their lives, oblivious that the creatures who had stood between them and death were just . . . gone. Had the Elite regrouped or were they still on lockdown? Had someone else already claimed the Signet? No . . . that couldn't happen. She was alive.

The Queen was alive . . . and she was alone.

Miranda wavered on her feet, nausea hitting her at the thought, but she clamped down on it. *No. Not now. Think about it later. Right now just keep walking.*

She should be going insane, shouldn't she? More than that—her power should be out of control, burning her out from the inside . . . but it wasn't. Her shields held firm, and if anything she felt stronger than she had before. This wasn't what was supposed to happen . . . was it?

She would have to look in the database of Signet history that David was building. He might know . . .

Miranda gasped and nearly fell, knees suddenly giving out. She threw herself sideways just in time to grab a tree trunk and stay upright. Again she had to fight the pain tooth and nail: *Not now. Later. Just keep walking.*

I can't do this. I can't . . .

I have to. Keep walking. Stand up, Queen.

She made her way back to Stella's apartment by sheer force of will. She was concentrating so hard on the simple act of walking that at first she didn't notice anything amiss.

As she approached the building, a slightly run-down but very Austin sort of place with lots of wind chimes and a concrete Virgin Mary birdbath, her eyes narrowed.

Stella's door was open.

Miranda knew her mind wasn't entirely on point right now, but she remembered very clearly locking the door when she left. The key was in her pocket.

Wary, hand moving up to the hilt of her sword, Miranda edged toward the apartment door, leaning her senses toward the building to catch any sound or flicker of emotion. She slipped around in the shadows, drawing Shadowflame slowly and silently.

She was nearly at the door when she heard a noise behind her: a car door slamming.

Miranda jerked her head toward the sound and bit her lip as she saw Stella walking toward the apartment from her beat-up old Camry; she had a paper coffee cup in one hand and her keys jingling in the other.

The Witch made a tiny squealing noise of fright when Miranda's hand closed around her arm and hauled her away from the door.

"What the—"

"Shh." Miranda pushed Stella behind her. "There's someone in there."

Stella went pale. "In my apartment?"

Miranda waved a hand to shush her again. "Stay here."

She inched toward the door, listening hard: one person, rooting around for something, not very concerned with stealth . . . which meant they either knew Stella was out or didn't care if she caught them. Miranda didn't like either idea. She also didn't like the certainty building in her mind that the intruder was a vampire.

Vampires moved differently from humans. Their energy was different. Now that she had spent the last few days completely separated from her own kind, that difference was almost startling.

She heard the intruder move toward the door and braced herself.

As soon as he cleared the threshold, Miranda's sword was at his throat, and she said quietly, "Don't move."

The vampire darted sideways, trying to bolt, but Miranda was ready for him; she lashed out with her booted foot and sent him flying into the column that held up the front porch. He stumbled but regained his equilibrium and threw himself back at her with a flash of silver: Two long knives appeared in his hands.

They fought from Stella's front door out into the courtyard, Miranda spinning in midair to avoid his blades, the intruder ducking Shadowflame with expert grace. He was obviously well trained, and though his fighting style wasn't as graceful as what Miranda was used to, it was effective; she felt one of his knives slip past her guard and slice into her forearm.

Annoyed, Miranda pushed energy into the cut and closed it. She spun again, this time twisting the sword when it met the knives, and one of the intruder's blades flew out of his hand, embedding blade first in the dirt nearby.

As he stepped back, trying to reach the blade, she returned his laceration with one of her own, opening a long red ribbon in his chest. He staggered, shocked, and his eyes locked on Miranda's throat, where her Signet had fallen out of her collar and hung shining in the darkness.

The intruder's eyes widened with realization, and before Miranda could move in for the kill, he turned and bolted.

She was so surprised that he ran, she hesitated, and he disappeared into the night while she was still gaping at the spot where he'd been.

"Son of a bitch," she panted, sheathing Shadowflame.

Miranda stepped over to where his knife had fallen and yanked it out of the earth. Behind her she heard Stella let out a breath. "What . . . the hell . . . was that about?" the Witch wanted to know.

Miranda turned toward her, but something caught her attention: a glint in the corner of her eye, on the sidewalk in the intruder's flight path. She bent again to get a closer look . . .

"Son of a bitch," she said again.

She picked up the small metallic device and shook her head.

"What's that?" Stella asked.

Miranda held it up so the Witch could see it. "An earpiece," she said. "I've seen one just like it before."

"So . . . what does that mean?"

The Queen faced the Witch, pondering the blade in her left hand and the earpiece in her right.

"It means it's time for me to go home," she said softly.

Three

That night Stella did arguably the first smart thing she'd done all week: She called her father.

He arrived at her place inside ten minutes, took one look at the mess of Stella's apartment, and said, "All right, start at the beginning."

Just then Miranda emerged from the bathroom, where she'd been washing the dried blood off her already healed arm. "Detective Maguire," she said. "Nice to see you again."

Stella's dad blinked at the Queen in astonishment. "You're alive?"

Miranda smiled slightly. "Seems that way."

"What about—"

Miranda shook her head. "The Prime is dead," she said, the words hollow. Stella knew she was trying to push as much distance between herself and her grief as she could, at least for now.

Maguire sat down on Stella's couch. Stella had never seen her father look quite so bewildered. "And Faith?"

Miranda closed her eyes for a second, then said, "She's gone."

He stared at her for a moment. "I'm sorry," he told her. "For your loss . . . I know the entire Shadow World is poorer for it."

"Thank you. We have a more pressing problem, though—someone knows I'm here. I don't know who they are or what they want, but they have this place marked, and that means your daughter isn't safe."

"She'll come stay with me, then," the detective declared.

"Dad—"

"No arguments, Stella. I'm not going to let you get eaten by these people. Just because the whole city's been a tomb for a week doesn't mean you should be alone—"

"A tomb?" Miranda interrupted. "There hasn't been any gang violence, any territory battles?"

He shook his head. "I expected there to be. Everything I know about Signets tells me that after one dies there should be a surge of attacks—I had extra men on the street, even covered the Shadow District, but it's like everyone in Austin is scared shitless."

"Why?" Stella asked. "I mean . . . aren't your people out there doing their jobs like always?"

Miranda sighed. "No. We have . . . had . . . protocols in place for our deaths. The Haven and our entire network is on lockdown, and all the Elite will be in hiding until either a new Prime claims the Signet or we send the recall signal. Often when a new regime takes over, they start by killing off all the old Elite and destroying anything connected to the former administration. We didn't want to make it easy for them, so not only is the sensor network down, the Haven itself is locked tight. Even the cars are locked down."

"So if your guys aren't policing the streets, why aren't all the bad vampires out there having a people-eating party?" Stella asked.

"I don't know. But we have to assume that whoever came here knew who you are, Stella, and that means they probably know who your father is. Staying with him might not be as safe as you think."

"Don't worry," the detective said sternly. "I've got a really big gun."

The Queen smiled again, this time with a touch of pity. "You know that won't help if they come for her."

"Then what do you suggest?"

Miranda looked at Stella. "I take her back to the Haven with me."

Both Maguires must have looked flabbergasted; the Queen chuckled. "Only for a few days. I need to recall the Elite and get the network back up, and then I can have the evidence the vampire left behind analyzed and learn more about what he wants. Once I know what I'm dealing with, we can make a more sound decision about Stella."

"Do I get a say in this?" Stella asked.

"No," Miranda and the detective said at the same time.

Maguire rubbed his chin, and Stella almost smiled herself; he'd always done that when he was worried about something. She suddenly felt a little amazed by her father: All this time she'd thought he was so ordinary, but he had been up to his badge in vampires, knowing what they were capable of. His constant fretting over Stella's safety made a lot more sense now . . . Stella was fretting a bit, too.

She couldn't help it, though—the thought of seeing where Miranda lived gave her a thrill that overrode her sense of self-preservation. Lark would shit herself when she found out.

"Can you guarantee Stella will be safe with you?" Maguire asked. "I know you regulate your employees' feeding, but I can't say I'm too keen on the idea of her being surrounded by vampires."

"Whoa . . . how many vampires are we talking about?"

Miranda glanced at Stella. "About a hundred, assuming they're all alive. I give you my word, Detective, Stella will be under guard every moment she's there. I'll give her a com and put her on the network so even after she's back in town she can call for help instantly if she needs to. Believe me, I won't let anything happen to her. We've . . . we've lost enough already."

Finally, Maguire nodded. "What do you need from APD?"

"Right now, nothing. Let me get my people back home and get a status report on the territory; as soon as I find out anything about the intruder I'll send you the data and you can send out an alert to your officers."

Which was how, two hours later, Stella wound up driving her car out Loop 360, a duffel bag full of clothes in the trunk, a cat carrier in the backseat, and a vampire riding shotgun.

She left Lark a voice mail calmly explaining the situation, though she anticipated a frantic call whenever her friend managed to check her phone. She also called in a "family emergency" to Foxglove at the shop; Foxglove knew her father was a cop, so she would probably assume something had happened to him. Stella hated lying, but she tried to be as vague as possible, hoping she could come up with something close to the truth by the time she got back to town.

Stella had no idea how to act in a car with her idol, but within ten minutes on the road, after giving her basic directions, Miranda fell asleep. With her head leaning against the window and her feet tucked up under her in the seat, the Queen looked so vulnerable and young—except for her face. Even asleep, there was pain in her face, and a kind of exhaustion Stella couldn't even fathom.

How old was she really? Stella wondered, eyes on the road ahead. Miranda's website bio said she was thirty, but how much of that was actual fact? She could be a hundred years old for all anyone knew, and looking at her now, Stella could believe it. There was so much weight on her heart . . . Stella remembered the night the call had come about her stepmother, shot in a robbery, and how she and her father had wandered the earth like ghosts for months . . . What must it be like to lose a soul mate?

"How old were you?"

Stella started, shooting Miranda a sideways glance. "Hey, no mind reading."

A slight smile. "I can't always help it. Plus . . . after all that suicidal energy work you were doing on me, I think we're linked for a while. You might want to keep an eye on your shields for a few days."

Stella bit her lip, then said, "I was twelve."

"I was fourteen when my mother died . . . but she had been lost to me for a long time before that."

"Lost, as in . . ."

"As in, committed to a mental institution. It turns out we had the same gift, but no one ever recognized hers for what it was."

"Who recognized yours?"

Miranda closed her eyes again. "David."

Stella immediately cursed herself for asking. "Sorry."

"It's all right."

"Can I ask . . . I mean . . . how did you meet?"

The Queen looked out over the darkened Hill Country, and her eyes were bright with tears, but her voice was steady enough as she said, "In line at the grocery store."

Stella laughed. "No, really?"

She gave a flicker of a smile. "Yes. He was buying ice cream."

"So you can eat . . . other stuff?"

A nod. "Some of us do. Too much can make us sick, though. Most of us stick to liquids."

"When you met, were you already a vampire?"

"No. Not for about a year."

"Does it hurt—turning into one?"

"Yes." Miranda looked at her gravely. "It was my choice, but it was excruciatingly painful . . . and it's not an easy life, or a kind one. So don't get any ideas."

Stella laughed in spite of herself. "No freaking way. I'm not some goofy romantic teenager. I have no desire to be immortal."

"Really? Most people seem to think it's one hell of a prize, at least until they get it."

"That's because people are afraid of death."

"And you're not?"

Stella shrugged. "Maybe . . . I'm a Wiccan, though. We look at death as part of a greater cycle, not as an end. It's a doorway to whatever's next. Besides, I can't imagine living forever, watching everything else die and change . . ." She trailed off, realizing that she really, really needed to change the subject, given what Miranda had just been through. "But . . . at least the clothes are cool."

Miranda raised an eyebrow, not fooled by her lame attempt at steering the conversation away from death, but said only, "Take the next left turn."

They were heading deeper into the hills, and the road wound around like a snake, guiding them farther and farther from the city. Stella began to feel a creeping sense of unreality pricking her spine. *Out in the middle of nowhere in a car with a vampire . . . you are fucking brilliant, Stell.*

She would never have seen the odd little unmarked turnoff that Miranda pointed out to her. It was so dark and the trees so dense it felt like they were in another world . . .

. . . until the trees opened out onto a wide valley cupped in the hands of the hills, and Stella caught sight of the magnificent house . . . no, mansion . . . no, that didn't even cover it . . . at the end of the long, circular drive.

"Holy shit," Stella breathed. She heard Miranda chuckle.

It was hard to really get an idea of what the place looked like. There were no lights anywhere, and the only real sense she got of its size was based on the enormity of the blackness where it blocked out the half moon's light. It was gigantic, though, and she could see the edges of several other buildings behind it, all of them dark, like haunted houses, a ghost town.

They pulled up to the massive double doors at the front entrance. Stella grabbed her bag and Pywacket, who complained loudly from inside the carrier until she shushed him.

It was so quiet, and so dark. There was sound everywhere, crickets and night birds, but no traffic noise, no hum of the ever-wakeful city around them. The sky overhead seemed to go on forever.

Miranda walked up the steps and off to one side of the doors; she obviously could see just fine, though Stella had to pick out each step carefully to avoid stumbling and dropping the cat. Once she was closer to the building, Stella saw that the doors were actually made of steel, and it looked like all the windows were blocked off with metal, too.

Miranda reached out and pressed one of the bricks, which turned out to be a façade; it flipped up out of the way, revealing a touch screen of some kind.

The Queen pressed her hand flat against the screen for several seconds before there was a faint beep.

A small camera lens shot forward from the wall until it was close to Miranda's face, and Stella saw a blue line of light travel over her eyes. Another beep, followed by a female computer voice requesting verbal authorization.

"Star-two," Miranda said.

"Identity accepted. Access granted."

There was a deep clanging sound, and a moment later the steel doors slid back like something from *Star Trek*, revealing a pair of equally enormous carved wood doors behind them. Seconds later the windows began to follow suit, making surprisingly little noise other than the soft *flap-flap-flap* of the metal shutters retracting.

Above Stella's head, two electric torches blazed to life, banishing the eerie darkness.

Miranda took a deep breath. "Welcome to the Haven of the South," she said. "Follow me."

As they crossed the threshold, the interior lights began to click on, and Stella finally got to see exactly what she was dealing with here: The doors opened into a grand vestibule with a staircase that rivaled any Hollywood plantation set. The room was cavernous, their steps echoing as they crossed the marble floor. Even Pywacket didn't seem to know how to react; the cat was quieter than he'd ever been in his life.

They took a long hallway and several turns. Stella was good and lost before a minute had passed, but Miranda's stride was purposeful, her expression fixed on her goal.

She led Stella to another steel door and held her wrist up to the scanner on the wall beside it; the weird bracelet thing she wore was some kind of key, and the light on the scanner changed from red to green, allowing her access.

"You can leave your things here for now," Miranda told her.

Stella saw why: The door led directly to a staircase, and there wasn't much room to spare. Getting her bag and Py down there would have been awkward to say the least. At the bottom of the stairs was yet another door.

The Witch wasn't sure what she expected to find on the other side, but it wasn't what she got. They walked into a windowless, freezing cold room full of computers—cabinets of servers, monitors, an entire store's worth of laptops and other equipment meticulously organized on shelves.

Miranda went to a console where a red button was locked inside a shield, just like in a nuclear submarine movie. She held her wrist-thing to it, unlocking the shield, and flipped it up to expose the button.

She shot Stella a grin. "Watch this."

She hit the button with her palm.

Around them, servers and CPUs leapt to life, whirring and beeping and clicking; Stella felt a faint vibration beginning all around her, the entire building seeming to wake up. A monitor nearby lit up and Stella watched, fascinated, as it showed the system booting up, running through script after script that switched on other monitors, other subsystems.

SOLAR POWER SYSTEM: ONLINE.
EXTERNAL LIGHTING SYSTEM: ONLINE.
COM SYSTEM: ONLINE.
SENSOR GRID: ONLINE.
VEHICLES: ONLINE.

A window popped up asking for a password. Miranda typed in what looked like more than two dozen characters. Finally, another window appeared, saying, CONFIRM ELITE RE-CALL?

Miranda said aloud, "Confirm, Star-two, Queen Miranda Grey-Solomon."

RECALL MESSAGE?

She smiled softly, and when she spoke, her voice was clear and firm and held the barest touch of triumph: "Attention, all Elite and Haven personnel. Recall Code Omega-Nine,

Star-two. Report to the Haven immediately. I repeat: Recall Code Omega-Nine, Star-two."

RECALL SENT.

A flicker caught Stella's attention: On a monitor showing a citywide grid, red lights had begun to appear in clusters throughout Austin, and after a few minutes they began to converge.

"Now," Miranda said, still smiling, "Let's get you settled in."

Across Austin, in hidden shelters and safe houses scattered throughout the silent city, a woman's voice broke into the darkness, and in every corner of the Shadow District, there were cheers.

Four

She couldn't go in. Not yet.

She stood with her hands on the door, head bowed, for several minutes, but nothing she told herself could give her the will to open it or go inside.

She knew what she would see: everything just as it had been that night. Her guitar would still be on her chair. The book on string theory he had been reading would still be lying on the side table, his place held with a sticky note. The pair of boots she had almost worn, then changed her mind about and tossed on the floor, would still be there. A silver pen engraved with *David L. Solomon, PhD* would still be in the groove in the desk.

There was a gentle voice beside her. "May I get you something, *reinita*?"

Miranda turned to the woman standing there. "Welcome back, Esther. Is everyone all right?"

"Yes, my Lady. The Haven staff was in the safe house—we were the first ones back." Esther pursed her lips slightly and added, "I would have liked to stay, to watch the house until you came home."

Miranda smiled. "I appreciate that . . . but it was more important that everyone stayed safe. You never know what might happen."

Esther seemed to fight with herself for a moment, but then suddenly bundled Miranda into a hug. "Thank God you are home," she murmured into Miranda's hair. "I am so sorry about our Lord Prime."

"Thank you, Esther . . . so am I."

Miranda squeezed her back, and then Esther moved away, flushed a little at the emotion that had made her breach propriety for a moment. "I will go in and freshen things up," Esther said. "It will be ready for you when you are ready for it."

Miranda nodded, but she didn't speak and didn't stay to watch Esther go into the suite; she had to walk away.

She could hear the Haven coming back to life—the Elite were arriving in groups, the servants had returned, all systems were humming happily as if nothing had gone wrong. He would have been pleased, she thought, knowing how perfectly all the safeguards and contingencies had worked; everyone had done exactly as they were supposed to, waiting until they got the signal to emerge from hiding. If there had been no word for fourteen days, they were to disband. That way if a new Prime came forward and didn't try to wipe them out, they could choose whether to pledge themselves to his rule or to leave the territory. If the worst happened, he had wanted everyone to be safe and for the Haven technology to be as difficult as possible for his killer to steal.

She stopped, hands going to her face, unable to breathe through the upwelling of pain in her heart. *Oh, God . . . David . . . this can't be real. I'm going to wake up . . . and he'll be there, and he'll laugh at me for crying, and then we'll make love and go back to sleep . . . oh, God . . . please . . .*

Miranda held down her emotions, forcing them aside again. She couldn't fall apart. There was too much work to do. Later . . . later. Not now.

Stella was installed in a small room a few doors down from the Signet suite; Miranda had made the girl promise to stay put until Miranda returned with a com and guards for her. She knew better than anyone that even the Haven couldn't keep out every nightmare, but it was better for her to be here than vulnerable in the city—that, Miranda knew, too. Whatever that vampire had been after, even if it had nothing to do with Stella, Miranda wasn't going to have another death on her conscience.

She resumed walking, headed for the Great Hall, where the Elite were gathering to await their orders. Had it been only a week since the Council had been here? Since she had been shot? No wonder she was so tired. So much had happened so fast . . . did the Council know what had happened? Was Hart celebrating?

She walked out onto the balcony where the staircase opened onto the Hall . . . where a lifetime ago she had walked into battle with Sophie, and time had come to a halt as she and David stared at each other, his eyes full of shock that she was alive and a kind of love she had never, ever expected to find . . .

Not now.

They were waiting for her. Dozens of faces, expectant, tilted up toward her.

At first she didn't know what to say. There were no protocols for this. She had no script, no idea where to go from here. None of the scenarios that involved a Haven lockdown ended with only the Queen alive. The very idea was absurd. Pairs died together; that was the balance of the universe, the nature of their bond.

She took a deep breath. "Welcome home," she said.

Applause. She could feel their joy. They had believed her dead, but in defiance of all logic and history, here she was, returned to them again.

"I wish I knew what to say to you," she told them. "I wish I could tell you that everything can go back to the way it was. I wish I had inspiring words to rally us all . . . to bring some sense of meaning to all of this. But I don't. That was always the Prime's department . . . and Faith's. They should be here now to lead you . . . but they're gone. They're gone . . . and we have to go on. To honor what they lived for, and what they died for, we have to be strong and stand together. I don't know what god or fate or luck kept me here, but I remain. And I'm going to need your help."

She could see tears on several faces, and her own threatened to rise up, but she swallowed hard and continued. "For now, we'll adhere to Contingency Delta Three—modified duty, double patrols—to remind the Shadow World that we're still here. I'll be . . . I will take applications for a new Second in Command starting next week. In the meantime, shift leaders report to your lieutenants as usual, and lieutenants report directly to me. Patrol reports on the server as always." Miranda managed a smile for them and finished with, "I don't know what the future holds for us . . . but I know we can face it together. Dismissed."

As one, the entire Elite bowed to her. She nodded back, then said, "Elite Twenty-four and Forty-three—please report for guard duty at the Signet suite. Elite Eighty-one, with me."

Elite 81, a muscular dark-skinned man named Javier who had served on door guard duty many times, was at her side in moments. "My Lady."

"I have a human guest in East Wing room seven who needs twenty-four-hour guard. Coordinate with the other door guards to make sure she is never left alone."

"As you will it, my Lady."

"Also—grab one of the housekeeping staff and see to it that our guest's cat has a litter box and they both have food."

Elite 81 looked a bit bemused at the order but didn't question it; he set off for Stella's room without comment.

"My Lady, as your medic, I must insist you go and get some rest," came another familiar voice.

Miranda smiled. "Hi, Mo."

His warm eyes were sympathetic, though his tone was stern. "You will not do much good for anyone if you fall over from exhaustion."

Miranda looked down at herself. She had taken Stella up on her offer of a new shirt, but the black pullover the Witch had lent her was a little baggy and faded; still it was better than a bloodstained shirt full of arrow holes. Stella had washed Miranda's jeans, bless her, and by some miracle or magic spell the blood had come out of them almost completely. Miranda was clean, but she still must look a fright.

"If you insist, Mo," she said. "I'll be in the suite."

As she had when she went out to hunt, she concentrated only on taking one step and then another until she was back at the door again; now there were guards outside the way there always had been, and she could see light coming from underneath the door.

This time she had to open it.

She stood for a long time just inside the threshold, so many emotions hitting her at once that she went temporarily numb. It was a blessing, really—the numbness enabled her to move, to cross the room to her closet and pull out a change of clothes. She stripped off her shirt and jeans with shaking hands that felt nothing. The shirt she draped over a chair so she could have it washed for Stella. She tugged one of her own T-shirts over her head, put on her well-worn old yoga pants . . . but once the chore was done, she stood still again, staring around her yet not really comprehending the room.

Esther had built a small fire, not so much because of cold as to cheer up the space; she had also tidied things up a bit and turned down the bed.

Everything was so normal . . . as though, if she could turn her head fast enough, she would catch a glimpse of David in her peripheral vision, sitting at his desk or dozing off on the couch. Any minute now he would walk in, shake out his coat and hang it by the door, unbuckle his sword and hang it on the wall . . .

Miranda sank down on the bed, the shaking in her hands spreading up her arms and into her chest. She was so cold all of a sudden. She groped for a blanket with one hand and a pillow with the other, pulling the pillow up to her chest.

Instantly the smell overwhelmed her. Almond-scented soap, warm skin, the scent of wild immortality like the earth itself . . . she gripped the pillow to her, wrapping herself around it, burying her face in it, and the tears finally came.

Her sobs turned to screams, muffled by the pillow, long

wails of desolation, her abandonment so complete she could barely draw breath. The sound wasn't human, was far past hysteria; she screamed, and screamed, her entire being pushed under black water of a new kind, drowning her, stripping everything away from her but a loss she couldn't understand . . . that she couldn't survive. She wasn't *supposed* to survive it. That one hope of peace had been taken from her, after everything else had been taken . . . what was left?

Gradually, so very gently, she felt something at the edge of her awareness, an offer of warmth given with nothing but love and shared pain. She felt a kiss of energy against her forehead, and that warmth spread through her body, calming the shaking, quieting her sobs. It had a softness to it like a shadow cast in moonlight, and there was something familiar about it she couldn't place . . . but soon it solidified, and changed subtly into something else she knew . . . healing energy . . . arms around her.

Miranda took a gasping breath. This time she smelled whiskey, cologne, a faint wisp of hair dye, leather . . . and that same immortal edge, only deeper . . . older . . . and infinitely sadder.

She blinked and looked up into the lavender eyes. "Deven?"

He was holding her close, her head on his shoulder, his arms around her tight and protective like nurturing wings. "Easy, love," he whispered. "Just rest and let me work."

She closed her eyes and relaxed against him. All questions of blame, of guilt, were meaningless now; they had both, she understood now, lost their great love, though in different ways, and no one walking the earth could possibly understand what that felt like except another Signet bearer. His power enfolded her, not taking the pain away—that wasn't in his power to do—but gentling it, giving her enough distance that she could breathe. She would still have to face it, learn to live with the great emptiness inside her . . . but for now, it didn't claw at her so badly, didn't leave her bleeding.

She wept still, but the panic was gone. She curled up on her side on the bed, still clinging to the pillow, and Deven lay at her back, his arm around her, his breath warm on her neck. The energy flowed between them, and she felt his mourning as clear as her own. So much pain, and so much guilt . . . he truly believed, she realized, that he was damned, had always been damned, and that all of this was his fault. For hundreds of years he had drifted around the planet afraid to die because he knew what was coming. And then, finally, his faith had died instead of him, and then there was nothing . . . until there was love . . . until it, too, died. David hadn't been his Consort, but their souls had touched, and loved . . . and lost.

Moments, or hours, later, Miranda turned over, and they lay facing each other like two children sharing a secret. To her wonder, Deven's eyes were wet, too, and their irises had darkened almost to the color of actual iris flowers.

Deven's hand lifted and brushed stray locks of hair from Miranda's face, then cupped her chin lightly, fingers reaching up to wipe the tears from her eyes. The touch was more comforting than she would have believed possible. She had not expected to find comfort anywhere, ever again.

Deven smiled softly. "I remember a night that I came to this same room, to offer comfort in whatever clumsy way I could to a man who had lost the one woman in all the world who fully and completely understood and accepted him."

Miranda couldn't seem to stop her tears, but then she decided not to try; she had nothing to hide, not anymore. "I felt him die."

"I know, Miranda. I did, too. We all did—me, Jonathan, Cora, and Jacob. All of us."

"Did you . . . see him?"

Deven lowered his eyes, and when he met her gaze again there were more tears. "Yes. Jonathan and I found him on the roof. I brought you his ring and what's left of the Signet."

"Did you find his sword?"

"No, but we're looking for it."

"Was there . . . anything . . . of Faith?"

Pain creased his forehead again, and he said, "Only the hilt of her sword. Everything else in the room was pulverized."

She turned her face into the sheets for a moment. *Oh, Faith . . . I'm so sorry . . .* "Where's Jonathan?" she asked.

"Debriefing your Elite and ours to get a status report. I didn't think you would mind a hand with organization for a day or two, just to get you on your feet—Jonathan isn't much of a warrior, but he's one hell of a commander in chief."

Relief, sweet and dark, washed through her. "I'm so glad you're here."

Deven looked away again. "Even though . . ."

"Even though." Now it was her turn to touch his face. "Whatever you did, you did because you wanted to save us. It was batfuck stupid, yes, but I can't hate you for acting out of love."

The Prime looked at her as if she were some rare bird that had ventured into the yard. "He always said you had a blind spot when it came to me, but he never understood why, given . . . what happened between us."

"It's not a blind spot, Deven. My eyes are very much open. I see you. He . . . it's hard to explain to people who don't have this gift, but things like blame and forgiveness have a whole different meaning. I can't hold on to hate or it will poison me. And there's something . . . something connecting us . . . all of us. You know that. We're more than just friends and allies, all of us."

"I never wanted any of this to happen," he whispered, unable to meet her eyes any longer. "I never wanted to hurt anyone. When I found out about you, I sent Sophie, thinking I could set things right with him, help him be happy . . . and after all of that, he's . . ."

"I know," Miranda whispered back. "I want him back, Dev . . . I want him in my arms. None of this makes any sense without both of us here. It's just not right. I . . . I don't know what to do, Deven. What am I supposed to do?"

He reached for her again, pulling her close, and again she was surprised at how safe she felt in his arms, above and beyond the thought that he could easily disembowel anyone who tried to hurt her without breaking a sweat. He just felt . . . something about him . . . she wished she knew what to call it, but the closest word she knew was *holy*. Strange that things between them had changed so much since they'd met.

They settled into the pillows quietly, as morning rose from the ashes of the night, and between her absolute exhaustion and the gentle waves of energy he kept bathing her with, Miranda drifted off into sleep, feeling safe—not just that, feeling *loved*—for the first time in many days.

A week of nights seemed to float by in a watercolored blur. Miranda slept, woke, fed, and moved from one activity to another in a dream state, listening to Jonathan's advice about reorganizing the Elite, letting Deven fill her in on what they'd learned about Jeremy Hayes, hearing the patrol leaders report on the continued quiet that held Austin in its fragile hands. She barely remembered, from moment to moment, what she was supposed to be doing and could hardly carry on a conversation for more than a few minutes without her attention simply . . . fading away.

Deven and Jonathan watched her falter and decided between them, without even having to discuss it, that Jonathan would manage the military and Deven would manage Miranda herself. Back in California Jonathan was the one to whom their Second reported; Deven had to split his time between the Haven and the Red Shadow, so it was easier to let the Consort handle organization and leave things like weapons training to Deven.

It would take Jonathan only a few days to establish a temporary new chain of command for Miranda that could run without a Second for the near future; the choice of a Second wasn't something to rush unless a suitable candidate was already clear, and no one stood out in Miranda's mind. For now, the best thing was to delegate the Second's duties to the lieutenants and have them all report to Miranda every night in a group briefing. Once she got a better idea of who might work as a Second, she could shift back to the old way of running things.

They were lucky David had organized everything so

relentlessly; the outer cities of the territory could continue to run without any changes, except that they reported to the Haven lieutenants now instead of to Faith. David had structured his Elite with care so that they didn't need micromanagement on his part, and as far as Deven could see he had chosen his second tier of lieutenants very well. If Miranda was very lucky, there wouldn't be too much trouble.

As the nights passed, however, Deven began to realize that *lucky* was not a word he would use to describe the surviving Queen . . . in fact, neither was *survivor*.

Had she been a human woman, the loss of her husband so suddenly and so young would have likely destroyed her, at least for a year or more; she was entitled to her mourning, and no two people grieved on the exact same timeline. But she was Queen, and the Signet would not wait for her to recover.

All Deven wanted was to be sure she could stand on her own. He couldn't bring David back; he couldn't ease the great emptiness that constantly threatened to suck Miranda down into its hungry mouth; all he could do was take care of her, offer her the kind of solace he knew she needed, and pray—pray! him!—that somehow, Miranda would make it through this.

The next night he found her at her piano, her head bowed and resting on its shining lid, her fingers resting on the keys but not playing, her eyes closed but not sleeping.

"Am I needed?" she asked when she heard him enter the music room.

"No," he replied. "Not just now."

He sat down next to her on the bench. "Were you playing?"

She shook her head. "Sometimes I just come and sit here. She and I understand each other."

Deven laid a hand on the piano's lid. "I understand."

Miranda raised an eyebrow. "Do you?"

He smiled. "I lived in medieval Ireland, remember? I come from the time of wandering bards who were magically bound to their harps . . . back when it's said the Faery folk still lived among mortalkind. Mothers had to hang charms over their children's cradles lest the babes be snatched away, an Elf-child left in their places."

Miranda looked at him curiously. "Is that where you came from?"

His stomach clenched, and he started to snap at her the way he had Jonathan for asking something similar, but Miranda seemed to recognize she'd put her foot in it, and said, "I'm sorry . . . I just meant . . . healers can't be that common. I bet someone had the idea, back then, that you weren't . . ."

"Human?" he finished for her. The instinctive anger— and fear—that rose up when anyone made mention of the subject of his birth faded back into amusement. "Yes. Why do you think I spent so much time at church? It was the only place I could be alone with God, who loved me . . . or so I thought."

"So are you . . ." She sighed, shaking her head. "Never mind. I don't know what I was going to ask, but it probably would have pissed you off."

He smiled slightly. "It's all right, Miranda. It isn't your fault . . . It was a difficult childhood I had, and it never really got much better. My mother died giving birth to me. She was cold and still . . . until the midwife laid me on her breast, and five minutes old, I healed her. Half the village women saw her come back to life. From that moment there were eyes on me, whispers, knowing glances from the priest. My mother was terrified of me . . . the Faery boy, the Elf-child . . . the demon child. You can only be told you're damned for so long before you start to believe it, even when your soul cries out it's a lie . . . A dozen voices drown out the single voice of a child."

Deven frowned. He'd never spoken about his childhood to anyone—not even Jonathan, at least not to this depth. No one knew about his mother.

Miranda's eyes were bright with tears, and she leaned on his shoulder, her hand wrapping around his arm protectively. "That shouldn't have happened to you," she said. "They should have been grateful God gave them a healer."

Dev leaned his head against hers. "Perhaps. But they were only human, after all."

They were silent for a moment before Miranda asked, "Do you really think I can do this?"

"If anyone can, you can. I suppose the question is, do you want to?"

"Would you think less of me if I said I don't?"

"No. I wouldn't either, in your position."

"But I have to," she concluded.

"For David?"

"And for me. I have to believe I'm here for a reason, Deven . . . as many times as I've come close to dying, as much as I've lost, there has to be a point to it all. There's something I'm here to do . . . and if I have to do it alone, I'll just have to figure out a way to keep walking."

The Prime sighed. "I hope you're right. I hope there's meaning in all of this. But whether there is or not, Miranda, you're not alone."

She smiled and kissed him on the forehead. "Thank you."

Miranda turned back to the piano, her hands moving down onto the keys. Deven started to rise and leave her to her communion, but she looked up at him, and the pain in her eyes made him stay, remaining at her side on the bench while she sang softly, the weight of her sadness drawing tears from his eyes as well.

> *Till my body is dust and my soul is no more*
> *I will love you . . . love you . . .*

* * *

Jonathan hung up the phone with a sigh and leaned on the pasture fence, looking out toward Isis and Osiris, who were grazing contentedly, happy to be back home like everyone else. He wasn't really sure where the horses had been during the lockdown, though he would guess that their groom had taken them to a safe house—or safe stable in this case—until the recall was sent. What was supposed to happen to them in the event of the Pair's death? he wondered. Would the groom simply keep them, or did David have a will stashed somewhere that designated a new owner as well as the fate of his various research projects, labs, and foundations?

Normally these kinds of questions were moot. The new Prime would take over everything he could get his hands on and get rid of whatever he didn't want, including servants, Elite, horses . . . everything that David had built in his tenure could be tossed out like garbage. If the next Signet was friendly to David's allies, he would offer them access to some things, but more often than not, the post was taken by whoever killed his predecessor, and that meant a total blank slate.

He turned from the pasture and made his way back to the main building, feeling heart-heavy. He wasn't looking forward to this conversation . . . but then, lately every conversation with Deven had been hard, and most ended in arguments.

This time, though, Jonathan had to be the bad guy—it was time for them to go back to California. Thomas had reported a sharp rise in vampire-on-human crime in the territory this past week, and while they had a handle on it, it was clear that the word had gotten out: California was without its Signet, and every night they were away things got worse.

The truth was there wasn't much more they could do here, anyway. Miranda was as ready as she would ever be to assume full control; grief aside, she was perfectly capable of ruling on her own. She would eventually need a new Second, but for now things were as settled as they were going to get. Deven and Jonathan were only a phone call—or a few hours by plane—away, but they couldn't stay here any longer.

Jonathan didn't want to drag Deven away, not like this. He and Miranda had forged a new kind of relationship that Jonathan was loath to interfere with—he'd never seen Deven so open with anyone, as if their shared tragedy had gotten through the Prime's armor and let the Queen see what Jonathan knew was underneath. He was almost jealous, seeing the warmth between them, but right now they needed each other. Even apart from their relationships with David, Jonathan had simply never lost a love that way; he often wondered, in fact, if he was the only vampire on earth who didn't have massive piles of baggage to deal with. Deven had enough for them both.

He rehearsed what he was going to say all the way to the Haven, all the way down the hall, following his sense of Deven's presence; the Prime was leaving the music room, headed for the suite they'd commandeered.

Jonathan reached the suite a moment after Deven did and took a deep breath as he opened the door, bracing himself for the fight he was sure was about to erupt between them.

But as soon as he saw Deven, he forgot everything.

The Prime had sunk down in front of the fireplace, knees drawn up to his chest. He held David's broken Signet in one hand, the setting dangling in the firelight.

He was crying.

Jonathan all but Misted to his side and pulled the Prime into his arms, tucking Deven's head under his chin. He felt Dev's hands clench in his shirt, shaking.

For a long time, Jonathan just held him, letting his emotions work themselves out from the tangled, confused knot that had tightened around the Prime's heart since the moment they had found David dead on the roof. It wasn't just that loss, Jonathan realized; Deven blamed himself for every tear Miranda had shed, and the guilt was killing him as much as the grief: guilt over Miranda, over David, over Faith, over Eladra . . . the list kept going, stretching back hundreds of years until the heaviness was simply too much even for a Prime to bear.

If he could have stepped back from the situation, Jonathan might have been flabbergasted. Not once in all their time together had he ever seen Deven break down like this. Never. It was frightening.

But all he could do was hold him, and rock him gently back and forth, until the wave of emotion passed, and Deven grew quiet again.

Finally, sounding like he had completely given up on strength, on distance, on everything that had held him together as well as holding him apart from the rest of the world, the Prime whispered, "Take me home."

Five

The Queen watched the car pull away and stood there on the front steps of the Haven for a while after it was gone, a broken Signet in her hand, a broken heart limping around in her chest.

Her other hand held David's wedding ring; she had his phone now, too, tucked in her pocket, but the ring she couldn't seem to let go of. She tried slipping it on her middle finger, then her thumb, but it was way too big—funny, she'd never thought of him as having large fingers. They'd always seemed so nimble and deft, whether attaching a circuit to a bunch of wires or tracing circles on her skin.

She took a deep breath and turned back toward the Haven, where two servants held the doors open for her as she passed. She felt the weight of her own Signet around her neck as if it had doubled just crossing the threshold.

How had David done this on his own for fifteen years? How had Jacob managed for so long without Cora?

She paused. Was that why Hart was such a bastard, underneath it all? Or was he alone because he was a bastard? If he'd had a Queen, would he have been so full of hate he needed to lash out?

Miranda was surprised at herself; in that moment, she didn't feel any real hatred for Hart, only something like pity. If ruling alone felt like this, he had to be in pain every day, the pain of knowing he was only half complete.

But no . . . David had managed to lead without becoming a monster. So had Jacob. Even the ache of longing for something he'd never had was no excuse for what Hart had done.

Still, she couldn't summon any anger. She knew she should. Deven had offered, quite seriously, to have Hart killed; Dev had always avoided using the Red Shadow for Signet business, to help keep his two worlds separate, but it had finally come to such a pass that, knowing Hart had fully intended Jeremy to kill both David and Miranda, if it was war Hart was after, war he would get.

Miranda told Deven not to make a move on Hart. Surely that was what Hart wanted—he got the South destroyed, and one of David's allies would declare war, giving Hart a chance to rally other Primes against them in Council. Wait, she said . . . wait . . . just a little longer.

She wasn't sure why, but she knew Hart's time was coming. Whoever would take his head . . . it was important that it be the right person at the right time.

Knowing that didn't make it better.

She wondered if Jeremy had gotten his daughter back. That much, Dev's agents had discovered: Hart had Amelia Hayes, had imprisoned her in his harem to force Jeremy to do his bidding. Why Jeremy was so important to Hart, they still didn't know, but it had something to do with Australia, and they suspected McMannis was involved as well.

That was another reason why Miranda cautioned against Dev having Hart killed. She wanted to know more about what the hell was going on. There had to be more than just a personal vendetta at stake, or David's death was all for nothing . . . and so was Faith's.

Miranda found herself close to tears again, but this time

for Faith. Brave, wonderful Faith, who had given her life to save them—even though she had loved David, whom she could never have, she had freely died for Miranda . . . because she loved Miranda, too, as a friend and a Queen. It was the kind of death Faith would have wanted if she couldn't die in battle at her Prime's side.

As much as Miranda felt David's absence in every room of the Haven, she felt Faith's, too. The Second had been as much a part of her daily life as the Prime. Not a night had gone by in Miranda's entire tenure without talking to Faith, training with Faith, running patrols with Faith—and she knew that the entire Elite felt the same way. They had all settled into their new division of labor without complaint, but Miranda could feel what they felt, their confusion, their missing her. And there was no one to replace her . . . not even Jonathan had seen a suitable candidate among the remaining Elite. It was going to take time.

Time . . . time was all she had now. She had lost Faith, lost David . . . Kat had left . . . Miranda looked forward into her future, into every possible fate that could befall her, and she saw nothing but years stretching out, endless, as she wandered the Haven alone, anchored to the South and to her duty as Queen, forever . . . until some assassin got lucky, or she simply gave up and walked out into the sunlight.

And she couldn't do that. She wouldn't. She would go on.

Miranda checked her own phone, where the patrol reports were now routed: situation normal. Austin was still eerily quiet. She didn't really blame the Shadow District for reeling under the news that she was alive; she was reeling a bit herself. Everyone knew she should be dead. The fact that she wasn't was scaring a lot of people. There were whispers all over the territory that the Queen could not be killed.

She made her way back to their—her—wing of the Haven, and thought about Stella for the first time that night. She hadn't heard much from the girl, and hadn't heard from Maguire and the police, either. Stella must be going out of her mind with either anxiety or plain boredom.

Miranda stopped off at the study and raided the ice cream stash, then headed to Stella's room, which now had a guard at the door.

"Anything to report?" she asked.

"No, my Lady," he replied with a smile. "She's no trouble at all."

Miranda knocked, heard a welcome, and walked in, not sure what she'd find.

The Queen was a little taken aback. Stella had rearranged the entire room—she'd pushed the bed off to the side, rolled up the rug, and moved armchair and side tables out of the way, leaving a large swath of floor bare in front of the fireplace. Stranger still, there were drawings in chalk all over the floor—both in a circle in front of the fire and right under Miranda's feet at the door . . . and under the windows.

As Miranda passed into the room, she felt like she was suddenly walking through water, and she realized what was going on.

Stella had shielded the room. Heavily. She had in a matter of days put so much protection on the space that it was as strongly warded as the training room where Miranda worked with her telekinesis. Nothing could pass through the door or the windows without Stella knowing, and Miranda imagined if someone were to try with ill intent toward the Witch, they would get a lot more than the feeling of walking through water.

On the far side of the barrier, the room felt pretty normal, though there was a lot of energy moving around in it.

"Sorry," Stella said from the bed. "I wasn't taking any chances."

Miranda smiled. "You are a wise Witch . . . and even stronger than I thought."

"That's the thing . . ." Stella was sitting on the bed cross-legged, a thick leather volume in her lap, her cat curled up against her leg kneading the comforter. "I'm stronger than I was a few days ago. Ever since you did whatever you did to me . . . it's like you leveled me up or something."

Miranda's eyebrow lifted. "How could I do that?"

"I have no idea. Whatever weirdness you were channeling—"

"Channeling?"

"Yeah, didn't you feel it? After you freaked out, and I almost got lost in it, you sent all this power into me, but you were drawing it from some other source, not just yourself. Whatever it was, it was immense. And now I'm . . . I don't know how to explain it."

"You don't have to." Miranda went over to the bed. "How are you doing, other than that?"

"Bored," she said. "Although your guy did let me go to the library—it's pretty awesome. I . . ." Stella blushed. "I hope you don't mind."

"Of course not. I'm sorry I've been neglecting you this week. We had to get things in order."

"You and your . . . friends?"

Miranda smiled. "I didn't think you met them."

"I didn't. But I could sure as hell feel them. I'm guessing those are other Signets?"

"Yes . . . old friends of ours, from the West. They went home tonight."

"They just left you by yourself?"

Miranda shrugged. "They had to . . . they'd been away from their Haven for nearly three weeks, and that's asking for trouble. There were some things they had to deal with, and it was time I stood on my own two feet again."

Stella held her eyes for a moment, then asked, quietly, "What can I do to help you?"

Miranda couldn't help but smile at the girl. "Stella, you've been through more than enough because of me. I just want to get you back to your life."

"You don't get it, do you?" Stella asked, shaking her head. "You really have no idea how much you mean to us—to your fans, I mean. To me. I don't really know what you see yourself as . . . how much your music matters to you compared to all of this." She gestured around at the generalized grandeur of the Haven. "But you should know . . . the week I bought your CD I was going to kill myself. My dad had thrown me out, and I had never felt so alone in my life. I felt like there was something wrong with me, because I was different . . . like I was cursed. I thought, what's the point? Nobody will miss me. And this is gonna sound stupid, but . . . I was on my way to meet a guy who was selling me a bottle of sleeping pills, and the bus was late, and I ended up walking past Waterloo Records, and there you were—your poster—in the front display."

Miranda felt tears in her eyes again, but this time it was from such a different kind of emotion, she didn't try to hide it; it had been so long since she'd felt anything but mourning. Stella seemed to sense that, and went on.

"So I went into the store, and it was like I was in this trance—I bought the CD without ever having heard of you. That was back when Waterloo had those listening booths, so I took it in there, and . . . I knew you. You knew me. And for the first time in my life I felt like someone had heard me, had been there—you knew what it was like to feel crazy, to feel like damaged goods. But something in your voice told me that it was going to be all right. And I believed you, and I survived."

Stella sat forward and took Miranda's hand. The Witch's eyes were filled with a kind of light. "And you're going to survive. I promise, Miranda. It's going to be okay. I believed you . . . now you believe me."

Miranda smiled through her tears, nodding. "Okay, Stella . . . I believe you."

"Good. Whatcha got?"

Miranda laughed and held up the two pints of Ben & Jerry's. "Cherry Garcia or Chunky Monkey?"

"Monkey all the way."

"Here . . . now tell me why the hell you named your cat Pywacket."

At the sound of his name, the cat lifted his head and gave Miranda a baleful glare, then deemed her unworthy of attention and started licking himself with one leg sticking straight up in the air.

Stella grinned. "Wait . . . you've never seen *Bell, Book and Candle*? With Kim Novak? It's like the quintessential old Hollywood Witchcraft movie. I thought you were supposed to be, like, two million years old."

Miranda snorted. "I'm thirty," she said. "I just look two million years old."

"Any two-million-year-old would kill to look like you."

Miranda handed her one of the pints and a spoon she'd found in the study's drawer; Witch and vampire clinked spoons before digging into the ice cream, and for a while, at least, there were no tears in the Haven, only the bright sound of two young women laughing.

If either the South or the West had been in any shape to notice, they might have been pleased to see that the Northeast was in something of a disarray.

Prime Hart's Second had vanished into thin air, and the communication network had been infected with a virus that David Solomon himself would have admired: Rather than simply bringing the network down, it took the signals and misdirected them, resulting in patrol teams showing up at the wrong locations and communications getting lost all over the place. Suddenly none of the lieutenants' passwords were working, and everything from e-mails to training schedules went randomly missing, so the whole network had been rendered essentially useless.

It was a lovely virus. Jeremy had paid the programmer handsomely for it.

He was listening to the chaos, though he didn't derive any real pleasure from it; he had access to several of the Elites' phone logs and listened in on their voice mail—those few that went to the right phone—to find out just how well the virus was working.

Hart was, to put it mildly, in a bit of a temper these days . . . but it had very little to do with the computer virus, and not much to do with the lack of a Second.

On his way back from Austin, Hart stopped off in several cities, taking care of various forms of business, mostly illegal. The day he was set to return to New York, he got a frantic phone call from his Haven Steward . . . and it was really too bad Jeremy hadn't been able to listen in to *that* conversation. That, he thought, would have been quite satisfying.

As it was, he had quite a vivid mental image built up of what came next: Hart stormed into the Haven, threw open the doors to the harem, and found . . . an empty room.

Lydia had kept her word.

The harem guards were found dead, and every single girl in the harem had been kidnapped—or, rather, freed. Given how tight security on the harem was—Hart kept all his collections under guard—Jeremy had no idea how Lydia's people had managed it, but without even stirring the wind, the girls had vanished, and not a single person in the Haven saw or heard anything.

Hart and McMannis no longer had any leverage over Jeremy Hayes. Jeremy had never returned to work after completing his mission in Austin. He had simply gone to the apartment he had set up months before and waited.

He stood in the doorway of the dark bedroom for hours, just watching her sleep, wondering when the feeling of triumph would come, when he would feel some sort of relief.

Perhaps when she spoke.

If she spoke.

For three weeks she had lain there, barely moving. She hadn't acknowledged her freedom, or her father. She hadn't said a word. He had fed her, tipping a cup of blood into her mouth a little at a time, and she had swallowed, but she'd given no sign she knew where she was, or who he was.

He had wept when he saw her. She was so thin, so weak, a wraith in a slip of a dress, old bruises that couldn't heal mottling her body in patterns that left his chest clenched with impotent rage. The smudges of purple and black had faded once she fed, but her eyes were still sunken and stared sightlessly off at nothing, no matter what he said to her. He could count all of her ribs. Her clavicles stood out in sharp relief against her sallow skin.

She had been such a beautiful girl.

They had all been human once; he remembered the night

she was born, her first steps . . . seeing her run in the sunlight, ribbons undone, in gales of laughter . . . It wasn't until
she was a teenager that the sickness came on her, stealing
her life away little by little. They had tried everything, spent
a fortune on doctors and cures from all over the world, but in
the end, there was only one thing that could save her.

He and Melissa had chosen to come across with her, so
she wouldn't have to be alone in her eternal youth. She was
sixteen.

He remembered her dancing outside in the moonlight.
She always loved to dance.

For seventy years they had lived as a family, happy, while
he worked his way up the ranks of the Australian Elite; he only
got as high as lieutenant because Olivia had been so outstand-
ing at her job, but that was fine by him . . . unlike McMannis,
he had no problem answering to a woman. Unlike McMannis,
after Bartlett's murder, the Signet had chosen him.

He thought of how things could have been, if he had kept
his Signet, if Melissa had been his Queen, the three of them
living in the Haven, a royal family—Amelia had expressed
interest in learning to fight, but he had never let her because
he feared she would want to join the Elite and put herself in
danger. If he had taught her, would she have been able to
escape the men who came to kill her mother and drag her into
the hell of Hart's lusts? Was there anything he could have
done to stop all of this?

It no longer mattered. He had her back. It might take
years, but he would nurse her back to health, help her find
herself again. She was still in there somewhere, her sweet
smile hiding underneath months of torment. There was only
so much violation one person could take without shutting
down, but she was free now. Everything would be all right.

She would heal, and one day they would go home to Australia, and Jeremy would take his Signet back from the
usurper whose filthy hands were all over it. Jeremy would
expose McMannis and Hart to the Council.

He sighed. It was a lovely thought. There was just one
problem:

If he ever showed his face, Miranda Solomon was going to kill him.

He deserved it. He knew the kind of death he had dealt David; he knew the kind of future he had left the Queen. David had said she would come for Jeremy, but even without that assertion, Jeremy was well aware of the fate waiting for him if he let anyone in the Council find out where he was. Between her and Prime Deven there would be no escape—especially if Jeremy's suspicions were true and Deven was the Alpha of the Red Shadow. A great many Signets underestimated the South, but deep down everyone—even Hart—feared Deven. Their combined wrath would be Jeremy's doom if they found him.

He couldn't risk that. He couldn't leave Amelia alone. So they would disappear and create a new life somewhere . . . somewhere quiet, far away from this madness, where Amelia could dance in the moonlight again, and he could learn to breathe without the sharp pain in his heart that was both grief over Melissa and fear for Amelia. Someday they would both learn to smile again.

Someday he would learn to live with what he had done to Faith.

Someday, perhaps in a hundred years . . . but not today.

The surest way to hide was in plain sight.

In Austin it was not possible for a vampire to go off the grid, because there actually *was* a grid—the Signet sensor network tracked them, one and all. Those among them who lived for the kill had to find somewhere else to live. In Austin, vampires fed discreetly, kept their heads down, and got used to the feeling of being watched, because it meant they were safe from the violence of their own kind and the humans who hunted them.

It took nearly eight years for her to start to relax, to stop jumping at shadows and looking over her shoulder.

Eight years to feel safe . . . and one night to destroy everything.

She was having a drink at the Plague Rat when she heard the name. It froze her entire body, her mind; she could hear her heart racing in her chest, but around her time stopped. Seconds later she slipped out of the bar and ran.

She locked herself in her apartment and didn't leave for nearly a week. That fear she had fought for so long came roaring back, and she barely slept, couldn't feed, couldn't work; her supervisor left a message on her voice mail that she had been let go, and she didn't even spare a moment to worry about the rent. It was a part-time thing anyway. It sure as hell wasn't worth her life.

By the time she emerged from hiding, the Prime was dead, and that name she'd heard was no longer invoked around the District. As far as anyone knew, Jeremy Hayes had returned to New York and was no longer recruiting. Almost everyone he'd hired to go up against the Signet was dead, and those who weren't had fled Austin fearing reprisal. Once the Signet's dark gaze fixed on you, you were dead, and that was all there was to it; Hayes must have been offering obscene amounts of money to persuade anyone to join his cause.

But he was gone now. And there was no way he or anyone else would know she was here.

She was dead, after all.

The nights passed without anything calamitous happening. Life went on both in the Shadow World and outside it. She had to make a choice: either give up her life in Austin and run again, or find a new job and stick it out.

She decided to stay.

For once, luck favored her—she called George at Madre Luna to see if he had a chair open, and wonder of wonders, one of his artists had been fool enough to moonlight as a thug for Hayes and was now deceased. After months of waitressing she finally got to reclaim a little of her dignity, trading in the sound of clattering dishes and irritable humans asking if they could get their dressing on the side for the warm, familiar hum of a tattoo gun.

Tattooing vampires took a lot of skill, but it also took patience; a lot of vamps who wanted ink didn't understand that they had to be actively involved in the process and couldn't just sit there and bliss out from the endorphins. If they didn't consciously slow down the healing process, the skin would reject the ink and heal over before she even finished the outline, wasting her time and theirs.

She'd had more than one customer scream and yell at her for what was essentially their fault, and she'd had to resort to violence at her last job, which was how she ended up waitressing. Old instincts had flooded through her, and she'd nearly killed the dumb bastard who was yelling in her face. She'd scared herself as much as she'd scared him and had steered clear of the District for weeks afterward just in case anyone had gossiped, even idly, about the dreadlocked tattoo artist who seemed unusually skilled in martial arts.

That was the best thing about working for George—he was big and scary and nobody fucked with his artists. He was also upscale enough that she could be more selective with her clientele, so she mostly picked vampires who had experience with getting tattooed. When it was right, when the client knew what he was doing and so did the artist, the experience was amazing, even borderline tantric.

"How long have you been a tattoo artist?" the woman asked, sounding a little nervous. It was her first time, but they'd discussed the process and she had signed the waivers.

Olivia, hands encased in latex, looked at her over the needle she was preparing. "Fifty years, give or take—off and on."

"That's longer than I've been alive." The woman laughed. "I only came across four years ago."

Olivia didn't say what she was thinking—that wearing a butterfly on her shoulder for all eternity was the sort of thing only a baby vampire would go for—but the woman was nice enough, and it would be an easy hour's work assuming she could handle herself.

"So why do you have to wear gloves?" the girl asked. "It's not like you can give me HIV or anything."

Olivia smiled. "Health department regulations—as far as

the state of Texas knows this is a regular tattoo parlor. We follow the rules and nobody sticks their nose in our business."

The woman seemed to accept that and went into the deep-breathing exercise Olivia had shown her in the consultation, and she had obviously been practicing; Olivia could feel her energy slowing down, and even after the initial shock of the needle scraping into her skin, she'd maintained her calm, holding off the healing like a seasoned professional. Olivia knew from experience that the girl would be sitting there with her silvered eyes closed, her canines out as if she'd just fed.

After a few minutes their breathing fell into sync, and Olivia guided the girl's energy with her own, siphoning off the sparks of heat and electricity that shot from the skin of every person she'd ever tattooed and grounding them to help the girl last longer. She didn't have much of a pain tolerance, but with Olivia's help she'd be fine.

She was the last client of the night. Olivia cleaned up her station feeling closer to happy than she had in months—she'd missed this. The ritual of setting up, working, cleaning up . . . she liked every part of it when it went well.

She left work about two hours before the sky began to lighten. She was hungry—funny how quickly she'd forgotten what a drain the work was—but she didn't stop to feed until she was well out of the Shadow District. The less time she spent there, the better.

Once upon a time she'd spent nearly every waking hour in a District very similar to the one in Austin, stalking around the city with a sword at her hip. Now she slunk home with her tail between her legs, living not in a Haven, but in a crappy warehouse loft on the East Side, surrounded by humans.

If Jeremy could see her now, he'd laugh . . . right before he killed her.

It was possible he didn't hate her. It was possible he understood she wasn't to blame, and that what happened after that night was punishment enough . . . but she wasn't going to call him up and ask, show him the scars, swear she had tried to protect them . . .

She shook her head with a sigh. There was no use thinking about it. What was done could not be undone. She had failed, broken her promise to him, and the best she could hope for now was to live out her life here, where no one had the slightest idea what she had once been.

Still, when she heard the Second was dead as well as the Prime, part of her had the idea, for just a minute, that she could go back to her old life, this time working for a new Prime—

Oh, hell no.

She had built something of a life here, and as long as the Queen still lived and the regime didn't change, she could keep living it. The kind of people she had worked for, who would know her, didn't live in this territory. Now that Jeremy was gone, as long as she kept her head down, she would be safe.

She was no fool. Not anymore. Maybe once in a while she missed having a purpose larger than etching butterflies into skin, but that part of her life was over. She was just a vampire now, just a tattoo artist and painter, and she had no intention of getting within ten miles of a Signet ever again.

Really, she should have known better.

The walk home was long, way longer than from the café where she'd been working, but the buses didn't run again until way too close to dawn for her comfort. If she had been human, she might have been nervous as a woman alone in East Austin at night, but muggers and gangbangers were pretty laughable as a threat to even the weakest vampire, let alone one who had once been trained to kill. She didn't travel with a sword—that would draw more attention than she wanted if she happened across any Elite—but she had a stake in her bag and a knife in her boot. Outside the Shadow District, she had little to fear other than the sun.

She came around the corner of her building and froze.

Her unit was up a short flight of rickety wooden steps; it was the only one that had its own entrance, which was part of why she had chosen it. Everyone else who lived in the converted warehouse had to go in through the front of the building.

The streetlight was dim and tended to flicker, but it shone brightly enough to warn her: There was something on the ground in front of the stairs . . . no . . . someone.

Olivia's hand snaked into her bag and pulled the stake, and she moved sideways out of view, approaching silently. Her body automatically slipped back into guard mode, senses on alert; it was probably just a homeless guy, passed out drunk, but she hadn't survived this long without being paranoid.

She got close enough to see that yes, it was a person, face down on the ground, unmoving. He or she was clearly unconscious, but Olivia wasn't going to let her guard down until she was safely inside with the door bolted. She approached in a wide circle, sniffing the air; if it was a homeless person she'd be able to tell pretty easily by scent.

Strange. No smell of alcohol or accumulated filth. In fact . . .

Oh shit. Oh shit oh shit.

Vampire.

There was no way a vampire showing up outside her home was a coincidence. There simply weren't that many of them in this part of town.

Closer still, and she saw something else that made her stomach twist with dread. He wore a long black coat, but something metallic that caught the light stuck out from under it.

A sword.

Elite. Goddamn it.

Most likely he'd been on patrol and gotten injured, which meant there would be others arriving any second now. She had to get inside, and quickly, before they saw her.

She didn't stop to look any closer. She jumped over the unconscious vampire, her boots thudding dully on the steps, and started to run for the door.

"*Olivia.*"

Terror, instant and overwhelming, short-circuited her brain, and she spun around toward the voice, stake at the ready.

There was no one there . . . except the body. And while the vampire on the ground was male, the voice had been unmistakably female.

Breathing hard, she looked around the street, just barely stopping herself from calling out.

No one in Austin knew her name was Olivia.

Since arriving in the States after her flight from Australia, she had gone by her mother's name.

The street was silent; even the wind had fallen still. She saw movement in a tree across the street and clamped down on a horror-movie scream as she realized it was just a bird— a raven, sitting in the branches, watching her. Well, *it* certainly hadn't called her name.

She stared down at the man on the ground, heart in her throat, and before she could make herself run and hide, she descended the steps to the body and, with her free hand, took him by the shoulder and shook lightly.

"Hey. Hey, mister . . ."

The only answer was a soft groan. Cursing herself inwardly, she cast one more hunted look around the scene and then turned him over.

"Oh my God," she gasped.

Ten years ago, she had flown to London in service of the Signet; she had taken part in the Elite tournament . . . and she had seen the face before her once, standing among the others of his kind, watching the fights through deep blue eyes that held the quiet power and nobility reflected in the red stone at his throat.

It was impossible. Completely impossible. But she knew, even as she wanted to deny it and escape while she still could, that this was no lost Elite.

Prime David Solomon lay on her doorstep . . .

. . . and he was alive.

Six

"What are your orders, my Lady?"

Miranda walked from one end of the line to the other, examining each of the five vampires her Elite held captive. They all looked petrified, and with good reason.

She nodded to the lieutenant, who gestured at the others; they shoved their captives to their knees, and seconds later, the sounds of steel swinging and the dull thud of heads severed from necks ended the last handful of Jeremy's thugs.

They were out in full view of the Shadow District, and Miranda knew she was being watched—she could feel eyes peering out at her from the windows of the businesses and clubs that rose up on all sides of the execution. She wanted them to see her, to know that the rumors were true: The Queen lived, and she would suffer no disobedience. Nothing had changed in Austin. They all had to understand that.

She stood over the bodies as the Elite piled them on plastic sheeting and dragged them away, up to the roof of a nearby building to wait for the sun; another Elite opened a fire hydrant and sprayed the blood off the street, and all the while the Queen stood, impassive, watching with her arms crossed, allowing herself a moment of grim satisfaction at the sight of those who had brought such chaos to her city getting what they deserved.

If there were any more out there, they would most likely flee now. She was fine with that. Hunting down these five had been more of a show of dominance than anything else, to make an example of them and reinforce the fact that she was still in charge.

Dawn was coming; she could smell it, feel the fragility of the night air. Time to head home . . . to spend another morning locked in the music room, losing herself in the piano until her body gave out and she had to sleep.

Harlan piloted the Town Car back toward the Haven, and she sat in the back trying to stay awake even though the motion of the car was hypnotic and she was constantly on the verge of falling asleep these days.

The thought of sleeping filled her with the kind of dread that made her stomach hurt and her hands shake. She didn't want to sleep . . . she didn't want to dream.

It was the same every night, over and over until she thought she would go mad: She dreamed his death, feeling him fall, the night torn by her screams . . . then the horrible, endless emptiness, the cold in her mind where his presence had been, that safety and surety ripped from her forever.

She didn't know how much longer she could take it. At night, when she was awake and active, it wasn't as hard; she never stopped moving, never ran out of things to do. There were patrols to coordinate, network reviews to conduct, spats among members of the Court to mediate; the night-to-night business of the Signet didn't stop, and she was thankful for that, as it left her with little time to think.

She had the earpiece and knife she'd taken from the vampire at Stella's apartment sent to Novotny and was waiting to hear back; she made rounds of the Shadow District while the Elite hunted down Jeremy's hired hands; she took condolence calls from a wide array of Primes who didn't seem to know how to talk to her.

She couldn't tell if they were afraid or simply in awe. No one had ever heard of a Queen surviving a Bondbreaking by more than a week. By now she should be raving insane and throwing herself out a window into the sunlight, but instead she was lucid, strong, as perfectly composed as her Prime had always been, managing her territory with total confidence as if she'd been doing it for years.

Then the day broke, and she had to face the afternoon hours alone . . . at first she tried sleeping, but the bed was so empty, her mind so full of memory, that it forced her to her feet, down the hall to the music room, or the psychic training room, or through the tunnels to the Elite buildings where she could work out until she literally fell over from exhaustion. The more tired she was, the less she dreamed.

There weren't enough hours in the night, but there were far too many in the day.

It was not fair of her dreams to do this to her. She wanted to keep going, to accept David's death, not wallow in her mourning for all eternity; though the thought of curling up and dying was tempting sometimes, she had no intention of letting this defeat her.

Her heart apparently had other ideas. She woke every evening weeping, so lost and haunted, and there was no one to hold her, no one to reassure her that she would be all right.

She could call California if she needed to, but she was afraid of letting them become a crutch . . . she had to depend on herself now. No one else could do it for her. She had had three years of Pairhood, three years knowing what it was like to have a soul mate—those years had hardly been perfect, but she had never been happier, never been more sure of her place in the world.

That was over now. *It's over,* she told herself again and again, *and you have to keep going. You can do this . . . you're strong enough. You didn't go through all of this for nothing; this is why you're here.*

And as night became day and her nightmares continued, she fought like hell to believe her own words.

*   *   *

Olivia sat staring at the bed for nearly an hour, trying to figure out what to do and coming up blank.

Whatever madness had seized her and prompted her to drag him up the steps and into her home, depositing him on his back on her bed, had passed, and though the smart thing would have been to reverse the action and drop him back on the street, she didn't. She sat and stared at the man, who stubbornly refused to stop breathing, and waited for something to happen.

She had no idea how he had ended up at her door, much less still alive but without his Signet, but she knew she was right about who he was; even if she'd never seen him before, she would have known what she was looking at. She could feel it, that aura, the same one they all had.

Whatever he'd been through, he looked dreadful. His skin was drawn and ghostly pale, with dark circles around his eyes; it was obvious he hadn't fed in days, maybe even as long as he'd been missing, and even unconscious it looked like he was in pain. His breathing was shallow but steady, and she felt for his pulse, which was weak.

He didn't stir when she spoke to him, shook his shoulder again, even lightly slapped his face—the sort of thing she knew in different circumstances would probably have gotten her beheaded. Nothing.

She supposed she should call . . . someone. But who? It wasn't as if there was a Haven hotline, and he didn't have a phone on him so she had no access to his emergency contacts. The sun was up now, but after dusk she could venture out and try to find a patrol team; there was one that passed through her neighborhood. For now, though, they were stuck with each other.

Olivia tried to busy herself straightening up the apartment; she was way too wired to sleep, and somehow the idea of the Prime waking up to a room with dirty laundry in the corners was more than she could take. Her bed was in the loft, with her studio space taking up most of the main floor, and she ran around nervously rearranging stacks of canvases and wiping the rarely used kitchen counter for a while before giving up and returning to her vigil. She thought about trying to paint, but she didn't think she could concentrate with him there.

A couple of hours after dawn, something changed.

She had just sat back down by the bed when she saw his eyelids flutter. She sat very still, waiting, watching.

Slowly, his eyes opened, staring up at the ceiling.

She said quietly, "You're safe, my Lord. It's all right."

At the sound of her voice, he turned his head toward her, and she sucked in an astonished breath.

The eyes that lit on her were black as damnation, without even the narrowest ring of iris showing, they seemed to glow, lit from within, like a night sky full of stars. She couldn't look away . . . it felt like falling, or flying, or dying . . .

Now he gasped, shutting his eyes tightly against some sudden pain, and she flinched as he cried out, curling up on himself, hands clenching the comforter so hard they shook.

Olivia watched, horrified, as agony gripped the Prime's body, and he writhed against the torment with strangled moans—one minute he was trembling like a leaf, the next drenched in sweat, struggling weakly to get his coat off.

Again she acted before she could think better of it. She dove to his side and helped remove the coat, then unbuckled the sword and pushed it off on the floor. She could feel heat radiating from his skin. She got the shirt off him, which seemed to be enough—he twisted onto his stomach, giving her a look at the black-line tattoo of a hawk that covered his entire upper back.

It was, she thought crazily, beautiful work—she would place it at around sixty years old, given the technique, and had been done by a master of the art. She couldn't help but touch the lines, out of curiosity; most vampire tattoos were raised a little more than a human's would be.

The line beneath her fingers shifted.

She gasped yet again and jerked her hand back, then shoved herself back from the bed, eyes going huge with shock. Her heart was in her throat—what she was seeing couldn't be real, couldn't be happening—

The tattoo was *changing*.

Mesmerized, she watched some of the lines fade, others darken . . . The bird's head, which was in profile, changed shape, the skin erupting in blood as if a needle were digging into it. The wings altered, their edges seeming to sharpen. Blood ran down the Prime's back onto the bed, but within seconds the flow had stopped, the lines healing themselves.

Another spasm of pain hit him, and he turned his face into the pillow and screamed.

Olivia wanted to run, to hide; she had never felt fear like this, never seen anything like what she was seeing . . .

. . . except something about it was oddly familiar . . .

Her hand flew to her mouth as she made the connection. Aside from the tattoo, she had seen something like this before . . . when a human became a vampire. She had been one of the lucky ones whose transition occurred peacefully in her sleep, because she was prepared for it and it was done with care; she'd woken up wanting to shag everyone in sight, but with rest and feeding she was fine, no screaming required. But many of them went violently, awake and able to feel every second of their bodies changing, and the way it hurt . . . it looked just like this.

But he was already a vampire . . .

It seemed to go on forever, but later she would check the clock and see that the whole thing lasted about two hours, with the pain coming on him in waves, periods of intense fever alternating with screaming torment, and there was nothing she could do but stand watch.

Finally, the fever broke one last time, sweat soaking the bed. He began to shiver, and she could sense it was almost over; she grabbed a blanket and started to cover him. He whimpered softly and curled up again, as if the touch of the fabric were painful, and she got another view of his back.

The tattoo had finished its transformation. Once a raptor, it had redrawn itself line by line into a raven.

* * *

"David!"

In the middle of the afternoon, Deven woke with a start, sitting bolt upright in bed trying desperately to catch his breath.

Jonathan jolted awake, too, but not quite so violently; he stared at his Prime, blinking confusion from his eyes. "What the hell was that?"

Deven could only shake his head; his heart was hammering wildly, and before he could even frame a sentence, it felt like a giant invisible hook had dug into the skin of his back and was dragging itself through the flesh.

Jonathan saw his facial expression and was clearly alarmed. "Are you all right? What's happening?"

"My back," Deven hissed. "Is it bleeding?"

Wide-eyed, Jonathan looked, then said, quizzically, "No . . . it's fine. Does it hurt?"

The pain was already starting to fade, but it left him dizzy, nauseated. He fell back onto the pillows, hands over his eyes to try to block the faint light of midday that had seeped into the room. His head began to pound, and suddenly the room felt like it was a hundred degrees. He kicked the covers off with a grunt.

"Talk to me," Jonathan said.

Deven let out a long breath, pushing his pulse lower with his will. "I'm fine."

"You said David's name," the Consort told him. "Were you dreaming about him?"

"No . . . I don't know. I don't remember. Are you sure that's what I said?"

"Very sure." Jonathan watched him, eyes slightly narrowed now, appraising. "You know, I've seen you have a lot of nightmares, but nothing like that has ever happened— most of the time you just mutter for a while and that's it."

Deven absently bent his arm back around to touch his back, reassuring himself that there weren't any welts or jagged gashes. Nothing.

"Do you need a Coke?" Jonathan asked with a smile.

Deven smiled back in spite of himself. "No . . . I think I'm all right, love. As far as I know it wasn't a precog episode . . . unless you've ever had one that felt like being tattooed by a chainsaw."

"You didn't flail like that when you were actually tattooed, did you? If you did, I hope you tipped your artist extra."

"No . . ." He put his head in his hands, and Jonathan tugged the blankets back up around him, adding his arms for good measure. Deven let himself relax back against Jonathan's chest. "I remember . . . I remember the night David got his back done . . ."

He didn't go any further. He suspected Jonathan wouldn't want to hear how unspeakably sensual it had been watching the needles dig into David's skin, blood welling up ruby-bright in the wake of black ink . . . It had taken all of Deven's will to wait until they left the studio before he tore the shirt from David's back and baptized the barely healed black lines with his tongue.

"Do I really talk in my sleep?" he asked, hoping to change the subject.

He could hear Jonathan smiling. "Mostly in Gaelic, so I can only pick out the curse words. Sometimes you pray in Latin."

Deven was glad, in that moment, that Jonathan didn't speak Gaelic.

He tried to think back and remember what he'd been dreaming this time, but his mind felt like it was full of mist; the most he could summon was a feeling, the slightest pale whisper of . . .

"I was dreaming about him," Deven said softly. "I don't know what, but . . . it was like, just for a second, he was here."

Jonathan sighed into his hair and held him close. "Where do you think he is now?"

"Nowhere. Gone."

"Do you really believe that?"

Deven didn't answer right away. He knew what he wanted

to say: that death was just the end of the story, fade to black and that was all. But the thought hurt, now more than it ever had. He had never wanted so much to believe in an afterlife as he did now.

"It doesn't matter," he said, winding his fingers through Jonathan's.

Jonathan didn't contradict him, but he knew what the Consort was thinking: that it *did* matter, very much, and while the thought of either heaven or hell for a vampire seemed ridiculous, they were both thinking . . . hoping . . . that wherever David was now, he had found some measure of peace.

After the pain, there was only darkness.

Then there was turpentine.

The ceiling came into slow focus: exposed ductwork, industrial lighting. Metal creaked, rattled. Beyond that, the faint sound of something rasping . . . no, brushing. A brush hitting a flat surface that gave slightly with each stroke.

Painting. Someone was painting.

The room smelled like turpentine, acetone, toluene. Paints and solvents. Underneath that was the old, faded smell of automotive exhaust, as if the building had once been used as a garage.

There was another sound, too, that took a moment to understand: a whooshing in and out, expansion and contraction . . .

Breathing.

Breathing.

Alive.

A shift, creaking bedsprings. The scent of laundry detergent, sweat, blood . . . dried blood . . . not human.

The brushstrokes stopped. Feet on stairs.

A face came into view.

Compassionate gray eyes ringed with blue-green, a lovely olive-mocha skin tone that suggested mixed race; long, dark dreadlocks that fell down around her shoulders. Black tank top spattered with paint. Her neck, chest, and all the way down her arms were covered in complicated tattoos of vines, roots, and snakes that seemed to almost move in the dim light of a nearby candle.

Her voice was a soothing contralto. "Awake at last." She stared down for several minutes, seeming to search for something, before asking, "Do you know who you are?"

Silence. Her words seemed to translate through several languages, inflection and vocabulary so alien at first, twisting around themselves—English. American English, touched with a faint accent. *Do you know who you are?*

Do you know who you are?

A breath in, a breath out. Words. There had to be words there somewhere. "No."

She nodded, unsurprised. "Let's take it slow, then. Can you sit up?"

Her hands were warm and strong, capable. An artist's hands, perhaps—but also a warrior's. Muscle, tendon, bone engaged, inch by inch, lifting, the room spinning for a moment. A breath in, a breath out.

The bed was in a loft overlooking a room full of easels. Paintings in various stages of completion leaned everywhere: strange landscapes that morphed into the garments of shadowy figures, a woman's hair becoming the ocean. All of them seemed to move like her tattoos did, undulating, waves cresting, tides going in and out . . .

. . . like the moon, cycling, waxing to fullness, waning to darkness . . . like life falling into death, clawing its way back to life, like black wings against a starlit sky . . .

"Whoa," she said gently. "Calm down . . . there's nothing to be scared of. Just breathe . . . in and out . . . there you go."

. . . black wings . . .

. . . enfolded in wings, rising . . .

"I think we need to feed you," she said. "You look like you might pass out again."

Panic. Where was this place? What was this? Who was she? Where . . .

. . . Where was the forest? Why was there no sound of wind rustling through leaves? *Where was this?*

"Take my hand, child. Come . . . you have work to do."

. . . wings . . .

There was the sound of glass breaking, of things falling over—the metal walls of the building shook.

The woman dove into the corner, arms over her head, terror written in every line of her body. "Stop it!" she shouted. "Please, stop!"

Stop?

It stopped.

She peeked up through her arms, her eyes bright with tears and wide with fear. "I'm just trying to help you," she said quietly. "I didn't want this."

Words. "I'm sorry."

She swallowed hard and unbent herself, rising gracefully. "I should never have brought you in here in the first place— I must have been out of my mind."

Even as she spoke, though, she was righting the shelf that had tipped over, relighting the candle; she shook her head again and held out her hand. "Come on . . . let's get you cleaned up."

The hand that took hers was pale, a little shaky, and strangely bare, missing something. It was, of course, connected to a wrist, and then to an arm, a well-muscled bicep, a shoulder . . .

. . . a body.

Breathing. Alive.

"I'm alive," he said softly.

The woman sighed. "It was a shock for me, too."

"Who . . . who are you?"

She looked relieved to get a sensible question. "My name is Olivia," she said. "You probably don't remember me, but I remember you." She seemed to sense what was coming next, because she squeezed his hand firmly, and said, "Your name is David Solomon. You're the Prime of the Southern United States . . . Does that ring a bell?"

He listened, but didn't hear any bells. "No."

Another sigh. "I'm sure it will come back to you. You've . . . been through a lot."

She helped him stand, and the room pitched and spun, but she was strong and held him up. This close, the mingled scents of paint and coffee were both alluring and strangely comforting. Her body was solidly built, curvaceous, and she had a proud bearing, the posture of someone comfortable in her own skin. The best word he could think of to describe her was *present*; she occupied her own aura, where many people seemed to be halfway aware of themselves at best.

She was very familiar, somehow, almost as familiar as the name she had given him. The memory was there somewhere. Everything was twisted around itself in his mind, like trying to make sense of ten lifetimes at once, a thousand voices clamoring to be heard, a thousand threads of meaning trying to coalesce into a single reality. He sensed it would right itself, given time, but he also sensed he was not going to be patient about it.

Taking each step carefully, she led him down to the bathroom, pausing to grab a shirt that had been tossed over a nearby chair. She sat him down on the closed toilet lid, facing away from her, and soaked a washcloth in warm water.

"You're all bloody," she explained, swabbing his back. It didn't hurt.

"Why?"

Olivia chuckled. "I haven't the slightest idea how to answer that."

Sudden discomfort clenched his stomach, a deep hot itching blossoming along his jaw. He felt his teeth pressing down and again, the room swam in his vision, physical sensation fighting its way to the front of the vortex of strangeness in his mind.

Hunger.

She finished her work and handed him the shirt. "Yours," she said.

It was dirty, he noticed. It smelled vaguely of battle and fire. His fingers stumbled briefly on the buttons as dozens of mental images intruded, flashes of remembered pain, of eyes . . . green eyes, full of fear and anguish . . . a scream . . .

Olivia shook her head and took over buttoning for him, finishing the last few quickly.

Once he had the shirt on, she walked him out into the main room of the loft, guiding him like an invalid. She left for a moment, and he peered around at the paintings, trying to make sense of them. The same figure recurred throughout the series: female, sometimes cloaked, sometimes arising from the night itself, sometimes entwined with serpents or the roots of a tree, much like Olivia's tattoos.

As Olivia came back down the stairs, he asked, "Who is that woman?"

Her eyebrow lifted in surprise. "I don't really know," she replied. "I dream about her sometimes. I always paint from my dreams."

He turned in a slow circle, eyes moving from canvas to canvas. "She grows closer over time," he observed. "Why doesn't she have a face?"

"I'm not sure. Sometimes she almost seems to, in the dreams, but it changes." She held out the length of black leather in her hands. "Coat."

It, too, was familiar, as was the weight of it as it settled on his shoulders. He straightened its collar, and one hand came to rest on his throat . . .

"What's wrong?"

He looked down, seeing nothing where there should have been something. "It's gone."

Olivia nodded. "Right . . . your Signet. I'm sure your people have it—we'll get you fed, and then maybe you'll be able to remember more and we can get you home."

"Home . . ."

She held up the other item she had brought from the bedroom: a sword.

"Is that mine?"

"Yes." She pulled it partway out of its sheath, admiring the blade, which was carved in an intricate design from the hilt midway down. "It's a beautiful piece," she noted. "Order of Elysium, looks like . . . and . . . I didn't notice that until just now, but there are words carved on this side. Gaelic . . . I think."

Curious, he took the proffered weapon and looked at it more closely. She was right; at a certain angle, he could see that the pattern he had mistaken for vines was, in fact, lettering. Somehow he knew he had never noticed that before.

"What's so funny?" she asked.

He hadn't realized he was smiling. "The Oncoming Storm," he read. "It's . . . it's funny, for some reason."

Olivia went for her own coat, and as she gathered up her keys and phone, he buckled the sword to his belt, his hands moving of their own accord as if the action had been performed so many times it was a reflex.

She eyed him from head to foot. "You look a little less frightful. After you've fed, I'm sure you'll lose that zombie quality." She turned the deadbolt on the door, slid back a second lock, undid a chain.

"Wait . . ."

She paused with her hand on the doorknob. Their eyes met. Uncertainly, he asked, "How long was I gone?"

She seemed to understand the enormity of the question, as well as of the answer, and chose her words carefully. "You've been presumed dead for three weeks."

"But . . . where was I?"

Olivia gave him a small but genuine smile. "That's a very good question. Let's see if we can find you some answers."

She reached out and grabbed his hand again and, with another reassuring squeeze, led him out into the night.

Seven

"You're sure you don't see anything."

"I promise you, my Lady, there is nothing on your back."

Miranda lowered her shirt. "Thank you, Mo." She smiled slightly at the look on his face. "Do you think I'm cracking up?"

The medic laughed. "I think you are burning the candle at both ends and the middle, my Lady, and you need to get more rest. I also think that, whatever I say, you will keep working yourself past your limits until something forces you to stop. It is a common affliction among Signets."

He had come running to the suite at her frantic call, and she was embarrassed to have summoned him to an emergency that didn't exist; but he took it in stride as always and left her to finish getting dressed for her meeting with Novotny.

She had woken in so much pain . . . but this time it was purely physical, an intense burning and scraping all over her upper back. She could feel herself bleeding . . . but there was no blood, no welts, nothing, and now she wasn't even sore.

It had to have been a nightmare. She put her head in her hands for a moment, trying to remember what she'd been dreaming about; she'd been reliving that night over and over, but this was the first time she'd felt any real physical pain from it. As far as she could remember, neither she nor David had been injured that way. She'd been shot, yes, but those were arrow wounds and hurt the way stakes did. This was very different.

Her phone rang, and with a sigh, she groped sideways on the bed for it. "Hey, Dev."

"I have a weird question."

"Yes?"

"Did you have a nightmare about your back?"

She nearly dropped the phone. "Um . . . yes. I woke up freaking out, but nothing was wrong . . . Why?"

"I did, too."

"I don't understand. Why would we both dream that?"

"I'm not sure . . . but Jonathan had a hunch that it happened to both of us. He woke up when I did, but he wasn't in pain. Maybe I picked it up from you somehow?"

"You mean the way you felt my meltdown at Stella's the other night?"

"Yes. And the way we all knew that Jacob and Cora's car was bombed, and . . . about David. I called Jacob, and he said that Cora had some sort of dream that woke her up, but it wasn't nearly that bad and she doesn't remember it actually *hurting* her."

"I really, really don't want you guys to have my dreams, Deven."

He chuckled softly. "Same here, love. But I think it's something more than that. Jonathan said that when I woke, I called David's name . . . and I don't remember the dream, but I know he was in it. What about you?"

She took a deep breath. "I don't know. I've dreamed about him every day, but it's always the same thing. This wasn't that. This didn't feel like a memory—I don't have any memories of him being carved up with a hot poker."

"I . . ."

"What? Spit it out."

"I had a terrible thought, but . . . it's ridiculous . . . and I don't really believe it, but . . . what if, wherever he is . . ."

Miranda felt cold inside, understanding what he meant. "You mean he's in hell."

"Of course not. I just . . ."

"But we can't have a physical connection anymore . . . you said yourself his body went to dust."

"I know. And like I said, it's ridiculous. If you have another theory, I'd love to hear it."

"I don't." She closed her eyes. "I don't understand why any of this is happening. Why I'm alive, why we're all connected . . . I should have gone stark raving insane by now from the power imbalance, but . . . there isn't one. I'm stronger than I ever was, but I don't feel unbalanced. I feel . . . right. In fact, that's the only thing that does feel right."

"You haven't by chance been manifesting any new abilities, have you?"

"No . . . aside from whatever I did to Stella. Why?"

He hesitated. "You started moving things with your mind after you Paired, which was unheard of. If we're all connected, we should keep an eye out for anything like that happening to the rest of us."

"Did you tell Jacob?"

"Yes. He said if he or Cora starts making things float, he'll give me a call."

Her com chimed, and one of the front door guards informed her that Harlan was ready for her. "I'm headed into town to talk to Novotny about the earpiece," she said, forcing herself to stand up and find her coat. "I'll copy you on the results." She grabbed Shadowflame with her free hand and asked, "How are you holding up?"

"Don't worry about me. I'm fine."

She smiled. "You know, I can tell when you're lying now."

She could hear him smiling, too. "I was afraid you'd say that."

* * *

It was a cloudy, cold night in Austin, unseasonably so for the beginning of June; it looked like another round of storms was moving in from the north. The wind had an edge of desperation to it, the last gasp of a mild early summer before hundred-degree temperatures took over and suffocated the region for the next five months.

As they walked through the slick, rain-shining streets, Olivia watched the Prime keenly for signs that he might panic again. In her apartment he had only knocked over a few books and paintings, but out here, who knew?

She had heard rumors that he was telekinetic but hadn't really believed it. There were some powers only Signets had, true, but there were also some things vampires simply couldn't do, and she had thought it was just another myth built up to give the Prime more of a reputation than he had earned.

It didn't take long for her to understand that the myths were not myths, at least not where Solomon was concerned. She could feel the power building in him with every step he took, even before he had fed. Something else seemed to be feeding him, some current of energy she couldn't quite place.

He walked beside her, biddable as a baby chick, but gradually regaining more and more of his confidence. He looked around at the city at first with an almost innocent curiosity, but she could see sparks of recognition here and there the closer they got to the Shadow District.

She didn't grill him on his identity or history. It would come—it was coming, bit by bit. She wouldn't call his condition amnesia so much as a state of shock, and she couldn't blame him . . . if he had, indeed, come back from the dead, whatever had happened to him might be even worse than death . . . and whatever Olivia had witnessed happening to him had taken its toll as well.

"Over here," she said, tapping his arm lightly. "Humans."

They looked around the corner of a building at a rather

typical Austin street scene: plenty of mortals hurrying to get wherever they went, a homeless man with a dog sitting on a bus bench, a vendor selling tacos from a cart. It wasn't all that busy; now that the music festival was over and the university out for the summer, the city was quieting down, breathing easier.

"Call one over," Olivia told the Prime. "Discreetly."

He was staring at the mortal crowd as if he'd never seen such a thing in his life, his expression shifting from apprehensive to understanding, and then to something like pity.

"They're all dying," he said softly.

"Yes. Eventually."

"They're afraid."

"Probably."

His gaze traveled from human to human, and she wondered what exactly he was seeing, or feeling, that she couldn't. Like any vampire she could pick out the healthy ones, evaluating them by scent, and she had a talent for sensing energy as well, but it was clear he was looking for something else.

Finally, his eyes narrowed. She saw a silver ring appear around each iris. "You," he murmured. "Come here."

A man who was about midway across the park changed his trajectory and veered right. He seemed ordinary enough—a businessman of some kind, midthirties, briefcase in hand, likely on his way home from a late evening at the office.

The Prime stepped back into the shadows, and a moment later the human had reached them. Olivia cast a quick glance around to make sure no one had noticed.

The man blinked, confused. "What's . . . what's going on? Who are you people?"

"Be silent," the Prime snapped.

Olivia wasn't sure what to make of his behavior. He circled the man, sizing him up, his eyes cold and hard; his innate grace had become predatory, which was normal on the hunt, but there was something strange in his eyes, something *angry*.

He attacked the man so fast she barely saw him move. The human tried pathetically to struggle, letting out a strangled cry, but there was no escape. The Prime's mouth clamped onto his throat, one hand snaking up to cover the man's mouth.

Olivia felt her own body respond to the waves of satisfaction he was giving off. Hunger raced through her, hot and needy. She could barely concentrate enough to return to the corner and call another human over.

She chose a young brunette woman and dealt with her quickly, efficiently. Blood flowed over her lips and soothed the burning; she wasn't one to toy with her prey usually, preferring a more clinical approach. Five minutes, not a drop spilled, and the girl was already on her way again, barely wavering on her feet.

Olivia turned back to the Prime and gasped.

The human sank to the ground, released from both the Prime's power and his bite, his face blank, eyes staring fixedly at nothing.

Solomon stood over him, eyes closed. His tongue flicked out over his lips and he sighed, a slight smile touching his face. Olivia stared, speechless, as the power of the human's death flooded through him, dark tendrils of energy curling around him that reminded her, unexpectedly, of the design of the raven tattoo that now dwelt on his skin.

The eyes that met hers were black, and she took an involuntary step back.

"You killed him," she breathed, just at a whisper.

He looked down at the human with obvious loathing. "He raped a seven-year-old."

"How can you be sure?"

He lifted his eyes back to hers. They were blue again, to her relief. "I am sure."

"There are laws about killing humans. You made those laws. Even if he had it coming—"

"It was necessary."

"Necessary for what?" she asked, but she already knew—whatever transformation he had undergone in her loft, if it was anything like becoming a vampire, it needed human blood to seal it . . . and if it was more than that, it might have required death. He didn't answer her question—it was possible he didn't really know himself but was simply following some new instinct that had compelled him to kill.

He started to walk away.

"We have to do something with the body," Olivia hissed. "Someone will find it."

He paused and looked back at her over his shoulder. "Who?"

"The police, your Elite—"

A moment passed in which he apparently weighed whether to ignore her and keep walking or stay and argue; finally, he returned to the body and, giving it one last disdainful glance, held his hand out over it, and . . .

. . . it vanished.

"What the hell did you just do?"

Her surprise surprised him. "You said to do something with the body."

"Where is it?"

The Prime tilted his head to the right. "In the Dumpster."

"Did you just . . . *Mist* him?"

He considered that. "Yes."

"That's not possible," she said. She almost laughed at herself. As though if she reminded him he couldn't do it, he would remember she was right and suddenly lose the ability. "You weren't even touching him."

A slight frown creased his forehead. "So?"

"That's not . . . fuck, never mind." Exasperated—and massively discomfited—Olivia threw up her hands. "Let's just get out of here and get you back to your people so they can deal with you."

Confused, the Prime looked from the Dumpster to Olivia before falling into step beside her again. "You're upset."

"That's one way to put it."

Another frown. "You're afraid of me."

"Generally, my Lord, I think you'll find most sane people are."

"I won't hurt you."

She stopped and looked at him. "I'm not afraid you'll hurt me. I'm afraid for the same reason humans are afraid of death."

"They don't understand it . . . it's an unknown."

"For starters."

He held her eyes for a long moment, then said, "Olivia."

"Yes?"

"Olivia Daniels . . . Second in Command of the Australian Elite."

She felt her mouth drop open. "You remember me?"

"Aren't you supposed to be dead?"

"You're one to talk."

He smiled. It was a rather attractive smile, aside from the faint edge of menace about it. "Did you die?"

She looked away. "It felt like it. I think part of me did."

"Then you know death. Therefore you have nothing to fear." He looked around at the buildings on either side of them, then started walking again, beckoning to her. "This way."

The only thing she could think to do was follow. "Do you have any idea where we're going?"

He looked around again. "West."

"I meant the destination, not the direction."

"Not really. I just know it's this way."

"All we need to do is find a patrol," Olivia said. "I'm sure they'll recognize you. Assuming they don't all drop from coronaries, they can take you home."

"No . . . not yet. There's somewhere I need to be right now."

"But you don't know where."

"Not as such."

"Great." She rolled her eyes. "Tell me again why I don't leave your ass right now?"

He looked at her. "I have no idea," he replied thoughtfully. "Perhaps because you miss being part of the Australian Elite and you unconsciously hope to find a place among us."

Olivia snorted. "Not on your fucking life, Sire. Just because you've got a dead Second and I used to be a Second doesn't mean I'm going to hop right into that role like some red shirt on *Star Trek*. I'm done with the Signets. If you want to know the truth, I think I just have to see how this turns out. I want to see the look on their faces when they realize

you're not dead. And I'd like to know a little more about
what the hell happened, just for my own peace of mind."

He tilted his head to the side, again looking like he wasn't
sure what language she was speaking or what species she
was. "You're in hiding," he said.

"Well, it's no wonder you're in charge, if you're that clever."

His lips quirked in a smile. "They think you're dead, but
you're alive, and you're hiding, which means you did something wrong, or they think you did, and if anyone finds out
you're alive they'll kill you."

She felt cold seep into her veins. "Is that a threat?"

He blinked. "An observation. I have no reason to threaten
you, Olivia. You did save my life."

"Did I?" Olivia wasn't sure of that; she had given him shel-
ter, yes, but at this point, could anything kill him? "Besides, it
wouldn't be the first time a Signet turned out to be a traitorous
snake."

There was an edge in his voice that surprised her. "Do not
compare me to the other Signets."

Exasperated again, she started walking, continuing in the
direction he'd chosen. "Fine," she said. "Here it is: I knew
Jeremy Hayes. He was a friend of mine . . . a good friend. He
and his wife and daughter . . . they were family to me, once."

"Jeremy Hayes . . . the rightful Prime of Australia."

She stopped short again. "You know?"

Solomon's brow furrowed as he groped after the memory.
"He told me," he said, nodding his head. "Yes, he told me.
About Amelia, and how they stole his Signet."

"Did he tell you where Melissa and Amelia were when
Hart's men came to kill them?"

"No . . . just that they were taken, his wife murdered."

Olivia couldn't keep walking; the truth made her whole
body ache with sadness and guilt that she had shoved as far
down as possible for as long as she could. "Not right away," she
said quietly, backing up until she was leaning against the side
wall of a building. "I was guarding them. Jeremy asked me to
keep them safe—Bartlett was dead, the territory had been in

chaos for three years, and Jeremy was going to make a play for the Signet. I was to keep them under cover until I got the all-clear, but . . . they found us. Somehow they found us, and . . ."

"They killed her."

"Not right away . . . first they . . ." She put her hands up over her face. "They made it last awhile, and they made the child watch. I was chained, tortured . . . for information, but mostly for sport. I heard Amy crying for her mother . . . begging them to stop . . . and I heard one of them go over to her and strike her, and he was about to rape her but his friends told him, 'That one's for Hart.'"

She kept speaking, though she wanted desperately to fall silent; but somehow she couldn't, couldn't stop the story coming out for the first time since that night. She had never been able to speak of it to anyone, but by sheer dumb luck here she had fallen in with the one person she could tell, who wouldn't kill her for it, not with Jeremy as his enemy.

"They had beaten me so badly I was able to lie there and pass for dead . . . so they left us there to rot until sunup, and took the girl. Hours later Jeremy arrived, and I heard . . . I heard him find Melissa. His grief . . . I swear, it tortured me in ways the men couldn't begin to. And I knew if he found out I had failed him, he would kill me. The fear drove me mad—I just had to survive. To run. So I did."

She felt hands on her shoulders and looked up into his deep, lake blue eyes, which were, just now, full of compassion, which she would never have expected given how cold they had been. With everything that he was going through, he still felt compassion for her . . . perhaps, just perhaps, he was the man they said he was. She felt a glimmer of hope for the first time in years.

"It wasn't your fault," he said to her gently. "You couldn't have known what McMannis and Hart were planning. You did the best you could."

"If he ever finds me, he'll kill me," she said.

Solomon made an indefinite motion with his head. "I wouldn't be so sure, Olivia. I think . . . whatever his actions, Jeremy Hayes is a noble man."

Now both her eyebrows shot up. "You can say that after he killed you?"

A nod, slow and measured, but certain. "He did what he had to do for his daughter. I would have done the same. It gave him no pleasure to kill me or anyone else. He just wanted it over."

He took a step back, and she could breathe again. Something about him in close proximity made her pulse skyrocket, though whether it was regular old attraction or mad atavistic terror, she couldn't quite decide.

"At any rate, Olivia . . . whether you want a place with us or not, you need not fear for your safety. You've helped me, and that alone earns you the right to our aid."

"I don't want aid. I want to go back to my life and live it in peace."

"Do you really?" He smiled. "I find that hard to believe—you were a Second in Command. That kind of authority and power is hard to shake off."

She smiled back. "Clearly."

The compassion was still in his eyes, as was a glint of humor, but he turned back to the road, and said, "Come on . . . it's not far now."

Once again, it all came back to Morningstar.

The Queen pondered the data readout on the monitor. "Give it to me in small words, Doctor. I've had a long week."

Novotny grinned. "Basically: Ovaska, your new mystery attacker, and the earpiece Hart handed over three years ago are all connected. The transmitters used by Jeremy Hayes to blow up Monroe and Prime Janousek are not. All of the transmitters and earpieces are made of similar materials, but when you compare them all very closely you can see that they were made by different people, in different places."

"So whoever's after Stella works for the same group that's been killing Hart's Elite—how does Ovaska figure in?"

"It's a tenuous connection, I admit, but it can't be a coincidence that the Morningstar people who had Ovaska on their payroll to kidnap you also made a large payment to a development firm in New York that specializes in exactly this kind of technology. We ran a search for this particular titanium alloy and they're the only company using it for tele-communications. Morningstar, I believe very strongly, was behind both Ovaska's mission and these unknown assassins."

"And none of it has anything to do with Hayes."

"Not as far as we can tell, my Lady. He was working on Hart's behalf, but whatever his associations with the Order of Elysium or anyone else, he is absolutely not connected to Morningstar."

"What about the knife the attacker left behind at Stella's?"

"We're still analyzing it. So far there doesn't seem to be anything remarkable about it at all—it could have come from any military surplus store. And, unfortunately, there are no prints on it, either."

"We need to find these people," Miranda said. "I need to get an update from . . . our intelligence operatives . . . on whether they have any useful information or actual names we can dig into. Thank you, Doctor."

Waiting for the elevator, she called Deven, but surprisingly Jonathan answered.

"He's in the middle of a debriefing," the Consort told her, "and that's not a euphemism for once. What did you learn?"

She related the highlights of Novotny's report. "Do we have anything new on Morningstar?"

"That's part of what Dev is up to right now. I'll have him call once they're done. In the meantime . . . how are you?"

"Me? Right as rain," she said as the elevator lurched downward.

"That bad, eh?"

Miranda leaned back on the handrail. "I'm okay, I guess. I mean, I'm not bouncing off walls and I'm not dying. Somewhere in between."

"Did you hear about Hart?"

She straightened. "What about Hart?"

"Apparently whatever deal Hayes had with Lydia paid off. Hayes got his daughter back and disappeared with her—and the entire harem. And Hart's whole Elite's in a tizzy; they'd been working on getting a computer network going for communications, but it mysteriously got a virus and went belly-up."

"What happened to the girls?" she asked. "Does Cora know about what happened?"

"I have no idea, and yes—Jacob's the one that gave us the news. He's been keeping eyes and ears on the Council since they all left Austin, and things are, in his exact words, 'exceptionally weird.' Rumors flying, allegiances shifting. No one has come out and said that Hart had a hand in David's death, but he seems to have lost quite a few of his followers."

"Couldn't have happened to a nicer sleazeball," she replied.

"We don't have a lot of details yet. I'll let you know if I get anything."

Just thinking about Hart—about the Council—drained her emotionally, and as she hung up and stuffed her phone back in her pocket, she found her eyes aching.

She didn't want to know what Hart was doing. It didn't matter what the other Signets thought. She didn't have the strength to care about anything beyond her own borders right now. It felt like, for the moment, the South was insulated from the rest of the world; the whole Council, as far as she could tell, was watching them, equal parts horrified and mystified, their understanding of their own existence shaken by the thought that the one thing they counted on—not dying alone—might fail them.

After everything Hart had done to destroy the South, he had failed. She imagined that once he was over his outrage at the harem escaping him, he would go right back to gathering up innocent girls to abuse and turn his attention back on Austin. He had tried everything to nullify their power, and not even sending Jeremy to kill them had succeeded. The South would not be taken down.

The thought gave her only a hollow sense of satisfaction. It was a Pyrrhic victory . . . if it was a victory at all.

"My Lady," Harlan said as she approached the car. "Where to next?"

She stood by the car for a moment, breathing around the sudden knot in her throat. "I need to stop by a couple of District businesses. There's been some unrest."

"My Lady—"

She turned back to the driver and was surprised; he looked genuinely concerned and for just a second abandoned his seamless professionalism.

"You should cut yourself some slack," he said. "When my wife died . . . we'd been together for nearly four decades. I didn't even leave the house for most of a year, and we didn't have a mystical bond. You have a right to hurt. No one here would judge you for taking some time off."

She had no idea what to say to him. She'd had no idea he was ever even married, but of course he had been—they all had their histories, they'd all lost loved ones. Mortal or immortal, everything died eventually. She barely knew anything about most of the vampires who worked for her, but she knew they were all in pain.

Miranda just nodded, eyes bright, and said, "Just . . . going for a walk. To hunt. I'll be back in half an hour."

Harlan bowed, cleared his throat, and ducked back into the car.

She set off down the street blindly, not caring where she was headed. She just needed to be . . . away . . . for a moment.

There were too many things for her to feel. She wished she could simply turn off her heart for a while, run on autopilot for a few years; she was surviving, and thanks to Deven's healing ability—that was the only explanation she'd come up with—she wasn't going mad, but it seemed like every night her wounds grew new scabs that were ripped off the next night by a sound, a smell, a memory. How long would this take?

She knew the answer, and it filled her with despair. Normal people who lost a spouse suddenly and violently would take years to recover, and some never did at all. She of all people knew the depths to which pain's serpentine roots could dig into the soul and coil around, squeezing out every breath of happiness. The prognosis for a woman losing her soul mate was even grimmer.

Once again, the enormity of the future before her sprawled out in her mind, and she wanted to curl up and wail; she could rule the South, she could live without David, but could she do it . . . forever?

She felt bent beneath the weight of her life as she wandered through the Shadow District, passing the front windows and entrances of bars and businesses that only a few weeks ago she had laughed in, danced in, drank in. The thought of laughing—really laughing, hard and breathless, to the point that she snorted loudly and made everyone around her laugh even harder—seemed so beyond comprehension it might as well have been some curious phenomenon she'd read about in a magazine.

She might have felt guilty, or at least self-indulgent, over how poorly she was handling things, but so far no one had suffered; the territory was safe, her Elite managing just fine. She hadn't retired to her bed to waste away. And Deven had said that even David had lost his mind for a few days when he thought she was dead; Faith had mentioned that once, too, that the Prime hadn't moved or spoken, just curled up in a ball.

Miranda couldn't imagine him doing that. She couldn't imagine her Prime being so completely lost that he simply stopped functioning. But Dev swore it was true, swore he'd had to call David out as he had Miranda, set him back on his feet.

She paused, suddenly amused. At some point she had apparently decided to love the Prime of the West, and he her, with a fierceness that she would never have believed possible only three years ago. David would be pleased.

Wavering on her feet, she dug in her coat for the broken Signet, her fingers closing around it. "I miss you, baby," she whispered. "I don't know how . . . what the . . ."

Something felt odd. She flipped the Signet over in her hand, feeling along its polished surface, the stone cool against her fingertips. It took a moment to realize what was wrong.

It usually hurt.

She yanked the amulet out of her coat, walking over to the pool of a streetlight, even though she could see just fine; it was an old human habit, wanting to verify things in light even when they were obvious.

Miranda stared at the Signet, unable to breathe.

When she had put it in her coat that evening, the stone had been cracked, several shards missing; they were mostly in the box in her room, but she guessed a few tiny slivers would never be found. The edges of the shattered stone were sharp and hurtful when her hand had squeezed it, the pain grounding her out of her thoughts and into the harshness of reality.

Now the stone was whole.

Not only were the cracks healed, the missing shards were no longer missing. It might as well have regrown itself in the course of the night.

It wasn't possible. *Was it?* Was this what happened after one broke, so that whoever was in charge of such things didn't have to make a new one? How could that even happen?

David would have had a theory already, something to do with crystalline molecular structures.

She stared into the ruby for a long moment, willing it to relight, but it remained dark . . . whole, yes, but still asleep, waiting, she supposed, for whoever came to take it after she finally died.

She was so focused on the Signet that she almost didn't hear the footsteps before it was too late.

The noise hit her ears a split second before the stake sang through the air where her body had just been. She twisted backward, the cylinder of wood grazing the sleeve of her coat, and spun downward into a crouch, one hand stuffing the Signet back into her pocket and the other unclipping Shadowflame.

She straightened in a blur of motion, drawing the sword just in time to meet the blade that swung for her neck.

There was no time to think, no time to do anything but act; she parried the first attacker's sword while another tried to dive in on her left, her leg flashing out sideways to connect a boot heel in his rib cage. She rammed Shadowflame into the first one's throat and pulled the blade on the same breath, spinning around to slice open a third attacker on the follow-through.

She leapt backward, giving her a few feet to sweep the situation with her senses: seven of them, one of her, all of them armed, all of them thirsty for exactly one thing—her blood.

They had no idea what hell they had just unleashed upon themselves.

The Queen made no move to escape, no effort to call for backup. She flung herself into their midst with a hiss and gave herself over to the bloodred haze of rage, letting her body take over, meeting sword slash and fist with such force that even seasoned fighters who knew their quarry were caught by surprise.

She had three of them down in less than a minute, and the other four circled her, suddenly made wary by the groans of their dying comrades.

"Come on!" Miranda snarled at them. "If you've come for my life, take it! Four against one, you can do better than that!"

Shadows moved beyond the streetlight, and four became eight . . . became ten. She was surrounded.

She knew she should Mist away, reappear back at the car and call in Elite to pursue them . . . but something deep within her, perhaps her precognitive gift or perhaps just wild suicidal desperation, kept her rooted to the spot, her heart clamoring for their blood.

One of the attackers turned his head just enough that she saw the glint of something in his ear.

"Morningstar," she spat at them. Her voice rang off the night air. "You can take a message back to your boss, then. I am Queen of this territory. I paid for my Signet with blood and death, and neither you nor anyone else will take it from me. *You cannot defeat me, you bastards. I dare you to try.*"

They accepted the dare.

* * *

Olivia heard the sounds of battle long before she saw it: the old familiar clang of steel on steel in its age-old rhythm, the cries of pain, grunts and yells of both male and female voices, heavy sounds of bodies hitting walls.

Warring instincts flared up: Part of Olivia wanted to run toward the fighting, and part of her wanted to run away.

But the Prime had already decided for them and had broken into a run.

Olivia caught up in time to see a rather surreal scene playing out before her: a street in the Shadow District, out in view of everyone, where at least a dozen black-clad men and women were attempting to take out a single opponent. All around them, Olivia could see faces peering out windows, watching fearfully, all of them no doubt terrified that gang violence had at last erupted to destroy the tentative peace of Austin.

But, she realized as she drew closer, that wasn't the issue here. They weren't watching the whole fight . . . just its epi-center, where a single woman was engaging every one of her attackers two, sometimes three at a go.

She was as graceful as a dancer; her sword was a silver flame in the night, almost liquid in motion, so fast the blood that sprayed from the wounds it inflicted didn't seem to even touch the steel.

But there was something more at work here—Olivia had seen someone fight that way before, throwing her entire body and mind into the fight as if she had nothing to lose . . . someone who didn't care anymore whether she survived the fight. Her desires had contracted to a single pinpoint: make someone pay.

Olivia saw a sword slip past the Queen's guard, saw it pierce her shoulder; the Queen hissed, but merely spun toward its wielder and beheaded him with a single stroke. She paused long enough to pull the blade from her body and throw it on the ground. She was bleeding badly, but it didn't stop her, nor did the half-dozen or so other wounds she had sustained already—a couple of lacerations on her arm, bruises on her face, and the way she held herself suggested a cracked rib or two.

She had six of them down before she truly began to wear out, and Olivia saw her falter.

At her side, the Prime sucked in a breath that was half a gasp and half a snarl. Olivia looked at him, saw how mesmerized he was by her—and before Olivia could ask if he recognized her, he had already set off for the fight, sword drawn.

The attackers fought the Queen until they had driven her back toward the wall of the building behind her, but she didn't give up, even though she was growing weaker from blood loss and, it seemed, the waves of sorrow she was emitting so strongly that Olivia felt tears in her own eyes. Whatever her intention in taking on this fight, Olivia knew that the Queen was at the end of her strength . . . she was about to give up.

It happened so fast. One of the men parried her sword's stroke and knocked the blade from her hands, another kicking her in the side; she went down to her knees, then rolled onto the ground with a groan of pain, arms clenched in front of her abdomen. Olivia could see blood seeping out between her fingers.

The attacker stepped in closer, raising his sword to swing down in the final strike—

—and it met another blade, hard enough to throw off a spark as the two swords grated along each other's edge, bringing the attacker face-to-face with his own death.

Olivia saw the shock in the man's face turn into instinctive horror as he realized what he was looking at—who was on the other end of that sword—and tried, in vain, to turn and run.

He made it about two steps before his body jerked, and a loud, sickening crack split the air, his body twisting violently and falling to the ground.

The Prime took his head in a graceful arc and turned, slowly and deliberately, to face the others.

They were all staring at him in petrified silence.

He tilted his head to one side. There was nothing human, none of that compassion Olivia had seen earlier, in his hell black eyes. "Run," he said softly.

And they did.

Olivia watched his gaze travel from window to window around the scene and catch the eyes of all those watching the fight. No one would mistake him for another vampire; he was too well known in this city. They all understood the implications of what they were seeing.

Shutters and blinds flipped closed. Deadbolts shot up and down the street. Lights went out.

Only then did he turn to the Queen.

She was curled up on herself, one hand on the pavement while the other was still held against her middle; she stared at the ground, eyes dull.

He went silently to his knees before her, still unspeaking. Her pale, graceful hands, hands that had swung a sword and killed half a dozen vampires, were shaking, and Olivia watched with her heart in her throat as he reached out and took the one that lay on the ground, covering the Queen's hand with his own.

The Queen was still.

Her eyes shut tight.

"No," she whispered. "Don't do this to me."

He didn't speak, and she went on, "If I open my eyes and I'm dreaming . . . if I wake up and I'm alone again . . ."

He lifted one of his hands from hers and cupped her face, palm against her cheek so softly, as if she were made of spun glass.

Slowly, she lifted her head and opened her eyes.

A ragged gasp passed through her lips, and she lurched backward, away from him. "No . . . no . . . no . . ."

When he didn't say anything, she reached out to him, shaking even harder this time, until her bloodstained palm met solid flesh, his shoulder, then his neck, then his face. Her hand slid back down over his chest, seeking a heartbeat.

Her voice was barely a whisper, as if giving words to the

thought made it real, and she was too far gone for even that much hope. "Is it . . . is it really you?"

He nodded.

"You died . . . I felt you die . . . the others saw you . . . you went to dust . . . there was nothing left but a shadow."

Softly, he smiled. "And of shadow I was reborn."

The sound of his voice seemed to break something inside the Queen. She lost her balance and fell sideways, landing almost in a fetal position, so far past hysterical she barely moved as shock waves of emotion wrenched her heart in all directions. She was screaming—a ghostly, keening sound, the kind of sound that was all that remained in a broken heart after every last hope had been stripped away and all that remained was too raw and bloody to even bear a loving touch.

The Prime moved over to her, gathering her up in his arms, bundling her into his coat and holding her tightly, rocking slowly back and forth with her; his face was turned up to the sky, eyes closed, but Olivia could see the tears running in silver rivulets down his face, and she knew that whatever holes still riddled the Prime's memory, this much he knew: He was home.

Eight

She fully expected to open her eyes to her bedroom, her solitude, and feel the brief moment of terrified joy ripped away from her as reality settled back in.

What she got was a little different.

She smelled antiseptic, industrial cleanser; she could hear beeping, and whirring, and the sounds of people milling around. As her eyes fluttered open she saw a white curtain, and looking down, white sheets, and her arm stretched out across the bed, a plastic tube taped to her wrist, the needle a thin but very real presence in her arm.

"There you are, my Lady," came a voice, and a blurry face resolved itself into Mo. "How are you feeling?"

She had no idea how to answer that. "What happened? Why am I here?"

"You were in deplorable shape," he said, his voice becoming a little stern. "Wounded, dehydrated, underfed, exhausted—your electrolytes were, as they say, extremely out of whack. You've been receiving fluids and blood for several hours . . . and a little Xanax thrown in with some pain medication for a few superficial wounds you sustained during your . . . altercation."

"Altercation." She remembered, vaguely: blood, and screaming, adrenaline coursing hot and violent through her body. It didn't even seem real. Had she really been attacked by a dozen vampires? How many had she killed? With numbers like that, she should have been dead.

Mo sensed her confusion. "I wish I could have been there," he said. "According to witnesses it was like nothing they had ever seen. Even those used to watching Signets fight were beyond words."

"I don't understand . . . it feels like a dream . . . even . . ." She gasped.

Her hands tightened in the sheets, and she heard the heart monitor's beeping begin to accelerate. "No," she whispered. "It couldn't be real . . . Mo . . . tell me . . ."

His face softened, and he smiled at her gently. "Look to your right, my Lady. I warn you: It may be something of a shock."

Miranda couldn't do it. She was seized with such fear, she was paralyzed, unable to even acknowledge the hope that . . . It couldn't have happened . . . it had to have been a hallucination brought on by exhaustion or the fight . . . Things like that simply didn't happen, not in this world. If she looked, she would see nothing, and even that tiny thread of possibility would be lost to her.

But gradually, a quarter inch at a time, she forced her head to turn, forced herself to confront reality.

The heart monitor shrieked out an alarm. She heard Mo fussing with it.

She was shaking, she knew she was shaking, so hard she could hear her teeth chattering. Disbelief dug its teeth into her like a wolf snapping its head back and forth to break a rabbit's spine. Her mind, her heart, everything . . . stopped.

A man lay asleep in the bed next to hers. He, too, was hooked up to a variety of monitors but slept peacefully, hands folded over his stomach, breath slow and even. Black hair fell into his face, and though his features were drawn and he was dangerously thin, that face was unmistakable.

She heard Mo murmuring to a nurse about sedatives and heard him say, "My Lady, please, you must calm down. Your poor heart is going to explode at this rate."

She couldn't answer. She couldn't even move. All she could do was stare.

She took a breath and pushed words out one by one, each taking a herculean effort to speak: "But . . . you're sure it's him."

He smiled. "You would know that better than I, my Lady."

Miranda struggled to sit up and scooted toward the edge of the hospital bed. "Help me up," she gasped. "Mo, help me—"

The medic looked like he wanted to push her back down, but, obviously realizing it would be pointless, he sighed, nodded, and lowered the rail on the side of the bed. "Slowly, please," he said. "Wait—"

He quickly clipped off the tube from her IV and plugged it, freeing her from its tether; she slid onto her feet but nearly collapsed, her legs buckling beneath her. Mo caught her and steadied her patiently, then stepped away to let her stand.

Miranda, heart racing, took one step and then another, forcing strength into her limbs, the four feet from one bed to the other feeling like a mile. At last, her hands wrapped around the rail, and she leaned on it heavily, pulling herself closer, holding her breath.

Mo came to stand beside her.

She couldn't stop shaking, and her voice trembled as she asked, "Mo . . . in your professional opinion, as a doctor . . . have I gone mad?"

She looked over at the medic to see his expression lose its usual genial professionalism; for a second it looked like he wanted nothing more than to hug her, put her back to bed, and tuck her in safe and sound. "No, my Lady," he said. "Nor are you dreaming, or delusional. This is very real."

"But it's not . . . possible . . ."

As she spoke, she remembered the last thing she had heard before the world went black: *And of shadow I was reborn.*

"We don't know what happened," Mo said quietly. "He and his companion brought you here, but before anyone could interrogate her she disappeared, and our attention was diverted to the two of you. As soon as we got you on a gurney he passed out cold."

She reached out, letting her palm rest for a moment on his chest, feeling it rise and fall, feeling the thrum beneath her hand. A good, strong heartbeat; a slow, even breath. Just in the few moments since she'd woken his face had softened, the blood pumped into his veins reinvigorating the flesh, giving it back its warmth and life. She stood there, watching, feeling his heartbeat, still so afraid . . . so afraid she would wake up, despite Mo's words, or that this dream would dissolve into the nightmare she had faced over and over. Her heart could not accept this, not yet.

"If you need anything," Mo said, "press the call button."

She nodded, and the medic left; deprived of his reassuring presence, Miranda felt even more terrified, smaller and more vulnerable. She kept her free hand wrapped around the bed rail, gripping it tightly, lest her knees give out again.

Even with all the machines beeping and whirring, her breath on the air seemed loud, her words strangely young and childish. "David? Can you hear me?"

After an endless moment, she saw a flicker of movement and his eyes slit open, blinking against the room's relatively bright light. Miranda reached over and snapped off the examination lamp; the clinic had lighting options for both sectors of its clientele and staff.

Eyes opened, first unseeing, then gradually focusing on her face.

She nearly sobbed. Oh, God, how she had missed that blue . . .

. . . but . . .

Despair choked her. He was blinking at her, confused . . . without recognition.

"Please," she whispered. Tears were already falling, and she didn't try to stop them. "Please tell me you know who I am."

He stared at her, and she could see the pain in his face—
he was trying, reaching for the memory, and it was so
close . . . his history, their life together, everything, it was
so close . . .

Miranda took a deep, slow breath, closed her eyes, and
sang softly,

> *You're in my blood like holy wine*
> *You taste so bitter and so sweet . . .*

There was a choking, gasping noise, and she opened her
eyes to see that he was pushing himself up, struggling against
the wires and IV, blue eyes full of tears—and memory—
trying to reach her.

She flung her arms around him, not caring if the monitors
got dislodged and the whole staff came running; she was
weeping again, and so was he, murmuring her name over and
over, his hands moving over her body, pressing against her
shoulders and back, proving to himself she was there—and
she did the same, touching him everywhere she could, kissing any place she could find with her lips, her sobs giving
way to first a gasp, then another, and then laughter.

They clung to each other, neither able to speak at first
through the overwhelming relief, the joy that was so immense
it hurt, the creeping hell of the last three weeks finally, finally
over with, her heart almost unable to contain it all.

"Where were you?" she finally sobbed into his shoulder.
"Where have you been? Why didn't you come home?"

"I don't know," he whispered. "I don't know . . . Please
forgive me, beloved . . . please forgive me . . ."

She shook her head, though what she was denying she
couldn't say for certain, and put her lips to his at last.

They held on to each other until the flood of emotion had
moved through them both, and Miranda could pull away far
enough to look in his face. Their eyes locked, his still murky
from the struggle to remember everything, hers anguished
and confused.

"I remember dying," he said hoarsely. "I remember the

darkness. And I remember waking up and feeling the daylight coming . . . I must . . . I must have crawled to the stairwell before the sun hit me. After that it was black again . . . I was so weak . . . I didn't know where I was, or who I was, but everything hurt, and I knew I had to find . . ." He looked up, around at the room. "Olivia . . . where is she?"

"Olivia?"

"The woman who brought me here. Who saved my life. Where is she?"

Bewildered at his desperation to find this woman, Miranda said, "Mo said she vanished before they could question her."

"She took me in the other night and kept me safe while . . ."

"While what?"

"I don't know," he said helplessly, putting his head in his hands. "I don't understand what this means, what it's done to me. My back . . . my back hurts . . . it itches so badly I want to claw the skin off."

The second he said it, she was pulling the gown off his shoulders, sudden knowledge gripping her heart. When she saw the tattoo . . . the remains of the red-tailed hawk that were now . . . something else entirely . . . her dream, and Deven's, made sense.

"I think I may be sick," David said softly.

Miranda slammed her hand against the call button, and a cadre of nurses and Mo swept into the room, taking over with no little relief of their own. They eased David back down onto the bed, checking his vitals, adjusting the fluids they had dripping into his body; she heard Mo ordering Valium, and something called Phenergan, for the nausea.

"You must relax, Sire. Please. You are safe, and your Lady Queen is here with you. There will be time for understanding all of this later once you are strong again, but for now you both are in desperate need of quality sleep. In fact, I shall have your people return you to the Haven tonight— once this batch of sera is in, you should be fine on your own as long as you keep feeding regularly. You will be more at ease in your own bed."

The nurses tried to usher Miranda into a chair when she

refused to leave David's side; finally they compromised and wheeled her bed closer so that she and David could at least hold hands while Mo pushed another bag of fluids and blood into Miranda's IV, just to make sure she was stable.

There was definitely something more than blood in the bag—Miranda felt woozy almost immediately, and the nurses had a much easier time guiding her back to bed after that.

She kept her face turned toward him, though, waiting for herself to wake up and all of this to end, but it didn't. The drugs coursed through her, relaxing her gently away from the room, carrying her in their safe, somnambulant arms into the darkness that welcomed her, but she kept watching his face, as long as she could, just in case when she woke it had been the last time . . .

But gradually the room faded, the sounds faded, and she began to drift in a silent sea of shadows that buoyed her up, cradling her softly. She relaxed, feeling safer than she had in weeks, and listened to the movement of the shadows, so much like water, with tides and breakers as the darkness lapped over her, warming her, soothing away the horror she had been living in.

She looked up at one point to a starlit sky—or was it the reflection of the ocean of stars she now floated through, shining back down at her from overhead? The stars turned in their own endless waltz, through time and space and nothingness.

She felt a hand on her face and looked up.

There was a woman kneeling above where she lay in the dark water-shadows, thin black robes like wisps of smoke flowing down over her moon white skin. She stared down at the Queen through fathomless black eyes—black, without pupil or iris, simply the night sky caught in their depths. Hair the color of old wine, or perhaps blood, flowed down over her shoulders much like Miranda's own, but it seemed to move of its own accord, almost serpentine around her shoulders.

When the woman spoke, her voice was the wind through a cold winter thicket, the *slip-slip-slip* of sleet, the whisper of snow. *"You have done well, my daughter, and I thank you."*

Miranda stared up at her. "Who are you?"

"Now your work truly begins."

"What work?"

"First you have to make a choice . . ."

Miranda tried to grab her arm, to hold her there until she gave a straight answer, but her hands wouldn't cooperate; they seemed to be made of mist, and the room was mist, and mist flowed forward and into every corner of her vision, and gently lathed the room away until it was just her, drifting in the shadows, resting, cocooned in that diaphanous mist that was so like a raven's wings wrapped around her, feathers holding her safe, safe . . . safe.

There was little comfort to be found, even in the hunt.

His teeth broke through the woman's skin, sliding through muscle and into vein, before withdrawing to allow the hot rush to spill forth. She was too far under his thrall to struggle, but she tensed at the pain and moaned softly, the sound lost in the neverending noise of the New York streets.

Jeremy found the city barbaric and disgusting. Humans died here every night and no one took any notice; it wasn't so much that he cared about their lives as the idea that fifty feet away pedestrians kept walking, oblivious to the violence a stone's throw away, and even if the woman were screaming, they would in all likelihood simply walk faster, not wanting to get involved. When a murder was reported it didn't generate the kind of scene they portrayed on television; there would be perhaps two police officers, neither particularly invested in the crime, stretched thin as they were.

For that reason the Northeast had always been ruled by vampires who turned a blind eye to killing. There was really nothing to stop them here. London was just as bad, and as he understood it Los Angeles had once been even worse. And even with no-kill laws in place in the South, only the advent of the sensor network had put an end to the fun in New Orleans . . . and still, if one was discreet, there were ways around it. Vampires would always, always find a way to kill.

He didn't kill her. There was no point, really. The momentary high of her death would do nothing to assuage his true hunger.

Drunk as she was, he didn't have to bother with altering her memory. It would be a minor miracle if she remembered the night at all once her head was in the toilet in a few hours.

The alcohol in her bloodstream hit him a moment later; he'd chosen her for that very reason. For a few minutes the world spun and swam, and he felt himself relax, worry . . . everything . . . blurring until nothing mattered. For just a moment, he was free.

It passed, leaving faint nausea in its wake that also faded quickly. Jeremy left the alley as sober as he'd entered it, and also just as heavy-hearted.

He was only a couple of blocks from the apartment. He had a blood supply there, but after the last few nights he'd needed to get out . . . just for a little while. Even the most devoted parent needed a moment away. He had given Amelia a phone, promised he'd be back soon and wouldn't go far.

She had simply looked at him through her big, empty eyes and nodded vacantly.

At least it was something. He'd gotten a few words from her here and there but still couldn't tell how much she understood about where she was, or even that she was free. In her sleep she whimpered, begged invisible assailants to stop, her child's voice numbly repeating phrases she had been schooled into reciting to entertain Hart during his use of her body. Listening to it had been a new form of torment, and up until now Jeremy had thought he was familiar with them all. It had taken a monumental act of will not to head straight for the Haven and fight his way through the Elite to draw and quarter Hart with his bare hands.

Not now. Later. One day he would have his vengeance. For now, Amelia was all that mattered.

To that end, he was preparing to get her out of the country. Perhaps once they were home in Brisbane and she was surrounded by sights and sounds and scents she had grown up with, she would rally. At the very least it would be more comforting to her than this place.

His phone rang, startling him, and his heart immediately set to pounding. The only person who had his number was Amelia.

"Hello?"

There was a pause, and then a soft, young voice said, "I'm sorry, Dad."

He froze where he was, midstride. "Sweetheart, are you all right? I'm on my way back now, I'll be there in five minutes."

"I'm sorry, Dad."

"What are you—"

He heard the faint sound of glass breaking, but not heavy like a window or mirror—more like a jar, or a bottle. Then there was a scraping, and the noises in the room got suddenly louder; he could hear traffic going by down below. "Amelia . . ."

"It wasn't your fault."

Something in her voice triggered an instinct older than time, and he broke into a run, heading toward the apartment.

"I can't do it, Dad. I'm sorry."

He came around the corner of the building, and as he heard the phone clatter to the ground, someone across the street yelled in surprise.

A dark shape fell from one of the fourth-floor windows, nightgown fluttering in the wind, a cape of white-blond hair trailing behind.

He was halfway across the street, desperately calling her name, when she hit the ground and the explosives in her body went off, throwing him back into a parked car with a blast of heat and a shower of blood.

My name is David Solomon. I am Prime of the Southern United States. I hold a PhD in Engineering from MIT and have a Stanford-Binet IQ of 187. I was born in . . . in England . . .

His hands wrapped around the cool sides of the sink, and he leaned forward, staring into the stream of water flowing into the vessel as he tried again.

I was born in England and married Elizabeth Cooke. She bore one son, Thomas, before her execution for Witchcraft. I came to America in . . . in . . .

The date would not come. He had to start over:

My name is David Solomon. I have black hair and blue eyes. I have a tattoo of . . .

His mind filled again with that cold, gray fog, and he had to try a different approach, something to cast light through the confusion.

My name is David Solomon, Prime of the Southern United States. My Queen is Miranda Grey-Solomon, an award-winning musician and singer, gifted with empathy and some of my telekinesis. I met her four years ago, as a human, and I brought her to the Haven when she was injured.

Yes, that part was working. It sounded right, it made sense. As long as he kept his mind focused on the connections to his heart, he didn't panic. It was only when he tried to remember anything else, anything outside his emotional world, that he felt the creeping madness begin.

He stood at the sink for far longer than seemed appropriate, and sure enough, a few minutes later he heard the soft knock. "Are you all right in there?"

"I'm fine."

"Can I come in?"

"Yes . . . of course."

She opened the door a few inches and peered in, and he saw the relief cross her face when her leaf green eyes settled on him. She was still expecting him to disappear, or for herself to wake up. He felt rather the same way.

"You still look so thin," she said, coming into the room in her bathrobe, her hair a damp fall of shining curls around her face. "I guess you couldn't feed . . . where you were."

He closed his eyes. "I don't know. I guess not."

He felt her hand, warm and real, on his bare shoulder, and reached up to link his fingers with hers.

"I called California," she said. "I'm pretty sure Deven fainted. He dropped the phone and Jonathan picked it up and said they'd have to call me back."

"What . . . who?"

She frowned, took a breath. "Deven . . . the Prime of the West. Your ex-lover . . . mostly. Our friend. Little guy, lots of leather, the world's oldest bitchy queen."

Again, he shut his eyes, this time against a sudden memory: mouth against mouth in the darkness, his nails digging into tattooed biceps, a gasp of pain that faded into pleasure.

"I hurt you," he murmured. "I went to him and hurt you."

Miranda nodded. "Three years ago."

"Why would I do something like that . . . to you? Why . . ."

She looked down at the tile floor, then back up into his eyes. "You love him," she said. "Not the same way you love me, but you do. You were both very confused about your relationship, and you made a terrible mistake. But it's been three years and we've grown so much since then."

He returned her nod; it made sense, and he believed her. He remembered that night, the desperation . . . both of them trying to claw their way into . . . something. Something they had lost long before. Something that should never happen again . . . and yet . . . it had . . . and . . .

"You do remember him," Miranda said with a sigh. "That's something, I guess."

She smiled. "Come on," she told him, tugging lightly on his arm. "Esther brought in more blood—doctor's orders. Then we can have a long sleep."

With a nod, he followed her back into the bedroom, to the fireplace, where two goblets of blood sat on the coffee table. They drank in silence for a while, both concentrating on the renewed strength and nourishment that seeped into all the still-raw places in their bodies and minds . . .

"I can't feel you," he said suddenly, head snapping up.

Miranda lowered her eyes. "I know."

"I should be able to. You should be in my head."

She set her glass down, staring at the fire. "The bond between us was broken when the Signet shattered. I don't . . . I don't know how to get it back."

His hand moved up to his throat. "My Signet."

"Oh!" Miranda, looking sheepish, rose from the couch

and took her coat from its hook by the door; she reached into the pocket and retrieved the heavy silver chain, then returned to him, sitting down and giving him an uncertain look. "Do you think that's all it will take?"

He held out his hand, and she placed the Signet in it silently. He regarded the amulet for a moment; he could feel its energy humming faintly, and as soon as he turned it over in his palm, the stone began to glow.

Miranda sighed. "Thank God. It remembers you."

"I thought it was broken."

"It was. Earlier tonight it fixed itself."

"You didn't think that was a little strange?"

She raised an eyebrow and said wryly, "Don't know if you noticed, baby, but much stranger things have happened tonight."

He lifted the chain and fastened it around his neck, letting the stone settle where it belonged between his collarbones . . . and waited.

The stone continued to glow, but nothing felt different. He remembered . . . vaguely . . . the first time he had put it on, and the rush of power that had overcome him; this time he could feel the Signet's aura, whatever it was, like warmth spreading through his skin, but there was no drama, no rush . . . no bond.

They were still two separate people. The wrongness of it made him feel sick.

Miranda's eyes were wet, and she looked away again. "Too much to ask that it be that easy," she muttered. Then her eyes returned to him, and she managed a smile. "But you look like yourself again with it on."

He let his hand rest on the stone. "I'm sorry," he said quietly. "I don't know what to do to make all of this better."

She smiled again through her tears. "You don't have to make it better. You being here makes it better. Just be patient—I'm sure it'll all come back."

He met her eyes. "But . . . what if it doesn't? What if . . . this is just how things are now? Do you still want . . ." He looked away, no longer able to bear the desperation in her gaze. "Would you still want to be with me if we couldn't have what we did before?"

"David Solomon, don't be a dumbass," she said, reaching over to swat him lightly on the back of the head, a move he was *sure* he remembered. "I didn't fall in love with you because of a mystical bond. I sure as hell didn't marry you for it. I married you because I wanted to spend as much of my future with you as I could, as your partner and Queen, and because I loved you. None of that has changed. I believe things will come back. But if they don't, we'll adapt. I lost you once already—no stupid soul mate thing is going to make me lose you again."

Her voice, fierce and strong, flooded his heart with love, and he smiled. *That's my girl.* "All right," he said. "We're in this together, then. For better or worse."

"Let's stick with better. We've already done worse."

"From your lips to God's ears," he answered automatically.

She smiled. "That's my boy."

They took each other's hands and just sat for a while, taking in the wonder of each other's presence. It seemed a silly thing, perhaps, but wherever he had been, he had missed just being with her, hearing her breathe, catching the scent of her shampoo. He had missed their conversations and the way she moved. Her wit, her honeyed voice . . . her skin . . .

"Bed," she said, softly but insistently. Once again, he obeyed.

Halfway there, he stopped and pulled her back toward him, into his arms, fixing his mouth to hers with a greater hunger than he had felt since waking up in Olivia's loft. He wove his hand through her hair, his tongue through her lips, kissing her until they were both breathless and dizzy from the heat that leapt up through them.

He took hold of her robe and pushed it off her shoulders onto the floor, running his hands down her back. Her fingernails scratched over his skin as she urged him toward the bed again, neither willing to break the kiss as they sank into the comforter together. She pinned him on his back, leaned down to nibble along his neck, while her hands busied themselves getting reacquainted with the rest of his body.

"Do you remember this?" she asked.

He grinned. "If I say no, will you keep doing it?"

Miranda chuckled. "You asked for it—how about this?"

She flicked her tongue at his navel, and he made an involuntary snorting sort of sound and tried to push her off. "No fair tickling," he said, laughing. In reply she repeated the motion off to the side, midway between his rib cage and hip bone, and he yelped.

She was giggling as he flipped her onto her back. "That's it, woman, you're in for it now," he informed her.

He wanted so badly to get lost in her, to feel their joined being merging and dissolving as their skin met and joined, but even through hours of renewing their love for each other, there was something . . . something not *wrong*, exactly, but not the same. They were both trying to find it, trying to return to what had been there before, but the reality was there, and incontrovertible: They were two people, separate, able to connect to each other only as closely as flesh would allow.

When, hours later, they lay entwined, sweaty and out of breath, he heard her sigh, her fingertips tracing the new lines on his back.

"I love you," she whispered into his ear. "So much."

He smiled. "I love you, too."

She kissed the back of his neck and rested her cheek against his shoulder. "What happens now?" she asked.

"Now we sleep," he replied.

He knew, without any sort of mystical bond, that she still had a thousand questions and was no more satisfied than he was—but she especially needed rest, and whatever answers there were to find would have to wait until they were both functional enough to face them.

But bond or no bond, they would face them together . . . and he gave in to sleep gratefully, knowing—not hoping, knowing—that if death couldn't keep them apart, nothing could.

Nine

To: Lark (lark1026@fastmail.net)
From: Stella (stellybeans@austin.mm.com)
Subject: Shit gets weirder.
YOU'RE NOT GOING TO BELIEVE THIS . . .

Stella stared at the monitor of her laptop for several minutes, then sighed and closed it.

She had absolutely no idea how to finish the sentence.

It would help if she knew more about what the hell was going on. All she had been able to glean from eavesdropping on her guards was that somehow, some way, the Prime had come back from the dead. It didn't sound like anyone had seen him, just that he was home and he and the Queen had been in bed for most of the last two days, recovering from . . . it, whatever it was.

She was dying to know more, but the only person she knew she could ask was Miranda herself, and she hadn't seen Miranda in days. Stella didn't blame her for not having time to come entertain her human guest, but still, Stella was getting bored and impatient, and there wasn't a damn thing she could do about it.

Sighing again, she slid down off the bed and stretched. Her legs were kinked up from sitting too much. Maybe she should go outside. She wasn't much on working out, but she was used to walking everywhere to save gas. That was one of the nice things about living where she did. In her part of town, everything she needed was within walking distance.

At this point she was starting to consider Austin itself within walking distance . . . it would just be a really long walk. It would be worth it, though, to get back to her actual life and stop grumping around her gilded cage.

Pywacket, who was much more lackadaisical about their predicament, looked up from his butt-licking cat yoga and gave her a wide-eyed look.

"I know, I know," she said. "Bad vampires, going to kill me, et cetera."

She left her room, giving the door guard a nod: "Just going for ice cream," she said.

Nobody minded if she wandered around, as long as she told her guard where she was going; if it was daytime, limited personnel were available to watch her, but it was unlikely anyone would try to hurt her during the day. This far from town, anyone with deadly intentions would be stuck at the Haven until the sun went down, and there weren't a lot of places to hide with all the sensors and so forth. The Haven was like Fort Knox. She also had one of their band-bracelet things now, set specifically to call Miranda.

She'd been to the library and the gardens, seen the big damn horses, walked around most of the Haven itself without poking her nose into too many rooms, and found the study where Miranda kept the ice cream stash; she could get almost anything she wanted brought to her, but there was something vaguely mischievous about hanging out in the study where Big Important Vampire Things probably happened. She'd spent several hours there poring over the bookshelves and the liquor cabinet, both of which boasted wares from all over the world.

She had in fact spent an evening embarrassingly drunk on

a bottle of tequila that later Internet research revealed cost $200; she kind of doubted they would care, but still, it was a good thing that it had been such high-quality booze that three shots had her on her face.

Her footsteps were quiet on the cold tile floor; everything echoed in this place during daytime, and there was something in the air that brought to mind a museum . . . or a mausoleum. Even though a handful of day guards watched the corridors, the whole building was basically asleep; the metal shutters kept all but the faintest pale light out, and aside from the distant sound of lawn and garden equipment coming and going, the Haven was dead until sunset.

Stella had been keeping odd hours since she'd arrived—she wasn't entirely nocturnal but tended to sleep from the wee hours of the morning to early afternoon. Just now it was around four, not quite true evening. In another three hours the Haven would rumble to life around her.

She had to admit she got a kick out of walking around the place alone. She doubted many people had the chance to do so.

She reached the study and opened the door . . .

. . . only to find herself in the company of the Prime of the Southern United States, tousled and sleepy, bare feet propped up on the coffee table, working his way through a pint of ice cream.

Stella squealed and jumped back. "Oh shit!"

He looked as surprised to see her as she was to see him but said, "Don't run off."

Stella, heart pounding, tried to think of an excuse for her being in what was, after all, one of his private rooms, and stammered a few seconds, flustered.

Amused, he said, "I'm sorry . . . I seem to have appropriated your Chunky Monkey."

"Well, I . . . it's . . . um . . . technically it's *your* Chunky Monkey."

A shrug. He gestured at the freezer. "After everything you've done for Miranda, the least I can give you is ice cream, Mistress Witch."

She had to smile at that. Funny . . . she'd met him only

once, at the clinic, when she'd been high on painkillers and shock; she remembered him being . . . different. He was still ridiculously gorgeous, but now he looked tired, thinner, like someone who had seen way too much and not had time to process any of it.

Still, the power-aura around him was insane. It, too, was different, but she couldn't quite put her finger on how without shifting into Sight and analyzing him . . . and that might be a little awkward.

She went over to the freezer and retrieved another pint of ice cream, this one a mocha something-or-other. There was a stash of spoons in one of the nearby drawers; always prepared, these vampires.

Not exactly sure what else to do with herself, Stella sat down in one of the other armchairs, crossing her legs, and dug into the ice cream.

"So you're not dead," she said, trying to sound nonchalant or at least non-freaked-out. "How'd you manage that?"

His mouth quirked in a half-smile. "I have no idea."

"I thought they said you burned up in the sunlight."

The Prime pondered the spoonful of ice cream in front of him for a moment before saying, "No one actually saw that happen. They just assumed it did because I wasn't there the next night."

"Where were you?"

"I don't remember."

Stella swallowed. "Amnesia? Kind of a cliché, don't you think?"

"It's not amnesia exactly. Everything's there, it just . . . I feel like my brain needs a defrag."

She snorted. "I forgot Miranda said you're a geek."

He looked down at himself; he was wearing faded jeans and a worn T-shirt with the slogan *Han Shot First*. "I've heard that about me."

"You haven't forgotten all of the techno stuff, have you? That would be really awful."

"No. It's there. I think once I actually sit down and use the knowledge, it will come back fully. Whenever I concentrate on something in the past it takes a moment to access the first time, but then it's more solid." He stared down into the nearly empty pint as if trying to divine the future—or the past—from the fudge chips. "Except for the last few weeks . . . none of that has come back."

"I'm sure it will," she said, trying to sound reassuring, though the absurdity of the moment was not lost on her. Here she was, eating ice cream with the most powerful vampire in the region, trying to make him feel better about the after-effects of being dead. It was nearly as surreal as having the Queen in Hello Kitty pajamas asleep on her couch.

He watched her keenly for a moment before adding, "You seem to be handling all of this vampire business pretty well."

"I'm a Witch. Strange stuff happens to us all the time. But I'll give you this: If I had even the slightest sense that you guys weren't the good guys, there would be a Stella-shaped hole in that door and my ass would be on a plane to Bermuda."

He smiled. "You are smarter than a lot of humans who find out about us."

"Don't most of them end up dead?"

"Precisely."

Stella frowned; she wished she could put into words what had changed about him, but she couldn't make sense of it any more than he could. "What exactly are you now?" she asked.

He raised an eyebrow. "What do you mean?"

"Well, I don't know much about vampires, but I've felt quite a few of them—their energy, I mean—while I've been here. There's normal vampires, and then there's Miranda, and there's the other Signets that were here . . . and then there's you."

The Prime narrowed his eyes, and for a moment she was afraid she'd crossed a line. He might sit here eating ice cream like a human, and might be dressed like one, but he wasn't human . . . she was the only human in this entire building . . . and for miles around. The thought made a ripple of fear run up her backbone.

His reply, though, wasn't what she expected. "Tell me about your gift."

"My Sight? Okay . . . when I look at things a certain way I can see energy. Auras, I guess, though it's not always literally visual. And I can see connections between people, even old karmic ones, in a sort of spiderweb of energy. Plus, with my training as a Witch, I can sense other sorts of energy from people, sometimes places. I can learn a lot about someone that way. It's how I figured out Miranda isn't human."

"If you were to use this Sight on two people, you could see how they were connected—and if they weren't, could you tell why not?"

"I guess so. I've never tried anything like that . . . but then I'm a lot stronger than I was before I met you guys. Why?"

Seeming to lose his appetite, the Prime set aside the pint and leaned back in his chair, hands folded. "Miranda and I have been severed. It is, essentially, what killed me . . . and I thought it would come back, but it hasn't. Nothing like this has ever happened among our kind. None of us have ever really explored the nature of our bonds—it never seemed necessary, since if one of us dies, we both do . . . or that's how it's supposed to happen."

"She should have died when you did?"

"Normally. But if you shatter one Signet, you break the bond itself and kill whoever bears that Signet, leaving the other alive. The power between us rebounds, basically, and the imbalance is deadly—the survivor usually goes insane and dies anyway; it just takes longer . . . and is far more painful."

"What good does that do, then? Why would anyone want to break you apart if whoever lives ends up crazy and dead?"

"The point of a Bondbreaking isn't divorce. The point is to make us suffer as much as possible before we die. It's the cruelest way to kill a Pair, destroying the one thing that makes our eternity bearable. In all our history it's been done perhaps a half-dozen times, and then never by another Signet; the thought of it horrifies most of us to the point that we won't even think of doing it to our worst enemies."

"But someone did it to you." Stella couldn't eat anymore, either, imagining what it must have been like . . . She remembered the shape Miranda had been in, how close she'd come to dying. "That's . . . God, I'm sorry."

"The interesting thing is, that wasn't all he did. There was more to it. The Bondbreaking was part of a greater ritual—the power it supplied was channeled somewhere, through Miranda's Signet and another amulet, supposedly to open a door."

"A door to what?"

He lifted his eyes heavenward, not quite an eye roll but definitely born of exasperation. "There's a vampire cult that is trying to bring back their goddess from some sort of astral exile."

"Vampires have religions?"

"Some do. This group is one of the oldest out there, and the nuttiest. They worship Persephone, the—"

"Greek goddess of the Underworld," Stella finished for him. "Queen of the Dead." She felt a chill of creeping recognition . . . It couldn't be a coincidence. She remembered looking at the image of Persephone on her altar as she turned the cards . . . the Tower burning . . .

"Are you all right?"

She shook her head. "I don't . . . I'm a Pagan, you know . . . basically a Goddess worshipper. I've had Persephone on my altar for years. I was doing a tarot reading when I had this vision that . . . It's how I found Miranda. She . . . Persephone . . . led me to her."

He was silent for the better part of a minute, then shook his head and said, smiling faintly, "They might make a believer out of me yet."

The second David stepped out onto the balcony, the Elite went absolutely wild with applause and cheers and didn't stop for more than a minute. When Miranda came over to stand beside him and they joined hands, the tumult was deafening.

Finally, smiling, Miranda held up her hand, calling for silence. A hundred twenty-nine faces stared up at their leaders, smiling, eyes bright with jubilation.

"Honored Elite, Haven staff," David said, "I want to thank

each of you for continuing your work in my absence. Your devotion means everything to us." He looked at Miranda, smiling, and added, "I'd also like to thank my beloved, our Queen, for refusing to be defeated even in the face of death. I am honored to have her at my side, and you are all honored to have her as your Queen."

Another cheer went up. Miranda smiled down at them and picked up where David left off. "For now, we'll stay with the chain of command we established while the Prime was . . . away. While he is definitely one hundred percent alive, he'll be taking a few days to get back in the swing of things, so lieutenants, please continue making your reports on my server. Again, thank you all so much. I couldn't have kept this place going without each and every one of you. Oh, and one more thing—check your deposits for this month; you'll each be receiving hazard pay for the time during the lockdown, and a bonus for all your hard work since then."

More cheers. David, who had made sure to wear black to set off the color and glow of his Signet and looked, at last, like himself, gave them one more smile, and said, "Dismissed."

Miranda breathed in, letting the Elites' joy sink into her body; there was plenty of it to go around, and she needed all the energy she could get.

She watched her Prime as he spoke to a couple of the lieutenants, wondering if they saw it, too, or if the Elite down below had noticed something different about their leader. Perhaps they dismissed it as mere tiredness, after whatever ordeal had taken him from them and then miraculously restored him. And perhaps that was all it was.

No. It was far, far more than that.

A hundred tiny things gave it away. He was still very much David, and yet . . .

This was the first time the Elite had really seen him. Rumors had flown for several days while he and Miranda rested, and finally David had decided he was recovered enough to at least address his people—they deserved to see him, to know that yes, he was back. He wanted the news to spread from the Haven throughout the city, the territory, and the world: David Solomon had returned.

Miranda knew it was true, but . . .

She told herself that it was the distance between them that was causing her to feel ill at ease; indeed, not feeling his presence in her mind, that warm touch throughout her being that reminded her she wasn't, could never be, alone, was painful, a part of her grief that had yet to be healed . . . if it ever could be.

She shook her head slightly. It could be healed. They would find a way. There had to be something . . . perhaps it would return in time. He hadn't even been back a week, and the Bond-breaking had been catastrophic for them both; something like that didn't just up and get better. It was a process.

The thought that it might never return . . . that they might forever be two separate beings, that soul-deep connection that had made them more than just a couple gone forever . . . she couldn't stand it. Despite her brave words to him, she couldn't imagine living a hundred, two hundred years without it.

But if it never returned . . . they would adjust. They would find a way to deal. There was no other alternative. If she could live without him, she could certainly live with him as a normal husband.

Miranda concentrated on the happiness. Having him back was a blessing beyond anything she had ever hoped for. Just waking up next to him again, knowing that when she opened her eyes his side of the bed would no longer be empty, made up for so much of the loss.

Every day he was regaining more of his memory and had even logged into the Haven systems to look around earlier, refamiliarizing himself with their layout and operations. Within a few minutes his fingers had been flying over the keyboard as always, and she had stood in the doorway watching him, tears running from her eyes. She had thought she would never see him sitting there, reading glasses catching the monitor's light, again; but there he was.

But then she would catch him staring off into space, his

expression one of faint bewilderment, as if he'd woken from a dream to find himself in a strange land where no one spoke his language. Or she'd start a sentence, expecting him to finish it, and he wouldn't; or she'd make some crack that he would have laughed at before, only to get a blank stare. The closest word she could come up with to describe his state was *distracted*, but that was inadequate.

Sometimes she lay awake staring at his back. The tattoo seemed an outward symbol of a much deeper transformation, one that neither of them understood.

"Are you all right?"

She felt his arm slide around her and leaned her head on his shoulder with a sigh. The contact did nothing for her energy—there was no sense of relief, no feeling of their power balancing itself—but it did everything for her heart.

"Just lost in thought," she replied. "How are you? Tired? Do you need to rest?"

"No . . . I actually feel fine." He kissed her forehead. "What's next?"

"Well, you have about a thousand phone calls to return—mostly variations on 'Holy shit, are you really alive?' You might want to draft a mass e-mail to the Council to let them know I'm not playing some kind of trick on them."

He nodded. "Any further news on Hart?"

"Not that I've heard. I'll have to check in with the West on that one—Dev has an agent in Hart's Haven somewhere who's keeping an eye on things."

"What about Deven? Have you spoken to him tonight?"

Miranda started to say she hadn't, but she broke off at a gasp from the hallway and smiled softly. "No, but you can."

She would never forget the look on Deven's face as David turned slowly toward him; she had never seen the Prime of the West so completely, totally stunned.

She grinned and stepped away from David, giving him space. For a long time, neither Prime moved, just staring at each other.

Finally, Deven said in a surprisingly small, young voice, "Is it really you?"

David smiled a little. "Shall I prove it to you? You recite the *Officium Divinum* in your sleep. You shagged Lord Byron up against a tree one night in Genoa. When you're depressed you drink peanut butter milk shakes, and—"

Before he could finish, Deven had crossed the room and flung himself into David's arms.

Miranda couldn't stop smiling, which might have surprised her a few months ago, but now all she could feel was gratitude. She had experienced Deven's pain as acutely as her own, and now she could feel its relief, an echo of her own.

David rested his chin on Deven's head for a moment, eyes closed, and sighed. "Yes," he said. "This I remember."

Deven looked up at him. "Do you remember being angry at me before?"

Miranda saw it in David's eyes: a conscious choice to let go. "No."

David kissed him lightly on the lips, and Deven smiled and moved away, taking a deep breath before turning to Miranda. "How are you, love?" he asked.

Miranda went over and hugged him tightly. "Better now. Where's Jonathan?"

"At home. I'm not staying, I just . . . I had to see for myself, before I could believe it."

Tilting his head to one side, David smiled at the two of them standing with their arms around each other. "This is new."

Miranda and Deven looked at each other, then at David. "Tragedy has a way of bringing people together," Deven pointed out. "That's how I ended up shagging Lord Byron." He shot Miranda a grin. "Long story. I'll tell you about it next time we're drunk."

David walked over to them and kissed first Miranda's cheek, then Deven's. "While you're here, I wonder if you could do something for me," the Prime said.

Deven raised an eyebrow. "Anything."

"There's someone I want to introduce you to . . . someone who I think can help us figure out what the hell is going on." He gestured at them to follow, and Miranda nodded, understanding what he meant. He wanted to have Stella use her

Sight on him and Miranda, and it would presumably work better if she had another Signet as a basis of comparison. Deven's Consort might not be there, but if Stella could see their bond, she'd at least know what to look for.

"Good idea," she said, and then to Deven, "Just . . . promise you won't terrify her too much. She's seen a lot, but she might not be ready for you."

Deven laughed. "I have no idea what you mean," he said with feigned innocence. "I am the very model of an average everyday vampire."

Miranda snorted. "Right. And I'm Mother Teresa."

David was still looking at them with bemusement, as if seeing the two of them genuinely getting along were the oddest thing he'd seen since coming back from the dead with a magically altered tattoo and partial amnesia. But he seemed to decide that if they had lost their minds, it was a pleasant enough insanity, and he shook his head with a smile before leading them toward the young Witch's room.

Whatever Stella was expecting . . . he was not it.

She felt the Signets' energy out in the hall; she was used to Miranda's, and she recognized David's, but the third she had felt only at a distance, and only once or twice. Still, she was pretty sure she knew who it was: Deven, the Prime of the West, and from Miranda's vague description Stella knew he was dangerous, powerful, and very old.

"Come in," Stella called at the knock.

The door opened, and she blinked.

The three vampires crossed the threshold, through the wards Stella had set up; Miranda had already felt them and didn't react, but David flinched as if he'd been poked in the ribs, and Deven stopped, looked around, and shrugged.

Miranda smiled. "Stella, I'd like you to meet our ally, Deven O'Donnell, Prime of the Western United States. Lord Prime, this is Stella Maguire, our friend and guest."

"*You're* Deven?" Stella blurted. "But you're so . . . cute!"

Miranda snorted, and David had to turn his head to hide his laughter.

Deven looked at her, and for just a second she wanted the earth to open up and swallow her. Then he smiled.

"So are raccoons," he pointed out, "but they'll fuck you up." His voice was a quiet tenor, the cadence of his words almost suggesting an accent but not quite. He looked like the kind of "vampire" she and Lark might have run into at the fetish club . . . yet something in the way he stood, the coolness in his eyes, told her there was no pretense or artifice here. Cute he might be, but he was every inch the real thing.

"I'm sorry," she said, blushing deeply. "I just . . . After feeling your energy around the place, I was expecting . . . like a huge scary dude of some kind. I should bow, or something, right?"

"You're not a vampire," he pointed out. "Therefore you aren't subject to our rule, so usually we let it slide."

David, still holding back laughter, said, "I thought perhaps if you had another Signet to Look over, it would be easier for you to make something out of our situation."

Stella nodded. "Good idea. Um . . . would you mind sitting on the bed with me? I need to concentrate, and it works best if we're facing each other."

Miranda and David waited on the love seat while Stella and Deven got comfortable, both sitting cross-legged. Meanwhile Pywacket came barreling out of his hiding place under the bed and leapt up into David's lap, immediately setting to kneading his thigh. Stella had never seen the cat do that before—he usually took weeks to learn to like new people.

She didn't know what to make of it, but she'd have her chance to get a good Look into David's weirdness soon enough.

Stella faced Deven. "Okay . . . I'm going to go into a light trance and shift into the Sight so I can get a feel for your energy and that bond thing you guys have. Any questions?"

One eyebrow lifted. "Is that a ColorWheel shade? Their reds are always so vibrant."

Stella couldn't help it; she giggled, reaching up to tug on a strand of her hair. "Yeah. It's A27-1, Price Above Rubies."

"Duly noted. Do you have any questions?"

She laughed. "Like a million. Such as, what happens if you take out a piercing?"

"It heals in about four seconds and I have to repierce it if I want it back. I had nine yesterday."

She counted: He had only four at the moment. Eyebrow, nose, one in each ear. "Yikes. Okay, so, do you know anything about energy work? If you don't, this might feel a little weird."

Deven gave her a slight smile. "I do indeed."

"And you're sure you're okay with me poking around in your aura?"

He smiled again. "I won't let you in any deeper than you need to go, Stella. This isn't my first rodeo."

She felt her own eyebrows go up. "Are you a Witch, too?"

"Not exactly."

Stella glanced over at Miranda, who chuckled. "Don't worry—he won't bite."

Deven grinned and made a slight snapping motion with his teeth; Stella laughed before she could stop herself and tried not to think about how his canines were more pointed than a normal person's. "Okay . . . just relax, then . . . try not to think about anything specific."

She took a few long breaths to ground herself, then reached for the Prime's hands; she could feel the strength in them—the kind of strength usually reserved for people who wrung necks in the dark, like her dad's Special Forces buddies. She wondered, wildly, if Deven had ever killed anyone.

"Stella," he said softly, "you are far too bright to ask such stupid questions."

She nodded . . . but then her eyes snapped open. He'd heard the thought—without even trying.

This was going to be interesting.

"Now," she said, "if you can thin out your outermost layer of shields for me, just enough that I can see the Signet bond—"

"It goes deeper than that," he replied. "It starts at the very core of our being."

She smiled. "Not your first rodeo," she repeated. "Okay, lead the way."

She shifted into her Sight, and for a moment, the man sitting in front of her seemed almost normal; like a strong Witch, perhaps. She had seen from Miranda's shielding that vampires structured their barriers kind of like onions—layer upon layer, each one with a slightly different function, some to deflect unwanted energy, some to keep others from Seeing in. Miranda's had been extremely complex to control her empathic talent—she had to be able to use it without it using her, and learning to do that must have taken her years and a lot of pain.

Once he'd let her in, Stella paused to learn the lay of the land. The way she Saw energy was in colors, but also in threads of light; each person's choices and interactions with other people created a spiderweb, and that web made up the individual's life, connected at its edges with everyone they loved, hated, knew, and eventually, everyone on earth, if you were powerful enough to See that far. Stella couldn't venture too far past the person she was Looking at—at least not for very long without burning out—but that was usually knowledge enough for her.

It was hard to explain to anyone who couldn't See it—the best comparison was watching a 3D movie first without the glasses, then with them, so that all those different versions of a person came together to form the solid, fully dimensional life before her.

He was only the second vampire she'd ever gotten this close to, and it was hard not to get caught up in her fascination—they were so different from humans, and so different from each other. The basic structure of the web was the same as a mortal's, but everything from the color of the energy to how it flowed made it obvious, unnervingly so, that the person before her was not human, and hadn't been human for a very long time.

She could feel every year of his age—the burden of all those years, of watching the world change while remaining essentially an eternal teenager, like one of the Lost Boys of Neverland without the fairy dust.

Except . . .

There was something . . . as she was learning how he worked, she happened across the thread of Deven's family line, buried deep among a lot of painful memories she couldn't access. That one line had a certain color to it, a silvery violet shade she felt like she had seen before somewhere a long time ago . . .

"Don't," Deven whispered into her mind, practically slamming a barrier down in front of the line. *"Please."*

"But . . . are you?"

He met her eyes. She felt him deciding whether to tell her. *"Yes."*

"But that's . . . that's amazing! You're so lucky . . ."

"Lucky?" His mental voice went sharp and bitter. *"Would you like to see how lucky I am?"*

Before she could say no, several flashes of memory exploded in her mind, and she gasped: a child lifting chubby hands to heal a puppy's broken leg, then dragged before a priest . . . an exorcism, to force demons out of the child's body, when there were none . . . the sting of a whip, each crack punctuating the drone of holy liturgy.

Stella could feel her eyes filling with tears. *"Stop,"* she whispered. *"That's enough."*

He sighed. *"I'm sorry, Stella. You didn't deserve that."*

"Neither did you!" She squeezed his hands, lifting her eyes to his. He looked surprised at the sorrow on her face, as if compassion was something he didn't entirely understand when it was directed toward him.

"Anyway, let's . . ." She went back to her work, seeking out the Signet bond, and after another moment, she found it.

Deep within the glowing energy of his heart center, reaching up to connect to the third eye as well as the solar plexus, was a black strand of energy—no, not black exactly, more like darkened quicksilver. She touched it lightly and felt it connecting all the way across the country, giving her a sense of a tall, broad man reading a book in front of a fireplace. Stella was amazed she could sense that far, but it wasn't so much her talent as it was the nature of the bond.

The man—Jonathan, she remembered—felt her presence,

but also felt that Deven had allowed her in, and though he was surprised, he didn't object.

The connection flowed back from him equally, and their two energies merged and blended, radiating love and unity all the way from one end to the other. Stella kept her hands on it for a while, just getting used to what it felt like . . . a true soul-mating, something she doubted most humans ever experienced.

It was strong—its thread was like steel compared to the gossamer threads of the rest of the web—and would be nearly impossible to break. Two people joined this way wouldn't just love each other—they would complement each other, and that kind of connection went way beyond romance. It was beautiful, heartachingly so, but she could imagine how much pain it could cause if something went wrong.

She followed it in both directions for a while, learning its weight and strength, before she noticed something odd.

It split.

No, that wasn't right. At first glance it looked like the Pair bond split, but looking closer she saw that there was another thread, a thinner and paler bond that wrapped around the Pair bond and then split off on its own again . . . and this one flowed right back around . . . into David, and even beyond that.

When she saw where it went, she snapped her gaze back to Deven's. *"Do you see it?"* she asked.

"See what?"

She showed him the second bond. He looked genuinely shocked when he saw it. *"I always knew there was something between us, but . . . this . . . how is this possible?"*

"I don't know. I'm new at this kind of bond. But from what I'm Seeing here there's more than just ex-boyfriendy stuff going on with you two—you have a secondary link of your own, just not a Signet bond. And if I follow it past David, it looks like all of you have something like it, and it weaves around your Pair bonds and to and from one another—like a half-finished braid. The Pair bonds connect you to your Consort, but this other bond is what connects you to the others, so that explains you all sharing visions and powers."

"I'm not sure whether that makes me feel better or worse," Deven noted.

She shrugged. *"It is what it is. Now, if I follow it over to David . . ."* She led Deven toward the other Prime, without alerting David, just yet, that they were looking at him. *"See, it should connect back into his own bond with Miranda."*

"But there isn't any bond with Miranda," Deven replied. *"It was broken . . . wasn't it?"*

Stella stared, trying to make sense of what she was See-ing, then said aloud, "David . . . would you mind joining us? You, too, Miranda."

She waited to dig any deeper until the Pair—or not-Pair—had come over to the bed and the four of them were sitting in a circle, knees almost touching. Stella released Deven's hands and took David's.

"Okay, let me in as much as you can," she said. "Deven, could you grab that notebook and pen from next to you? Thanks."

David might not be able to See what he was doing, but his shields parted as elegantly as a curtain, and she followed the thread of his connection to Deven as it merged back into the thicker, silver-black thread of his Signet bond . . . that should have gone to Miranda.

She could see now what had happened. Right where it should have connected, the bond had been burned off, the ends scorched, blasted away. The edges were sort of cauterized—that had stopped him from energetically bleed-ing to death, though how it had happened Stella couldn't say. The heart connection was still there, but it was partially torn off, hanging on by only a bare handful of frayed threads.

Did that mean that they were no longer *meant* to be Paired? But how could someone go from being a soul mate to nothing?

There was something else about David as well—some of the threads of his web looked almost blurry, like they were in the process of dissolving and re-forming elsewhere. He had changed, and changed profoundly . . . and he wasn't done. The last phase of the transition was waiting for something.

"What do you see?" Miranda asked softly. "Is there any hope?"

"Just . . . give me a little bit," Stella said, daunted by the task ahead of her. She wasn't sure she wanted to get nearer to those blasted ends, but she had to, if she was going to see a way to help them. "I need to get closer . . . I need to touch you both, if that's okay."

Suddenly she felt a line of energy wrap around her wrist; the tendril was gentle and cool and had silver-violet in its aura.

She looked up at Deven.

He smiled. *"An anchor,"* he replied. *"And extra strength should you need it."*

Stella grinned broadly at him. *"Thank you. That's . . . that's exactly what I needed."*

Taking a deep breath—and sending up a quick prayer to Persephone to keep her from doing anything that would make the situation worse—Stella settled in to tease apart the ragged edges of the bond, to follow the lines where they led, to try to find a solution.

It was strange, really, that of all the vampires in the world, she'd met one who had these gifts, this bloodline . . . one that stretched back to the making of the world, to people who had taught the first Witches how to harness the power of nature.

Her heart leapt with excitement—she could only imagine the things she might learn from him about her own gifts . . .

"Stay on point, Stella," the violet-eyed Prime admonished her gently.

"I'm sorry," she said, smiling breathlessly. *"Back to business . . ."*

The first question was, why did the end of the Pair bond that should lead to Miranda not seem to recognize her anymore? It was as if the roots wanted to stretch toward her but weren't sure what they would find there.

"Miranda," Stella said, "I need to dig around in you a little, is that okay?"

The Queen nodded. "I appreciate your asking."

"Just give me a tap on the shoulder if I make you uncomfortable."

"Gotcha."

Stella settled back into her Sight and reached for Miranda's web, first learning more about her energetic makeup. She could see the thread that represented Miranda's empathic gift—Jesus, it must have driven her insane back before she learned to control it. Any psychic gift that strong was a sure-fire ticket to a closed ward. It was under control now as firmly as it had been when Stella met her in the clinic. Nearby ran several other strands that she guessed were other powers Miranda had as a vampire, varying in strength and texture.

She approached the torn-out bond cautiously. Mentally she compared what she was Seeing to the same connection between Deven and Jonathan, and a picture began to form, one she wasn't sure she liked.

Finally she sat back to catch her breath. She had to be careful how long she worked with it, or she'd burn out as she nearly had saving Miranda. She had much better control than she'd had that day—in fact, since Miranda had come back and saved *her*, Stella's control and accuracy had bumped up by a factor of five at least, and this whole thing, which would have scared her shitless a week ago, felt perfectly normal, just a little draining.

They waited patiently but expectantly until she took a deep breath and said, "I think I know what's going on."

Miranda gave her an encouraging look, though from her face she already had a bad feeling about what Stella was going to say.

"First of all, you've all been finding connections among you that didn't exist before, and you don't understand where they came from. Well, I can't tell you that last part, but what we're dealing with looks like this." She grabbed pen and paper and hastily sketched out what she'd seen.

The three Signets stared at it. "It looks like an atom," Deven observed. "David, what element is that?"

David smiled. "The closest would be oxygen, although the electrons wouldn't line up quite like that, but rather in concentric shells with two in the first and . . . never mind. You're right, though—it does look like an atom. A circle with four Pairs placed around it, each Pair bound to itself, and the whole circle bound to all of them."

"You said that a Pair has to be made up of two vampires— that a human can't hold a Signet. Right?"

The Queen nodded. "It would be like trying to mate a deer with a horse."

"Well . . . you started out with two horses. When the bond between you was broken, it was broken on David's end since his Signet was the one smashed. But when he came back, it should have reconnected, except . . . he didn't come back . . . quite the same. Now, instead of a deer and a horse, or two horses, you've got a horse and a freaking unicorn."

This time Deven snorted. "David's a unicorn? That explains so much."

Neither David nor Miranda seemed to find it as funny. "So . . . what am I, then?" David asked hesitantly.

"I have no idea. I mean, you're still a vampire, at least mostly, but . . . the change is still going on. I wish I could tell you what it means, or how it's happening, but I am so far out of my league I can't even see my league from here."

Miranda sighed, defeated. "You can't help us."

"Even if I knew exactly what was different about David, I'm not nearly powerful or trained enough to go trying to reattach a bond like this. I don't think any garden-variety Witch has that kind of juice—not even a High Priestess."

David gave Deven a piercing look. "I don't suppose a vampire Priestess might be able to."

Deven looked away, shaking his head, but Stella went on. "It's not just the power that's the problem—it's ability, too. Sight. Deven can See almost as well as I can because . . . um, because of his healing talent. But even as strong as you two are, neither of you can See energy like I can, so you wouldn't be able to fix it—you'd be working blind. We need someone who can See *and* who has the strength, and frankly . . . I have no idea where to find that."

"If we're the most powerful of our kind, and that's still not enough, then we're screwed," Miranda said. "There aren't any Signets with Sight like yours, Stella . . . are there, David?"

The Prime thought a moment, then shook his head. "I've never heard of one."

Deven, who had been sitting with his eyes closed, said, "You're not old enough."

"What do you mean?" David asked him.

"I mean, the kind of magic we're dealing with here isn't just amulets and shields. It's not like what Ovaska used, or even what Volundr worked with. We're talking about reshaping someone's *soul*. No vampire—not even the High Priestess of Elysium—could do that."

"Then who can?" Miranda asked.

"No one. Not anymore. Once, long ago . . . there used to be people who worked that kind of magic, and their power was enough to cast even the greatest Signet into the shade."

Stella's breath caught. Was he going to tell them?

"Who?" David pressed. "And where are they now?"

"Dead. Hunted to extinction by both humans and vampires. By the time I was born, they were almost gone . . . almost."

Miranda and David both looked baffled. "What the hell are you talking about?" the Queen wanted to know.

Stella saw him struggling, trying to force himself to speak the truth after hundreds of years of hiding, and she realized she couldn't let him do it, not yet. "Elves," she finished for him. "He's talking about Elves."

Ten

Olivia knew that eventually they would come for her. She had run—again—but this time only as far as her loft. She was half-way through shoving her belongings into a bag when she simply stopped, dropping the bag on the bed, and gave up.

She had nowhere left to go.

She hadn't done anything wrong this time. But as soon as the Prime carried his unconscious Queen up the steps to the clinic, and the Elite guarding the place clustered around them, she knew they would have questions for her . . . too many questions. They would want to know where she had come from, who she was . . . and David knew. He knew, and others would find out. Any thought she'd had of hanging around to see what happened evaporated as the fear took hold, and she fled.

Perhaps the Prime could protect her. She might have thrown in her lot with them, gone back to work for a Signet, even joined the Elite and become Second . . . she certainly still had the skill. But the thought filled her with the kind of fear that had driven her over the face of the globe, from her old life in Australia to the anonymity of a tattoo studio in Austin.

And now they would find her. Now that David knew where she lived, he could go through old network data to track her and then follow her signal; she had no idea what the extent of his reach was outside Austin, but he had a lot of allies in the Council, and rumor was he had eyes everywhere. One way or another she would be running the rest of her life . . . it was just a question of how long that life would be.

So she just stopped. She put her things away, went out to hunt, then came home and slept; the next night, she went to work, letting the hum of the needle soothe her rattled nerves. She re-inked a piece that was two hundred years old and repaired shoddy workmanship that had barely seen a full presidency. She gave another young, naïve vampire a butterfly tramp stamp.

And she waited.

She watched blood roll down the back of one of her clients while he held the wound open as long as he could, and she wondered if her own blood would flow onto the street, or perhaps the concrete floor of her loft to mix with the paint that had been splattering its surface for months. She hoped whoever came to kill her wouldn't destroy her paintings. Of course, what difference would it make? There was no one to leave them to.

Sometimes she stood in front of her most recent canvas, another in the series trying to capture the faceless woman from her dreams. In this one the woman stood only a few yards from the viewer, looking back over her shoulder; her clothes seemed to be spun out of spiderwebs and shadows, and on her outstretched hand perched a raven.

Olivia couldn't stop staring at her, waiting . . . for what, exactly? For the painting to come to life and tell her fortune? She didn't need a painting for that.

The nights were growing warm, another round of rainstorms making its lazy way through the Hill Country and into Austin. Olivia still wore her coat—most vampires did, even here. Texas was warm enough that they didn't need the extra layer—at least not outdoors. Walking into an air-conditioned building was enough to give a vampire chills for hours, so most of the time they could be seen skulking around town in jackets no matter what the weather.

She'd had a long night. The entire city was practically vibrating with awe and fear; news had gotten out, and though so far only a few had seen him, everyone knew the Prime lived. He had either come back from the dead or survived in the first place—and either possibility was terrifying . . . as much to his allies as to his enemies.

No one knew what to think or how to react. Was their ruler a god? The devil himself? Had the whole thing been a hoax? So far the Elite weren't talking, and while the ordinary vamp on the street was grumbling about the lack of any real news, Olivia knew that the truth was the Elite had no idea what to say either, because no one did. Not even the Prime himself.

The anxiety hovering around the Shadow District made it hard to concentrate on work. She wasn't an empath, but she sure as hell could sense fear as well as any of her kind. She'd nearly committed a cardinal sin of tattooing and fucked up a word—fortunately she'd quadruple-checked the image and realized it was reversed in time to fix it without alerting the client. Granted, it was in Japanese, and she doubted he had any idea it really said *fish bicycle* rather than *inner strength*, but research wasn't her job.

She dug in her coat pocket for her keys as she rounded the corner to her building. It had become habit to check the ground outside for unfortunately placed bodies, although chances were when they came to get her they'd be on the front stoop instead of—

"Good evening, Liv."

She froze. *Oh God. Oh God, no. No no no . . .*

Jeremy Hayes, who was sitting on the steps waiting for her patiently, gave her a wry smile. "You look like you've seen a ghost."

She started to step back, to bolt, but he asked, "Where do you think you'll go?"

She was shaking violently as she took the last few steps and knelt. "My Lord Prime."

He rolled his eyes. "Oh, get up, for God's sake. I'm not here to kill you."

She clutched her coat tightly at her throat, standing up slowly. "You aren't?"

He smiled. She had missed that smile—once he'd been such a witty, lighthearted man, so apt to laugh. She'd never thought he was bloodthirsty enough to be a Prime, but she would have followed him willingly . . . she had tried. "If you hadn't rabbited that night, I would have told you then that I wasn't angry at you. You didn't do anything wrong."

"I failed you," she whispered, eyes burning. "I failed Melissa and Amelia. I should have gone down fighting to save them."

His smile faded. "No . . . I should have listened to you years before that and left the Signets alone. But fate had its own ideas, it seems." He shut his eyes a moment before continuing. "Amelia's dead."

"Hart—"

"I got her back from him, but it was too late. He had already murdered her in spirit. She just finished his work. After everything I did to rescue her, after all the blood and death . . . I lost her anyway, Liv. I killed a Prime . . . and Faith . . . for nothing."

They were both silent for a while, and then Jeremy asked, "Is it true? Did he really come back from the dead?"

Olivia nodded. "Nobody knows where he was or what really happened, but he showed up here on my doorstep."

Jeremy shook his head. "It doesn't make sense. The whole point was to take all of his power, send it through the Stone, and that would open the door. Who can come back from that? Who can just . . . wake up after having all the life energy sucked out of them?"

"David Solomon," she replied, going over to sit next to him on the steps. "Why did you do it?"

"Lydia, one of the priestesses of Elysium, came to me and said she would free Amelia if I performed the ritual. It had to be done by a Prime—even one without his Signet would do. She assured me that Hart's downfall was a guarantee once the door was open . . . maybe I did something wrong and it didn't work. If I had any idea where the Cloister was, I could ask them, I suppose. I haven't noticed any goddesses walking the earth, have you?"

"Not so much. Although if Solomon were a god it would explain a lot."

He stared off into space, and she wasn't sure how to interpret his expression. It was somewhere between anger and sadness, but it had an edge to it that made her deeply uneasy for reasons she couldn't name. "It wasn't so much the Pair . . . Signets die all the time. None of us really live that long once that thing's around our necks . . . it's a noose on a timer, that's all."

"You hate what happened to their Second," she guessed.

"I . . ." He put his head in his hands for a moment. When he spoke again, his voice was heavy with guilt. "I used her as a detonator. She shouldn't have gone out like that. She should have gone out fighting. I'm pretty sure she made the bomb go off herself—I never hit the switch. I think she was trying to give the Queen a chance to escape, assuming my people would have killed her."

"She gave her life for her Queen, then," Olivia said. "For a Second there's no better death, fighting or otherwise."

He almost smiled again. "Spoken like a true Second."

She shrugged. "Not much of one." She took his hand, squeezing it. "I'm sorry about Amelia. I should have helped you. I would have."

"I didn't want to drag you back into all of this. But now . . . there's no one else I can turn to. I have nothing left in this world . . . Hart and McMannis and their friends took everything from me. I have only one thing left, one purpose. For that I need your help."

"Anything," she said. "You have only to name it. I made an oath to serve you, remember? As far as I'm concerned you're still my Prime."

Jeremy met her gaze with eyes that had gone abruptly hard and steely. She had never seen the cold in his gaze before—the hatred she could feel roiling beneath the surface. He had never been a man who hated easily. The uneasiness in her gut redoubled. "Vengeance," he said. "I want you to help me bring an end to this. I want you to help me destroy them all."

David managed to find his voice first.

"Elves."

"Yes."

"Elves."

"Keep saying it, David, until you believe it."

"That's ridiculous," David said. "There's—"

"No such thing," Deven concluded with a nod. "You're right. They're extinct. The last few were hunted down and killed around the time I was still mortal. But they did exist once, and they had the kind of power Stella is describing."

Miranda wasn't sure what was funnier—Deven telling them there was such a thing as Elves, or the look on David's face trying to make sense of Deven telling them there was such a thing as Elves. For all that Deven insisted he was an atheist, he seemed to acknowledge a lot of odd supernatural things, and David kept having to readjust his idea of how far Dev was willing to suspend disbelief.

Stella cleared her throat. "Before you both dismiss the idea as totally bonkerdoodles, you should probably remind yourselves that you're vampires and I'm a Witch and you all wear magical amulets that light up."

Miranda had to chuckle at the Witch's choice of words. "Okay, so, Dev, have you ever *met* an Elf?"

Something tugged at her empathic senses, and she frowned, trying to figure out what Deven was feeling without violating his privacy. His expression remained neutral, but his voice had an edge to it she didn't know how to interpret. "Not in person."

"Then how do you know they existed?" David demanded. "I thought you didn't believe in anything you haven't seen with your own eyes."

Deven gave a world-weary sigh. "The same way I know most of what I know: none of your damn business. The point is, they're all gone and can't help you."

Stella was giving Deven an odd look, but after a moment she said, "There is one other place you could go: Persephone."

Miranda's heart skipped a beat. An image formed in her head: a woman robed in shadow, with endless black eyes. "And . . . how would we do that?"

The Witch shrugged. "Step between the worlds."

The Pair gave her a long blink.

"I'm serious," Stella told them. "Witches go between worlds all the time—trance journeys, vision quests, that sort of thing. Sometimes we even invite the Goddess to enter our bodies and speak through us. It's called Drawing Down the Moon."

Deven lifted his head from his knees. "Aspecting?"

"That's another term for it. I've never done it before, but I'd be willing to give it a try—the summer solstice is next week. That would be a good time."

"Is it dangerous?" the Queen asked. "I'm not putting you at risk."

"If you don't take the proper precautions, and if you're Drawing Down an aspect of deity that's too much for you, it can be. It's a demanding ritual. But I know what I'm doing—in theory at least."

David rubbed his temples, his classic headache tell. "So . . . you're going to invite an invisible superbeing to come hang out in your body and tell us what's wrong with me."

Deven shot him a rather aggravated look. "I can give you a list of what's wrong with you right here and now."

"Boys, please," Miranda said. "Stella . . . are you sure? We've already asked way more from you than we have any right to."

Surprisingly—or no, not really at all, given who she was—Stella looked excited at the prospect rather than nervous. "I'm sure. I can do it. I know what precautions to take. The worst that happens is nothing happens, and we know as little in a week as we know now. Besides, it'll be fun."

"I'm surrounded by crazy people," David muttered.

The Witch grinned. "You say that like it's a bad thing."

* * *

The next night, they decided it was time the city saw them again—alive, strong, and very much still in charge.

"Did Dev get back to Sacramento?" Miranda asked.

David, who was thumbing along the screen of his phone to read the network status report, answered absently, "No . . . he said he had a stop to make on the way."

She relaxed into the corner of her seat, listening to the steady thrum of the car's engine and feeling more at ease than she had in days. Something about being here, on their way into town with Harlan driving and David on his phone, was so comforting, a familiar ritual that made life feel almost normal for a moment.

"He was acting kind of weird," she added. "Did you notice?"

David lifted his eyes to hers and gave her a smile. "Beloved, with all the weird going on lately, I'm having a hard time keeping up. How was he acting weird?"

"I don't know, just . . . he was awfully quiet when he left. Preoccupied. And not with some matter of state or Red Shadow business. Something personal. It's not like him to let that kind of thing show." She fiddled with the lapel of her coat.

He finished what he was doing and gave her his full attention. "When you get to seven hundred years old you'll have a lot on your mind, too."

"I can't imagine being that old. When he was born the printing press hadn't even been invented."

"Neither had whiskey," David said. "Imagine what that must have been like for him."

"Do you remember what it was like when you were human? The world, I mean?"

He got that look—the one that meant he was trying to access a memory—and said, "It was dark, quiet, at least in the village where I lived. Cities were beginning to be lit up at night, but sleepy towns like ours were dark. Now . . . there's constantly light and noise everywhere, no matter what the hour. Everything moved more slowly back then, and life was short and hard. You didn't have time to think about much beyond work and food and babies and death."

"It sounds awful."

A shrug. "Not really. Most people were pretty content with what they had. There was joy and sorrow, loss and celebration, just like now. People are people. Then of course you had the oddballs like me, eyes on the horizon, a mind full of ideas—troublemakers."

She grinned. "You? Never." Miranda toyed with her buttons for a moment before asking, "Do you think he was right? About there being Elves?"

David leaned back, sighing. "At this point I have no idea. I want to laugh at the very notion . . . just like I want to laugh at Stella's delusions of goddesses, and I wanted to laugh at Marja Ovaska using magical talismans and at things like Awakening rituals existing . . . but it seems the universe is determined to make a fool of me." He held up his phone. "See this? When I was human, a device like this would have been considered demonic. The thought that you could use your thumbs to send words through the air to be read by people thousands of miles away—at the speed of thought, no less—was beyond impossible."

Miranda nodded in understanding. "It's possible, then, that there are still things that haven't been measured in a scientific way but are real all the same."

"I always said that about the Signets—that it was just some form of electromagnetic or other energy that couldn't be measured yet—but I tried not to analyze it any further because I think deep down I knew I couldn't explain it away."

"I never thought I'd hear you admit that magic might be real, even if it whacked you over the head."

"That's pretty much what happened, isn't it? I was killed by magic, resurrected by magic—my tattoo changed by magic."

Miranda thought of her dream, the one she couldn't remember that had woken her to searing pain in her back, and Deven, too. "So . . . the tattoo thing happened nearly three weeks after you disappeared . . . that means when you initially came back, you were still regular old you."

"I suppose so."

"I think we need to find this Olivia," she said. "She might be able to tell us more about what happened to you."

"I know where she lives . . . assuming she hasn't run. I wouldn't be surprised if she had. She's got as many ghosts as any Signet I've ever met."

"And you're sure she was the Second in Australia?"

"Positive."

He was quiet for a while, looking out the window, and when he finally flicked his gaze back to her, she shot him a questioning look.

"I was thinking about Faith," he said.

Miranda bowed her head. "I miss her."

"So do I."

"I don't think I ever realized just how hard she worked, how much she did for us. I wish I had . . . I don't know."

He nodded. "I regret so much when it came to her."

She thought a minute, weighing whether to say anything, then said, "You do know she was in love with you, right?"

He smiled sadly. "I know."

Surprised, she asked, "When did you figure that out?"

An eyebrow raised. "I don't remember exactly . . . but I know."

The car pulled to a stop and Harlan said, "The Black Door, Sire."

David and Miranda exchanged a look. "Ready?" he asked.

She nodded. "Let's do it."

The Shadow District was still recovering from the weeks of insanity that had gripped it—first with Jeremy's thugs causing mayhem, then with the uncertainty of the Prime's death—but a respectable crowd was out on the streets. Miranda could feel all the eyes on them as she straightened her coat, tossed her hair back over her shoulder, and took her Prime's arm.

They walked up past the velvet rope where a dozen or so

people were waiting to get in, and the bouncers both grinned broadly and held open the doors.

Miranda looked up at David, who gave her a quick kiss on the lips and, smiling, swept into the club at her side.

The deep stench of charred wood and flesh was beginning to dissipate from the ruins of the Cloister, but a silence hung over the blackened walls, both sorrowful and expectant.

Here in the Northwest the nights were cold, the damp an ever-present cloak over the redwoods, and while it was never entirely silent, the remains of the holy place caught hold of the quiet and held it close.

A small group of huddled figures moved among the ruins, looking for anything worth salvaging, but the fire had been ferocious, and there was little left besides the walls themselves.

One of the searchers, a dark-skinned woman in a black robe, paused in her grim work and stood apart from the others for a moment, hand to her face in grief.

She didn't hear the step behind her, but she felt the stake's point at her back.

"Easy," he said softly. "Don't cry out."

The hatred in her voice was iron-edged, but she kept it low as she said, "You have no right to set foot on these lands."

"I am aware of that, Xara."

"What do you want?" she hissed. "What more can you possibly do to us?"

Deven drew up close to her and said into her ear, "Never, ever ask that question."

He stood behind her, watching the other members of the Order, most of whom he recognized, if not by name, then by face. Xara's heart was hammering, her breath shallow with terror—despite her anger, she still feared him, and rightly so.

"Have you been through Eladra's quarters yet?"

Xara shook her head.

"Good. Walk with me. There's something there I need."

Her eyes on the others, she did as she was told, carefully

picking her way among the fallen timbers, following his lead until they reached what was left of the High Priestess's rooms.

Here, the fire had not been as destructive; parts of some of the furniture still stood, and the Order would probably find a number of artifacts that were still useful.

"She trusted you," Xara said, tears in her voice now. "How could you do this?"

"Eladra foresaw her fate long ago. She made peace with it. If you're going to lead them, so must you. I'm not here to ask your forgiveness, Xara . . . I don't deserve or want it. Now, pick up that box."

She bent over a pile of debris and, with hands shaking violently, brushed aside wood and ash to reveal a half-hidden silver coffer.

"Your ring," he commanded quietly.

Nodding, Xara held her right hand to the lid of the box, her priestess's ring fitting into the lock; it clicked open, and she lifted the lid.

"A Speaking Stone?" she asked. "What do you want with this?"

He reached around her and took the palm-sized piece of polished labradorite from its cushion of velvet. "I need to make a call."

She drew a shuddering breath. "Are you going to kill me now?"

Deven reached up and touched the side of her face, kissed her softly on the cheek. "I know it changes nothing, Xara, but . . . I'm sorry."

He was gone before she could reply.

Jonathan knew, of course, when his mate returned from Texas, but even so he was a little surprised to walk into their bedroom and find Deven lying on his back in the middle of the floor, still in his coat, an empty bottle of Scotch on one side of him, a bloody knife on the other.

"Good Christ, who did you kill now?" the Consort asked.

Bleary eyes looked up at him. "Nobody." Deven held up

his hand, displaying a cut down the center of his palm that, as Jonathan watched, healed over and vanished. He groped sideways and produced an odd object: an ovoid, flat piece of dark stone that shimmered blue, gray, and green in the candlelight. There was a dark smudge on the stone's surface. "Blood calls to blood."

"How drunk *are* you?"

Deven smiled faintly and put his forearm over his eyes. "Drunk enough to do magic."

"Magic?" Jonathan went over and helped him up, steering the Prime, who was more than a little wobbly from the alcohol, over to the bed. "Deven . . . what did you do?"

Deven flopped onto his back and stared up at him for a moment before grabbing Jonathan by the neck and pulling their mouths together.

Jonathan knew perfectly well what he was doing, but turning down a kiss from Deven was simply not something he was capable of, so he sighed and returned it, stretching out next to his Prime on the bed. Deven tasted of whiskey, which he often did, but there was desperation in the kiss that Jonathan wasn't used to.

The Consort drew back from him and said, smiling, "You're not changing the subject that easily, baby."

"I'm not trying to. I just wanted to remind you that you love me before I tell you what I have to tell you."

Jonathan rapped his head against the mattress theatrically. "And what, pray tell, is that?"

"Two things, really . . . First of all . . ." Deven laid his hand palm up on the bed with the weird stone in it, closed his eyes . . .

. . . and as Jonathan stared, mouth dropping open, the stone rose into the air, spun around a few times, and lowered back down.

They stared at each other for a long moment.

"How long have you been able to do that?" Jonathan finally asked.

Deven bit his lip. "Since the three of you banded together to heal me that night in Ovaska's hideout."

"*Three years?* You became telekinetic three years ago and you didn't think it was worth mentioning?" Jonathan took a deep breath. "I suppose you've already told David."

"No. I haven't told anyone but you."

Clamping down on his anger, Jonathan counted to ten silently and then said, "Okay . . . you said there were two things."

"The second one is far, far weirder, and I'm not sure you're going to believe me."

"What? You can fly? Shapeshift? Start fires with your brain?"

"Weirder than that, I'm afraid." Deven sat up, picking up the stone and showing him that the blood smear had disappeared. "Remember when we were talking about the Order, and the Persephone myth, and you asked me about the other side of it?"

"Other side—oh, right. How one goddess made vampires to kill people and the other goddess made, what was the word you used . . . the Elentheia?"

"Yes. I told you it was true, that they did exist once, and you laughed at me and told me I had clearly done too much acid in the sixties."

"Right . . . I still think that, by the way."

"You also said that if it were true, there'd be a lot of pointy-eared people walking around."

"And you got pissy and changed the subject."

"Yes."

"So? Where are you going with this?"

Deven sighed and looked up at the ceiling. "Just looking at the ears wouldn't tell you if someone had Elven blood. Only the pure-blooded Elentheia had the ears. But there's another trait that did pass down for a few generations before it finally faded."

Jonathan suddenly realized he was gripping Deven's hand very, very hard, and his heart had begun to race. "And . . . what's that?"

"The eyes," Deven said softly. "We all have violet eyes."

Eleven

"Where am I?"

She smiled, crossing her arms. "Put it together, Sire."

He looked around at the dense forest that surrounded them, starlight seeping through the trees; she was standing in what looked like a pool of light, though the moon was not visible . . . and oddly, she seemed to be in a sort of grayscale instead of full color, like . . .

"You're dead," he said. "We both are."

"Looks that way."

Sorrow and guilt wrapped around his heart. "I'm sorry . . . Faith, I'm so sorry."

"Don't be," she replied with a shrug. "It wasn't your fault." Her gaze sharpened, and she came toward him, laying her hands on his shoulders; the contact felt real. "It wasn't your fault, David," she said firmly. "Remember that. I'm okay."

He reached up, took her hands, and squeezed them. Strange how comforting such a small gesture could be in a place like this . . . wherever it was.

"What happens now?" he asked.

"Don't ask me. I've been dead about three minutes longer than you have. Not a lot of time to explore."

Again, he looked around, confused. "If this is the afterlife, why is it a forest? It seems familiar, but . . ."

Faith stepped away suddenly, her eyes drawn to something behind him. He turned.

The fabric of the night seemed to turn into water, an area about six feet tall going blurry until light poured out of it. They stood together staring at it for a long moment, both knowing, deep down, what it was, neither willing to go any closer.

A light breeze lifted the leaves all around, and he heard a voice whisper, "Faith . . ."

She took a deep breath. "It's for me," she said softly. "It's time to go."

Before he could answer, she pulled him into a hug, and he could feel her heart beating fast as she whispered, "I love you."

There were tears in her eyes as she stepped back and turned to the portal, but her steps were sure, her shoulders squared, no fear in her body as she walked into the light . . . and was gone.

He was alone . . . but only for a moment.

The hair on the back of his neck stood up and his senses prickled with alarm. There was someone . . . something . . . behind him . . . and for once in his life, he was paralyzed with terror.

"Face me . . ." that same feather-light female voice whispered over the wind, the words cutting through him. "Be not afraid, child."

Steeling himself, barely breathing, he turned . . . and met silver-black eyes full of stars.

"Earth to Prime."

He looked away from the window, where he'd been standing and staring for several minutes. "Sorry," he said sheepishly.

Miranda paused in tuning her guitar and scrutinized him.

"Are you sure you want to go alone? I can come with you if you're not ready."

David shook his head. "I'll be fine. I just . . . I had a weird dream today, is all."

"What about?"

"I don't really remember. I was trying to, just now, but I can't. It felt important, and . . . I could swear Faith was in it."

She smiled softly. "I would be surprised if you didn't dream about her. I do. Mostly wishful thinking, rewriting the ending. That's probably all it was."

He nodded, even though he didn't agree. The problem was he didn't have the words to frame how the dream felt, or why he knew Faith was in it; it was just a feeling, and feelings had never been his specialty.

Sometimes he remembered snatches of his dreams, fluttering remnants that fell apart in his hands when he tried to examine them. It seemed to be the same location over and over again: the woods somewhere, under a moonless night run riot with stars. Sometimes he heard wings—dozens of them.

He turned away from the window and finished getting ready, buckling on his sword, putting on his coat. As he did the former, he smiled.

"What's so funny?" Miranda asked. She had been watching him this whole time—she watched him a lot these days, as if unsure what she was looking at.

David chuckled and drew the sword, holding it out where she could see the carving on the blade. "Have you ever noticed this?"

"Noticed what?"

He changed the angle, tilting it down away from her. "Look again."

The Queen's eyebrows shot up. "Whoa! I didn't think you had anything written on it."

"I didn't. *Someone* sneaked it in, and all this time I never noticed it until Olivia pointed it out to me."

Miranda grinned at him. "So I assume it's the sword's name—what is it?"

"The Oncoming Storm."

She sat back, pondering the words. "I think it fits you."

"It's a *Doctor Who* reference," he told her.

"Then it definitely fits you." She laughed. "Even when you're not wearing a geeky T-shirt, you're carrying your geekdom with you wherever you go."

He laughed, too, and bent down to kiss her. "I'll be back in a few hours."

"Be careful . . . and I hope you find her."

"I hope so, too."

David sat brooding in the car halfway to the city, not even sure what he was brooding about; he wanted to know what was going on, and on the other hand he didn't, because he had a feeling it wasn't good.

What if, when he came back, he hadn't come back all the way? What if part of him was gone—the part that had bonded to Miranda—and could never return?

And *how* had he come back? It wasn't possible. It wasn't as though he'd just seemed dead; he knew, even without Deven and Jonathan's verification, that he had really been dead. Besides, they would know the difference. No seven-hundred-year-old vampire could be fooled by fake death.

On impulse, he called California.

"Yes, David?"

He frowned. "Are you all right?"

"Right as rain."

It took David a minute to recognize the relaxed tone of Deven's voice—it had been a long time since he'd heard it. "I've interrupted something," he said.

"Actually your timing is impeccable as always. Jonathan's in the shower. I'm being disgustingly lazy."

"But it's ten P.M. You stayed in bed three hours late?"

"Rank hath its privileges. Besides . . . it was very important business. Negotiations for a cease-fire between warring parties."

David rolled his eyes. "You could just say makeup sex. What were you fighting about this time?"

"Whether Alexander or Hannibal had the sounder military strategy. I said it was an unfair comparison on account of the elephants."

David snorted. "In other words, none of my business."

"Was there a reason you were calling?"

"Yes . . . I mean, no, not really. I just wanted a distraction from my thoughts, I suppose. I'm on my way to Olivia's loft to try to persuade her to tell me more about that night."

"Are you sure she's still there?" Deven asked.

"Well, there are two vampires inside the building, and they've been coming and going for days—I've been watching."

"I remember Olivia from the last Elite tournament. Gorgeous tattoos. She was fierce in battle. I considered trying to poach her from Australia, but she was too loyal to Bartlett—and to her commanding officer, Hayes."

"Any news on that front?"

"No. No one's seen him. It would seem he got his daughter back and ran for the hills. Idiot."

"Why idiot?"

"Because if he had asked for help, we could have conspired together, all of us, to bring Hart down and expose him and McMannis."

"This from you?"

A sigh. "All I'm saying is that we could have helped him."

"We still can. All it would take is someone demanding to see McMannis's Signet up close. If we turn the matter over to Tanaka, no one could accuse us of harboring a vendetta."

"Not yet. There's something bigger at work here, and I want to know what it is. Somehow all of these events are linked—I can feel it. Can't you?"

"Deven, I have no idea what the hell I'm feeling. I don't even know what I am. I'm wandering around a stranger in my own life—I can barely keep the details of what happened together, much less draw any conclusions." He leaned back.

"Well, just relax, and stop trying to force everything. Go see what Olivia has to say. One way or another we'll get answers." There were a few muffled sounds, and Deven said,

"I have to go, darling—I have an immense load of work that I need to sort out."

David snorted. "You're just going to shag again."

Wicked amusement entered the Prime's voice. "Jealous?"

He sighed. "Yes."

There was a pause, and then Deven said, "David . . ."

"The bond, Dev. You still have one . . . I don't. Of course I'm jealous."

"Oh." David couldn't tell whether Deven sounded relieved. "About that . . . hopefully you won't have to go without it much longer."

"Why not?"

"Remember how I said the Elves were extinct? Well, there's still some of their blood around, especially in Witches. So I sent out a call looking specifically for someone with the ability and the Sight to help rebond you."

"Sent out a call how, exactly?"

"I happen to know someone who collected magical relics, and among them was a particular kind of stone that can be used to more or less ping people with Elven blood."

"That's the most ridiculous thing I've ever heard."

"Oh, surely not. Now, if you'll excuse me . . ."

"Right. Enjoy."

He heard a murmur, but whether it was a farewell or not, there was no telling; Deven hung up without clarifying.

The Prime shook his head. He had hoped calling Deven would make him feel better. Instead he felt worse, whether because he didn't find the idea of magical stones making magical calls particularly comforting, or because the thought of Deven and Jonathan spending the whole evening enjoying the luxury of a connection David no longer had . . . or just the idea of them . . .

Oh for fuck's sake. Let's not go down that road again, Prime.

"Sire, we're within half a mile of the address you specified," Harlan said from the driver's seat. "Did you want me to drop you at the door, or were you intending a stealthier approach?"

"To hell with it, Harlan. Let's make a spectacle of ourselves."

"As you will it, Sire."

This was not the part of town where one would often see a Lincoln gliding up the street; no matter where he had Harlan park, it would be noticed. Might as well let his presence be known.

"Are you sure you don't want backup, Sire? At least a bodyguard?"

"I don't want to spook her. I'm in no danger here. Don't worry."

Harlan opened the car door for him, and David disembarked with a sweeping look around the block; he could feel eyes on him from one of the buildings, but other than that, the neighborhood was quiet.

Olivia's front stoop was just as it had been. He paused, looking down at the ground where he was pretty sure he'd fallen . . . or crawled . . . or magically appeared . . . in front of the building, then took the steps up to the door.

He heard movement inside at his knock, but no one answered. Eyes narrowing, he tried again.

Still nothing. Curious, he tried the door handle . . . it was unlocked.

Quietly, he said into his com, "Patrol Team Nine, what is your current location?"

"East Cesar Chavez and Matagorda, Sire."

"Divert to my coordinates. I want you approaching this warehouse from all four sides. Alert me when you're in position."

"As you will it, Sire."

David quickly checked the grid on his phone again; the situation was the same, two vampire life signs inside. There was no way to differentiate between strong and weak, male and female—only whether a vampire wore a Haven com or not. Signets themselves showed up differently, as white dots instead of red or green, and Jeremy Hayes had proven that that part of the system was unreliable. Whether it was the lack of an actual Signet around his neck or the fact that he hadn't displayed Prime-level power until he Misted, David couldn't say yet, but somehow Jeremy hadn't shown up as a white dot until the night of the Awakening. David wasn't sure how to compensate for it, though—he rather suspected it was a onetime issue.

There were not, however, any white dots here. These were green; not his people. Very slowly, he lifted the latch on the door and eased it open, thankful for well-oiled hinges that didn't squeak. He wasn't going in until the team had arrived, but he didn't want the sound of a bolt to tip off whoever was in there.

He leaned close to the door, listening. For a minute there was nothing, just the sounds of an ordinary night outside and the settling of an old industrial building inside, but then suddenly he heard a creak and a raspy noise that had to be a door on the other side of the building. Sure enough, the signals inside were approaching one wall. Whether they knew he was there or not, they were about to get away.

Or so they thought.

The loft was dark, and though it still smelled like turpentine, there were no paintings standing around the room, no art supplies in haphazard configurations that would make sense only to a creative mind.

David moved into the room with all his senses on alert, listening for any movement, a breath, a shift of weight . . . He knew someone was still here . . . he could feel it . . . and it probably wasn't Olivia.

A click, a whistle.

Before he could even realize he knew that sound, he felt the impact of the stake as it buried itself in his heart.

A standard punching bag wouldn't do it for vampires. It would just burst like a piñata after a minute or two. Fortunately centuries of training warriors had given rise to quite a few innovations among the Signets, one of which was a steel-reinforced system that could withstand all but the most enraged pummeling.

"Good!" Bax pronounced as the Queen slammed her fists into the bag. "But less force, more precision. Targeted strike, my Lady."

Miranda nodded, blowing out of her face a sweaty curl that had escaped her ponytail. She hit the bag again, this time remembering to keep her wrists straight and *place* her punches rather than throwing them.

For the most part the Haven vampires didn't need extensive hand-to-hand combat training; they usually fought with weapons in their hands, so it was more important to learn how to kick the shit out of someone before beheading them. Still, Miranda didn't like having holes in her training, and since losing David, she had tried to fill all her waking hours with exhausting work, so she enlisted Bax, a longtime Elite lieutenant who specialized in violent things to do with one's fists. By the time Bax was done with her, her arms would be noodles, and any tension she had in her body would be good and worked out.

Over the last few weeks she had imagined several different faces on the punching bag. Her favorite was Hart, but Jeremy Hayes came in a close second.

She was still trying to have compassion for him—to have lost his wife and daughter, and his Signet, all at once, then be forced into indentured servitude for Hart to try to buy his daughter's life back . . . it was horrible, sickening. And if he had come to Australia's allies for help, she would have been more than glad to band together with him against the bastards who had usurped him.

But instead, he had killed Faith, and killed David . . . and if Miranda ever saw him again, she wouldn't waste time with pity. He would know exactly why she took his head—if he was so noble, he would be ready for justice, and the Queen of the South would deliver it with a smile on her face.

She wasn't used to being quite so bloodthirsty . . . but some crimes were unforgivable. Sometimes a raised fist didn't earn the other cheek; sometimes it earned a stake through the heart. This time, she didn't let her empathy overwhelm her anger; she had a right to be angry.

Miranda's fists collided with the bag so hard that Bax, who was standing behind it holding it still, was pushed back a few inches, no mean feat for a 250-pound former heavyweight boxer.

"Sorry," she panted, lowering her arms. "Got carried away there for a second."

"Not a problem, my Lady," Bax replied with a grin. "I'm just glad I'm not who you were thinking about just now. At least I hope not."

Miranda summoned a smile, though she was drenched and out of breath. "Not today," she told him.

"Time for one more round?"

She started to say that she'd had enough for one night—

—but pain crushed her, forcing her to cry out and fall to her knees. Her hands went to her chest—she could feel something, something piercing her flesh—

—but there was nothing—

No, no, no . . . not again . . . it can't be happening again . . . please God no . . .

David.

You've got to be fucking kidding me. Again?

He dropped to the ground, grasping at the stake with hands gone numb with shock. It was slippery, bloody, and he couldn't get a grip on it . . . but it didn't matter anyway; he could feel the wood in his heart, feel his heart shuddering to a stop, leaving him with only a moment to live.

Except . . . it didn't happen.

David was dizzy and nearly unconscious from lack of oxygen, but he managed to get hold of the stake and, with all the strength he could muster, pull it from his chest. The stake hit the ground, splattering blood, and he fell forward onto his hands, desperate for breath.

The pain in his chest amplified for just a second, and then he heard a thundering noise in his head, once, then again, then stumbling around until it fell into a steady rhythm.

His heart was beating.

Distantly he heard a second click, another whistle.

He snatched the stake out of the air a foot from his face, turned it around, and threw it back where it had come from, extending his telekinetic power to make sure it struck true.

A strangled cry. The clatter of a crossbow hitting the concrete floor, followed by the heavy thump of a body.

Breathing hard, grateful to breathe at all, David sat back on his knees, vision swimming. His mind was spinning in circles.

His phone rang: Miranda.

His bloody finger left a smudge on the phone's screen. "Beloved," he said hoarsely.

The Queen was practically screaming with fear. "What happened? I felt a stake—"

"Yes, you did." He swallowed his own reaction and spoke calmly, for her sake. "It's all right . . . I'm fine. This shirt, however, is a goner."

"But . . . I don't understand—it felt like it was a heart shot."

David stared down at the stake, then lifted his eyes to the far end of the room where his assailant lay. "It was," he told her. "I took a stake to the heart . . . and I lived."

By the time he summoned a second patrol team to help tear the building apart looking for the other vampire he'd seen on the grid; sent the stakes and the attacker's fingerprints to Hunter Development for testing; reassured Miranda that she didn't need to come to him; essentially told a severely rattled Jonathan the same thing when he called; and ascertained that Olivia was not, in fact, tied up somewhere in the building or lying dead anywhere nearby, the Prime had a splitting headache and excused himself from the scene to hunt.

As he walked down the street toward an area where he could hear more activity, he found himself wishing Faith were with him. She would have something reassuring to say, and she would do whatever needed doing to solve the problem, if it was a problem. If nothing else, she would tell him not to look a gift horse in the mouth.

Gift unicorn, he thought crazily, remembering what Stella had said.

The part of his mind that was still rational was analyzing the incident: Not only had he healed from a stake to the heart, the wood itself hadn't impeded the healing process any more than a blade would. Normally a wood wound took twice as long to heal, if not longer, which was why it could kill them.

Somehow he had become immune to wood. It was so beyond weird he didn't even know where to begin to analyze it.

He approached the cross street, pulling his coat closed over the ruin of his shirt so it wouldn't alarm the mortals. Sure enough, there were a few out. A café on the corner was doing a brisk late-night business, and it looked like a ways down the street a live music performance of some kind had let out. In a city like Austin, with a flourishing nightlife, vampires never had to worry about going hungry.

David stayed in the shadows, watching them pass in twos and threes, until he saw one walking by himself.

He reached out and took hold of the human's mind, pulling him over.

He was an attractive young man, a musician by the look of it—they had a certain similarity of nonconformity in Austin and were rather thick on the ground. David recognized guitar calluses on his fingers—Miranda had them after a show, though hers faded almost as soon as she was finished playing. The human smelled like clove cigarettes and beer. Not an ideal choice, but David wasn't in the mood for a serious hunt. He just wanted the headache and the exhaustion to go away.

"Hey, man," the human said. "Do I know you from somewhere?"

"No talking," David replied, teeth already extending like a cat's claws. "Just hold still."

The human's blood tasted surprisingly healthy considering the marginal lifestyle so many young musicians led, and within a few swallows David felt renewed strength flowing out to every cell of his body, both soothing and enlivening where it touched. It was difficult not to take too much in the state he was in, but this lad had no stains on his soul, unlike . . .

A man in a suit slid to the ground, face caught in an expression of eternal surprise, a brutal death for a brutal man—

David lurched backward, pushing the human away. "Oh God."

The human was starting to come around. David seized him quickly and blanked the incident from his mind, then all but shoved him back out onto the street and away.

He remembered the look on Olivia's face. The satisfaction from the glut of blood as well as from knowing that there was one less predator in the world . . . bold thoughts, coming from the predator that had killed him.

He had killed a human.

That in and of itself wasn't so shocking—he'd killed a lot of them, back in the day, and that one was far more deserving than most—as the idea that he had done it so casually, without a second's hesitation or remorse. Since taking the Signet he had found it much more difficult to excuse any death, whether among his own people or theirs. If he had been himself, he would have . . .

. . . wait . . .

How had he known the human he'd killed was an evil-doer? He remembered fixing his attention on the man and knowing, somehow, the black and filthy secrets of his heart . . . normally vampires could scent a lot of qualities in their prey and could sense fear and stress; that, coupled with subtle body language cues, gave them a pretty good idea of who might be walking around with a guilty conscience, but he had *known*. He hadn't needed to psychically interrogate the man to know his crimes; he had known specifically what the man had done, and . . .

"Oh, bloody hell," David groaned aloud, startling a passerby. "Empathy."

Miranda had "caught" telekinesis from him. It stood to reason he could have picked up some of her empathic talent, although that posed a bigger question: *How?* He and Miranda were sundered. This hadn't happened before his death, so somehow he had caught her gift after the bond was broken.

Not to mention, she had felt the stake tonight. Either their bond wasn't as broken as it seemed, or there was something even stranger and bigger going on here than any of them knew.

He made his way back to Olivia's loft, where Harlan would be waiting with the car and the Elite would still be poring over the scene. More than anything, he wanted to talk to Miranda, but a phone call wasn't going to cut it. He had to tell her everything, and he had to do it face-to-face.

The leader of the Elite units he'd called in approached him to give a status report, but he waved her away, telling her to send it in to the server later. There were a few curious and concerned looks from the Elite who watched him all but fall into the car.

"Home, Sire?" Harlan asked.

"Please. And if you could break a few traffic laws, that would be lovely."

Harlan steered the car toward the highway, saying, "I certainly can, Sire."

"All right," Miranda said calmly, each phrase sounding progressively more insane to her ears. "You killed a human, you're mildly empathic, and you're immune to wood."

"There's more."

She held up her hand. "Hang on a minute." He waited while she poured and knocked back another tequila shot. "Okay. Go."

"After I killed the man, I . . . did something with his body."

Miranda put her head in her hands. "Baby, I love you, but I'm telling you right now, necrophilia is a deal breaker for me."

He stared at her for a minute before laughing. "No, it's nothing like that. I Misted him."

"What do you mean?"

"I . . . sent the body away. He didn't float, or slide—he transported, the way we do. Only I wasn't touching him."

This time, she just drank right out of the bottle, then handed it to him so he could do the same. He took a long swig and capped the bottle, setting it on the side table. They were in the study; he had told her they needed to talk and that she would probably need liquor. He was right.

He took a deep breath and held his hand over the tequila bottle.

It vanished.

Miranda stared, wide-eyed, her heart hammering so hard she could hear it. She felt suddenly cold. She'd seen him move plenty of things with his mind, but they never just . . . disappeared like that, exactly the way a Prime or Consort did when Misting. "Where . . ."

He let out the breath and gestured toward the other side of the room. Sure enough, the bottle was there, sitting unharmed on its shelf in the liquor cabinet. It had been transported not only across the room, but through the glass doors.

When he looked back at her, she saw . . . no, it must have been a trick of the light. His eyes were blue as they'd always been.

"What?" he asked. "Miranda . . . please don't look at me like that . . . like you're afraid."

She swallowed and shook her head. "No, it's . . . I'm fine. I'm not afraid, just a little freaked."

He accepted that . . . and for the first time, she was glad the bond wasn't working.

Before Miranda could summon the wherewithal to ask another question, David's phone rang—the West's ring tone. David sighed and took the call. "Yes?" He looked at Miranda and mouthed, *Jonathan*.

She knew immediately something was wrong . . . but if either of the Pair had been injured she was fairly sure at this point she'd have felt it. This was something else . . . and the slowly dawning astonishment on David's face confirmed the stroke of her intuition.

"How long have you known?" David asked. "Well, of course they're trying to keep a lid on it, but I assumed Deven had an operative in his Court . . . damn." The Prime's expression hardened. "Investigation, my ass. Any idiot would know who's behind it. Let me know as soon as there's anything else."

He sat for a moment staring at the phone, until Miranda couldn't take it anymore. "What the hell happened?"

David didn't seem to know how to feel about his next words. "Chicago is in chaos—Joseph and Abigail are dead."

Miranda's mouth dropped open. "I knew the Mideast States were contentious, but . . . they've held the Signet for ninety years. Has someone claimed it?"

"No. Whoever did it assassinated Prime Kelley, left his Queen to die, and then burned down the Haven and vanished. Dozens of Kelley's Elite were trapped inside, including the Red Shadow agent Deven had there."

Prime Joseph Kelley had never been an ally of the South, nor was he really an enemy; his territory had been seething with gang warfare for decades, and he and Abigail had sometimes held on to their Signets by the skin of their teeth. Miranda had never even met them—they hadn't been able to get away for either the Magnificent Bastard Parade or the Council meeting.

"You said any idiot would know who's behind it," Miranda repeated. "You were talking about Jeremy, right?"

"It had to be."

"Why? Why would he go after Kelley?"

David made an indefinite gesture and said, "I'm not sure. I think I remember Kelley having some sort of tie to McMannis, but I'd have to research it. The thing is . . . preliminary reports from the scene indicate liquid explosives."

"Oh, hell. Jeremy's trademark."

"So either he killed the Pair, or someone wants it to look like he did."

Miranda didn't like either possibility, but either way, it

seemed her vacation from Signet politics was over; now that David was back and things could return to mostly normal, she couldn't keep ignoring the problem of Hart, McMannis, and Hayes for long. The sticky part was . . . what should they do about it?

"Maybe we should just sit back and let Jeremy kill them off," Miranda mused. "Much as I'd like to hang his head from the front gate, if he can take out Hart, it might be worth leaving him alone."

The Prime was giving her an odd look. "Would you really kill Jeremy, even knowing what the others did to him, and knowing he was only trying to save his daughter?"

Her eyebrows shot up. "Since when are you the compassionate one? He *killed* you. He killed Faith. He hired thugs to burn and pillage all over the territory. All of those lives seriously outweigh his wife and daughter."

He frowned. "So it's a zero-sum game."

She couldn't help but stare at him, unable to comprehend his attitude—but then she smiled and said, "Empathy?"

David frowned, then looked dismayed. "Christ, I hope not."

Miranda laughed. "So do I. It's not fun. So . . . what do you want to do about this whole situation, if you don't want to pop some popcorn and enjoy it?"

He smiled at her idea, but said, "We can't be a hundred percent sure it's Jeremy yet, and even if we could, we'd still need to know a lot more about what's going on before we decide how to deal with it. In the meantime we've got Morningstar to occupy us, if for no other reason than to get Stella home."

"True."

"The question, then, is this: Why would Jeremy want to kill Kelley? Did Kelley have a connection to his enemies that put him in the crosshairs? That's the only reason I can think of."

"Unless . . ." Miranda felt dread sneaking into her stomach, the kind of horrible certainty that Queens were cursed with—the kind that never chose a good moment to assert itself. "There's one other possibility."

David lifted his chin, thoughtful, indicating she should go on.

She met his eyes. "Unless Kelley was just practice . . . and this is only the beginning."

Even as she said the words, a horrible but familiar feeling gripped her chest and sent her mind into a whirl. Fear and anger washed over her—not her own—

The phone began to ring.

PART TWO

An Unkindness of Ravens

Twelve

"Are you sure you're all right?" Deven asked. "If you need more hands, I can send someone to you from Vienna."

Jacob chuckled. "Do I get to know why you have someone in Vienna?"

"Absolutely not."

"Very well. We're fine. The crossbow bolt missed Cora by several inches, and my Elite got to him before he could make it out of the square. Cora was shaken, but unhurt."

"And the assassin?"

"Dead, unfortunately," Jacob said ruefully.

Deven heard David sigh on the other end of the line. "Tell me he didn't blow himself up with liquid explosives."

"No, actually, it was definitely—what's the phrase humans use—suicide by cop. He resisted detainment and made sure they had to kill him, thereby keeping him out of interrogation. There is, however, one detail we got that I think you'll find intriguing . . . or incredibly disturbing, I'm not sure which."

"Oh?" David asked.

"An earpiece," Jacob told them. "Identical to the images you've sent me of the ones used by Morningstar."

"I don't get it," said David. "Why would they be after you now?"

"Because he's an easy target," Deven said.

"Thank you," Jacob replied wryly. "Good to know I have your confidence."

"No, listen to me. I know what you're capable of, and so do David and much of the Council . . . but if you were trying to take out one of us, who would seem the most vulnerable? You, Jacob. Your Elite has fewer than sixty swords, you're isolated from the rest of us, and your Haven isn't a technological powerhouse because it's never needed to be. Your population is lower and both you and your predecessors kept it peaceful, so the likelihood of reprisals is low. From the outside, you make the perfect target."

David and Jacob were both silent for a beat while they digested that. Then David said, "I still don't understand. Jacob is hardly the only Prime with a small Elite and a peaceful territory. There are at least half a dozen others they could have gone after."

"Do you really think so?" Deven asked gravely. "Or do you think, perhaps, that this connection among the six of us might not be as much of a secret as we'd like?"

Another pause, this one longer.

"First they used Ovaska to go after Miranda, and caught you in the process, intending to kill you but take her alive." Jacob added it up. "Then they sent someone after Miranda who would probably have killed her mortal friend as well—a mortal friend who could help you get your bond back. Now they've come after me. You're right, Deven . . . it can't be a coincidence."

"But what the hell is so special about us?" David wanted to know, and Deven could practically see him, in his mind, leaning his forehead in one hand, the line between his eyes appearing both from tension and from the inevitable headache.

"How would you like that list? Over e-mail, or verbally?" Deven asked archly. "I think the fact that we all keep having the same premonitions and feeling each other's pain would be enough to make us pretty damned special."

"But that's just it. Why is it happening to us? Why now? And what the hell does Morningstar have to do with it?"

"Good questions, all," Jacob noted. "None of which we have the answers to."

There really wasn't much more to say. A few minutes later, when the call ended, Deven looked over to where Jonathan sat listening. "What do you think?" the Prime asked.

Jonathan interlaced his fingers and sat back, considering. "Well, I think . . . no, I've got nothing."

Deven had no intention of leaving the situation alone. He switched over to the Red Shadow network and sent out a divert command. "I don't care what Jacob says, 7.4 Carmine concluded his op two hours ago and didn't have a new contract yet. I'm sending him to Prague."

"I had a feeling you'd say that."

"You're sure you haven't had any sort of premonition or even an inkling as to what's going on here?"

"I wish I had, Deven. Things are getting a little out of hand."

"Understatement, love. You were right about one thing: Lydia set the dominoes falling. But we thought the last one was David . . . Now I think we might have underestimated the scope of her plan." He pulled up a global map of the Signet territories with each Haven location marked, linked to information about whoever held it. One of them was vacant. "Kelley is dead . . . but that was almost certainly Hayes."

"Did you figure out why?"

He touched the screen and brought up another image, enlarging it so Jonathan could see. "Credit card statements," he said. "They put McMannis and Hart in Chicago a week before the Council meeting. That's a long way to travel from Australia just for a pub crawl—Kelley was up to his ass in the plot to overthrow Hayes. I don't know exactly what he did to earn a fiery death, but I'm one hundred percent certain he had it coming."

Jonathan looked like he was trying to decide whether to say something.

"Out with it," Deven told him.

The Consort smiled slightly. "Do you really want to stop Hayes?"

Deven held his eyes for a moment, and Jonathan added, "I mean, this is Hart and McMannis we're talking about. If Jeremy can kill them, why not let him?"

Suddenly, uninvited, images flashed in Deven's mind: terrified faces, blood flowing . . . the sound of screams . . . Eladra's agonized, but accepting, eyes. Smoke in black, choking clouds . . . the lick of flames . . . and a whisper over and over again: *Nothing. We died for nothing.* By the time he managed to shove the memories out of his mind, his hands were shaking.

He put his hands over his face for a few seconds before saying, almost too quietly for Jonathan to hear, "Kelley had eighty-seven Elite, twenty-two servants. There were twelve Elite out on patrol, and they all came home to the Haven on fire—the security systems overridden, window shutters locked, bolts on the doors. Do you think they could hear their comrades screaming inside as they burned to death? We can't die by smoke inhalation, after all. They would all have been conscious for every second until their flesh was burned past the point of no return. No matter who they worked for, they didn't deserve to die that way, and neither do McMannis's or Hart's Elite."

When he lifted his eyes back to Jonathan, the Consort was staring at him as if his Prime had morphed into a new creature, one Jonathan had never seen before . . . and then his expression changed slightly, to something Deven recognized, that look Jonathan got just before sweeping him up in a breathless kiss.

But Jonathan merely nodded, gave him a soft smile, and said, "All right . . . what are we going to do?"

* * *

Fire—

Miranda woke with a start, eyes on the fireplace and heart pounding. She looked around in confusion.

What she'd been dreaming faded into a much less dire reality: She had dozed off on the couch. Her guitar sat leaning on the coffee table near a scattering of notebook paper covered in her scribbles. Right, she'd been working on another new song, taken a break, and fallen asleep.

She frowned, trying to make sense of the dream. It was painful, laden with crushing guilt. An old stone building somewhere in a forest . . . populated entirely by vampires, but not a Haven . . . burning from the inside, destroying the corpses of the inhabitants who were already . . . dead . . .

"Oh, God," she murmured. She knew what she had seen.

Suddenly she couldn't stand to sit there anymore. She grabbed her guitar and pushed herself up off the couch.

The guards were used to her bursting out of the suite hellbent on the music room; their Queen's idiosyncrasies had stopped worrying them no more than a year into her tenure. She waved them off, so they wouldn't feel it necessary to follow her, and all but ran down the hall.

Once inside, she returned the guitar to its stand and dropped heavily onto the piano bench.

Even the worst realizations felt a little less overwhelming with her fingers on the keys. She shut her eyes and let her hands talk for a moment, starting with one of her favorite pieces— the main theme from *The Piano*—and then improvising her way around it for a few minutes. The rolling melody translated through the dark echoing depth of the Bösendorfer eased some of the tension that had tightened all her muscles even before she woke from the dream. Still, the thought remained:

He killed them all for us. All those people. And . . .

Something occurred to her that she hadn't really put together before, and she found herself fighting back tears.

He knew them. From a long time ago. They were his friends once, and he killed them . . . for us. To stop the Awakening . . . but it happened anyway.

She stopped in the middle of a chord, causing a rather harsh sound from the piano, but she needed one hand to pull out her phone.

Without a greeting, she said, "They were your friends."

He didn't seem surprised to hear from her. Nor did he pretend not to know what she meant. "Yes."

"Even after David said he didn't want to see you again, you did that for us."

"Yes."

"And it's killing you."

A pause, then: "Yes."

The weariness, the ache in that one word nearly made her weep, but she held herself together and asked, "What can I do to make it better for you?"

Another pause. "Don't waste it," he said.

He started to hang up, but she interrupted, "Deven—"

"Yes, Miranda?"

"I know you would do it for David . . . and you have to save me to save him, but . . ."

"Miranda," he said, a sort of gentle firmness in the word that brooked no disagreement, "I thought by now you would understand—things aren't like they were three years ago. If I never expected to still love him after all those years, well, let's just say I was utterly blindsided by you."

"By me?"

"Yes . . . I would do anything for you. Anything. Ask for the stars and I'll do what I can."

They sat in silence, he thousands of miles away, she safe in the Texas Hill Country, sitting at a piano. "I don't need the stars," she finally said. "But I would like to see you happy for a change."

A quiet chuckle. "I'll do what I can. Good night, my Lady."

"Good night."

She was still sitting there, staring at her phone, when

David found her a little while later. Still in his coat and armed from his night in the District, he poked his head into the room first as always and inquired, "Clear?"

Miranda lifted her head and nodded.

As David approached her, he saw her expression and frowned. "What is it? What happened?"

She looked up at him, down at her phone, back up. "I think Deven just sort of told me he loves me," she said.

David stared at her. "He did?" He sat down in one of the chairs nearby.

She recounted the conversation, and his expression grew more and more thoughtful.

"I'm sure he says that to a lot of people," Miranda ventured, but even without the *Are you kidding?* look David gave her, she knew better.

David said, "I wonder if perhaps he's picking up on your empathy, too. He's always been something of a guilt-ridden mess on the inside, but I've never known him to show it. Whatever this connection thing is could be changing all of that. Of course, it might also be that the two of you have something now that you never did before—genuine friendship, which for Deven is a rare and precious thing."

Miranda looked down at her hands, still on the piano keys. "For me, too." She smiled a little. "All of my friends have a tendency to get killed or justifiably run screaming."

He got up from the chair and came over to her, leaning in to kiss her forehead. "Not all of them, beloved."

She leaned against him for a moment, closing her eyes. He couldn't give her the kind of reassurance she craved, but the solidity of his presence was no trifling thing. She remembered how she had broken down over his scent, and here it was, warm and real and alive, with her.

"Tomorrow is the solstice," David said, voice vibrating against the side of her head. "Have you spoken to Stella about this ritual of hers?"

"I have. She asked if her friend Lark could help her, and I didn't see any reason not to let her. They're going to work in one of the unused rooms in our wing—I'm having the furniture cleared out tonight so they'll have all the floor space they need."

"Wouldn't they be better off in a shielded room?"

"Stella said that the way they do their rituals, they create a sphere of energy that protects them, then take it down when they're finished. Plus they often work outside, where it's a lot harder to keep a permanent shield. There's a storm in the forecast or they would have found a place in the gardens somewhere." She shrugged. "Stella swears there's nothing I can do to help. She gave me a list of things she needs, and I gave it to one of the Elite to take care of."

"What kinds of things? Eye of newt?"

She leaned back to give him an irritated look. "Candles, incense resins, that type of thing. And white paint."

"Paint?"

"To draw some sort of symbols on the floor." Before he could object, she said, "Nobody's used that room for anything in ten years—Esther told me so. And I looked at the floor; it's in pretty rough condition. If we need the room later, we can refinish the floor. I think it's worth some sanding if we get answers."

"True." He looked like he wanted to say more, but he returned to the chair, something troubling in his eyes.

"What is it?" she asked.

"This thing they're doing . . . I have a bad feeling about it."

Miranda groaned. "God, you don't have precog now, too, do you?"

He laughed. "I don't think so. It's nothing that strong. Just a feeling of unease I can't shake. Do you feel it?"

"Well, I will now, thanks a lot."

"It's not that I can see anything going wrong, but . . ."

She missed being able to simply intuit what he was thinking and finish his sentences; she had depended on the bond so much for that, it was difficult to read him just as an individual. Even when they'd met and she was human they'd had something connecting them, that force of nature that had driven them together.

Still, she had some idea what he was thinking just because she knew him. "You don't know what would be worse: for the ritual to work, or for it not to work."

"That's it in a nutshell. If it doesn't work, we're still adrift, not knowing anything. But if it does work, we could learn something we really don't want to know—something that makes it all worse."

"I'm not trying to tempt fate here or anything, but . . . what could possibly be worse?"

He smiled faintly; she couldn't help noticing, in spite of the conversation, how amazing he looked sitting there in his coat, hands on the arms of the chair, utterly and effortlessly regal. He no longer had the drawn, exhausted look he'd had when he returned. She had always thought he had the most ridiculously perfect posture—straight but not rigid, every inch a king, unless he was sprawled out on the couch or bed, in which case he reminded her more of a drunken octopus.

". . . staring at me," he said a little more loudly, and she felt herself blushing. She hadn't heard a word he said.

"Sorry, what was that?"

The smile grew a tiny bit. "I said that I have an irrational dread of the whole thing—some part of me knows I'm not going to like what we discover."

Miranda closed the piano and stood up, coming over to slide into his lap. "I think even learning something awful is better than knowing nothing," she said. "I also think there's not a thing we can do about it right now. The sun's coming up."

He was staring at her mouth. "I hadn't noticed," he replied.

She grinned and kissed him, her hands winding around his neck. The response was as enthusiastic as she'd hoped; he wrapped a hand around the back of her head and the other arm around her waist and pulled her as close as he could, kissing her hard enough to bruise her lips.

"Come on," she said breathlessly, all but jumping off his lap and hauling him to his feet.

They had barely reached the door when she felt his hands

on her hips, spinning her around so her back hit the wall. He pinned her there, gripping both of her wrists in one hand above her head.

In between kisses she frowned . . . He knew she didn't like being held down or pinned. "Hey," she murmured, pushing against his arm as a reminder.

The only response was a low hiss in her ear and a tightening of the hand around her wrists. He pushed her harder into the wall and bit her solidly on the neck.

It was hardly the first time he'd done that, and usually it was an intense turn-on, but something about it made her stomach lurch this time. She could feel something akin to anger radiating from him . . . that wasn't right. Miranda twisted hard to the side, wrenching her wrists free. "What the fuck is wrong with you?" she demanded.

Their eyes met, and she gasped.

She hadn't been imagining it before. His eyes were black, two cold obsidian chips that seemed to glow in the room's low light. There was no humanity in them whatsoever, nothing she recognized, only darkness.

"David!" she said desperately. "Wherever you are, get back here!"

He blinked, frowning, and in half a second the black was gone and he jerked back, almost stumbling away from her, blue eyes wide and horrified.

"What . . ." Confused, he looked around the room, then back at her, a touch of fear making its way into his voice. "What just happened?"

Miranda leaned back against the wall, crossing her arms over her chest. "I don't know."

"God, Miranda . . ." He groped sideways until he found the chair and sank into it, putting his face in his hands. "What's wrong with me? How could I even think of hurting you?"

She took a few deep breaths to steady herself. "Don't freak out about that," she said. "Honestly, you being a little more aggressive than usual isn't the scary part. You checked out on me . . . your eyes went black. I don't know what I was looking at, but it wasn't you, or at least, not all you."

Shame, fear, and repulsion were all evident in his face as he replied, "You mean you *hope* it wasn't all me."

"Tell me what you were feeling," she said. "Did you go somewhere? Did you feel . . . possessed or anything?"

"No," he answered. "I was there. As much as I ever am anymore . . . but sometimes . . . just now . . . something comes over me, like a shadow wrapping its hand around my throat. I can feel it . . . like when I killed that human. Or when I saw you fighting in the city that night. All question of reason or logic is swallowed whole and all I can think of is blood. I'm off-balance in a way I never was when we were bound."

Miranda bit her lip, watching him for a moment. Finally she recalled, "Stella said it looked like whatever was changing you wasn't done yet. Maybe that's the problem—you're caught between two lives and they're at war with each other."

David looked up at her, anguished. "I don't want that one to win."

"I know you don't. Neither do I."

"You were right," he said, closing his eyes. "No matter how awful it is, we have to know what's happening. We can't go on like this. The Witches may be our only hope."

Thirteen

Lark's reaction on seeing the Haven for the first time was priceless.

"Come on," Stella told her, bumping her forward with her shoulder, laughing. "We've got a lot to do."

Lark snapped her mouth shut and nodded. "Lead the way," she said, shifting the backpack she'd brought.

Once she was inside the building, Lark's mouth fell open again and she made a squeaking sort of noise. "How much money do these people have?" she wondered, falling into step with Stella down the hallway.

"Enough that nobody's batted an eye over anything I've asked for," Stella said.

Lark's eyebrow lifted. "What's that thing on your arm?"

"This?" Stella held up her wrist. "It's a communication device. They all wear them—it keeps track of where you're at and even records your DNA so they know who's who. This one's limited access, though—I can only call Miranda or my door guard and I can't spy on the others."

"How does that flat little thing record DNA?"

"Beats the hell out of me. There's a lot of crazy-ass technology around here. Hell, all I did was mention my laptop is a couple years old and David upgraded it in about four minutes. With his *phone*. While eating ice cream with the other hand." Stella held her com up to the lock on her suite's door; it beeped and opened.

It was still daylight so she didn't have any guards—there was one at the end of the hall and another posted at each exit, and special network alarms were turned on during the day. They'd had a regular cab bring Lark out, and Stella had special permission to open the front door with a day guard standing around the corner. They could have waited until dark, but Stella wasn't sure how much preparation they'd need before the exact moment of the solstice, and she didn't want to leave anything to chance.

"Not bad," Lark noted, looking around the room. "I see you've got your hard-core shields rocking. Not as trusting as you seem?"

"Yeah, well, I trust Miranda and David, and mostly anyone they've vouched for, but I only have to be wrong once."

"Are we doing this in here? There's not a lot of space."

"Nope. Down the hall. Did you bring everything?"

Lark nodded and hefted the backpack onto Stella's bed, unzipping it; there were overnight clothes and sundries, but also a cloth-wrapped bundle that turned out to be Lark's ritual robe with everything else wrapped up in it for safekeeping: a ritual chalice wrapped again in a velvet altar cloth, a package of round charcoal tablets, a stone incense burner, and a wood box.

"Did you find all the ingredients?" Stella asked, picking up the box and opening it. Inside was about a quarter cup of mixed herbs and resins. The combined scents wafted up to Stella's nose and gave her the impression of some wild place in the woods, heavy on evergreen trees, with a faint berry-like undertone.

"Foxglove gave me one hell of a look when I bought this stuff," Lark mentioned as they transferred the ritual items from her backpack to a tote Stella had already loaded halfway with other tools. "Mugwort, myrrh, wormwood, pomegranate leaves . . . the makings of a hard-core trance-inducing blend."

"Did you get the critter bits?"

"Yup. Snakeskin, a pulverized raven's feather, and hair from a black dog. You do know all this is going to stink like ass when we burn it."

"I'm hoping this will even it out," Stella said, pulling a bottle from the tote. "I knew this stuff would cost an arm and a leg, so I asked Miranda to get it."

"*Liquidambar orientalis v. nigrus* . . . Pure Black Storax oil," Lark read. She gave Stella a wide-eyed look. "There are only like five dozen of these trees in existence. This bottle's worth about five hundred dollars."

"Like I said," Stella said with a grin. "Money is no object around here, especially when it's this important. Just don't spill it."

Lark, who had lifted the bottle's cork just a little so she could smell the fragrant liquid inside, immediately recorked it and looked sheepish. "Right."

Stella laughed and hauled the tote up onto her shoulder. "Come on."

She'd spent most of the previous afternoon preparing the room. The Queen had offered help, but Stella wanted to make sure it was done right, and the only way to do that was to take care of it herself. She had, however, asked for extra hands moving the furniture out—two vampires had done in twenty minutes what would have taken her all day on her own.

"Wow," was all Lark said when she saw it.

In the center, Stella had hauled a small rectangular table to use as an altar, and she'd started painting based on its position. Radiating out from the altar and filling most of the room's scuffed and scratched floor were glyphs, protective sigils, and a variety of other symbols standing out stark white against the dark wood. They lined up with the four directions and with several celestial bodies including Pluto and

Mars; she'd researched the entire configuration for days before settling on exactly what she wanted.

Lark walked slowly around the circle, reading the glyphs to herself, until she got to one: "A triple moon and the infinity symbol? What does it do?"

"The Order of Elysium—the vampires that worship Persephone—use it as their seal. I figured it would be a good idea to include it. The version of Persephone I'm used to and the one they call on aren't exactly the same, so I thought we should specify."

Lark paused in front of the altar, then looked over at her friend. "Are you sure you want to do this?"

Stella had been expecting that very question. She sighed, opening up the tote to start pulling everything out, and said, "I'm sure."

"Did you tell your friends everything that could go wrong?"

"They didn't need to know about all of that. They would have just tried to stop me. I need to do this, Lark. They need answers, and nobody else can help."

"You know, I get that you love Miranda and all, but . . . it's an awfully big thing for you to do just out of fangirl loyalty. Let's not forget you almost died for this chick once already."

Stella set a pair of thick candles on the altar and added the incense burner. "It's more than that. I know you don't remember much of it, but that night we were attacked, it was Miranda's Elite that saved us. If another Pair had been in charge, we would probably be dead. In most parts of the world, the rules about feeding on humans are lax, if not nonexistent. Miranda and David are working to change all of that. If they can't do their jobs, they're vulnerable, and someone could take them out—for real this time."

"Stella Maguire, indirect savior of the human race," Lark laughed. "I like it. Maybe they'll make you their official Haven Witch. Like a mascot."

Stella shot her the finger. "I'm not wearing a big animal head for anybody, I don't care how awesome they are. Now get changed."

Lark grabbed the robe Stella held out to her, sticking out her tongue in the process. "You, too. Persephone isn't going to hang out in your skin if you're wearing that ratty-ass tank top."

Once they both had their robes on, they sat down in the middle of the floor with Stella's notebook to go over the details of the ritual. They had about an hour before it was time to begin—astronomically the Earth's axis was tilted just right at 10:34.

It wasn't that Drawing Down was so difficult—every High Priestess was trained to do it, and disaster was rare. But Lark was right; there was always a possibility of something going wrong. The darker deities tended to be a little less gentle with their followers and could be almost cruelly demanding. The rewards, however, were equally great: They could confer amazing strength and new abilities, and if you wanted justice or vengeance, they were the way to go. Stella couldn't imagine vampires having been created by a soft-and-fluffy goddess.

At precisely ten o'clock, they both rose from meditation and got to work.

Stella drew a line of salt over the circle she'd painted to contain all of the glyphs, marking the outermost boundary of the space they were creating; Lark got the incense charcoal burning and sprinkled powdered frankincense on it, sending up a fragrant billow of smoke that filled the air in the room and almost instantly changed how it felt. That smell was so familiar, it put them both in a ritual frame of mind without even trying.

"You cast," Stella said. "You'll need to hold on to the boundary if anything goes kaput."

Lark made her way around the boundary, pausing at each compass direction to invoke the powers of its associated element. She spoke aloud, using invocations they'd used before but adding an extra request for protection.

Stella could See the Circle taking shape, a sphere of energy that reminded her of a soap bubble, shimmering in the candlelight. It was far stronger than a soap bubble, though, and once it was up, it would keep unwanted energies as well as unwanted people from entering. The way they'd set it up it was like a magical electrified fence, and only Persephone herself could walk through.

Finally the two Witches met in front of the altar.

"Okay," Lark said. "You ready?"

Stella met her eyes and nodded. "Let's go."

Lark took the incense and mixed the oil into it, then dropped a spoonful onto the glowing charcoal. This time the smoke wasn't a comforting, familiar scent. It was thick and acrid, and Stella felt her lungs rebelling against breathing it in; she calmed herself, though, and inhaled.

Her senses spun off axis. She blinked, trying to make sense of it, watching as Lark's aura doubled in intensity and everything around them began to glow. She could feel her shields opening up—without any effort on her part—and could, at a great distance, hear Lark intoning the words they had agreed on for the invocation.

> *Lady of the darkened moon,*
> *Queen of the endless underworld,*
> *We ask for your presence here in this Circle.*
> *Descend into the body of your priestess . . .*

Stella didn't know how much time passed. It could have been seconds or minutes. The smoke had clouded her mind so much she couldn't form a coherent thought, and realizing how helpless she was, she felt herself hyperventilating out of panic. Fear overcame her—what was she doing? Who did she think she was, calling on a deity whose children were predators of the human race? Was she expecting hearts and flowers? She'd been such a—

Just as the terror began to buckle her knees, time seemed to slow down. She could see Lark in front of her, but the Witch was barely moving, her lips forming words but no sound coming out. The candle flames froze midflicker. Stella saw the ladders of smoke climbing toward the ceiling stop halfway there and hang, suspended, waiting.

For a moment the only sound was Stella's labored breathing. Cold crept up over her skin.

The room fell away, smoke obscuring her view and then clearing, without anything actually moving.

She heard the rush of wings.

She stood in a woodland clearing, feet rooted to the spot, staring all around her with her heart in her throat. It was deep night, the sky overhead heavy with starlight, a soft breeze lifting the leaves of the forest that surrounded her.

The voice that filled her ears was made of that breeze, of wings, of stars . . . of shadows.

"You are brave, child."

Stella took a deep breath and said, "I come seeking knowledge to help my friends."

She felt something sort of like eyes on her, as if holding her up to a jeweler's lamp to look for flaws. A presence circled her slowly: weighing, measuring.

"You are strong," the voice observed, *"but not strong enough to contain that knowledge. Should I speak through you, your own voice may be lost."*

"You know why I'm here?"

She almost heard a smile. *"Of course. I have been waiting for you."*

"Then you know I have to try."

The voice became sympathetic, gentle. *"To step into this world is to accept a life unlike any other of your kind . . . a life that may bring you to grief. If you do this, there is no turning back . . . and it will not be only your life that changes."*

Stella asked, almost in a whisper, "Is there any other way?"

"No. To speak to my children I must speak through one with your abilities. It is not yet time for them to come to me directly—only in dreams. With your help they will find me soon, but without your help, it may never be, and when war comes, my children will be unable to win."

"I take it that would be bad."

"Do you consider the loss of many thousands of human lives bad?"

She nodded, understanding. The vampires couldn't come here yet. They weren't ready. Without the knowledge she would bring them, they might never be.

"What do I have to do?" she asked.

She could sense approval, even pride. *"Only open your-self to me, child, and I will do the rest."*

Stella closed her eyes.

A scream split the air.

Miranda was on her feet before she could even register where it was coming from. She hit the music room door at a run, and emerging into the hallway she saw the suite door guards as well as several other Elite running toward the sound.

She knew, with a sinking heart, where it had originated: the room where Stella and Lark were doing their ritual. And even in that single scream, the Queen knew it wasn't Stella's voice.

She also knew it was a bad idea to burst in on them—but there was no other choice, if they needed help. She flung her arm up to unlock the door, not even waiting for the lock to beep before she turned the knob.

The scene inside was surreal. The air was hazy with smoke that smelled like burning dog hair and church; the floor was, as she anticipated, covered with white symbols in concentric circles around an altar. On the floor in front of the altar, one black-robed young woman lay in a heap, and another knelt beside her, sobbing incoherently.

"Stay back!" Miranda yelled at the Elite, remembering the dizzying sensation of walking into Stella's room. She braced herself for something even worse.

It seemed, however, that whatever had happened had blown the Circle to smithereens. There was no barrier at all when she ran into the room, though the entire place was crackling with energy. Miranda dove to the girls' side and dropped to her knees next to Lark, who was cradling Stella's head in her lap, begging her friend to stay with her.

"She's not breathing," Lark moaned. "Please, do some-thing, please—"

Miranda spared a second to call out to the others: "Get Mo down here now!"

She felt Stella's chest for a heartbeat. It was there, but faint. She wasn't exactly CPR certified, but she had to do something— she blew hard into Stella's mouth, hoping against hope that something would happen, that she hadn't sent a friend into this room to die. At the same time, she *reached*, willing Stella's lungs to work, her heart to keep beating.

Footsteps thundered outside the room, and Mo appeared, just as Stella drew a ragged, gasping breath.

Relief made the Queen feel weak; she sagged backward, letting Mo get to the Witch. Lark was still sobbing, clinging to Stella's hand.

"We must get her to my clinical room," Mo said urgently. "She needs oxygen and an EKG." He stood up, taking the Witch with him, and carried her out the door, Lark running to keep up behind him.

Miranda rose, intent on following.

Before she could take a step, thunder seemed to roll through her head; the room pitched and spun, and she collapsed where Stella had lain.

Austin was quiet that solstice night.

A summer storm was rolling steadily across the Hill Country and would reach the city in an hour at most, but for the moment the air was calm, even as high up as the roof of the Winchester Bank building.

He stood watching the city's heart pulse with the rhythm of hundreds of stoplights. People were trying to get home before the rain started. The blare of horns punctuated the relative quiet, but from up here, the sound was just part of the symphony.

Waiting. Too much waiting. The Prime had no choice but to be patient, and it was maddening.

They were waiting on the Witches. Waiting to find out more about Morningstar. Waiting for intelligence about Jeremy Hayes.

In the meantime, Miranda was talking to her agent about

going back onstage, and the Prime was standing on a roof, so all was right with the world again.

He hadn't slept that day; between the stress of all this waiting and the fear that he might lose himself in his sleep and hurt Miranda, there was simply no rest for him, not yet.

He was afraid of himself. His entire life he had been reasonably self-aware, able to think his way through any problem. The only thing that had ever caught him off guard was love—and who could blame him for that? Love caught everyone off guard, after all. But this new thing, this darkness that had taken root inside him . . . he feared it . . . and he was not used to fear.

There was nowhere to turn, no one who would understand. He had no Second to turn to, and even if he had, he couldn't imagine confiding in anyone the way he had Faith. The closest, he supposed, would be Olivia, since she had been there to witness some of what had happened, but he had no way to reach her.

There was something he trusted about her implicitly; he couldn't put his finger on what, but he knew, once again somewhere deeper than logic, that he hadn't seen the last of her. There was some kind of strength in her, some kind of power that his own power seemed to recognize. Olivia's part in this was not yet over . . . and if he could find her, he would tell her so.

The first few drops of rain fell on his coat, and he sighed. Time to head home.

It was getting harder. He wasn't sure how much longer he could face his Queen, seeing the way she looked at him when she thought he wasn't aware of it. Now that they were separate, there was a very real possibility that she could turn away from him, even leave. She didn't need him anymore. He didn't truly believe she would give up on them, but it was still possible and never had been before. Who could blame her, after all she'd suffered because of him? It seemed that whether living or dead, he brought her nothing but pain.

Self-pity, Prime? Very nice.

Things would be clearer once he got some sleep. Before, he'd been able to push through entire weeks with only a couple of hours snatched here and there, but for some reason since he'd come back from the dead, he found it incredibly difficult to function without enough sleep. Whatever he was dreaming about, it was obviously very attractive to his subconscious.

Having done the math, he estimated that he had regained 98 percent of his memory; the things that had always been fuzzy, like his human life, were still fuzzy, and parts of his life that had been a blur were still a blur, but almost everything else was back where it belonged.

Unfortunately that 2 percent was the part he needed right now. He needed to know where he had been, how he had come back. He needed to know how to make things right again. There had to be something. Things couldn't just . . . be like this now. How were they supposed to work as a Pair this way? How could he rule his territory if he couldn't even control himself?

His thoughts were not helping.

He needed to focus on something normal for a while to stave off the creeping madness. Programming, perhaps. He'd been digging through the sensor data to figure out how Hayes had confused the network; he had come up with a couple of algorithms that might make detecting Signets more accurate even without the presence of a Signet itself. Knowing how powerful a vampire was would be very useful, but he had to figure out what kind of data to collect to calculate it.

There was also the camera project he'd left unfinished. He'd made a lot of progress before everything had gone to hell, but it needed more than a few refinements to be genuinely useful. If Miranda was going back onstage, she would probably need the camera/mirror illusion again, so he needed to get back on it.

David shook himself a little, then stretched, rolling his head from one side to the other to unkink his neck. He'd been standing there staring far too long; it was beginning to rain in earnest, and if it weren't for his coat he would be soaked. As it was, his hair was already dripping.

He couldn't help but laugh at himself. Brooding in the rain in a long coat—all he needed was a British moor to wander around and he could be a reject from any Brontë novel.

"All right," he muttered, stepping down from the stone surround and turning toward the stairwell, "enough gargoyling for one night, Prime."

As he walked across the roof, though, he felt something strange; his mind got suddenly blurry, as if he were drunk. It almost seemed that time was slowing down—he was afraid for a moment he would pass out, but everything was moving so slowly . . . or was it moving backward?

He pushed himself over to the door and leaned against it, trying to center himself and figure out what was going on, but the strangeness only grew. It wasn't painful, really, it was . . . *wrong*.

What the hell . . .

He could hear something—someone speaking, or rather reciting something that had a rhythm, but the sound was far away, and it wasn't possible; he wasn't anywhere near another person, and neither his com nor his phone had alerted him to a message. The longer the voice went on, the harder it was to think. He could feel something . . . something coming closer . . . reaching for him . . .

David slid down the door to the ground, weak all over. It felt like the inside of his entire body was shaking, poised on a knife's edge between nausea and pain, and something was reaching into him—

He gasped. Thunder seemed to split his skull, wave after wave of tremors starting in his mind and rolling outward. Was the thunder outside, or inside? He could barely feel the rain; there was nothing but that horrible shaking, and something trying to force him open, trying desperately to get in before it was too late—

Lightning struck the Prime's mind . . .

. . . and with it, *memory*.

Fourteen

"Hello, David."

He stared at her, uncomprehending. "Who . . ."

Her eyes, black and full of stars, lit on him with kindness. "I think you know."

One moment, she seemed to be just a woman, as Faith had been, a little colorless but still real. Her hair trailed around her shoulders, dark and bloodred, its tendrils moving almost like snakes; she was robed in mist, in shadows, in the suggestion of iridescent black feathers. Her feet dissolved into the ground beneath them, as if she had arisen from the night itself . . . or was the night itself.

He took a step back. "Persephone."

She inclined her chin in confirmation.

"It was true," he said. "The Stone, the Awakening . . . my death freed you."

"Yes. Thank you."

"Who was holding you captive, then?"

She smiled. It was a familiar smile . . . a predator's smile. "You will find out soon enough."

Suddenly he remembered—"*Miranda,*" *he said.* "*She's alone, and hurt—*"

"*She is safe for now. Worry not, child . . . you will be reunited soon. But first you must listen to me; there is not much time before dawn . . .*"

Dawn . . . he could smell it in the air . . . he was so weak, and so afraid . . . ten feet to the stairwell might as well be a thousand miles . . .

It would be so easy just to give up and let it happen.

No.

Miranda.

The name brought strength from somewhere too deep to understand, and with agonizing slowness, he moved one hand . . .

Cold. So cold.

First one abandoned building, then another; the second had recently been a squat and still had the remains of a vagrant's camp inside. There was a blanket, filthy but warm, and nearby a closet that would block out light. He collapsed inside, pulling the door shut, and hit the ground already unconscious.

In the squalid depths of the city, he was no one; no name, no memory, no purpose except to stay alive. This much he knew: He had to feed. Neither he nor she could keep their promises until he was strong enough to survive what was coming.

The first was a homeless man. He was old, mentally ill; it was a miracle he'd survived another winter, even one so mild as Austin's. His blood tasted like loss. Like a family long gone, like service in war, like being left out in the cold. But it was blood, and the man died peacefully, to be found by police the next day. They wouldn't look hard for a cause.

The power of the man's death wasn't enough. It burned out quickly. There had to be more.

One by one, he took them from the streets, choosing easy targets that, by coincidence, were those least likely to arouse suspicion. Each one helped, but by the time another day had passed, he thirsted for more. His body was still so weak that it took days, and days, to even leave the block.

There was someone he had to find. Someone who would help. Someone who had to be a part of this . . . was already a part of this. She would take him in, she would know what to do, and then she could be . . . what she was meant to be.

That knowledge drove him, step by stumbling step, a block turning into half a mile, a mile turning into half the city, until he found the warehouse . . . just in time for his few precious scraps of energy to exhaust themselves.

"This is your choice," the goddess said to him. *"You can go through this portal, and move on from this world . . . or you can go back, and serve me."*

"If I do this," he replied, *"You give me your word that Miranda and I will not be parted again."*

She looked amused, perhaps at the idea of a mere Prime—and a dead one at that—demanding anything from her. But she nodded. "David . . . in order to take up your work, you will have to be changed. You won't be what you were ever again; you will be something far greater, and far more frightening. And I will not force Miranda to stay at your side if she is unwilling to be joined to what you become—it will be her choice, to be bound to you again, or to go her own way."

He nodded. "I agree. She has to have a choice."

"If she chooses to stay with you, I give you my word you will never die apart."

He was aware of how carefully her words were chosen, but at the moment it was promise enough for him. "Good."

"You understand what I have told you—what you must do."

"Yes, my Lady."

"You understand the consequences of your return—that traveling backward along a soul's path through life can cause untold damage to the soul."

"I understand."

"Knowing all of that, is it your will to enter into my service, David Solomon?"

Their eyes held for a long moment.

"It is my will," he said softly.

Still holding her gaze, he knelt before her.

She lifted her wrist, and two puncture wounds appeared in the flesh; as the dark blood began to flow, she held it out to him.

He drank.

Miranda came to in a rush, flailing all around, to the consternation of the servants who were puttering around her bed.

"Ah, *reinita*," Esther said with a smile. "Just relax where you are; I have called Mo."

"I'm fine," the Queen insisted, sitting up . . . then fell back into the pillows, dizzy. "Okay, I'm not."

She tried to straighten out the convoluted tangle of her thoughts. What had happened? She remembered Stella nearly dying, but after that, something very weird had happened in her head, and she'd passed out. Was it from the Circle? Maybe she'd been wrong when she thought the barrier was down; she'd been running on adrenaline, after all.

Still, the uneasy, almost sick feeling in her stomach remained.

Across the room she heard her phone ring. Curious, Miranda held out her hand and reached with her mind. The phone rose up out of the pile of clothes on the floor and floated to her hand. One of the remaining servants saw it, squeaked, and jumped back.

Miranda closed her eyes and held the phone to her ear. "What now? Another dead Prime? Space monkeys attacking?"

Deven ignored her weak attempt at humor. His voice was tense. "What happened?"

"I have no idea. Something went wrong with the Witches' ritual—Stella almost died and I think she's in some kind of coma. Then I passed out."

"Have you heard from David?"

She frowned. "No . . . have you?"

"No. I just felt this sick dizzy thing happening, but I couldn't figure out who it was coming from. Cora called not twenty seconds later—she felt it, too."

"I'll call him," Miranda said. "Then I'll have him call you."

She pulled up David's number and waited . . . and waited.

Voice mail.

Feeling the first twinges of panic, she tried again.

Voice mail.

She held up her com. "Star-one."

"Right here."

Miranda looked up at the doorway, where David was standing, soaked to the skin and looking like nine kinds of hell.

She jumped out of bed and went to him. "What happened to you? Are you all right?"

He was trembling, his skin clammy and cold. "I don't think so."

"Come on, let's get you warmed up . . . I'll run a nice hot bath. You look exhausted."

She got him into the bathroom and sat him down on the closed toilet lid while she got the water running.

Her com chimed. "Go ahead," she said.

"My Lady, this is Mo; I wanted to give you an update on your human friend's condition."

"Yes, please do."

"She is stable for now. I have run a few preliminary tests, and while all her bodily functions are human normal, her brain seems to be . . . switched off, is the phrase. She is breathing on her own, without any trouble, but we cannot rouse her."

"Can Lark tell you anything about what happened?"

"It would seem she tried to stop whatever was happening and got caught in the goings-on, which did not damage her but put her in shock. If we can get her talking, I will ask for details. For now, both are as comfortable as we could make them."

"Thank you, Mo."

"Are you or our Lord Prime in need of my services?"

Miranda looked over at David, who was trying to undress, his hands shaking so hard he could barely manage his buttons. "I'll have to get back to you on that," she said.

She went to her Prime. "Let me take care of it." She gently moved his hands away so she could unbutton him herself. They were silent as she eased the shirt from his shoulders, then knelt, unbuckled his boots and pulled them off; she removed The Oncoming Storm from his belt before unbuckling it, too, setting the weapon carefully aside. By the time she got the rest off, he was staring into space, unseeing.

"David," she said, poking him in the ribs. "Bathtub."

He nodded vaguely and climbed into the tub. Miranda stripped herself much more quickly and joined him, sighing at the perfect temperature of the water.

David was leaning back against the side of the tub, eyes closed. He looked so tired, and so careworn, almost as badly as he'd looked when he first came home.

"What happened?" she asked. "You can tell me."

He looked at her, and in his eyes she saw at least part of the answer; they had the same weariness she had seen in the eyes of nearly every Signet, especially the Consorts: knowing too much.

"The ritual worked, didn't it?" she said.

David nodded. "I'm afraid so."

"Whatever Stella learned, she transferred directly to you?"

"That's the best guess I could come up with."

"So what did you find out?"

He didn't answer right away. "Come here," he said softly.

Miranda smiled and moved across the tub into his arms. For a while they just held on to each other, grateful to hear each other breathing, to feel each other's heart beating. She did her best to soothe him with her empathy, since she couldn't work through their connection anymore. Together with the heat of the water and the peace of the room, it worked, and he began to relax.

Still holding her, he said, "I remember everything now."

She swallowed hard. "And?"

"I saw Faith after we died."

Miranda's eyes filled with tears. "In the afterlife?"

"It wasn't really the afterlife—more like a meeting place, or maybe a holding area. She left from there to go . . . wherever."

"Was she okay?"

"Yes. She was ready to go. She hugged me and told me she loved me, and then she was gone."

Sniffling, Miranda wiped at her eyes, and asked, "Then what happened?"

"Then I met Persephone."

Miranda pulled back and looked him in the face; no, he wasn't joking. "Persephone?"

"Yes. The Awakening was a success. She thanked us for freeing her. But there's more, Miranda, and . . . I'm afraid of what you'll say when I tell you."

"Try me."

"I told her I didn't want to go without you—that it wasn't right for you to be alone when we were meant to die together. She said that she could send me back, give me another chance . . . but there would be a high price for violating the natural order that way."

He lifted a hand and plucked a stray curl from her face, tucking it behind her ear before cupping her chin in his hand and kissing her. Then he took a deep breath and went on.

"A long time ago there were three races: humans, Elves, and vampires. The first vampires were monsters—they had no reason, no conscience. They destroyed everything in their path and before long had upset the balance among the races, so Persephone had to destroy them. She created a second version, an upgrade, and buried the Firstborn deep in the earth. The Secondborn were the first Signets. From them, all other vampires were made, to help keep the human population from spreading. But as time went on, the Secondborn grew more and more power hungry and wanted autonomy; they pushed the idea of service to the goddess off on the zealots and revered only money and power.

"Meanwhile, humans had multiplied faster than anyone

expected, and their religions grew stronger, strong enough to suffer no competition. They turned on the Elves and hunted them to extinction until all that was left were humans and vampires. Meanwhile, all the old gods were being forgotten or forcibly usurped. A particular group of humans dedicated themselves to wiping out Persephone and her followers. We know their modern incarnation as Morningstar."

Miranda just stared at him, trying to take in as much of the story as she could before asking the thousand questions building up in her mind. "Morningstar . . ."

"They managed to banish Persephone herself—you can't destroy a god, but you can create a barrier that keeps her from reaching into the manifest world. But the Secondborn banded together one last time and, combining their powers into one, destroyed Morningstar completely. Wiped them from the earth. After that, the Secondborn split—their titanic egos and power-lust got in the way of cooperation, and from there, the Council was created, mostly to keep a check on each other's territories. Centuries passed."

Miranda nodded, guessing the next part. "Then along comes this group of Signets who have a connection like the old Secondborn did."

"Exactly. The barrier was growing thinner. With a new threat rising—the return of Morningstar—Persephone knew the time had come when her children could free her from her exile and she could bring her chosen back together to fight. So she inspired the High Priestess of Elysium to begin preparations for the Awakening, if they could verify that this group was the one they'd been waiting for. Turns out, we are."

"All six of us," Miranda murmured.

"No," he told her, shaking his head. "We're not a complete circle yet. That's part of the problem. We'll all continue to share power, and our abilities will cross from one to the other, but it will be hard to control until we have four Pairs who can stabilize the circle. Only then will we come into our full power."

"So who is the other Pair?"

"I have no idea."

"What does any of this have to do with what's going on with you?"

"I'm getting to that. The price for my return to you was that I accept leadership of the circle and pledge myself to her service—not as a worshipper, but more as a Second in Command. In doing so, I would have to be . . . changed . . . into something stronger than even a Prime. Something that's never been seen in the world before . . . I would become, in other words, Thirdborn."

"And for you to do that, we can't have a bond," Miranda said, tears welling up again. "So you got to come back to me, but you can never *be* back with me, not like you were."

"No, beloved . . . that's not it at all. I refused to force you to change. I wouldn't make you do it against your will just because you had to be bound to me. So we agreed the bond would stay broken until you made your choice, and then, if you underwent the change yourself, it would return."

Silence. Miranda sagged back against the side of the tub, taking in everything he'd said, not sure she really understood any of it—no, she understood it, but she couldn't accept it. Not this quickly.

She could feel his eyes on her, but she didn't look up; she was afraid that if she did, she would burst into tears and not be able to stop. "I think I . . ." she tried, but she didn't know what to say, so the words trailed off into the silence, hanging between them.

"You don't have to decide now," David said. He, too, sounded overwhelmed by his words, as if he'd realized their enormity only after saying them aloud. "There's time . . . and, beloved, if you decide not to . . . we can still be happy together. Now that we know what really happened, maybe it won't be so bad."

She shook her head, unable to answer, trying to deny the entirety of the last ten minutes. Miranda turned away and pushed herself up out of the water, having to move slowly and carefully not to slip on the tile in her rush to get away, far away. She grabbed a towel and left the bathroom. David didn't call after her—he knew her well enough to know she would need a little time and space to work it out for herself, and that it had nothing to do with him.

She had no idea where to go, but she couldn't stay there. She needed to be away, somewhere she could breathe. It felt, all of a sudden, like the Haven's walls were closing in.

She threw on the first clothes she grabbed and ran from the suite, ignoring the questioning looks of the guards. She threw open one of the Haven's side doors, bolted into the garden, and didn't stop running until she had reached the edge of the woods. It wasn't nearly far enough, but it would have to do for now.

Too much. It was too much. She didn't want any of this.

Stella . . . poor Stella, who had given herself so they would know the truth and had fallen just like Faith . . . and for what? So that some moldy old deity could demand they change themselves for her? So they could be her slaves and give up even more than she had already taken? David had already died once because of Persephone. They had both suffered more than any Signet bearer was ever meant to suffer. And now, what, they had to sign up for more? What kind of deity would do that to her children? Why did it have to be them? They'd done enough!

She sat down bonelessly beneath a tree, curled up in a ball, unable to keep the tears from falling. "I hate you," she whispered. "You should have stayed locked away."

There was movement off to one side—rustling in the treetop, something small and nonthreatening. A bird, most likely. The noise made her lift her head to see if it was an owl.

To her surprise, it wasn't a bird that should be out at night. A large, jet black raven perched in the tree, its shining black eyes fixed on the vampire Queen who wept below.

The oddity of it brought her out of her fit for a moment. Odder still, the bird jumped off the branch and landed on the ground in a rush of wings, not five feet from her.

They stared at each other. There was something familiar, she realized, about its eyes.

"You're watching me," she said. She wasn't talking to the bird.

The raven tilted its head to one side and came closer, not even the slightest bit afraid, but she supposed it wasn't a normal bird, so she shouldn't expect it to act like one.

"I don't want to work for you," she said, holding on to her anger just enough not to shout. "I just want our life back. We were happy before all of this. Neither of us wants to be all-powerful or fight a war for someone who won't even show her face."

To her amazement, the raven hopped even closer, and next thing she knew, it was standing on her knee.

"Planning to peck me to death?" she asked. The raven puffed up its feathers at her almost playfully.

"All right, fine," she muttered, and reached up to pet it.

The raven's feathers were surprisingly soft, and it was solidly built—she hadn't realized how big they were up close, but this one was easily a match for a hawk. She'd always thought birds were a little creepy; mammals were much easier to relate to. Still, it seemed this guy was enjoying having his head scratched; he made little clucking noises of approval.

As she petted the raven, a thought came to her: Perhaps Persephone *couldn't* talk to them directly yet. David had said something about a barrier; maybe the Awakening only made communication *possible*, not automatic. So far the only person who had seen her was David, and he'd been dead. It wasn't as if gods made a habit of dropping in on people— that had been the way of things in ancient Greece, maybe, but here and now, things were different. It might be that they had to go to her, not the other way around. Asking for a burning bush at this point might be pushing it.

"I'd feel a lot better about this whole mess if I could . . ." She wasn't sure how to articulate what she wanted. If she could meet this goddess, talk to her, get some sense of what it all meant, it might not be so horrible. She didn't want to serve someone whose motives she couldn't identify.

But then again . . . right now, it wasn't about serving anybody. Right now it was about Miranda and David, and their future together. She didn't have to fight a war right now. She just had to decide what she wanted.

She could run away. Be free of all this Signet crap. Live as an ordinary vampire somewhere.

The thought made her smile in spite of herself. Ordinary? And what would she do with her eternity, play open mic nights at coffee shops? After living as Queen, having that responsibility and authority around her neck, how on earth could she ever be satisfied with less?

When she thought of all she would have to give up, the idea of running seemed ludicrous. She had been happier here than ever in her human life, and even with all the pain, she knew it was where she belonged. But the thought of staying was almost as crazy—neither she nor David had any real idea what his transformation really involved, or what they would both be like when it was done. She thought of his eyes, black and cold, and a shiver ran through her.

She remembered those terrible weeks while David was gone, and how much she would have given just to have him back. How she knew she could go on without him, but the prospect of living alone was like a long nightmare she couldn't wake from. But now, against all odds and by an actual miracle, he was home, and they had finally found a way to restore their bond. Could that be worth whatever price they had to pay?

Fear or love; it all came down to fear or love.

Miranda pulled her hand back and eyed the raven critically for a moment. "Well played," she told it wryly.

The bird made a half-squawk that sounded suspiciously like laughter and bounced back onto the ground, stretching out its wings and giving her one last look before it launched itself into the air. Its wings beat against the night as it rose and winged off toward the forest. Between one blink and the next, it had vanished completely.

She rested her head on her knees for a moment. Something black lay in the grass, and she picked it up: a feather.

With a sigh, she laid her head back down and stayed beneath the tree's sheltering arms until nearly dawn.

* * *

"You're going to owe me a fortune in jet fuel," Deven said, taking the steps to the Haven's front doors, where David was waiting.

"Put it on my tab," David replied mildly. "And don't act like the minute I called you, you weren't already packed and ready to come out here."

They smiled at each other. "Where's Miranda?" Deven asked.

David's smile faded. "I don't know. She's been avoiding me—she needed time to think. I don't know where she's been disappearing to . . . I can't feel where she goes anymore."

They headed down the hall to the Elite wing, where Mo's clinic was located. David had waited to call California, loath to drag Deven back to Texas again, but they had run out of ideas. They'd even brought in a human doctor, but she had been as mystified as Mo. David didn't know if Deven could help, but it was worth a shot.

The rarely used hospital room was cool and dimly lit, the beeps and whirs of life support equipment the only real noise. David couldn't remember the last time it had been needed other than for Miranda's video blog after she'd been shot; vampires tended to either heal right away or die, but Mo had wanted it just in case. There were a handful of scenarios David could think of where they would need life support for a vampire, but Mo was more concerned with the ones they *couldn't* think of.

A comatose Witch was one of them.

Stella looked small and young in the bed. Her bright red hair stood out vividly against the white sheets. Her hands, with their careful manicure in alternating black, white, and red, were curled at her sides. The aura of power, and wisdom beyond her age, was nowhere to be found now. She was just a girl who needed help, a nerd-Goth-punk Sleeping Beauty.

Deven circled around to the other side of the bed and stared down at her, seeing—or Seeing, David mentally corrected himself—more than just flesh.

It had never really occurred to David to ask Deven exactly how his healing talent worked. Even when he'd first learned about it seven decades ago, he had assumed incorrectly that it was just a matter of pushing power into a body, but it seemed to be far more complicated than he'd realized. Stella had learned more about that part of Deven in an hour than David had in decades. David's stubborn denial of the mystical had kept him from knowing something important about his lover, and now, years and years later, he regretted it.

After several minutes, Deven lifted his eyes to David. David felt his heart sink. "I don't think I can help her," Deven said. "Her body is fine—it's her energy that's been overrun. Whatever went through her basically fried all her circuits. There's a high probability she'll come back on her own, but it will take time."

"How much time?"

"Weeks. Or longer. Honestly, seeing the damage it's a miracle she didn't just die right then and there. If it weren't this severe, I might be able to give her energy to replenish her, but right now, it would be like bailing out the *Titanic* with a thimble. I'm not a mind or energy healer."

David placed his hands on the bed rail, defeated. "She had to have known this would happen."

"Why do you say that?"

"Because Persephone wouldn't have just burned her out without giving her a choice in the matter. That's not how she operates."

Deven knew; David had told him two days ago. So far no one else did, although David assumed Jonathan would by now. Typically one didn't tell a Prime something without expecting his Consort to hear about it. He wasn't really sure what to call Deven's reaction, but it definitely wasn't surprise.

"Can you be sure of that?" Deven asked. "Stella is human,

after all. She's not as strong as a vampire, even with all her power."

"I'm sure."

Deven didn't say what he was obviously thinking: that David had no way to know, and that he was assuming Persephone cared about them, had their best interests at heart, or viewed them as anything but disposable spear carriers for her war.

"Bringing someone back from the dead is unnatural," David said. "It violates the order of the universe. Yet she gave me the choice to return."

Deven's eyes narrowed. "Serve whatever master you like," he said. "Just leave us out of it."

"But—"

"No, David. Did you really think you could tell me this wild story, offer no proof whatsoever that it wasn't a near-death hallucination, and expect me to fall to my knees worshipping this thing? Are you some kind of Persephone evangelist now? Because it may have escaped your notice, but *I serve no god*. My days of blind faith ended in the dungeons of the Inquisition. And what about Jacob and Cora? Have you forgotten they're devout Christians? Are they supposed to abandon a lifetime of belief and just follow you and your savior?"

It had been a long, long time since David had seen Deven so outwardly angry, at least not without someone's head literally rolling.

"That's not what she wants," David said, but the words, though true, sounded like pathetic denial even to his own ears.

Deven made a disgusted noise. "Would you just take me to the other girl?"

With a wordless nod, David led him out of the hospital room and across the hall to one of a handful of empty Elite barracks. He hadn't wanted to move Lark too far away from Mo's immediate vicinity, at least not until they were sure she was going to be all right.

Lark was sitting up on her bed, hands clasped in her lap,

staring off into space. It was exactly the same position she'd been in three nights ago after the Elite brought her here and changed her into a hospital gown. When Miranda had found the girls, Lark had been alert and responsive, but the longer Stella stayed under and the more hopeless it seemed, the more Lark faded away.

He hung back near the door and watched Deven kneel in front of the girl, peering into her eyes, one hand resting lightly against her cheek. Again, he stayed still for several minutes.

Deven glanced back at David, and this time his expression was far less grave. "This one, I can help," he said. "It looks like she tried to reach in and pull Stella out of whatever was happening, but the energy tripped a breaker in Lark's head. As her last stores of energy were depleted she wound down like a clock, but it doesn't look like there's any real damage."

"What can you do?"

"I can give her a pulse of energy, and that should bring her out of it. She just needs the equivalent of a good slap. I think a lot of the problem is emotional, though, and that's not my area."

David nodded. "I'll ask Miranda if she can help. Next time I see Miranda . . ."

With a sigh, Deven said, "David . . . darling, you dropped a ridiculously huge bomb on her with all of this. We only just got you back and now everything is changing again—that's too much for anyone, even a Queen, to just accept without a little meltdown."

"There you go again," David remarked, "being sensible."

"One of us has to be, if you've lost your damn mind," Deven muttered. He returned his attention to Lark and closed his eyes.

Moments later, the girl shuddered. Her eyes lost their glazed-over look, and she blinked, staring down into Deven's face.

Comprehension and memory came on her at the same time, and she burst into tears.

* * *

Once Deven had left, claiming he had things to deal with back home but, in all likelihood, simply unwilling to deal with David and his delusions any further, David had two conference calls with various members of the Council, a patrol leaders' meeting, and a glitch in one of the sensor sectors to contend with before he could really sit down and think.

He understood why Miranda had made herself scarce; the Haven felt unusually confining. He wanted the open sky overhead and free air to breathe.

It was the first time he'd been to the stables since his return, and the minute Osiris heard him coming, the horse started making whickering noises, tossing his head, and stamping his hooves impatiently, excited as a puppy.

"Hey there, boy," David said, stroking the Friesian's nose. "I missed you, too."

He looked over at Isis's stall, but the mare was pointedly ignoring him.

"That's all right," he called over to her. "I'm still glad to see you."

She snorted and went back to her oats.

He took his time saddling Osiris, letting the familiar motions calm his racing thoughts. Even without this new insanity, he had plenty to deal with. The Council was in an uproar over Kelley's death; everyone knew, though no one would say in so many words, that Hayes was behind it. Word about Hayes's true identity was still need-to-know, but even those who didn't know the true extent of what had been done to him knew about his daughter now. Deven and Jacob had made sure of it, and while David was gone, they had gotten unofficial promises from nearly every Signet to extradite Jeremy Hayes if he was found.

McMannis and Hart had both essentially barricaded themselves in their Havens. Right now the only thing that was public was that Hart had held Amelia prisoner to force Jeremy to work for him, but without Jeremy himself to make further accusations, it would be hard to prove that Hart himself had been involved in David's death. To really take Hart down they needed Jeremy's testimony, or some other undeniable proof. David intended to be sure they got it . . . whatever it took.

Everyone wanted to know how Hayes had killed David, and how David had come back, but he didn't want them to know the specifics just yet. The story they were perpetuating at the moment was that David had only been *mostly* dead, but had recovered and returned home as soon as he was able. He knew not everyone was buying it, but nobody had objected yet.

And now that he knew what Morningstar was really about, they were even more of a mystery—they were supposed to hate vampires, but they'd sent vampires to attack Miranda twice now, and Cora once. Why would they employ what they hated, and what exactly did they want with a Signet? If all they wanted was to kill vampires, surely Ovaska would have killed both Miranda and Deven three years ago when she had them captive. There had to be something else.

He leaned his forehead on Osiris's shoulder for a moment, frustrated and weary. Osiris responded by whuffling his hair, and David laughed.

"All right, let's go," he said, patting the horse's neck. "We'll both feel better after a good run."

He and Osiris both knew the trails around the Haven property by heart, of course, so he barely had to hold the reins; he leaned into the Friesian's neck and let him take to the wind.

An hour later, back in the stall grooming the horse, he did feel better, but still, as he brushed Osiris down and gingerly combed a few burs from his tail, David couldn't shake the pervasive sorrow that he had been carrying since his memory had returned.

Life had been so good, for a while. Oh, he'd known better than to think it would last forever—that simply wasn't possible for Pairs. Eventually everything fell apart; entropy was the nature of the universe. But for a brief three-year period he had felt invincible. As long as his Queen was standing with him, all those decades of loneliness, the pain of leaving California, everything felt worth it.

But now . . .

"Hey."

Startled, he looked up from the hoof he was examining. "Hey."

Miranda stood at the stall door, as usual keeping her distance from Osiris. She was dressed as if she'd been in the city.

"I had a meeting with Cynthia," she explained before he could ask. "Picking a venue for my big comeback."

He straightened. "You look tired," he said.

"I guess."

"You haven't been sleeping."

She looked at the ground. "I had a lot to think about." She raised her eyes to him and added, "I wasn't angry at you, I just . . . needed some space."

"I know. I'm glad you had it." He returned to his work, running his hands along the horse's legs, looking him over carefully; it had been a while since Osiris had been ridden, and David wanted to be absolutely sure everything was sound. The grooms had been taking excellent care of him, though, as usual.

He was aware that Miranda was watching him, but he didn't comment. He went about the old routine as he always had, waiting for her to speak.

Finally she said, "Lark went home tonight."

"Did she? Good."

"Maguire wants to come see Stella. He thinks she should be in a regular hospital. I think once he sees her he'll change his mind. People who don't understand what's really wrong with her would only make things worse."

"I agree," he said.

"We need to talk."

The words made his heart tumble down even further, somewhere around his feet. He felt like he already knew what she was going to say . . . and it was the death knell for what little hope he'd still had. "Okay. Here?"

"No . . . why don't you get cleaned up and we'll talk in the suite?"

He nodded. "I'll be there in ten minutes."

He finished up the last few tasks and paused to touch his forehead to the horse's, seeking comfort wherever he could find it. Osiris seemed, as always, to understand, and again stuck his big nose in David's hair, having learned over the years that his warm breath was comforting to his master. Finally there was no more putting it off; David left the stable and made his way back to the Haven.

Miranda was already in their suite, showered, and in her off-time uniform of black cotton pants and a tank top. He had to smile at that; even the most powerful vampires in the world were always creatures of habit. She had her yoga pants and tanks, he had his old worn jeans and T-shirts. They both tended to go barefoot around the Haven except when on duty, which had led to some sideways looks at emergency meetings when the Pair showed up without shoes on to confer with Tanaka on the other side of the world.

She was sitting cross-legged on the bed, holding something in her hand and staring at it: a black feather.

"Be right with you," he said, bypassing the bed for the bathroom.

He stood under the blast of near-scalding water for as long as he could, but there was only so long he could stall; he had to face this and move forward. In a few minutes he'd know for sure if he was facing it alone.

She was still sitting where she'd been, and he joined her there as soon as he was dressed again.

Miranda smiled. "Thank you for not getting horse funk on the bed."

He smiled back. "You've trained me well, my Lady."

She stretched out on the bed, saying, "Lie down with me."

He did as she asked, and she moved closer, pressing herself against him with a sigh, her head on his shoulder and one hand around his upper arm. David held on to her tightly, trying to memorize every last sensation: her scent, the weight of her head, her bare foot curved around his ankle. To have known such grace, even for a little while . . . he had been blessed.

The minute stretched out into several before she asked, "Why did you come back?"

"What do you mean?"

"You were done," she said. "You could have gone on, not had to deal with this world anymore. I know how tired you always were . . . you could have gone to rest. Instead you came back, knowing the risks, knowing it would hurt . . . why? Was it a sense of duty, to fight Persephone's war?"

"No," he replied. "That was a condition of my return, not the reason. As far as I was concerned, she could find another vampire to be her Second. All I cared about, the only reason I agreed to any of it, was to get home to you." He sighed into her hair and said softly into her ear, "I love you so much, Miranda. Nothing could keep me away from you, no fate could stop me from finding you. And no god could win my allegiance if you weren't by my side."

He didn't look at her face, but he could hear the tears in her voice. "I know," she said. "I just needed to hear you say it, just to remind me why I'm doing this."

"Doing this . . ."

"I'm scared," she whispered. "This whole thing is too big for me . . . but after everything we've been through, I can't give up on us." She drew back and looked in his eyes, and in that moment his heart rose up from the floor and remembered how to fly. "I am still, and will always be, your Queen," she said. Then, she smiled. "Any questions?"

Fifteen

It was one thing to watch a building blow up from a distance, too far away to hear the screams of the dying. A rumble of thunder, a flash, flames, smoke . . . then sirens shrieking out into the night as the human authorities raced to extinguish the inferno . . . too late to save anyone. From nearly half a mile away, it might be any city fire. Perhaps a faulty gas line had ruptured in a restaurant.

Most people would hear the noise, maybe even smell the smoke, then go back to their lives, uninterested, perhaps seeing a news story about the accident and remarking to a friend that they had heard the explosion.

From that far away Olivia could almost pretend it was an accident and not mass murder.

This time would be different. This time the Haven had once been her home.

She had at least earned clemency for the servants and Elite—she had begged Jeremy to see reason, especially since nearly all of McMannis's Elite had been hired after Jeremy was deposed, so they had nothing to do with what happened to Amelia and Melissa. Perhaps they worked for a villain, but their complicity in his deeds didn't make them deserve the same fate. He had to see that. He *had to*.

But it wasn't until she threatened to leave that he relented. He needed help, and he was basically out of allies. If the choice was only kill the Primes or kill no one at all, Jeremy was willing to spare the others. He wasn't happy about it, but Olivia didn't really care. After seeing what had happened in Chicago, she couldn't let him do it again.

It turned out that Jeremy couldn't use the same method for Hart or McMannis as he had for Kelley, anyway. Just in the brief span of days since Kelley's demise, the other two Primes had overhauled their security systems and had barely left their Havens. Both had brought in extra hands—hired thugs off the street, she supposed—and locked down their Havens as much as possible. With all those eyes on the Havens there was no way to plant bombs, no way to even get close enough to bar the windows and doors shut. They'd be killed before they even reached the building. A different strategy was called for.

"All right," Jeremy said, spreading a roll of blueprints and plans out on the table in their shabby, anonymous motel room. "Jameson finally came through—we've got a new diagram of the system."

Olivia leaned over and studied it. "It looks a little patched together."

"Very. McMannis was in a hurry to get new alarms in place—I suppose he expected me to strike all three of them within days of each other. I'd rather give it time for him to let his guard down."

The lamplight made him look sinister . . . or at least it didn't hide it. Olivia held back another gut reaction, which was to flinch when he leaned closer. She'd been deliberately shoving away her intuition for days now, but she knew one thing: This would not end well.

Still, she waited . . . waited to figure out what to do. She didn't want to stop him from killing McMannis or Hart, but the more time passed, and the more plans they made, the more she realized that he might not stop there. If he looked far enough, every Signet in the Council had something to do with Jeremy's downfall, even if it was just turning a blind eye . . . and that blind eye would be taken for an eye.

"The good thing is, in his haste, he left a security hole," Jeremy was saying, bringing her back to the table before her. "The guard shift changes at two A.M.—the standing guard isn't allowed to leave his post until the new guard arrives, but if you compare the personnel lists, you see that over here"— he tapped an exterior Haven door with his pen—"the incoming guard for this station is returning from a patrol, meaning he has to enter the building from the outside. If we catch him and use his key, we get in without tripping the system."

"What kind of identification are they using?" Olivia asked. "It can't just be a key."

"Key cards and fingerprint scanners," Jeremy replied. "McMannis is working on a more sophisticated system, but the kind he really needs only exists in the Southern U.S. and there's no way in hell he's getting those designs."

Olivia snorted softly. "Solomon would probably give him fake plans anyway to make sure they failed."

"I was thinking of doing something like that with Hart— his system is already more secure than McMannis's, but after what happened with the harem I'm sure he's working on an upgrade."

"This is probably a dumb question, but why don't you just Mist inside? You did it to set the explosives in Chicago."

"That was outdoors in line-of-sight," Jeremy replied with a self-deprecating smile. "To be perfectly honest I'm dreadful at Misting. My control is iffy at best if I can't see where I'm going and haven't been there before. Since McMannis took power he remodeled the west side of the Haven, so I have no idea what I'd be Misting into. You should have seen me sneaking around the Southern Haven peeking in all of the interrogation rooms so I wouldn't accidentally land in a wall."

That was news to Olivia. "I thought all Signet-level vampires could Mist the same."

"Oh, no. There are a few who can't at all, and then there

are others, like the West, who can go great distances and even take someone with them. I wish I could—that would simplify things quite a bit."

"All right, so we get in at two A.M. at this location. What then?"

Jeremy pulled another sheet of designs out of the stack and laid it over the security grid. "Knowing McMannis, he'll figure his security is sufficient and won't have bothered moving to a bunker. I made sure my style was obvious enough in Chicago that they'll be assuming I'll stick with what worked, an external attack. They won't be expecting a surgical strike."

Olivia's stomach twisted remembering Chicago. So many dead . . . and she had helped lay the bombs and block the exits. She had honestly thought that most of the Elite were out that night . . . or that was what Jeremy had led her to think. She had racked her brain trying to remember their conversations, trying to pinpoint whether he had said for sure how many would be trapped in the Haven, trying to figure out if he had lied or just been vague . . . The difference between the two was huge when there were a hundred lives at stake.

At least the Australian vampires wouldn't have to suffer the same agonizing fate. She told herself it was enough.

Her hope—a faint and fading one, but a hope all the same—was that after McMannis was dead, the Signet would remember Jeremy and Jeremy would remember it, and he would be loath to throw it away; he might give up on Hart for the time being, choose to stay and rule his territory, and look for a less hands-on way to get rid of Hart. Plenty of people wanted Hart dead. Surely if they all pooled their resources they could make it happen no matter what kind of security the bastard had.

When trying to decide whom to attack after Kelley, Olivia had lobbied for McMannis for exactly that reason, though she'd told Jeremy it was because they would need more time to strategize for Hart since he already had better security and getting hold of the plans would be difficult, if not impossible. Australia's Haven was isolated from the rest of the world, and despite McMannis's being a cowardly jackass, things had remained peaceful here since he stole the Signet.

The plan was straightforward, which Olivia liked—the more complex something got, the more places it could snag. They would get into the Haven, find McMannis, kill him, and get out in a matter of minutes, hopefully before a single alarm went off. She knew they could do it—once she had slipped back into her role as Second, her training came back to her in full force, and she knew they were both up to the task.

Still . . . that morning, lying awake in her bed in the motel, blankets over the windows and the staff paid not to ask questions, she considered the growing likelihood that she would have to kill her boss.

She didn't want to. She had killed plenty of people, but she never liked taking life, especially that of her own kind. It was one reason she had stayed in her homeland when looking for a career; she knew it was less likely she'd have to take heads in war after war the way other territories required. Western Europe had offered her a position just based on her reputation as a fighter, but Western Europe tended to explode into violence every few years, and the Prime there wasn't terribly invested in brokering peace.

But if Jeremy couldn't be satisfied with revenge, if his hatred continued to metastasize and destroyed what was left of his conscience, many more would die to slake that thirst for blood, and she wasn't going to let that happen. She had been caught off guard in Chicago—she honestly hadn't been able to believe what was happening and at first thought it was a mistake, that he had accidentally locked all those people in the Haven and would help her get at least one door open . . .

The look on his face when she wanted to run and help them was acid-etched in her memory. She had been genuinely afraid, for a moment, that he would turn his sword on her.

One way or another, after he got his vengeance, he had to stop. She would do what she had to do.

She put her hands over her eyes and did what she often

did when sleep eluded her: She painted. In her mind, she started with a blank canvas and gessoed over it to smooth out the substrate, then began the background. What was this one? A night scene, of course, but the idea that came to mind was of a forest beneath a blanket of stars. Black, but with a touch of indigo and phthalo blue, applied thickly in swirls so that the texture would be visible . . . or maybe starting with Prussian blue, adding in black to get the right level of darkness, and masking off the stars so pure white shone through.

Would the woman be in this painting? Probably. Olivia never planned for her, she just sort of showed up. She was strangely comforting to Olivia—whatever kind of delusion or dream the woman was, she kept Olivia from feeling entirely alone.

Olivia wished she were here now.

Under her pillow, her phone vibrated. Olivia held still, keeping the pillow over it so Jeremy wouldn't hear from the other bed and wake demanding to know who she was talking to.

She listened, but he didn't stir. Good.

She slid her hand under the pillow and pulled the phone out. She wasn't expecting to hear from anyone—it was a burner phone she'd gotten in Illinois, so it had to be either a telemarketer or a wrong number, probably from Chicago or thereabouts.

A text message. She frowned. The originating number was blocked, and the message said, *Your technical support request has been forwarded to your service provider, Raven Telecom. Please call 512-555-2976 for more details.*

Wrong number, then. She'd never even heard of . . . Raven . . .

Her heart began to pound.

It was an Austin number.

Deven disconnected his laptop from the satellite and shut down the triangulation program, satisfied.

"Well?" Jonathan asked from the bed. "Did it go?"

The Prime smiled, stretching and standing up. "Oh yes."

Jonathan nodded, but asked, "How can you be sure this is going to work? We don't know anything about this person or her loyalties."

Deven climbed into bed next to him and settled into his arms with a sigh. "I can't be sure. But seven hundred years of learning how people tick tells me that as soon as she realizes what she's gotten herself into, she'll make the call."

"You've been wrong before."

"Maybe twice."

"True." Jonathan squeezed him around the middle, and Deven chuckled and wound himself around his Consort, nipping his ear in the process. Jonathan growled and in one quick motion flipped Deven onto his back, pinning his wrists up above his head. "But both of those times were in the last couple of months, so you can see my concern."

Deven sighed. "True. Perhaps one day I'll learn to stay out of things . . . after a few more people have died and I'm left without friends."

Jonathan frowned down at him. "This time no one's going to get hurt," he said. "All you did was send her a phone number that might save her life. What she does with it, and what he does, is not up to you. Most of the things you've done over the years have worked beautifully—don't judge yourself so harshly."

Deven smiled ruefully. "I don't know any other way to judge myself."

"What do I have to do to get your mind off such unpleasant things?" Jonathan asked.

He decided, just for now, to let Jonathan have this one. He deserved at least a few hours where he didn't have to worry about Deven's mental health. He gave his Consort a mischievous grin and pushed Jonathan off him easily, reversing their positions. "You know what I do to people who question me."

Jonathan smiled up at him hopefully. "Shag them blind?"

"Damn it, my torture methods are supposed to be a secret. Who told you?"

The Consort chuckled. "I'm familiar with your work, my Lord."

Deven lowered his head and began leaving kisses along Jonathan's jawline, down over his throat, and around to the other side of his neck, where he bit down hard.

Jonathan groaned. "You bastard."

"Language, Mr. Burke."

"Oh, fuck off."

"That's more like it." Deven grabbed Jonathan by the collar of his T-shirt and dragged him upright, whereupon he immediately seized the shirt and stripped it from him. "I intend to draw quite a few more obscenities from your mouth in the next couple of hours; you might as well accept it."

"Really?" Jonathan asked, laughing, joining in the effort to get them both undressed as quickly as possible. "Well, that works out very nicely, because I have a use for your mouth, too."

The Queen looked pleased as she walked out of the office building, red hair and coat both caught by the wind and lifted up behind her like a cloak. As she passed, he noted a pair of humans near the end of the block whispering to each other and pointing at her, but they were either unsure it was her or too intimidated to ask for an autograph.

David smiled. Harlan opened the door for her on the other side, and she joined her Prime in the car. "A productive meeting, I trust," he said, taking her hand and kissing it.

She nodded. "Everything's falling into place—a small show, indoors, at either Travis Auditorium or the Keeton Arts Center. The main thing is having enough security, both ours and theirs."

"Do you have a date nailed down?"

"We're looking at July thirteenth . . . that is, if . . ." She bit her lip, looked out the window for a minute, then finished with, ". . . if I can perform."

He still had her hand, and he squeezed it. "You'll be

there," he said, with as much certainty as he could put into the words. "I'll move heaven and earth to make it so."

She sighed. "Can we take a walk before we head home? I'd like to see the city before . . ."

He wanted so badly to allay her fears, but he couldn't, really; they had no idea what the next twenty-four hours would bring, and there were so many ways it could go wrong . . . but if it went right . . . they had agreed the possibility of regaining their bond was worth the risk, but that was yesterday, a little further from the reality. In truth he couldn't be completely sure what would happen, and he wasn't going to lie to her to make her feel better when, bond or no bond, she would see right through it.

They disembarked at the edge of the District. David told Harlan to meet them in the usual place on the far side.

Miranda was smiling at him as he straightened from the car window. "What?" he asked.

"Sometimes at random I just wonder how the hell I ended up in this life," she responded, taking his arm. "I'm not even talking about the big stuff—I never thought I'd get married. At all. The whole idea was absurd. And ending up married to a guy who looks like a model and has a brain like a super-computer is even weirder."

He gave her a dubious look. "I can't decide if that means you had low self-esteem or just a completely inflated opinion of me."

"Oh, come on. You're not prone to fits of false modesty, which is another thing I've always loved about you—you know your own abilities and your limits, but you never let that stop you."

"Even when it should," he pointed out with a laugh. "But let's not forget my tragic flaw."

"Which is?"

"In emotional matters I turn into a jibbering idiot and make absolutely horrible decisions."

She burst out laughing. "Not *every* time," she said.

"Often enough. And badly enough."

Miranda paused and turned to face him, taking his hands and regarding him seriously, her eyes searching his. "I've never said it," she said, "but David . . . I forgive you."

The words hit him hard, and he actually felt his eyes start to burn. "You do?"

"Yes. I never could really say it before, but losing you . . . I realized I was done with the past. I was still carrying around some anger until then, so the words still rang false to me, but . . . not anymore. And if anything goes wrong tonight, I want to be sure you know."

He looked down at the ground a moment, unable to say anything at first. "Thank you," he said softly.

She kissed him, and his arms tightened around her. For a moment, standing there on the sidewalk while the Shadow District buzzed all around them, everything was perfect again.

She was panting, the pain in her ribs stabbing through her with every step, but she didn't stop running until she was well away from the building. She had to get to the rendezvous point . . . even if there was no one to meet there.

Every step was excruciating. She pushed energy into her ribs—she had lost a lot of blood but she still had the strength to at least hold herself together—and into what felt like a broken ankle, then leaned back against a tree to catch her breath. She couldn't rest long. They would be on her scent by now.

At least the earthquake had bought her some time. She could tell the Elite weren't prepared for what would happen. She hoped none of them had been killed, or at least no more than the ones she had killed herself.

Olivia sagged back and put her hands over her face for a few seconds, fighting back a few screams of her own. She knew she should go back, but if she did they'd kill her. As hurt as she was, and as weak, she'd be easy prey.

Not that they weren't already.

There was no way to have known how many guards McMannis would have. Australia didn't have a sensor network or any kind of tracking system they could tap into. They'd researched where all the Elite would be at the appointed hour.

She heard something in the distance. Shouting? Dogs? It didn't matter, she couldn't stay here. She pushed herself off the tree and started running again.

It took nearly an hour to reach the rendezvous point, where the car was hidden off the road. Olivia fell onto the seat with a cry of pain and lay there a minute to try to get her thoughts back in order.

Go. Go. He told you to leave him if things went wrong. Go back to the motel and wait.

She stared at the treeline, willing Jeremy to appear, but after ten minutes she had to get moving; he wouldn't want her to get caught waiting for him.

She pulled into the motel parking lot and rested her head on the steering wheel. Her heart was still hammering. She could still feel the ground moving. She could hear battle sounds and her own breath coming hard. She had lost one of the twin blades she had taken to using in Chicago, but she didn't care—it had saved her life.

She dropped the key card twice trying to get into the room and cast a hunted glance around the parking lot before locking the door behind her. It wasn't likely they would have followed her this far, and the motel was far outside the Shadow District of Brisbane.

Collapsing on the bed, she took out her phone, checking just in case . . . she might not have heard the ring in the state she was in . . . but no, there was nothing.

She needed blood. Soon. In the mini fridge there was a bag left that was just on the edge of expiring, but it would keep her going until she decided where to go from here.

They'd been so stupid. The plan had made sense, but it depended on one thing: McMannis didn't know when they were coming. How had he found out . . . how could he have? She and Jeremy were working alone, so there was no one to turn on them. Unless the room was bugged somehow . . . but how would McMannis have known where they were?

A few minutes later she felt calm enough to get up and fetch the blood, which she warmed a little in the microwave before gulping down half the bag. She wanted to leave a little, in case . . .

Olivia leaned forward, elbows on knees, taking deep breaths. It was probably better this way. The Jeremy she had known—from before his family was murdered—was long gone, and the new one was not a creature whose story would end well. Whether he succeeded in killing Hart or not, what happened after would most likely result in his death anyway.

What was she going to do?

Her phone was still in her hand; almost without meaning to, she pulled up the last text she'd gotten, Jeremy giving her the all-clear outside the Haven. She'd joined him at the door where he'd killed the guard and used the guard's finger on the print scanner; they'd slipped inside, exactly according to plan. There would be only a few minutes—eight, if his calculations were correct—before someone came along and saw the dead Elite, but it was thirty seconds to McMannis's quarters, thirty seconds to the exit on the other side, leaving seven minutes to kill McMannis. Minimal loss of life was her goal, and there should have been only three or four casualties other than the Prime himself.

She stared at the text, then deleted it.

The previous message popped up . . . the Austin number.

Sudden hope leapt in her chest. Maybe . . .

There was a faint knock at the door.

Olivia froze, every muscle tightening to launch her at an intruder, but no one burst into the room. She approached the door sideways and avoided the peephole in case someone thrust a blade through it—she'd seen it done—and risked a glance out the curtain.

"Oh my God—" She threw the door open.

Jeremy fell into her with a grunt, the smells of fire and blood heavy in his ripped and stained clothes. She dragged him inside and locked the door again.

"I thought you were dead," she all but sobbed, helping him to the bed.

"Very . . . nearly," he said hoarsely.

"Here," she said, handing him the blood. He took it gratefully and finished off the bag; the bruises and lacerations on his face began to fade immediately. "How did you get out?"

"No idea," he replied, coughing. "One minute I was surrounded, and the next . . . someone set off a charge. Not me," he said at the look on her face. "I told you I wouldn't kill any more than necessary, and I kept my word. But someone didn't. Bodies were flying everywhere—I Misted outside, but it nearly killed me to. I could see Elite streaming from the doors—I don't think there were more than a half-dozen casualties."

She sat heavily back down on the motel's rickety chair, which creaked a warning. "I don't understand," she said. "Who would have done that?"

"Whoever they were, I owe them a beer."

"It had to have been a traitor in the Elite," she mused. "Who else could've gotten in?"

"We did," Jeremy pointed out.

"And it must have been someone who knew we were coming and knew we would be ambushed."

Jeremy pushed himself up onto his feet and got them each a glass of water; she just stared into hers, but he drank his quickly, and between it and the blood his voice was far less scratchy when he spoke again.

"Did you feel it?" he asked. "The earthquake?"

She nodded. "I knew before that, though. I knew you'd kill him or die trying."

With a hand that shook slightly, he reached into his coat and pulled out the Signet.

The stone was lit up brightly, but Jeremy flipped it over, revealing a tiny battery attached to an LED. He ripped it from the stone and stomped on the device. Olivia watched, transfixed, as the darkened stone began to glow, first almost uncertainly, but then firmly as it seemed to recognize its true bearer.

They sat in silence for a while, digesting what amounted to a nearly Pyrrhic victory. They'd both almost been killed . . . but they had still won.

"You did beautifully in there," Jeremy said quietly, offering a small smile. "It was an honor to fight with you again."

Olivia smiled back. "Likewise, my Lord Prime."

He regarded the Signet in his hand. "I don't want it," he said. She could hear the grief in his voice, and it was perversely comforting. The last few weeks all she had heard was hate and rage. If he could still feel grief, there might be hope for him. "It isn't right for me to take it alone."

His mind was far away, his eyes on something she couldn't see, as he said, "I could break it, you know . . . smash the stone and die. No one else would get hurt since I don't have a Queen, but I would have control over my own fate. I haven't had that for years."

"Or you could stay here," she told him. "You could retake the Haven and start over. Band together with the others to take care of Hart. He doesn't have any leverage over you now—you could get help."

"I have help," he said. "I have you."

She met his eyes. "I'd rather be your Second than be the one to put your body to the sunlight."

For just a moment, she thought she had him; something in his eyes softened, his grip on the Signet tightened.

Then someone knocked on the door.

They both started and drew their weapons. "I'll go," he whispered. "Don't move."

He slipped around the bed and over to the door. He didn't seem to have her phobia of peepholes, and stared through it, making a noise of irritation. "No one," he said. "Must've been someone with the wrong room number."

Something in Olivia's heart clenched. She didn't want him to open it. "Don't—"

Too late. He removed the door chain, turned the deadbolt, and pulled the door open an inch or less.

Olivia heard something lightweight impact with the ground, sounding like it was made of plastic. Jeremy kept his blade out, but crouched down, eyes still on the cracked door in case someone tried to push past him. He picked up whatever it was and shut the door.

"What is it?" she asked.

He held it up: a flash drive and a business card.

They both looked at the drive quizzically. It was blue plastic, unmarked, and there was no explanation on the front of the card—just a phone number and the image of a blue star over an arc that brought to mind the curve of the earth.

When Jeremy turned the card over, however, she saw that someone had written on it in black pen: *YOU'RE WELCOME.*

"All right," Jeremy said. "I'll bite." He moved over to the table, wincing a bit at some pain still lingering from their escape, and flipped open his computer.

"It could be a virus," Olivia said.

"I borrowed a copy of the U.S. government's antivirus software," he replied absently, plugging the drive in. "Okay . . . there's a video file."

"Well, it can't be of us," she muttered. "What could it possibly . . . Whoa."

The video began, and she narrowed her eyes; the image was grainy, but the camera was trained on what was clearly the east side of the Haven, focused on a side door. As they watched, a slightly blurry figure darted across the yard to the door and hooked some kind of device to the fingerprint scanner. The door opened and the figure slipped inside the building.

"Look at the time stamp," Jeremy said. "We were already in there, about ninety seconds from killing McMannis."

The video continued for several minutes. At one point the camera started shaking—the earthquake, Olivia realized. They kept watching until the door opened again and the same figure came out; he (or she) looked right up at the camera and gave a thumbs-up before taking off running the way he'd come. The camera pulled back, giving a wider and wider angle, until the front of the Haven was visible. Seconds later brilliant light flashed through one of the Haven windows, and there was another vibration, much weaker than the first. The window blew out and belched black smoke. Within a minute Olivia could see flames through half the front windows.

The video went black, and a message appeared: WE HAVE SIMILAR INTERESTS.

Another image appeared for just a few seconds: a schematic of some kind, then another, then a photograph of a building in a city somewhere.

"That's the New York Haven," Jeremy said quietly. "Whoever this is, they have Hart's security plans."

IF YOU WANT TO ELIMINATE JAMES HART, WE CAN HELP YOU.
WE AWAIT YOUR CALL, LORD PRIME.

"Well, we don't need to do that," said Olivia. "You can just pause the video and take a screen shot of that—"

Lines of static appeared on the screen, and it went blank.

"Fuck!" Jeremy said, yanking the drive from the computer.

"This message will self-destruct in five seconds," Olivia muttered.

Jeremy rebooted the computer to see if it was permanently damaged, and Olivia sat with the business card in her hand, watching him.

"Lord Prime," she said.

He turned to her. "Yes?"

"No—the video called you that. They know who we are, Jeremy."

He paused, taken aback. "How is that possible?"

"I don't know. But it might be a good idea to find out what else they know."

"I agree." He took out his phone, shaking his head. "Maybe they saved our asses and maybe they didn't, but they must want something in return for their 'help.'"

He entered the number on the card and waited.

She heard a click on the other end of the line.

"I believe we have mutual interests," Jeremy said.

Olivia listened to him repeating an address, most likely a meeting place; then he listened for a moment before hanging up.

"They claim to have been watching us since Chicago," he told her. "Apparently they're fans."

"But what do they want?"

"A trade—their help in breaching Hart's security in exchange for some kind of artifact Hart has in his Haven."

Olivia gave him a look that was more than a little doubtful. "An artifact? They'd be willing to help kill a Prime for some pottery or something?"

Jeremy laughed. "I think it's something more than that. Something like the Stone of Awakening, only geared toward another purpose. Whatever it is, they can't get it on their own."

"Why not?"

"Because they're human," he answered. "At least that's what the man said. I thought there was something odd about the way the person in the video moved, so it makes sense; it was a mortal."

She didn't like what she saw in his eyes. "Jeremy . . . I know you want to get Hart, and I agree we should find out more about these humans, but getting in bed with them . . . it's a terrible idea. We can get into the Haven on our own."

Jeremy was looking down at the card thoughtfully. "I don't know," he said. "They might be right. We planned tonight for days and it still fell apart—we don't really even know why. They managed to get in, too, but you notice their agent didn't get caught. Getting updated schematics of Hart's system will be next to impossible unless I can figure out whom to pay off. Unless you'd rather I bombed the place," he added.

Olivia looked away. "You're going to use that against me?"

"I understand how you feel, Liv. But the fact is . . . I don't care about Hart's Elite. I don't care how much collateral damage we cause. As far as I'm concerned they can all die bloody and screaming as long as I get Hart. But you care, and as far gone as I know I am, I still care about you."

She shook her head, smiling in spite of herself. "I don't think I've ever had a man show his affections by not slaughtering a hundred innocents before."

"There are no innocents here. We're all culpable. I could find a reason to kill every single Council member and all their employees if I looked hard enough. God knows I'd deserve it myself."

Olivia looked at him, her face and voice gentling as she asked, "Would it solve anything? Or are you just piling death on top of death when you and I both know nothing will ever be enough to fill the hole they left?" She leaned forward and took his hand. "Look, if you want to kill Hart, we'll do it. But if we get involved with these humans, there are a thousand ways it could go wrong."

Jeremy pulled his hand back, stood up. "We were outmanned ten to one tonight," he said coldly. "McMannis's security wasn't nearly as sophisticated as Hart's will be. The same thing will happen in New York, and we won't have a convenient human to blow the place up for us. The only way to do this is to have a foolproof plan, and the only way to do that is to know Hart's systems inside and out. If these humans can give me that . . . we can get in and out without killing anyone, Liv. For real this time. Don't you think that's at least worth talking to them, finding out the details?"

She put her head in her hands. "All right . . . but this already smells rotten. Whoever we meet had better have a damned compelling case."

"I agree."

She looked up at him, wishing she could be heartless enough to put a stake through his heart here and now, before things could get any worse . . . but she couldn't. Not yet. Where else did she have to go now?

An image in her mind: the screen of her phone, a 512 number.

"So what are these crazy humans called, anyway?" she asked, giving up, for the moment, until she had time to think. She needed more information.

Jeremy was in the process of disarming himself, probably to take a shower and get the grime and blood off his skin, but he looked over at her. "The Order of the Morningstar," he said.

Sixteen

Dawn broke.

Miranda sat in her chair in front of the fireplace, hands clasped; her hands looked strangely small and pale to her right then, like a child's.

She realized she was rocking back and forth slightly and reached out to grab the arms of the chair, holding herself still. It was one of those things she associated with slowly losing her mind, and she wouldn't allow herself to do it again, no matter how anxious she felt.

A noise made her jump, but it was just David locking the suite door. She hadn't even heard him get out of the shower, but he was already dried off and dressed for bed, in basically the same thing he always wore. Today, however, he was wearing a plain black T-shirt without any nerdy slogans or diagrams, and she felt a little disappointed.

He took his own chair, and for a minute they just sat watching the fire.

She couldn't stop herself, though; she had to know. "How does this work?"

David lifted his eyes. "The same way it did last time."

She crossed her arms over her belly, and she knew she was rocking again, but couldn't make herself stop. "God . . ." Her voice became rough with tears as the memory came over her: cold tile, burning fever, and pain so intense the rest of the world faded to black. "I can't . . . David, I can't do that again . . ."

He came to her, kneeling in front of her chair and gently drawing her hands away and into his own. "No, beloved . . . there are two ways, remember? You and I both went the hard way."

She held his hands tightly. "And what's the other way?"

"It's how people become vampires when they do it on purpose. You're asleep for almost all of it and you don't feel a thing."

"How is that possible? Entire organs change shape!"

"It's the same basic principle," he said. "You have to die with a vampire's blood in your body, and you have to be strong enough to finish the transition. If your sire's blood is strong, you're more likely to survive. But the hard way, you die from a knife to the heart or a gunshot or something. The easy way, your sire drains your blood to the point of death and then feeds you his own before you lose consciousness; you die gently, and then he keeps you under until the change is complete."

She frowned. "I was stabbed. How did Lydia kill you?"

"She broke my neck, I think. It was the first thing that hurt when I woke up in the woods."

"How long does the whole thing take?"

"It depends on your own physical strength, your sire's . . . I would estimate two days, but you'll need to rest for at least a day after that, so . . . three, maybe four days total."

"But . . . draining blood will kill a human. It won't kill a vampire. Will it?"

"It will be enough damage that your heart will stop. Being drained takes a long time to recover from—it weakens you so badly that you can't hunt to replenish yourself, so you can starve to death without help. If it's too quick and too severe, it can kill you. It only has to be for a second."

"And this time . . . did you get to change the easy way?"

He met her eyes. "You felt me die, and later felt the tattoo changing—you can probably guess how the rest of it felt."

"You drank Persephone's blood," she realized. "You were sired by a god and then left to go through it alone."

"I was alone at first. But then Olivia was with me. I had no idea who or where I was, but there was still some comfort in that."

"And . . . you'll be with me," she said softly.

"I won't leave your side."

She managed a smile. "Liar. You'll have to pee eventually."

He smiled back at her. "All right. I won't leave the suite, and I'll be at your side as much as possible."

She nodded. "You're sure this is what we have to do."

"I'm sure. She told me."

"Okay . . . bed?"

"It would be best," he replied, drawing her up from the chair.

They lay down as they had a thousand times before, as if this were any morning after a hard night at work.

"Your heart is racing," he said. "If you're not sure . . ."

"Of course I'm not sure," she cut in, a little more sharply than she intended. "What if it doesn't work and I die for good?"

David's eyes narrowed. "Then I will kill myself, find Persephone, and drive a stake through her heart."

"Would that kill a goddess?" Miranda asked.

"Probably not, but even if it doesn't it hurts like hell."

He slid one arm under her head, the other around her, and kissed her forehead. "Just think," she said weakly, "in a few days this could feel like it used to."

He sighed into her hair, and said, "Close your eyes."

She obeyed.

He kissed her head again, murmuring, "I love you." She felt his lips against her cheek, and he said it again; then her lips, then down the side of her neck and over her collarbone, telling her he loved her with each kiss, nibbling along her skin in between, his hand curving around her hip and then sliding up her side, around over her breast, to tilt her chin up.

She remembered the first time he had bitten her, the first time she had tasted his blood—in her apartment, when neither of them had any idea what the future held . . . just like now. She had walked into that future with her head high; she would do the same this time, and not cower from it.

She turned her head toward him, offering the whole side of her neck, and wove her fingers through his.

She knew what his teeth felt like piercing her skin—it had happened plenty of times since that first night—but she wasn't used to what he did next, extending his will over hers, subtly pushing her to relax, raising his body temperature as well as hers. It was how they treated their prey.

The reason became clear very quickly. This wasn't like the other times. This wasn't for pleasure, it wasn't done as a prelude or addition to lovemaking. He was *feeding* on her . . . and fast approaching the threshold where the blood loss would hurt her, if she were human, and would weaken her . . . she could hear his heartbeat, and her own, falling into sync, then slowing down . . . and down . . . and down . . . and if it weren't for the loving hand wrapped around her mind, keeping her calm, she would surely have panicked.

She felt her whole body growing numb, detaching pleasantly from her mind. It felt so nice . . . but she was so tired . . . it would feel good to fall asleep . . .

Dimly she was aware that he stopped drinking, and a second later she felt something warm pressed to her mouth. "Drink, Miranda. Now!"

That last was said sharply, and it brought her back enough to understand the command; she had to drag up almost all of her remaining strength, but she opened her mouth, and sucked.

She was so weak . . . but she still recognized that his blood tasted different than before. That undertone of immortality had changed, darkened. Vampire blood didn't nourish vampires unless they drank gallons of it, so it was usually exchanged only during sex, but she knew his and he knew hers very well . . . and his was different now. Would hers be, too, when she woke up?

She felt the wrist lifted from her mouth, replaced with lips. She returned the kiss as best she could. Then she let her eyes open just a little so she could stare up into his.

They were black, but only for a brief second; between one blink and the next they had gone back to blue, and that was what she wanted to see, wanted to be the last thing she saw.

"Rest now, beloved," he whispered. "You're safe . . . and when you wake I'll be right here."

"I love you," she breathed, then closed her eyes.

He held her until she stopped breathing, then moved back a few inches to watch. If it had worked—if she was strong enough for this—she would come back in a few minutes, and she might wake up briefly, confused and frightened. He'd need to send her back to sleep as quickly as possible to avoid traumatizing her.

That was the real difference between the "hard" and "easy" ways; in the latter, the sire actually cared enough to stay close, to monitor the newborn and keep her safe and comfortable. That kind of intimacy created a bond even among ordinary vampires—it wasn't a Signet bond, but it was loving enough for most people, without all the added drama.

Two minutes rolled by, then five . . . six . . .

He leaned his head against hers and whispered, "Breathe, my love . . . breathe . . ." repeating it like a mantra until—

Miranda drew a gasping, violent breath, partway sitting up in the bed, her arms flailing wildly around her seeking something to hold on to.

David immediately caught her arms and eased her back onto the bed, sending more warmth into her body, sending her back into sleep. He held her, murmured to her that she was safe, and she could rest . . . just rest . . .

She finally dropped off again, and the relief was as great for him as for her.

He lay back down beside her, exhausted. He'd only ever turned two people, and Miranda hadn't been completely on purpose the first time. It wasn't something vampires of his caliber allowed themselves to do often.

His head had begun to hurt—to pound, actually. He sat up and rubbed his temples for a moment, but the pain only got worse. In fact, it wasn't even his head so much as his . . . jaw.

What the hell . . .

Pain coursed through his upper jaw, and it was a pain he remembered all too well from the night he had writhed and screamed in a cave, abandoned and alone. It was the pain of the jaw changing shape to accommodate longer canines, and . . .

What, was he going to end up looking like a saber-toothed tiger now? What the hell was going on?

He risked getting up out of bed to grab a bottle of Jack and drink four shots in a row; the pain dulled but was still there. And now his whole body had begun to hurt, his skin felt tight . . . and he remembered Stella saying his transformation was waiting on something . . .

. . . *it was waiting on Miranda.* As soon as he remembered the Witch's words, he grabbed his phone.

He had to talk around the intense pain in his mouth. "You have to get here now," he said without preamble.

"Why?" Deven asked.

"She's under, and she's fine, but something's happening to me now, too, and I might not be able to keep her asleep. If she wakes up and feels that pain again, it might send her over the edge. Help me, Deven. I need you."

Whether it was due to the words themselves or their panicked tone, Deven didn't hesitate. "All right, David, I'll do what I can."

"How soon can you get a flight? Take the jet, I'll pay for the fuel—"

"Just unlock the damn door," Deven told him.

David's head jerked up in time to hear the light *tap-tap-tap* at the door. He reached across the room and flipped the lock.

Prime Deven and Jonathan stood in the hall, each with an overnight bag, each in his traveling coat.

Deven saw David's expression. He pointed to Jonathan. "Precog."

David nearly passed out both from relief and from pain. He wasn't someone who liked to surrender control of a situation, but this time, he yielded it up gratefully. *Deven will take care of us. It's going to be fine.*

The Pair swept into the suite, their calm efficiency even more soothing to David's jangled nerves. They set their bags down, removed their coats, and came over to the bed.

He sat up, but Deven pushed him back down firmly. "Down, boy," he said. "Whatever's going to happen, you'll need your strength. How old is the supply in the fridge?"

"Fresh tonight."

"Good. Do you need some now?"

David nodded. "Please."

"All right. You lie down, and we'll take care of things. Just relax."

David smiled wearily. "As much as you've been here the last few months, we should give you your own wing."

Jonathan went around the bed to sit down next to Miranda, who lay with her arms crossed over her middle. "She looks like Snow White, or Rose Red— if Rose Red were Snow's vaguely Goth twin," the Consort remarked, testing her forehead for fever. "So the process went well? No complications?"

"Not so far," David said, hearing his words begin to slur. If only his mouth would stop hurting . . . he couldn't think straight . . .

"Dev, would you mind?" Jonathan asked, pointing at David. "He'll start flailing with his brain and break something—you know how uncoordinated he gets under extreme pain."

Deven sighed. "I do indeed." The Prime sat down next to David on the bed and handed him a glass tumbler of blood. "Drink this, darling, and let me see what I can do for you. No, wait—" He grabbed the tumbler out of David's hands. "I have a better idea. Tell me how you feel. What all hurts?"

"My mouth," David said. "My jaw is changing."

"Any internal organ pain?"

"No, not so far. But my skin feels wrong, like it's on too tight, and my muscles all feel like I've run five marathons in a night."

Deven considered that, then said, "I can do something—I can't stop it," he added, "because I'm assuming it's part of the transition. It needs to happen, do you understand? But I can give you something to dull it."

David's hold on the room was swerving wildly from side to side; the pain was obliterating all rational thought. "Like a Vicodin?"

Deven smiled. "A bit more precise than that. Give me a minute." Deven sat cross-legged on the floor in front of David, holding the tumbler of blood in his hands. He closed his eyes, and even through his addled mind David could feel Deven doing something, transferring energy into the cup.

Deven opened his eyes. Their pale-violet-sky-blue had darkened to genuine iris violet; David remembered the first time he'd seen them that color, and the circumstances then were disturbingly similar to now.

He felt Dev's hand on his knee. "This isn't like Anna," the Prime told him quietly. "Back then you didn't ask for my help until it was too late."

"That's why I called now," David replied. "I couldn't bear that again."

Deven held out the tumbler, and when David took it, the glass had warmed significantly. He took an experimental swallow. Taste: human, AB positive, from an athlete of some kind, probably donated by a university student.

Then the energy hit him. He started to fall backward, already losing consciousness, and the last thing he remembered was Deven taking the glass from his hand and telling him good night.

"Are you going to sit there all day?" Jonathan asked. "It's a little creepy."

Deven shook his head but didn't turn his gaze from the

bed. "We know how vampires are made, but we don't really know anything about this. If something goes wrong, I need to be able to act immediately."

"Dev, baby, you've been awake for fifty-two hours straight. You have to get some rest."

"I will."

He heard his Consort sigh and come over to him. "Why don't you at least lie down, then—you've been listing to port for the last half hour, and I'm afraid you're going to fall off that stool."

Deven smiled. "I rather doubt either of them would be happy to wake up with me in their bed."

"You've done it for Miranda. She's the one who's going to need your attention—that's the whole reason David called, to get someone to sit for her."

"That's what I'm doing. I'm sitting."

"Lie down," Jonathan said, pulling him almost roughly off the stool. "Next to the Queen, please, there's no need to cause drama. Good boy."

Deven shot Jonathan a dirty look but did as he'd said, and removed his boots so he wouldn't get blood traces from the previous night on their clean sheets. He climbed up next to Miranda, whose tiredness was contagious; the soothing psychic waves of restful sleep coming from her made it hard to resist.

"What about you?" he asked Jonathan.

"I slept on the plane—you saw me. I'll be fine."

Deven wanted to argue, he really did, but . . . his head hit the pillow, and that was that.

David woke to a completely unexpected sight, and for a moment he thought he must still be unconscious.

Miranda and Deven lay asleep not a foot away from him, curled up against each other and completely at peace. She was on her back, he pressed into her side, face buried in her neck. Her shirt had ridden up on one side, and his hand was curved around her waist, fingers splayed out, black nails stark against her ivory skin. Deven's other arm was around her shoulders, and her hand was entwined with his.

It was so beautiful. David just watched them for a long while, unable to take his eyes away.

Finally, though, other sensations began to intrude—his mouth no longer hurt, but his teeth felt weird, and he had a horrible taste in his mouth, sort of metallic; and, he had to admit, Miranda had been right about having to pee.

He inched his way out of the bed and wobbled to the bathroom. His limbs didn't feel entirely right. It was as though there were a delay between the neural impulse and the actual movement.

Standing in front of the sink, he gave his teeth a quick brushing and washed his face, the cold water waking him up a little more. Curious, he tongued his teeth to see if anything felt off.

It certainly did.

Vampires had sharpened canines, of course, which retracted into the jaw so that they looked more or less like human teeth, albeit a bit pointier. Feeling around, though, he realized that not only were his canines pointed, the first premolar behind each canine felt sharp as well. He touched one with his finger; the extension impulse could be triggered that way. Even though he'd touched the premolar, the canine in front of it extended. The molar did, too, but only a tiny bit, probably visible but not obvious. He wasn't sure what the purpose could be . . . unless it was purely ornamental. He couldn't see it, but he guessed it was pretty damn scary looking.

He left the bathroom and found Jonathan standing by the bed, staring down at their mates, who still slept in each other's arms, oblivious.

David came to stand next to him. "I had a dream like this once," he said quietly.

Jonathan held back a snort. "I'll bet you did." They watched in silence for another minute before Jonathan said, "He's not dreaming right now . . . he always dreams."

David nodded. "It must be Miranda's empathy—I dream

a lot less when she's beside me, and the ones I have are much less harrowing."

The Consort watched them another moment before saying, "You're a lucky man, to be so loved by two people."

David shot him a look. "Jonathan . . ."

"Don't worry, I'm not being maudlin, just making an observation. Even as weird as things have been with you and Deven, I've always found this irrational sort of comfort thinking that if anything happened to me, you'd take care of him."

David frowned. "But that can't happen."

"That's what makes it irrational," Jonathan reminded him with a grin. "But it's been on my mind a lot since you died . . . which couldn't happen either, but it did. As strong as you are, a few lines of Greek and a ten-dollar hammer were all it took to kill you. I would never leave him of my own free will—masochistic as that might make me."

David had to smile at that. "He's easy to love," he said. "Just kind of hard to like, sometimes."

"Truer words were never spoken, Lord Prime." The Consort eyed him critically. "How do you feel?"

"Better," David said. "Sort of. Everything's still a bit . . ."

"Wonky?"

"Yes. Exactly."

"Can you feel the bond?"

David reached toward Miranda in his mind, seeking that warmth . . . and finding nothing. "Oh, God," he gasped. "It's still not there . . . oh God, it's not there . . ."

"Easy there," Jonathan said, catching hold of his arms. "Sit down."

"But if this was all for nothing . . . if she lied to me, and I did this to Miranda for nothing . . ."

"Pull it together, David," Jonathan snapped.

David took a deep breath and nodded. He was right, of course. David clamped down on his emotions and forced himself to breathe slowly. "Thank you."

The Consort said reasonably, "You don't know for sure it didn't work. You said yourself you're feeling off; things might have to settle down, she might have to wake up. Don't panic yet. She's going to need you."

"Yes . . . you're right. She needs . . . Oh, damn it."

"What?"

David gestured at the bed. "She needs a live human," he said. "To complete the transition. A bag won't do."

"Call a patrol team and have them snatch one."

"I can't . . . It has to be a particular kind, and I'm not sure they would know the difference on sight."

Jonathan frowned. "What kind? I know she doesn't drink from men, but what else?"

"It has to be an evildoer," David said. "The more reprehensible, the better."

He looked dubious but shook his head. "We've all got our feeding quirks. I once dated a man who wouldn't drink from anyone who took yoga—he said the taste of sandalwood threw him off. How about this: I'll go. I can pick someone appropriate—I may not have empathy, but I can still spot one a mile away. You stay here as you said you would. I can be back inside two hours."

"Thank you."

"Can I get you anything? A nice blonde, perhaps?"

"No . . . no thanks. I'm fine from what Deven gave me earlier. I can hit another bag if I need to."

"All right. Go back to bed, and try not to worry." Jonathan fetched his coat and swept out of the suite.

David wished he could have sent Deven instead. If he'd told Jonathan the truth about his errand, Jonathan would still have done what was necessary, but like Miranda, he would feel guilty afterward, for they both cared far more about human life than either Prime did. David was firmly against killing mortals or causing them permanent damage unless it was absolutely necessary, but in a situation like this, he and Deven both would have been perfectly willing to bring back a human to die for the Queen.

With a sigh, the Prime returned to the bed, sliding back into his side; this time, though, he moved closer to Miranda, mirroring Deven's position next to her so that they essentially held her between them, safe and warm. David kissed her on the cheek and settled back in to try to rest, not expecting to be able to . . . but he was asleep within five minutes, and glad of it.

Darkness.

She could feel it flowing through her veins, like blood, suffusing her cells, altering them as it went. Her first instinct was to fight it—it was too big, too frightening, too much for her to face—but it beckoned so sweetly, she let it in and lay back, opening herself to its embrace.

There was no pain. She could feel things in her body changing; it wasn't anything as massive as the first time, but it seemed just as far-reaching. Some part of her had known that crossing over those years ago would change her whole being . . . now she knew that this crossing would change the world.

The darkness was soft and welcoming, whispering over her skin and teasing her almost unbearably. One minute she was on fire, the next drowning—burning, then drifting . . .

She didn't know how long it went on before she heard the voice. She recognized that whisper in her mind, words like feathers, like wind through a graveyard.

"Here you are at last, child."

She couldn't speak back.

"You have come to reclaim what is yours . . . but is it enough for you?"

What could that mean?

"You did not come to this place to serve me, but to take back what you lost. Perhaps when you understand what is truly at stake, you will want more from me . . . and as soon as you call to me, I will answer. For now . . . return to your beloveds, lest they worry."

She felt her body again, not so much a violent slamming into her skin as a sweet sliding—it felt so good to *feel*, to touch. So good to be alive.

Her eyes fluttered open, her vision blurry at first. There

were arms around her holding her tightly, the warmth of a body fitted perfectly to either side of her. She could feel two hearts beating with hers.

She tilted her head first to one side, then the other, making sense of what she saw: deep blue eyes, and pale violet, watching her intently. She could feel their concern—was she all right? Had it worked?

Her hands lifted, one touching either face, her fingers lightly tracing lips, wrapping around a neck. It felt so good . . . skin under her palm . . . so good . . .

Another feeling swept through her: *need*. She needed hands on her, to feel herself touched. She rose up partway and put her mouth to his, ignoring the gasp, unable to think, only to feel. He tasted like an autumn mist . . . like the slow turn of time through hundreds of years . . .

A hand slid up between them and gently pushed her away. "I'm sorry, love, but I think you have the wrong mouth," he murmured, his voice a wry tenor. "Turn to your right."

She felt another mouth touch her neck and travel along its line, at the same time that a wave of desire moved into her; she moaned softly and turned toward its source, recognizing that power and wanting it desperately.

This time his mouth took hers, easing her closer, holding her with hands that knew every curve of her body.

He lifted his lips from hers. "Miranda," he said, barely over a whisper, "you need to go back to sleep."

She shook her head, but he turned her onto her back again, and now each of them took hold of one of her arms and held it against the bed—not hard, not confining, just calming.

"Rest," said the first voice.

She looked up into his eyes, knowing that what she wanted was plain in her gaze.

A soft chuckle. "Dear one, you're going to feel very differently once you're yourself again."

He leaned down to kiss her forehead. She sighed; obviously she wasn't going to get her way. That was all right, really . . . she was starting to feel sleepy again . . . she wasn't sure if it was her own body or one of them pushing her into unconsciousness, but she acquiesced and turned onto her side, toward the door. A hand threaded through hers, comforting and strong.

She hadn't realized there was anyone else in the room, but over by the door, another familiar man stood, this one blond with muddy hazel eyes that were staring at the bed. The other two saw her staring and turned toward the third.

For just a second, the third man's eyes were full of a hundred emotions, but he covered it quickly. "Is this a bad time?"

"This is the exact right time," the first said firmly. "Thank God you're here."

The blond gestured toward the door. "I brought the human you requested, David."

David. The name ricocheted through her, and memories began to arise. *Yes. David.*

"What did you find?" David asked.

The blond reached out into the hallway and dragged another person into the room—a woman, dressed raggedly with sunken eyes that stared vaguely off into space.

"You know, female evildoers are a lot harder to find than male," the blond said. "There are plenty of drug pushers of both sexes, plenty of addicts, but that's sickness, not evil—this one took a lot of digging, which was why I was gone so long . . . much to my chagrin."

David sighed. "So what did she do?"

Jonathan pushed the woman forward. "She drowned her infant," he replied "She was acquitted—the lawyers blamed postpartum depression."

"How is that evil?" David wanted to know. "It's a terrible thing, but she can hardly be blamed for a mental illness."

"She was lying," Jonathan answered with a bitter smile. "Her husband cheated on her, so to get revenge she murdered his only son."

"Jesus," David said. "You're sure?"

"It was obvious she was corrupt as soon as I saw her, and my telepathy is strong enough to get the truth from her. Give her an empathic sweep and tell me I'm wrong."

A moment later, David nodded once. "Bring her here."

Jonathan hauled the woman over toward the bed, and David turned and said, "Come on, beloved, before you go to sleep, you need to eat."

"She smells like death," she said.

"Go ahead," David told her in her ear. "You'll like it, I promise."

She sat up as Jonathan shoved the woman to her knees beside the bed and pulled her head to one side, baring her throat.

Staring at the blue veins that showed up against sallow skin, Miranda felt her body begin to ache, her teeth pressing into her tongue. She could hear the human's heart beating, hear the blood pulsing through her veins, hot and dark, promising relief for the pain spreading through her body, her insides dry and itching madly.

Her teeth slid down over her lip. She heard someone suck in an astonished breath, but she ignored it and struck.

Jonathan let the human go, and she pushed her onto the floor, holding her down as she struggled—the woman was screaming in terror and pain, but that only filled her blood with power, made her taste even better.

"Miranda, that's enough," someone said.

"No." David's voice. "Let her be."

"David, if she keeps going—"

"I am aware of the procedure," David snapped. "I said let her be."

She kept drinking, forcing the woman back to the floor every time she tried to break free, until she became too weak to fight, too weak to scream.

A moment later something erupted from the human—a force Miranda had never felt before, strength so intense she fell back onto the floor, crying out. She understood at once: the last burst of life force, the power of death. It burned through her like an electric shock, and she writhed against it, unable to control it.

Hands took hers. "Focus," she heard. David. "Ground yourself and focus. Breathe, beloved . . . in . . . and out . . ."

She did as he said, matching her breath to his, taking hold of the energy and grounding it, letting it do what it needed to do to her body.

Silence fell. She lay on her side, curled up in a ball, her breath the only thing she could concentrate on.

She heard the door open. "I need Elite Seventeen and Forty-three for body disposal," David said to someone in the hall. "Immediately."

When she heard the word *body* she began to shake, comprehension starting to assert itself, but someone knelt next to her and put a hand to her forehead.

"Go to sleep, little Queen," he said kindly. "There will be time to worry about that later. Just go to sleep. Let go of the world for a while." She could hear him smiling.

She was already falling into the dark as he picked her up off the floor.

They all stared at one another.

Jonathan spoke first, and there was anger in his words. "So you've turned her into a killer, is that it?"

David, who had his head in his hands, looked up at the Consort. "Only once. The transition had to be sealed with death."

Jonathan shook his head. "So you sent me off to find a human sacrifice? Why didn't you tell me?"

David sighed. "I honestly didn't think it through that far, Jonathan. There was no one else to send whom I trusted to bring what she needed. We didn't have time for a moral debate."

"And you thought I would refuse to do what was necessary—even for Miranda—if I knew."

"I didn't want to burden you with it until it was too late to change your mind," David replied, then spoke over whatever Jonathan was about to say with, "And incidentally, neither of you gets to take the high ground when it comes to secrets and deception."

"What are you going to tell her?" Deven asked.

"I'll find a way to break it to her gently but without sugar-coating it. She may not even remember it happened." David glanced over at Deven. "She's going to be mortified if she remembers kissing you."

Jonathan's eyebrows shot up, and for a moment he forgot his anger, turning a wide-eyed look on Dev. "Wait . . . she kissed you? You?"

"It was the transition," Deven said tiredly, rubbing his neck. "You know how it works when you come across the gentler way—nature, or whatever it is, tries to deepen the connection between you and your sire. She had no idea who I actually was. I was just there, and when she woke up she was on me like bloodstains on a white shirt."

Jonathan stared at his Prime for a moment . . . then burst out laughing.

Deven threw up his hands, exasperated. "What the hell is so funny?"

"Sorry," he said breathlessly. "I just . . . I would have paid to see that."

David bit his lip, holding back a laugh of his own, but at least part of it escaped when he affirmed, "He looked like a deer in headlights."

"Have you ever actually kissed a woman before?" Jonathan asked.

Deven looked like he wanted to stake them both. "Of course I have," he said sharply. "Granted, it was five hundred years ago."

They both laughed again.

"Fuck off, both of you," Deven said, standing up. "I'm calling the airport—we need to get home. I think you two can handle things from here."

He left the room, and though he didn't slam the door, it was implied. Just as he left, the two Elite David had called for appeared with a tarp to wrap the human's body and take her away.

Jonathan sighed, sobering. "Is there anything else you need?"

David shook his head. "Only for life to make sense again, and I don't think you can give me that."

The Consort stood up and, as he walked by David, put a hand on the Prime's shoulder. "I apologize for my words," Jonathan said. "I know you're doing the best you can."

"Thank you. I apologize for not being open with you."

"Don't beat yourself up. We all do what we have to do for those we love."

After Jonathan left, David sat awhile, his mind too full of conflicting thoughts to organize into a coherent system. He thought about doing some work to focus his mind, but the truth was, he was worn out, even as much as he'd slept the last few days. Bringing someone across was always exhausting no matter who you were, and this had been out of the ordinary to say the least. He gave up and went back to bed.

Miranda was peacefully asleep again. He touched his forehead to hers, thinking of the sight of her on the floor, spasming against the human's death. If she were to do it again, it would be easier, and eventually killing became just like any other feeding, but its energy burned out quickly. It was a drug to many of their kind . . .

Their kind . . .

He hugged her tightly for reassurance. There were two of them now. At least he wasn't alone. And Persephone had promised they never would be again.

But Persephone had also promised their bond would heal. He still felt nothing.

He couldn't think about that right now. It threatened to send him into full-blown panic again, and he couldn't do that—not to Miranda. She needed him to be strong and, most important, calm; if they weren't to be bound, he could shield enough to fool her into thinking he was fine, just until she was recovered and used to her new life. He would hold himself apart from her for her sake. That was how things had to be, if they were never to be whole again.

In the meantime, as long as she was asleep, she wouldn't see him break.

Seventeen

Jonathan watched his Prime surreptitiously for the first hour of the flight, and though usually Deven would have noticed eyes on him within the first minute, he was either choosing to ignore it or too lost in his thoughts to be aware. He just stared out the window at the dark world passing by far below.

There was something very wrong with him. Jonathan had been aware of it for quite a while—since before David had died. A crack had appeared in Deven's armor, and it was getting worse. He'd first seen it the night Deven slaughtered the Priesthood of Elysium, and it was as if that one terrible act had broken some part of the Prime, one of the last pieces of him still whole.

Jonathan had been well aware when they'd met what a mess he was getting into. There were almost no vampires Deven's age left alive. To Jonathan's knowledge the oldest vampire to have lived reached about 840 before losing his mind and throwing himself onto a stake.

Jonathan had learned quickly that Pairing with Deven

was both the best and worst thing that had ever happened to him, but even if he had regretted it, there was no going back.

For the most part Jonathan was happy. He freely admitted he wasn't the most demanding partner; he was a man of fairly simple pleasures and with few enemies. As long as he had books, bourbon, and semiregular sex, he was quite content. Their relationship allowed him to get the latter from wherever he pleased during those long periods when Deven had no interest. He had a gift for strategy, which made him invaluable for organizing the Elite, but he was no warrior. He was not a politician, either, and had no desire to be. For the most part his role had been very similar to a traditional Queen's—support, confidence, and love.

He was perfectly fine with that . . . but as time went on, his contentment soured, because he couldn't do what he was meant, by fate, to do. He had tried a dozen different ways to help his Prime, but he was starting to believe, despite his usual optimism, that he had found Deven too late, and that the Prime was already too broken to save.

He had hoped, however faintly, that he could somehow nudge Deven and David back together, at least periodically, without any betrayal or anger. Clearly having a Consort wasn't enough to keep Deven balanced anymore. Perhaps if he had them both, between them they could ease the weight on his shoulders.

On the surface it was an insane idea, the sort of Hail Mary play that only a desperate man would try, but he'd considered bringing it up at least to the boys once all this business with David's death was over. He knew Miranda herself had suggested it three years ago, and though he didn't believe for a second she had meant it, she had at least entertained the notion. Some sort of arrangement might be possible down the road, given a lot of discussion and very specific agreed-upon circumstances.

Now, though, he was no longer sure it would help. Deven had formed an attachment to Miranda now, too, and while it wasn't exactly romantic, it was more than simple friendship—and after what had happened three years ago, there was no way Deven would ever, ever risk hurting her again.

"So," Jonathan ventured, keeping his eyes on his book nonchalantly, "are you planning to pursue that whole thing with Miranda, or . . ."

"What thing?" Deven asked, frowning.

"Well, change or no change, she did kiss you. And you did blush when we were talking about it."

"I don't blush," Deven insisted. "And by now I shouldn't have to ask this question, but, what part of *gay* do you not get?"

"Oh, please. As old as you are, you know sexuality is more fluid than that for our kind. That's how you landed David in the first place."

"I landed David because he had suffered a tragic loss and I give amazing head."

Jonathan snorted. "Exactly my point. He could get a shag from any woman not connected to another woman or life support machinery, but he tumbled into bed with you. Anyway, aside from the deer-in-headlights thing, what did you do when she kissed you?"

"Besides try to push her off? Well . . ." Deven crossed his arms. "I may have kissed back. Just to satisfy my curiosity."

Grinning, Jonathan asked, "Then what?"

Deven's eyes narrowed. "You're getting off on this, aren't you."

"I've just never seen you do anything remotely sexual with a woman. I'm sorry I missed it. What was it like?"

"Like? It was just like kissing a man. Lips don't really differentiate much."

"Maybe not, but breasts sure do."

Deven smiled a little at that. "That part was weird."

"So what if—strictly theoretically, of course—she actually wanted to sleep with you? Or better yet, what if they asked you to join in, and fooling around with her was just part of the equation? Would you try it?"

Deven was giving him a hilariously befuddled look. "What in God's name are you talking about?"

"I said it was theoretical."

"What are you fishing for, Jonathan? Are you trying to plan something?"

Jonathan laughed. "Of course not."

"Good, because nothing like that is going to happen. The whole thing was an anomaly that I'd appreciate you dropping."

Jonathan noted the rising ire in his voice and said, "Okay, okay. I was just curious. No plans, honest. I won't bring it up again."

There was a chime, and Deven took out his phone, unlocking the screen listlessly. A flicker of a smile crossed his face.

"What is it?" Jonathan asked.

The Prime held up the phone, letting Jonathan see the alert: An area code 312 number had called a 512 number. "Something's going right," Deven said.

"Dev . . ."

"Can we just . . . not?" Deven asked, sounding utterly exhausted, even flat. "I swear, Jonathan, I've had enough processing and emotional vulnerability to last me a fucking millennium. I just want to go home, go to bed, and maybe have a few nights of normalcy before the next fresh hell descends upon us. Please."

Jonathan smiled. "All right."

After a moment, though, Jonathan said, "You know, if you wanted to go to bed with them, I'd be fine with it."

Deven groaned. "What did I just say?"

"I just wanted you to know," the Consort said firmly. "I was mostly kidding—but if you wanted to shag the entire Council I'd make it happen. Whatever you want, no matter how ridiculous or impossible, I want for you. I want you to be happy, and I wish I could fix it. That's all."

At last Deven smiled. "Love, how many times must I tell you . . . you can't fix me. It's not your job. You're just going to make yourself crazy thinking it falls on you."

"Just tell me this, then. What would it take? What would it take for you to feel genuinely happy, even just for a moment? Anything. I just want to know."

The Prime sat quietly for a moment, then shook his head. "I don't think it's possible," he said. "I told you when we met that I'm a lost cause."

"I don't accept that. There must be something that would make you at least want to *try*."

They held each other's eyes until Deven closed his, and to Jonathan's surprise, when they opened again, they were bright with tears. "You don't want to know," he said.

"Yes, I do. Is it David? You can tell me."

"No . . . David and I could never make each other happy, you know that. If we tried to be real partners, we'd kill each other. I'm still surprised we didn't the first time."

"Then what is it?"

Deven leaned back in his seat, staring up at the ceiling, then closed his eyes. "I want to be loved," he said, almost too softly to hear.

Jonathan started to protest—whatever his faults, Deven was one of the most loved people he'd ever met—but the Prime wasn't finished. His last words, before turning his head back to the window and staring out again in silence, broke Jonathan's heart in half:

"I want God to love me again."

Miranda woke again, and this time she meant it.

She blinked in the firelight and sat up, a little confused for a moment, as though she'd just had an incredibly vivid dream. She was pretty sure it had been about sex but had ended in blood.

What had happened? Wasn't something supposed to happen?

She held up her hands, staring at them. They looked strange, and she didn't know why until she concentrated—and then it was like they suddenly went from two-dimensional to three-dimensional, and she could see things she had never seen before. She looked around the room, and the effect was the same: Everything was sharp and clear, even in her peripheral vision, and she registered things about the room that were so tiny . . . a minute crack in the bedpost, a delicate spiderweb in the far corner. She could focus her vision on one thing and still describe in detail something on the other side of the room.

She could hear the guards outside the door breathing. She could smell whatever the servants used to clean the bathroom. She could smell the residue of blood somewhere, too.

It might have frightened her had it not been so fascinating. She sat for nearly half an hour just listening, looking, smelling . . . and that wasn't all.

She didn't know what to call it, but it felt like another sense had heightened, one she didn't even know she had. It felt something like her empathy in the way it responded to her will, but instead of emotion, it told her how things were moving—she could sense a tiny fly's path as it flew into the spiderweb, even though she wasn't watching it. She could sense the flames in the fireplace dancing, down to each individual lick of flame.

Beside her, David stirred and woke, blinking as she had. "What the hell . . ."

His voice sounded different. It had layers and layers of vibration.

He sat up, too, and stared around him the same way she had. "Do you hear that?" he asked.

"The electricity? Yes." She raised an eyebrow. "Wait, weren't you like this before?"

"No. This is new." He held up one hand, stretched his arm out, moved it farther and farther back. "Whoa . . . my proprioception has intensified by a factor of three at least."

"Um . . . sure, mine, too."

"This is fascinating."

She smiled. "Thank you, Spock."

He swatted her lightly on the arm. "Aren't you freaked out?"

"No . . . I would be freaked out if this didn't feel completely normal, just new."

David nodded. "Yes . . . it feels right." He paused, staring

at her, and she waited a minute before giving him a questioning look. "Your hair," he said. "It's so many colors."

She giggled. "We sound like we're both stoned."

Miranda took his hand and squeezed it; he lifted hers to
his lips and kissed the palm. They held each other's eyes,
and she felt his love for her, as well as his surprise at—

Her mouth fell open.

He seemed to get it at the same exact moment and put his
hand to her face, swallowing hard. "I can feel you," he said
shakily. "It's back."

"I know," she replied, tears already flooding her eyes. "I
can feel you, too. It worked . . . it really worked . . ."

She flung her arms around him, laughing and crying at the
same time, and they held on to each other, overcome with
breathless joy.

She had almost forgotten how it felt, that warm touch in
the back of her mind. She had tried to push the memory away
so it wouldn't hurt so much, but now, as she put her mouth to
his, it all came back: the comfort, the surety, the beauty of it.
Suddenly, after walking around for weeks in someone else's
skin, she had her own back, and any fear she might have had,
any doubt about her choice, dissolved.

Just like the moment at the clinic when they had both realized he was alive, they kissed each other everywhere they
could, this time just for the wonder of feeling each other's
love radiating along the bond.

"Touch me," she whispered, pulling him down into the
pillows.

Joy curled up around itself and became desire. She felt
the echo of whatever dream she'd had earlier set her body
burning, and Miranda slid her hands up under his shirt, letting her new senses learn the lay of his muscles. Even the
slightest pressure felt a hundred times more intense; his lips
on her throat, against her ear, made her shiver. She scratched
lightly down his back with her fingernails, and he sucked in
a delightfully tormented breath.

They found their way into each other's clothes with hands
that felt so much more than before. His hand moved down

over her belly, and she gasped, arching her back; it felt like he was touching her everywhere at once, and every inch of her was so sensitive she wanted to scream, to demand that he hurry. She wanted him joined with her in every conceivable way and couldn't wait another minute—she had been waiting long enough.

Luckily he seemed to agree. They barely had the last of their clothes off before he had her on her back and took her, drawing a sound that was part moan, part sob, and part laughter from her throat.

This time there was no sadness, no sense of loss. This time body and mind united at the same time, with no separation, no distance. She opened herself to him fully, and he to her, their senses and thoughts merging so thoroughly there was no her, no him, not anymore.

Finally she could say she loved him without words—and with her entire being.

It was late in the afternoon when David woke; he'd been out for only about twenty minutes, and some noise had startled him.

He looked at Miranda, but she was fine, sprawled out carelessly across most of the mattress. She had fallen asleep in the same position she'd landed in, and he'd barely managed to push himself off to the side so he wouldn't knock the breath out of her. They were both utterly, deliciously spent.

What, then, had woken him?

The sound came again: his phone.

Sighing, he lifted it from the desk with his mind and drew it to his hand; the ring tone wasn't one designated for a particular person. When he saw the number, his eyes narrowed.

312 . . . Chicago?

Some impulse he couldn't really name made him hit Talk. "Yes?" he asked, keeping his voice down.

There was a moment of shuffling noises, and then a woman's anxious whisper: "Is this Prime Solomon?"

The accent was a dead giveaway. "Olivia," he said. "How did you get this number?"

"I need your help," she said. "I don't have much time."

"Are you in Chicago?"

"No. New Jersey. I'm with Jeremy."

She had his full attention now. "What's going on, Olivia?"

"I helped him," she said. "We killed Kelley and McMannis. I thought he'd stop there and stay in Brisbane, but he's determined to kill Hart . . . and I don't think he's going to stop."

"You need to get away from him," David told her. "Come back to Austin and—"

"I can't, not yet. There are people . . . humans. They offered him help with Hart, and I think he's going to take their bargain . . . I can't change his mind."

"What bargain?"

"They want something in Hart's Haven. Some kind of amulet. But they can't get it—their people wouldn't last one round with a vampire. So they want him to get it, and in exchange they'll give us plans for Hart's entire security system, blueprints of the building . . . anything we need."

"And you don't trust them."

"Of course not! Anything a bunch of humans could want from vampires isn't going to be good. Whatever that amulet really is, it's probably just as bad as the thing that killed you. I never trust religious nuts—"

"Religious nuts? Who are these people, Olivia?"

"I don't know for sure, but they're some kind of Order and they sound like zealots."

"Do you have their leader's name, the group's name, anything I can go on?"

"Morningstar," she said. "That's all I know."

David's heart did a somersault before freezing in his chest. "Olivia . . . you're right, you can't trust them. Listen to me—however you can, I need you to send me the plans they give Jeremy."

"I'll try. Shit . . . I have to go. I'll send what I can."

"Olivia, wait—"

She was gone. David stared at the phone, not sure he believed what he'd just heard.

Miranda had woken just as the conversation ended, as he had forgotten to keep his voice down. "What's going on?"

He shook his head, still thunderstruck. "I think we just had a break in the Morningstar case."

Eighteen

There was a sense of peace in the clinic room, a feeling of rest. It was very different from the way hospital rooms usually felt.

It certainly smelled better.

Perhaps because of her mother's fate, or perhaps because of the pain and grief she felt every time she entered such places, she had always had a morbid inner conviction that hospitals weren't places of healing, but were where humans went to die.

Miranda sat down in the chair beside Stella's bed, her eyes on the girl's still features, wondering what was going on in her mind—was she dreaming? Were they happy dreams? She didn't look like she was having nightmares.

The Queen reached over and straightened the girl's blanket, brushed her hair out of her face. Stella's hair had grown out a fraction of an inch from its red dye, but other than that, she looked exactly the same as she had when Miranda found her on the floor. "I'm sorry I haven't been to visit you until now," she said. "Things have been even weirder than they were before. You'd probably be overjoyed to dig into our energy now."

She felt her phone vibrate against her hip and took it out. She had a text from an agent at the firm that handled her money: the address and bank account information of Frank Hedelman, an insurance salesman whose mentally deranged wife had killed their newborn and then vanished—she would most likely never be found, as she was currently at the bottom of the lake. Mr. Hedelman's credit card and legal bills were piling up. According to the text he owed close to $122,000.

Miranda texted back quickly: *Pay it.*

As you will it, my Lady.

Sighing, she put the phone away and opened her guitar case. "I just wanted to thank you," she said softly to the sleeping Witch in the bed. "I'll tell you again when you wake up, but . . . what you did for us . . . there's no way to repay you."

Miranda wasn't expecting a reply, of course. She set aside the case and scooted the chair a little closer to the bed.

"I've got guards on Lark," the Queen added. "She seems okay. Your father is pretty angry about the whole thing—but you probably know that since he was here yesterday. He probably had a few choice words about us."

She searched the girl's face for another long minute—she wasn't sure what she was looking for, really. Her condition was essentially unchanged; she didn't seem to be wasting away, just on pause. Mo had her on some kind of glucose IV and had said he was ready to start a feeding tube . . . but so far Stella hadn't needed one.

"Anyway . . . I can't really do anything for you right now except this, so . . . if you can hear me in there, try to follow me back."

Miranda played quietly, starting with songs she knew Stella loved off the first album and then moving into a couple of covers and the two mostly finished new songs. She remembered how Stella's eyes had lit up when they were sitting on the bed talking and Miranda mentioned she was working on the new album; at the very, very least she deserved a sneak preview.

The strings felt different under her fingertips; her skin had become a lot more sensitive to pressure in the last few days, and her hearing was both more powerful and more precise, picking up nuances of tone and timbre that she'd never been able to hear before. She'd already made slight adjustments to her voice in a few places while she practiced, and the difference was amazing.

She was trying not to think about the implications. She couldn't focus on what it meant long term, only on the night-to-night changes and how to get used to them. Her teeth, her senses, the way people seemed to do a double take when they saw her, as if they thought she was someone else . . . She hadn't been into the city yet, as she was concerned about the sensory overload this soon—she remembered that night on the bus in Austin when she was changing the first time, and how close she'd come to a panic attack just from close proximity to humans. She was trying to give herself time.

Now that the transition was finished—and to distract him from worrying about Olivia—David had Mo helping him run a few dozen diagnostic tests to see what else had changed, and if there was any way to measure those changes. Miranda just laughed and left them to it.

She had, however, made it very clear that wooden stakes were *not* to be part of their experiments. After what she had felt the last time, when they weren't bonded, she could only imagine how it would be now that they were again. *No thanks.*

She was afraid to look at herself too closely. Right now it just seemed like a few new tricks, but . . . deep down she knew it was more than that. Soon enough she'd have to face it. Right now, she just played.

Using her empathy probably wouldn't help here, but nonetheless, she reached through the music to wrap a mantle of comfort around the Witch, trying to put all her gratitude and affection into each chord, hoping against hope that wherever she was, Stella might hear her and lift her head, reach out toward the sound, come closer . . . and if she did, perhaps Miranda could catch her hand, draw her across whatever distances separated her from her body, and coax her back in. Miranda knew she wasn't a healer, but if she let the music take her deep enough, maybe, just maybe . . .

With the new additions to her abilities, she found she could add more layers to the music, infusing it with new dimensions that she knew the Witch would like: the sound of wind in trees, the pale milky light of the moon, a rush of feathers. The only word she could think of for the new feeling was *darkness*; it made her think of the black keys on the Bösendorfer, lower notes that added a depth no other instrument could. She could now do with her voice what she could do with her piano.

She played for more than an hour, shifting from one song to another without really noticing. Usually using her voice that long without a pause would make her throat hurt, and the guitar strings would leave her fingers aching, but she didn't feel either. The well of quiet power within her seemed to have no end.

Finally, she brought the last song to a close, letting the final chord ring out into the room's silence.

Miranda bowed her head to let it rest on the guitar for a moment, strangely out of breath. She felt dazed, like she'd been working an audience of a hundred instead of a single young woman. As she breathed, though, she felt renewed strength flowing into her along the bond with David, gently rebalancing her as it always had before. She smiled.

A moment later, she looked up, and Stella was smiling at her.

"My goodness," Jacob said. "He's certainly elevating paranoia to an art form, isn't he?"

Thousands of miles apart, the three Primes scrutinized the scans Olivia had e-mailed David, which he had then combined with external photographs of the New York Haven to produce a three-dimensional image detailing Hart's entire security system as well as the building's layout.

"Based on the information Cora provided us, I've narrowed down the location of Hart's personal suite to this hallway," David told them, highlighting the corridor in question. "The harem room—former harem room, that is—is directly across from it."

"We doubt he's still staying there, though," Deven added. "Given the threat level he would most likely have moved. We can make certain assumptions based on the diagram that maps out where the Elite are stationed. He'll have heavy guard at his own door."

"So he's down on sublevel three in the corner there?"

"No," David told Jacob with a smile. "Basement one, actually. Apparently Hart doesn't like being that far underground."

"Then what's in sub-basement three? It has a high concentration of electricity and security equipment."

"Indeed it does," Deven said. He raised the diagram up on their monitors to expose sub-basement three. "And it's the focus of our concerns this evening. David thinks, and I agree, that this magical mystical Widget is in that room."

"I don't understand," said Jacob. "If Hart doesn't know Morningstar is after this thing, why would he have it so heavily protected?"

"I think he knows what he has," David replied. "I don't think he knows there are a bunch of humans after it, or that Jeremy will try to get it. He certainly doesn't know when. As far as he's aware, Jeremy just wants his head, not his Widget. But if you look at the system he's got in place: Notice there are no Elite guards on the room, which means he's not anticipating an immediate burglary. The system has been in place for at least five years, so he's confident it's enough."

"How can you tell it's been there five years?"

"Can you tell what it is?" David asked. "Look closely."

"Well . . . there are about three dozen or so separate devices placed along the walls and about two dozen cylinders that penetrate into the wall. Other than that, I have no idea. Schematics aren't really my area."

"Stakes," David said. "They're stakes. Each of those devices is a motion sensor. They're placed at random along both sides of the hallway. Each one triggers a stake launcher built into the wall. They're all wired individually, so the only way to deactivate them is to do it one by one, by which time the cavalry will arrive—there's an alarm connected to the junction box that will report a drop in power. They have a backup generator, so cutting the power to the whole building won't help. Here's the fun part: Some of them are dummies. They're electrified but not connected to stakes, so you could waste your time deactivating one that wasn't a threat. It's really rather ingenious."

Jacob sounded impressed. "There's no way Hart came up with that. He must have contracted out to a security firm. But how do you know it's five years old?"

"Two things—the signal quality and strength are identical to those of a particular model of transmitter, which is a five-year-old model. Also the kind of launcher he's using is modified from a type of spear gun that uses nitrogen canisters, and those date back about five years as well."

"You're a little terrifying, you know that," Jacob told him.

"Yes. The point is, you don't create a system like that for a room you go in and out of a lot. It's the only part of the Haven set up that way. I doubt the magical Widget is the only thing in there, but I'd lay odds everything in there is extremely valuable to Hart."

"So let's go over this plan of yours," Jacob said.

There was a soft knock at the workroom door, and Miranda stuck her head in and mouthed, *Clear?*

David nodded and gestured to the other chair; she sat on it backward, leaning her chin on the back and listening intently.

Deven made an uncertain kind of noise and said, "I know you're both going to look at me over the Internet like I've sprouted a second head, but I feel I should put this out there . . . We could warn Hart."

Miranda grinned at the look on David's face. "Close your mouth, baby," she whispered. "You look like a fish."

The astonishment was just as evident in Jacob's voice. "Wait . . . you're suggesting we save Hart?"

Deven sighed as if bracing for their inevitable reaction. "Yes."

"Who the hell are you, and what have you done with Prime Deven?" Jacob demanded.

"If he knows to anticipate Jeremy, he can move the Widget and himself elsewhere, and that way Morningstar can't get their hands on it. Anything else we do has the potential for a massive loss of life, not just Hart's."

"I'll be damned," David muttered. "Deven and Jacob seem to have switched personalities."

Miranda gave him a look, and he raised an eyebrow and mouthed, *What?*

She just shook her head. "Leave him alone," she replied.

David held back all fourteen sarcastic retorts he had already come up with for Deven and went with a less combative one. "You raise a . . . good point, Dev. We need a cost/benefit analysis of the situation, assuming we either take out Hart or allow Jeremy to do so. Cost one: potential deaths among Hart's Elite. Cost two: potential death for Olivia, who I think we can all agree deserves better."

"A caveat—if we warn Hart to expect them, Olivia will most likely be killed anyway," Jacob pointed out. "Benefit one: We get the Widget, and Morningstar doesn't. Another thing we agree on: Whatever the Widget is, we don't want Morningstar to have it. I'd also like to note that I'd really prefer Hart not have it either."

"Benefit two," David picked up. "We're finally rid of Hart, who enslaved Cora and countless other women; who had Miranda shot; who sent Jeremy to kill us in the first place; and who is a rabid donkey dick."

"Fine, do what you want," Deven said sharply; then his voice immediately switched to something like weariness. "I concede your point. I just had to put it out there."

David had no idea how to respond to that, so he went on.

"All right then, if you will both keep your eyes on the screen, I'll go through the other important features of the security system, and then we can get into the plan itself so you can offer your suggestions . . ."

Nearly two hours later, when they all disconnected, he felt Miranda watching him while he shut down the web chat program. He could also feel the twist of emotions she was feeling, and he knew what had brought it on.

"You have to admit it was weird," he finally told her.

She nodded. "I'm not disputing that. When was the last time you heard Deven suggest abandoning a plan in order to lower the body count?"

David frowned. "Pretty much never. But you said yourself he's been acting differently since I died. People do change."

"You've known him for most of a century. Has he ever changed before?"

"Only externally." David powered down the computer he'd been using and returned it to its slot on the shelf with the others. "My question is this: Can we really make any kind of assumptions about someone seven hundred years old whose history we don't fully know? Maybe once a century he has an existential crisis."

"The thing is, I can feel something from Jonathan, too—whatever's up with Dev is wearing Jonathan out. He's hiding it well, but it's exhausting him emotionally."

He thought back through the last time he'd seen Jonathan—the way the Consort had spoken, tiny alterations in his appearance that added up to a person who was frayed around the edges. He'd looked and sounded tired, and his trademark cheer was just a tiny bit dimmed—as Miranda had said, it was nothing obvious, but Jonathan was much easier to read than Deven, and the Consort was a canary in a coal mine when it came to his Prime.

Finally, David nodded. "All right. Once this thing with Jeremy is over with, maybe we can sit them down and see if there's something we can do to help."

Miranda seemed satisfied with that, at least as satisfied as she could be when she was worried about friends. She changed the subject: "Are you guys sure about this plan? An awful lot depends on trusting Olivia."

"I have faith in her," David said.

The Queen smiled. "Then I do, too. After all, she did help you get back to me."

He held his hand out to her, and she took and squeezed it. "How's Stella?" he asked.

"Back in her room. Lark's with her, and her father was here this afternoon. She says she still doesn't remember much of what happened, but other than that she feels great."

"Where have I heard that story before?" David said wryly. "And how are you feeling?"

She considered, then answered, "Okay. I'm not completely sure what to do with all of this. The enhanced hearing is doing odd things to my music; everything's taking longer because all the new layers I can hear make work that would have sounded fine before completely inadequate. But give me a few weeks and I'm sure I'll get used to it. Not to mention, it does make the finished product amazing. You?"

He smiled. "So much better. Having you back in here, I finally feel like myself again, although I'm having some of what you're describing, too—I can pick out all these details in code that I would have passed over before, but it's a good thing for me. I catch errors right away so I don't waste time trying to bug-hunt later."

"Do . . ." She looked uncertain about asking the question, but went on anyway: "Do you have any idea what all this is for? I get that Persephone wanted us to be megavamps or whatever, but I can't help but wonder if there's a specific reason she picked the alterations she picked."

"I have no idea."

Miranda frowned. "You didn't ask a lot of questions."

"Well, no. I was a little more concerned with getting back here than with debating the finer points." He was trying not to sound defensive, but he could tell by her expression that he wasn't entirely succeeding. "Plus I . . . I know this is going to sound ridiculous, but . . . I trusted her. I just had this inner conviction that she would take care of us, especially after everything we lost because of her."

Miranda eyed him critically for a moment, then nodded and said, "Fair enough." She let go of his hand and stood, pulling her leg over the seat of the chair as she straightened. "I have to call my agent in a bit—what are you up to for the rest of the night?"

"Dastardly planning. We've got three days before Jeremy and Olivia hit Hart—I want to make sure every aspect of the plan is seamless. Jeremy caught me by surprise once already. This time we have the upper hand." David stood as well; his next stop was a meeting with several Elite officers. "This time I leave nothing to chance."

"Hand me the mocha toffee chip."

Stella had never been so hungry in her life; she wolfed down the dinner the servants brought her—even eating Lark's leftovers—and then dragged her friend down the hall to the ice cream study.

"Are you sure we should be in here?" Lark asked.

"Shut up and get spoons!"

Quite happily ensconced in the plush chairs, the two Witches swapped pints and compared notes about the Drawing Down ritual.

"I don't remember a lot," Stella admitted reluctantly. "I remember I saw Persephone, but she didn't jump into my body—I went to her."

"What exactly did that accomplish?"

"Since she couldn't directly reach out to the vampires yet, she used me as a speaker, basically. The information she wanted to give them went through me to David. He would say I downloaded it, then brain-mailed it to him. But it was too much information for my puny human brain, so it blew my microchips or whatever."

"And you're okay now? Just like that?"

"All I really needed was rest. Profound rest. Then Miranda came in and plugged up the last couple of holes in my energy so I could wake up again."

Lark pondered her strawberry shortcake ice cream for a moment, then asked, "Do you ever wonder what normal people talk about?"

Stella snorted. "Normal as in normal Witches who don't know vampires, or normal people who aren't Witches?"

"Either."

"Whatever they talk about, it's probably pretty boring compared to all this." Stella crunched down on a toffee chip. What, she wondered, was Miranda doing tonight? Was she happy now that she was . . . whatever David was?

Stella knew they'd gotten their bond back, and that was good, but . . . seeing Miranda for the first time when she woke from her coma, she had known immediately she was no longer looking at the same vampire Queen she had known. She was almost certain that neither Miranda nor David had any idea just how deep the changes ran . . . or what they'd gotten themselves into.

"Do you remember what she was like?" Lark asked.

Stella took a breath and said, "She was fucking scary, Lark. Nothing like any deity I've ever worked with in Circle or seen Drawn Down by other Witches. She was a hundred percent darkness, but . . . the kind of darkness that heals, if that makes any sense. The darkness that comes from sleep and dreaming—and death, too, but . . . I don't really know how to describe it. But she was also kind. Really considerate of me and the fact that I'm not a vampire so I was taking a huge risk doing what I did. She made sure that it was an informed decision on my part."

Both Witches were silent for a while, each attending to her ice cream. Then Lark said, her voice a little hushed, "Something big is coming, isn't it? What we've seen is just the beginning."

Stella caught her friend's eyes. "Yes."

Lark nodded. "I guess there are worse reasons to die."

Stella grabbed her arm. "Lark . . . you don't have to be

involved in this stuff. I'm really grateful that you helped me, but I don't want you to get hurt. When I opened myself up to Persephone I pretty much signed up for this crap, but you don't have to."

Lark chuckled, set down her ice cream, and put her hand over Stella's. "Sorry, sugarbean. You're my best friend. Where you go, I go."

Stella sighed. "You're certifiable, you know."

"I've been told."

They grinned at each other.

"So," Lark asked, "got any sprinkles?"

Olivia had always found New York fascinating. She had visited many cities in her time, and had lived in several, but Manhattan confounded her; it was so packed with people living so closely together, with everything imaginable at their fingertips, most of it available for delivery.

She stood at the hotel window staring out at the waves of skyscrapers that spread out in all directions. She had no idea how people lived here, yet millions did, and moreover, they had a loyalty to their city and its relentless energy that reminded her of the loyalty Elite had for a Signet. To New Yorkers, there was no other place worth living.

"I haven't been here since the mid-1950s," she mused. "Even then I thought it was a strange place."

Jeremy, over at the room's nondescript desk, looked up from his phone. "I've always hated it here."

She took hold of the plastic rod that drew the curtains and shut them, then turned to him. "Are you all right?"

He held her gaze for a long moment. "I'm fine." Jeremy smiled slightly and added, "Tense, I suppose, about tomorrow."

Probably not as tense as I am. Olivia sat down on her bed. "Would it make you feel better to go over the plan again?"

"I don't think so."

She nodded, picking up her sword to give it a polish,

needing something to do with her hands. She was wound up so tightly it would be a minor miracle if she could sleep that day.

She didn't bother telling herself she was just nervous about invading the Haven. She was, but only marginally; it was a simple enough plan, and she understood her role very well. If anything went wrong, she had an escape route. No, what was really twisting her up inside was knowing what she was about to do to Jeremy.

He was probably going to die. Beneath his cool and calculating behavior she could see things unraveling . . . but still, she hated it, hated the duplicity.

She had never been above lying in service to the Signet when it was required of her. Her job had demanded occasional underhanded acts, but always in the name of what she believed to be the greater good. This time she was acting for the greater good *against* her Signet, throwing in her lot with others.

She had been surreptitiously texting with David for a week now, setting up the plot, giving him information. Every time she hit Send she felt sick. After all the betrayal Jeremy had faced, how could she do it to him, too? Olivia knew that whatever happened she would never forgive herself for it.

But she had made her choice. Regardless of her personal crisis of conscience, it was the right thing to do. She wasn't going back.

Despite her involvement with Kelley's and McMannis's assassinations, Prime Solomon had promised her asylum in her pick of three territories: the South, the West, or Eastern Europe. All three of those Primes supported her. If she didn't die in the attempt, she would likely be safe for however long she wanted to be.

There was always a chance Jeremy would survive, too, and be himself again one day. Olivia had asked for clemency for him because of what had been done to his family, and the Primes had agreed that they wouldn't deliberately kill him; they would let him have Hart but take the artifact so Morningstar didn't get it. From there, if Jeremy stopped in his killing spree, they would leave him alone, but if he made a single move on another Signet, all bets were off.

It was a much better deal than she'd expected them to offer. He had killed David, but David stood by what he'd said to her before, that Jeremy had only been acting to save his daughter. He agreed that Jeremy had become a threat and would probably need to be eliminated eventually, whether it happened tomorrow or not, but he hadn't been anxious to deal death to someone who had been victimized by Hart and McMannis.

She chose her words carefully as she asked Jeremy, "So . . . have you given any thought to what we'll do after this?"

He gave her another unreadable look. "After I get the artifact to my contact with Morningstar, we head for Mumbai."

She took a deep breath. "Why Mumbai?"

"India is next."

Ice formed in her stomach. "Why India? What did he do?"

"Varati was a known associate of Kelley."

"But . . . he didn't actually do anything to you directly?"

Jeremy snapped, "Are you questioning me?"

Olivia flinched at the sudden, unexpected rage in his words. "No, no, of course not. I just want to understand so I can help you plan."

He glared at her, then went back to whatever he was doing on his phone. "You have to trust me, Olivia. I know what I'm doing."

"Of course you do." She forced herself to smile. "You've gotten us this far."

After another tense moment, his gaze lost some of its coldness, and he said, "Good." He stood up. "I'm going out to hunt—I need some air, if you don't mind keeping an eye on things here."

"As you will it," she responded automatically.

He didn't quite slam the door, but close enough to startle her. As soon as he was gone she felt her entire body relax; she hadn't realized how tightly she was holding her muscles, her body understanding that it might need to fight or flee any second.

She put her head in her hands. One more night. Just one more night, and this would all be over. Maybe she would bear the guilt forever, but at least she wouldn't have to be in constant fear that her boss was going to snap and kill her for looking at him wrong. She didn't want to kill him, and she didn't really want him to die . . . but she had to get away. Tomorrow night, if fate was on her side, she would be on a plane to Austin, safe, and free.

Nineteen

I can't do this anymore.

It seemed to happen so quickly, but in truth it had been coming for a long time. Once the water had begun to seep through the dam, it was inevitable that the dam would eventually break.

He spent what remained of the night curled up on top of the Tower Bridge, staring sightlessly out at the river. He came here often to think, the way David liked to stand on tall buildings and survey his domain, but really, the bridge was more a place to hide. From atop one of the towers, as he sat cross-legged with one hand resting on the safety rail that was in place for maintenance workers, not visitors, the high cool air brought the smells of the river, of asphalt and car exhaust, of a dozen or more foods.

Eventually, as the night waned, he Misted down from the tower and began the walk to where the car would be waiting. Sacramento didn't have a dedicated Shadow District, at least not since the 1940s when the Blackthorn wars had caused such chaos; the District had spread out, blending in among the human businesses. As a result, there was no sense in strutting about to be seen. Here it was better to be known simply by reputation. Probably less than half the vampire population of the city would know him by sight.

Havens weren't always located near government seats, but most were. Several Primes back, the Western United States had kept its Haven in San Francisco, because of its much higher vampire population, but once the warring factions all over the territory were ruthlessly subdued, he was content to keep it here in Sacramento and allow Lieutenant Murdoch to run things in the Bay Area.

There weren't many humans about at this late hour, close to four A.M.; on some of the side streets he took to cut through the neighborhood, the sound of his footsteps echoed hollow on the pavement, louder than the sounds of passing cars a block over, louder than the buzz of streetlights.

Each step felt heavier than the last, as if the entire weight of the earth's atmosphere were pushing down on him—but not just down, in from all sides, very slowly crushing the life out of him, squeezing out anything remotely resembling a soul. Every night it got worse . . . harder to breathe, harder to move.

He was too tired for sadness, too weary for despair. All he really wanted was to curl up right here on the filthy concrete and fall asleep. Whether he woke again or not was irrelevant. He could stay asleep until the sun burned the flesh from his bones . . . except that would end Jonathan as well, and the one thing he would not do was have his Consort's death on his soul on top of everyone else's. Jonathan deserved better.

He nearly laughed. Yes, Jonathan deserved better . . . he always had. Whatever god had chained such a kind spirit to such a withered heart had inflicted cruel and unusual punishment on Jonathan—if there was such a thing as past lives, the Consort must have been an absolute dick in his last incarnation to deserve this life.

Tomorrow night the assault on Hart's Haven would go down, but now that the plan was set and the pieces in place, he had no further part to play. It was David's game this time, and he was glad of it; he was tired of intrigues, tired of things going wrong.

As if on cue, his phone alerted him to a text: *5.1 Claret. Mission complete.*

Without breaking stride he sent back an acknowledgment, then sent a message to the client informing her to make the bank transfer for the final payment.

Somewhere in Buenos Aires was a severed left hand where a drug lord had been.

Three more humans were scheduled to die in the next few days: an executive in a multinational corporation, a Japanese inventor, and the dictator of a small Mediterranean island nation. There was also a priceless relic stolen from the Iraqi Museum of Antiquities about to be stolen back, and a kidnapped child who would be on his way home to his wealthy mother by tomorrow midnight.

All in all it would be a billion-dollar week.

Only a handful of years ago, that would have pleased him.

He didn't realize he'd stopped walking until he saw the light.

Warm light saturated with color fell on the sidewalk through windows of stained glass, on either side of a pair of arched doors; over the doors were carvings of angels and saints, worn with age but still easily discerned.

St. Anthony's, of course. He'd passed it a thousand times, usually looking away to avoid any uncomfortable memories welling up. On the rare occasion he let himself linger, he ended up stopping at the bar between here and home and shooting whiskey until he was too drunk to walk, whereupon he had to call Wu and have the car brought to him instead of meeting it.

He hadn't set foot in a church in at least two hundred years, and he didn't now, but for once he let himself stand and watch the building for a moment.

What had it been like to have faith? He could barely remember. Somewhere in the mists of time he had worn brown robes and chanted the hours, thriving on the scent of frankincense and beeswax candles. Some time, long ago, even after he was no longer human, he had still felt the Divine Presence in the world, but it had faded, sliding inch by inch into a great ocean of regret.

He didn't remember the feeling of having it, but he remembered the moment the last spark of it was snuffed. He had held on to his belief in God through his uncle's abuse, through weeks chained in the dark amid the stench of rotting bodies and hours of screaming torment on the Inquisitor's table, through becoming a vampire, through Eladra's attempt to indoctrinate him into her cult, through decades of wandering and learning every martial art he could find in his desperation to strike back at anyone who raised a hand to him . . . but when the moment finally came, it was almost painless, like dropping a stone in a river.

He could see it all over again, such a simple thing: a young woman with dark hair, her face gaunt from starvation, sinking down before the doors of a church and dying there on the steps. It was Italy, in the early sixteenth century. All around her people just kept walking, ignoring the utterly needless loss of life at their feet. It was unremarkable, really. Humans died all the time. Many of them starved. Nobody cared. Yet something about that girl, lying before the church doors with her hand outstretched in silent, eternal entreaty, was the end of it.

He had almost forgotten about that moment until he met another woman who bore a striking resemblance to her; that woman was now the Queen of Eastern Europe. Now, every time he saw Cora, he thought about it again and remembered what had run through his mind at that precise moment:

Oh God . . . You have forsaken us.

Considering Cora's religious proclivities, it was rather tragically ironic. Perhaps to balance a nonexistent scale, he had made sure to take care of Cora as much as he could. He hadn't been able to do a damn thing for that nameless girl in Rome; he could at least give Cora a dog.

How many horrific sins had been committed in the name of the Church? He could hear, in his nightmares, the screams through the stone walls of the prison, life after life turning to demented agony as bones were broken, flesh peeled back, tongues seared. Then there were the wars, the genocides . . . midwives, gays, Witches, Elves, condemned and slaughtered. Corruption, institutional misogyny, hatred and greed disguised as piety.

And through it all, God remained silent, not once acting to correct the behavior of His followers. Perhaps there had been miracles once . . . perhaps the Church had murdered everyone who could perform them. There was nothing like that now, only a few pale threads of magic to recall the wonder that had once filled the world. Now, everything was dark . . . just dark. A silent heaven, a bereft earth, nothing ahead but the promise of hell.

David believed in Persephone now—he claimed she didn't want worshippers, just warriors. Deven had once been offered a chance to walk the goddess's path, and he had turned from it . . . and now that he had massacred her priesthood, there was no reason to believe she would want him any more than God had, assuming she was even Divine at all. Eladra had done her best; she had rescued him from the Inquisition, acting on some prophetic impulse he had never understood, and turned him, believing he was somehow special. She had wrapped him in her compassion and gently tried to teach him there was more to the universe than emptiness and brimstone.

All she had done was sire her own murderer.

Pain flashed in his body, and he blinked, momentarily coming back to himself to find that he had, at some point, moved closer to the church and gone to his knees on the steps, bruising them on the concrete. The stained glass filled his eyes, and all the world began to fade away, reality becoming a distant and unwelcome dream.

God, you have forsaken us.

A shadow passed between him and the stained glass, barely registering to his mind at first.

Then he felt a hand on his shoulder, and with that touch an inrushing of energy like he'd never experienced before: Soft, and warm, with the taste of clear water and a touch of moonlight, it moved through him, infusing every cell with calm clarity. The heaviness in his heart lifted just a little, enough that he could think again, and suddenly he felt so weak he tumbled forward toward the ground.

Hands caught him, kept him upright, their grip as gentle as a lover's but strong, reassuring. He blinked over and over, trying to make sense of it—he hadn't sensed anyone approaching, and the presence before him felt . . . strange . . .

He lifted his head.

Deep violet eyes met his.

Deven stared, uncomprehending, unable to breathe until the stranger offered a slender, graceful hand and said, "Come, my Lord . . . there is little time before dawn." He had an accent, Deven noticed dazedly, something like Irish mated with Italian, and precise diction that meant English was something he had only recently mastered.

Still speechless, Deven took his hand and stood, slowly and shakily. He had no idea what to make of what he was looking at: It was to all appearances a young man with straight, silken auburn hair nearly down to his waist, strands of it braided back from a fair, breathtakingly beautiful face. There was a scrolling vine sort of tattoo beside his left eyebrow, done in what looked like henna. He wore a strange cloak-coat hybrid that dusted the ground and obscured the shape of his body, and a silver ring on his left middle finger that looked remarkably like those worn by the Priestesses of Elysium.

Finally Deven found his voice: "Who are you?"

A kind, even affectionate smile. "My name is Nicolanai Araceith," he said. "Most people call me Nico." He held up one hand and, in it, held an oval-shaped dark stone . . . labradorite. At the same time he released Deven's hand and tucked his long hair behind one ear.

One *pointed* ear.

"You called," Nico said. He reached up and brushed his fingertips along Deven's jawline, the touch eliciting a slight shiver. "I am your answer."

* * *

Nearly midnight, and Olivia's entire body was one live wire of tension as she and Jeremy crouched behind the Dumpster in the back alley of the Haven. She could see the side entrance—and the guards flanking it—and the security panel that would allow access only to one of the Elite standing there. He would have the key card, and his fingerprint and voice would be recorded in the system.

"Are you sure you don't want to split up once we're in?" Olivia whispered. "I get the artifact, you go for Hart?"

"No," Jeremy hissed back. "You need a lookout and I'll need backup just in case the Elite find us before we're done. It's better if we stick together. Don't worry—just do as I told you and it will be fine."

Olivia sighed. She had hoped he would change his mind. It would simplify things. If she alone went to break into the storage vault and retrieve the artifact, she could slip back out of the building and rendezvous with the others. Then Jeremy could deal with Hart as he saw fit, and if he made it or not, fine. Now she had to find a way to separate from him once they had the artifact. He wasn't going to let her out of his sight easily.

"On three," he whispered. "One . . . two . . . *three*."

They both broke cover and made for the entrance, Olivia to the right and Jeremy to the left. She heard him toss the small glass bottle full of explosive he'd been gingerly carrying in a foam case in his belt.

It exploded in the pile of trash he'd aimed for—not loudly enough to raise the whole building's alarm, but enough to surprise the guards and draw their attention. In that momentary lapse, Olivia slipped up behind one guard and rammed a stake through his back.

The second guard realized what was happening and tried to call for backup, but Jeremy was on him already, his sword flashing through the darkness to take the man's head.

"Hurry," Jeremy said.

Olivia patted her guard down. "Here it is." She pulled the key card from a special pocket in the shirt of his uniform.

Jeremy already had out one of the numerous gadgets Morningstar had given them and helped her drag the guard up to the security panel; Olivia pressed his hand against the sensor while Jeremy ran the card.

VOICE KEY REQUIRED.

Jeremy clicked the device, which held a perfect, clear recording of a dead man's voice: *"Elite Twelve, Robert Eckhart."*

VOICE KEY ACCEPTED.

She heard the bolt shoot back, and the door opened. Grinning at each other, they dropped the body in the shadows with its companion and entered the Haven.

Jeremy gestured to the left, and she followed him to the stairwell. They had eight minutes until the patrolling guards came across the bodies and the unguarded door; at that point the alarm would go up and the building would lock down, though there was still at least one exit point they could use. Both moving silently, they made their way down to the sub-basement where the artifact was located.

She took down the guard at the door and dragged him into the stairwell. The sub-basement was a labyrinth of corridors, but they had been over the plans a thousand times, and even without him leading she would have found the hallway in question easily.

They both stopped. Olivia peered down the hall, eyes picking out all the little round sensors that dotted the walls. It looked exactly like the plans had indicated.

She dug in one of her belt pouches and removed four small pieces of equipment: a band to go around each of her hands and a pad that attached to the toe of each boot. All four were flat on one side but had spikes protruding from the other.

She hadn't believed such little things could hold on to a concrete ceiling, but they had tried them out, and they worked almost miraculously. These Morningstar crazies had some amazing toys at their disposal.

Olivia quickly slid the pads onto her hands and feet and turned to Jeremy, who gave her a boost. She smacked her hands into the ceiling and then lifted her legs up to do the same with her feet.

She had bound her dreadlocks up close to her head so they wouldn't drag, and she wasn't wearing a coat, so she was able to press herself flat against the ceiling and make her way toward the vault door without anything hanging down to trip the uppermost sensors.

"Careful, Spidey," Jeremy said, smiling. "You do have the charge, right?"

"Got it," she answered with a grunt, focusing all her energy on pulling one limb at a time and moving toward the door. She was considerably lighter weight than Jeremy, otherwise it would have been him up there. It took longer than she had expected, but they had allotted enough time. Three minutes later she was in front of the vault door.

She freed one hand and reached into her belt pouch again, this time taking out a small charge. She slapped it onto the door just above the lock and flattened herself against the ceiling completely. "Go," she said.

Jeremy hit a button on his phone, and with a muffled *POP!* and a puff of black smoke, the vault door swung open an inch. Coughing, Olivia pulled it open until it was just shy of the first sensor, then swung her legs down, around the door, and in, letting go in time to drop her hard inside the vault.

She landed in a crouch and looked around—exactly as the plans said, it was a ten-by-ten room with steel shelving, most of the shelves lined with orderly rows of boxes, files, and various containers.

Unable to restrain her curiosity, Olivia peeked into a black case; it held bars of solid gold imprinted with an eagle. Her eyebrows shot up—one of those would be enough for a vampire to live on for fifty years or better.

Focus, Olivia. Ebony box, carved lid.

It was where she expected it to be, in the back right corner, third shelf from the top. The box was five inches square at most and had the same symbol carved into it as had been on the business card left for her and Jeremy in Australia. She cracked open the lid to make sure the artifact was in there; it was.

She grabbed it and stuck her head out the door. "Got it! Stand back!"

Jeremy ducked back around the corner, and Olivia reached into her pouch one more time, this time for a handful of what amounted to digital firecrackers.

She took a deep breath. *Here we go.*

Flicking her wrist, she flung the tiny charges out into the hallway, where they went off as they hit the walls and floor. After the *pop!* of the charge, there was a click and a swish, then the hard thud of stakes flying from either side of the hallway to hit the walls. The noise was deafening for about thirty seconds, until most of the sensors had been tripped; then there was a brief respite of silence.

Olivia bolted down the hallway as fast as she could move, barely avoiding the two stakes that hadn't been triggered already. She skidded to a halt next to Jeremy.

"Give it to me," Jeremy said. "Now."

She frowned. "I thought I was going to carry—"

"*Now*, Olivia."

She knew that tone. Damn it. She handed over the box reluctantly. Now she'd have to get it back from him before she made her escape.

"Thirty seconds," Jeremy said. "Ready for phase two?"

They had waited to set off the stakes in case finding the artifact took longer than anticipated; the idea was that the alarm would bring the Elite running, distracting as many as possible so Jeremy and Olivia could get to the second floor, where Hart was tonight, with fewer enemies to face between here and there.

"Let's go," she said.

They ran for the stairwell again as the earsplitting klaxon of the alarm began to go off all around them.

Olivia heard the rushing clomp of boots. "They're coming!"

Jeremy shouldered the next door open and dispatched the guard there; it was the first floor, one floor down from Hart, but if they stayed in the stairwell they'd be easy targets. There was a plan for that, too, though—Jeremy led the way to an empty room that had once been used for Elite training.

The building had been designed with a wet wall—essentially a crawl space that held all of the plumbing for easier access. According to the plans it was wide enough for a fairly thin vampire to fit; they'd measured carefully to make sure neither of them would get stuck.

Olivia drew her knife and began prying the panel off the wall. "Remember," she said, "the panel one floor up opens into a bathroom, so we should have a few seconds to climb out without being seen. From there we take the left-hand hallway—there will be Elite from there all the way to Hart."

"I'm ready for them," Jeremy said. "And I'm ready for you."

Olivia started to ask—

Pain struck her in the back, right between her kidneys. She cried out and fell, scrambling to reach the stake jutting out of her body. "What are you *doing*?" she cried. "Jeremy—"

He stood over her, his face hard and impassive. "I'm sorry, Liv," he said. "I wish it didn't have to be this way. Thank you for all you've done for me . . . I mean that. But I knew you'd turn on me, and I was right."

She tried to think through the pain—she had to get the stake out or she couldn't heal, but all she could think of was making it stop hurting. "Jeremy . . . please . . ."

"Give my regards to David Solomon," Jeremy said.

She heard the scrape of the wet wall panel being pulled off, and he climbed into the crawl space and was gone.

Moments later, the door of the training room flew open and guards poured in.

* * *

David lowered the scanner. "Everything's going according to plan," he said. "Are you ready?"

Miranda nodded. "Let's do it."

The door where Jeremy and Olivia had entered was still unguarded, and David's scanner worked on the same principle as the sensor network but didn't need actual sensors; it couldn't tell the difference between a vampire, a human, and an animal, but would tell them how many living things were between them and their goal.

They went through the door and shut it just seconds before the patrol was set to come around the corner; there was no time to waste, so they hit the ground running for the second floor.

Miranda glanced around her as she ran—Hart's Haven was purely industrial on the first floor, utilitarian like an office building; but as soon as they reached the second, all of that changed and it became far more like the Austin Haven. Fine furnishings, elegantly painted walls and trim . . . the major difference was the lack of natural light, as there were far fewer windows.

Over their heads an alarm was blaring, and Miranda reached out with her mind, sensing the emotional signatures of dozens of vampires above and below her. A great many of them were headed to the second floor, and nearly a dozen were already there.

"This way," David said, checking the scanner again. "Hart's quarters are down here."

Suddenly Miranda froze in her tracks and half-screamed. A dull but piercing pain bit into her back and a wave of dizziness hit her. "I'm shot!"

David stopped and looked at her in confusion. "No, you're not."

"I can feel it! A stake—wait—there's nothing there?"

"I promise you're fine."

She realized what it felt like—not as if she had been staked, but as if David or even Cora or Deven had been staked, a distant pain that faded quickly. "It must have been one of the others—something's wrong."

"It will have to wait. Come on."

But the few seconds' lapse had been enough. Thundering footsteps from either direction turned into Elite running out of the stairwell at one end of the hall and the double doors at the other end. When they saw Miranda and David they immediately drew their weapons.

Miranda grinned. "All right, now we're talking," she said, and drew Shadowflame.

David shook his head, but he, too, was smiling, drawing his own sword. "You really are something, beloved."

She took the left, he took the right, and the fight was on.

Twenty

The guards dragged her up the stairs by her arms, blood trailing behind her as it dripped down her back. Every stair caused pain to shoot through her body.

Once they had her on the second floor, they opened a side room without much furniture. One of the guards stripped off her weapons and her belt; another one punched her in the stomach. She groaned, and they released her arms, letting her drop in a heap on the ground, where they kicked the stake deeper into her back, then kicked her in the stomach again when she jerked back to try fruitlessly to pull the wooden shaft.

"Tell the boss," she heard one say. "She wasn't alone—find the other one."

Yes, find the other one . . . and kill him, if you don't mind.

Olivia forced herself up onto her hands and knees, daring to look around the room for her weapons—they were on a table, her sword on top of the pile. If she could just get it . . .

The first guard kicked her again, sending her back to the

ground on her side; she tasted blood, and knew—didn't fear, *knew*—she was about to die. Jeremy had seen through her, had known her for a traitor; the others were waiting outside to ambush him and take the artifact, but he probably knew that, too, and would get the drop on them. At the very least he would escape. Another blow made her vision gray out. One of the guards leaned down, grabbed the stake, and yanked it from her back as hard has he could; Olivia screamed, and they laughed.

"Let's see how many places we can stick this before you bleed out," he said with a nasty smile. "Twenty-four, get her up."

I'm going to die. This is it.

Well . . . fuck if I'm going to make it easy for them.

As two of the guards bent to seize her arms, she summoned all of her strength and threw herself as hard as she could into his legs. He made a mew of surprise and flew backward, hitting the ground hard.

She rolled onto her hands and knees again but this time didn't wait for them to reach her; she jumped up to her feet, pushing as much energy as she could spare into the wound in her back. They were going to kill her—there were six of them and one of her and she had no weapons—but she would die as a warrior.

The first one was so shocked he didn't even have time to counterattack; he went down with a crushed larynx, gasping and clawing. He'd be back, but not before she could get to her weapons. The next took a swing at her, and she blocked it, spun around, and kicked him in the side of the head so hard his neck broke. He'd be down for an hour or more.

The man she'd knocked over was back on his feet and had his blade drawn. The other three did the same, and she was surrounded again.

All she had to do was move the whole thing over ten feet and she could get her sword—

Olivia dove into the man she'd knocked over before; he was still a little dazed from the impact with the floor, and now he and the tiles met again, even more violently this time. She aimed low and ducked under the sword that sliced at her head, hit the ground in a roll, and came up only five feet from the table. They were on her already, and she lunged forward, hand outstretched toward her weapons—she was so close—

Something smacked into her hand, and her fingers closed around it.

The hilt of her sword.

There was no time to wonder. She spun around and met the next slash with the clang of metal on metal. They hadn't been expecting her to reach the table, and she took advantage of their astonishment—not to kill them all, but to do the smart thing and run like hell.

Miranda pulled Shadowflame free of the guard's torso in time to meet the swing of another sword. It was almost unfair, the way the Pair was decimating the Elite who kept arriving from other floors to save their employer; the Prime and Queen together were an unstoppable force.

She felt energy that seemed endless flowing into her—from where exactly she wasn't sure—fueling her body and her reflexes, making her movements so fast she could barely see them herself. It was child's play. She'd always been a good fighter, and she'd learned even more from Faith and David, but overnight her skills had heightened exponentially . . . and so had David's.

She'd never seen anything like it.

They had the first wave of Elite down in about ninety seconds. When the second group arrived, they were confronted with the bodies of their comrades thrown all around the hall, most disconnected from their heads, some run through with stakes.

Through the din, as the next group attacked, Miranda heard the clang of a blade that sounded heavier than the Elite's. She tried to see through the mob, but she was too short to get much of a vantage point.

There was no need. The unfamiliar warrior fought her way through the Elite until she reached where the Pair were slowly edging toward Hart's door.

The woman was mocha-skinned, hazel-eyed, and dread-locked. Her arms were tattooed all the way down to her fingers. She was bloody and had dark circles under her eyes—the kind they tended to get when fighting through a significant injury.

"What the hell are you doing in here?" the woman yelled. "You were supposed to wait at the rendezvous!"

"Olivia," David called loudly to be heard over the fight. "Nice to see you again."

"Likewise, my Lord."

Miranda shoved a guard back into one of his comrades and looked at Olivia. "You're hurt," she said. "Move back—let us handle this."

"Jeremy's already in there," Olivia returned. "He staked me—he was on to me the whole time."

Miranda and David exchanged a look. "Let's get moving," David said.

"Come on!" Miranda told Olivia. "Stay next to me!"

They fought their way to the double doors at the end of the hall, adjacent to another door that Miranda knew had once been the harem room. Miranda grabbed the door handle and turned it, but of course it was locked, so she took a step back and kicked it in.

The doors flew back so hard they slammed into the interior walls.

Miranda charged into the room . . . and paused.

Sixteen Elite armed with crossbows pointed at her stood surrounding Hart, who was sitting casually behind a large oak desk.

Jeremy lay on the floor in front of him, bleeding, breath coming in harsh gasps. He had wounds from at least four stakes in his back—and that was just what Miranda could see.

David and Olivia took care of the last of the Elite that had come down the hallway, then they sought refuge in the room with Miranda, taking a moment to shut the doors before finally seeing what they were facing. Olivia stayed behind them, just as Faith would have done.

Hart was examining a stack of papers and didn't even look up at first. "There you are," he said. "What kept you?"

"Killing off half your Elite," David said, stepping forward.

Hart made a noise of amusement. "Bodyguards are a dime a dozen. Getting Jeremy Hayes to walk back into my Haven, along with you two, well, that's impressive."

He pointed toward Jeremy, and one of the guards went over to the fallen Prime and pushed him down, grabbing a small black box from him. "Here it is, Sire," the guard said, and set it on the desk.

"Let me guess," Hart said to Jeremy. "You're working with Morningstar."

"You know about them?" Miranda asked.

A quiet snort. "I know a lot more than you think I do. I'm sure you've been told by now that Lydia wanted my help in getting her ridiculous Awakening under way, but I refused. The last thing in the world the Council needs is all of you banding together like some kind of deviant sports team. I knew, as does Morningstar, that if any one of you dies, Persephone's little fan club can never exist."

"That's why they've been trying to kill me," Miranda said. "And Cora last week."

At the mention of Cora, Hart's energy suddenly flared with poisonous black rage. "That little bitch," he snarled, almost to himself. He turned hate-filled eyes on Miranda. "If you hadn't given her the idea to run away, I could have kept her on a leash until she died, and that would have been the end of it—before it even began."

"You knew Cora was one of us," David said, nodding slowly. "You found out somehow what was going to happen, maybe even a long time ago, and tried to stop it by enslaving her—and then when you couldn't, you tried to kill us."

Hart's anger faded, and he shrugged. "Oh well. A month's delay in the grand scheme of things is nothing."

"But *how* did you know?" Miranda demanded. "Who told you?"

He just stared at her. "Do you think Queens are the only people who have visions of the future? That's a rather arrogant assumption, don't you think? Prophets come in all forms."

"So what form was yours in?" Miranda asked.

"No," Hart said. "You don't get to die knowing everything. That wouldn't be nearly as satisfying for me."

"You do realize that if you kill us, the Council will come down on you like a sledgehammer," David pointed out.

"I'm not afraid of the Council," Hart said. "In fact, the one really good thing about Morningstar's holy war is that they plan to destroy the Council, down to the last Prime. I'm hoping to hold out till the end, just so I can see the others go."

Olivia said softly, "I can distract them, draw their fire. You can run."

David smiled grimly. "Don't worry, Olivia. Just stay where you are."

"All right, enough chatter," Hart said. He glanced over at one of the Elite. "Fire at will."

Miranda braced herself.

Almost in perfect unison, the crossbows fired, sixteen stakes whistling through the air at the Prime, Queen, and somewhat-Second in the center of the room.

Miranda and David each lifted a hand. Miranda grounded herself hard, pulled power from that deep and endless connection, and *pushed* . . .

. . . sixteen stakes froze in midair.

She saw the fear register on the faces of the Elite about a split second before the stakes spun and flew back the way they had come.

She held on to eight of them as David took the rest, and shoved them with her mind, burying each one in a guard's chest as deep as it would go, the force breaking through the sternum, nearly passing through the back.

One by one, the guards fell to the ground.

Hart had the decency to look shocked.

Miranda smiled at him, letting her teeth slide out where he could see the new pair behind her canines.

All the color drained from Hart's face. It wasn't the fear, however, that surprised Miranda; it was the recognition.

"You," he gasped, pushing his chair back as if trying to put as much room between himself and these strange creatures as he could. "It's you . . . just like they said . . ."

Miranda clicked her mouth shut and frowned. He wasn't staring at her, or at David.

He was staring at Olivia.

Miranda moved over so the woman was in plain view, and the minute he could see her, Hart practically came unglued. He was on his feet, one hand reaching beneath the desk for something. As he stood, the fear in his face became anger, loathing, losing all pretense of rationality and sophistication. He looked rabid.

Hart held up his hand: a throwing stake. *"Stay the hell away from me! I swore you would never set foot here!"*

He threw the stake at Olivia, and it would have been an excellent shot, but before either Miranda or David could catch it, Olivia twisted to the side in a blur of motion and the stake hit only the wall behind them.

Hart opened his mouth to hurl more rage at them . . . but he never got the chance.

As soon as the stake hit the wall, Miranda reached into herself and Misted.

She re-formed not twenty feet from where she'd stood, and Shadowflame sang through the air, catching the light and turning it to silver fire.

A thin spray of blood erupted from Hart's throat, and a heartbeat later, his head fell from his neck, his Signet falling on its own, his head striking the floor with a sickening sound as his body collapsed at Miranda's feet.

She stood over the body, satisfaction burning through her, and lowered her sword.

"That was for Cora, you bastard," Miranda said.

"And for you," David added with a smile.

"And for Amelia Hayes," said Olivia quietly.

It took a moment for anyone to notice that Jeremy was gone.

Bleeding, half-dead . . . no, more like two-thirds dead . . . he made his way down the stairs, leaving a smear of blood on the wall and bloody handprints on the rail.

On the last flight, Jeremy closed his eyes, breathing out slowly. Hart was dead. As soon as he had seen the Pair with Olivia, he had known Hart would die. As soon as he'd seen Miranda draw her sword, relief had washed over him . . . He hadn't delivered the killing stroke himself, but it didn't matter. Hart was dead.

It was over.

Right on cue, the ground began to shake, the walls pitching and heaving. He held on to the rail until it passed, listening to the shouts of the Elite still alive throughout the building.

He was so glad that Olivia hadn't died . . . he wanted her to live . . . he had killed Faith, but Olivia should at least get to survive, even if she had betrayed him. He couldn't blame her. Olivia had seen him for what he really was . . . and now so did he.

So much blood. He looked down at his hands. Such a waste. His life, Amelia's, Melissa's, Faith's . . . and nothing he could do, no vengeance he could ever exact, would bring them back again. Olivia was right about that, too.

He wondered why they weren't chasing him. Perhaps the deal Olivia had made with Solomon still held. He'd read all of her texts to the Prime, all of her fears, the plans they'd made—Miranda and David would wait outside for Olivia to bring them the artifact, and they would take her into protective custody. If Jeremy died, he died, and if not, he could slink off under a rock somewhere.

Jeremy nearly laughed. Solomon had well and truly outmaneuvered him this time.

He stumbled the rest of the way down the stairs, peering out into the hall, but as he'd expected, the guards who weren't already dead had run for their lives after the earthquake. They all knew what it meant.

Jeremy forced himself to keep going until he reached the exterior door where they'd come in, turned the handle with slippery hands, and all but fell out into the night.

He knelt there panting for a few minutes. He needed blood. He could find it a few blocks from here, outside the Shadow District.

But then he heard footsteps, and his heart sank.

"Did you succeed?"

Jeremy lifted his head. He knew what he must look like, soaked in blood, but the uniformed human staring down at him didn't seem to notice; nor did his ten friends.

Reaching down to his belt, Jeremy flipped open the pouch and took out what they wanted.

The human took it, pleased. "Well done. And Hart is dead, correct?"

He nodded.

"Excellent. There's only one more thing we need, then."

The humans surrounded Jeremy, closing in on him, looming over him, and suddenly he understood.

Jeremy shut his eyes, sighing, and a blow to the back of his head sent him into the dark.

"Son of a bitch," David said.

Miranda looked over his shoulder. "What?"

He held up the black carved box. It was empty.

Miranda shook her head in disbelief. "So not only did Jeremy get away, he took the damn Widget with him. Well, this was a rousing success."

David made an impatient noise. "Worth every minute just to be rid of Hart. It would have been nice to at least know what the hell that thing was, though."

Over at the door, Olivia, who was following the blood trail Jeremy had left, piped up, "It was a piece of metal."

"A piece of metal?" David repeated. "Could you be more specific?"

"Jeremy showed me a drawing of it so that if Hart had taken it out of the box I'd still recognize it. A flat metal oval, perhaps two inches long. Antique gold. It had some kind of script etched into it that neither of us recognized, and at four points around its edge were little prongs."

Prime and Queen looked at each other. "Did it look like this?" Miranda asked, flipping her Signet over and holding it out toward Olivia.

She came over to the Queen and got a closer look. "Yes, almost exactly like that," she said. "The writing was completely different, though."

"What would humans want with another Stone of Awakening, or whatever it is?" Miranda wondered. "Do they have Signets to clip it to?"

"I'll start researching it as soon as we get home," David said.

Miranda returned her attention to Olivia, who was leaning on the desk heavily. She looked exhausted. "Are you okay?" Miranda asked.

"Jeremy staked me," Olivia reminded her. "The wound is closed, but it still hurts like a motherbear. I tried to come after him once I got away from the Elite who caught me, but I blundered right into the fray—thank God you two were already there, or . . . wait, why were you there? You were supposed to meet me outside! You wanted to snatch the box from Jeremy on his way out but without risking your lives, remember?"

Miranda gave David a look, sheepish. "Why don't you tell her, Mr. Mastermind," Miranda told her Prime.

"I knew Jeremy was on to you," David said. "We planned all along to come in; we just didn't tell you because he was spying on you, reading your texts. He might have changed his plan if he'd known ours."

"But why come in at all?"

"Because we knew Hart was on to Jeremy."

Olivia's mouth dropped open. "You've got to be kidding me."

"No. We have an ally with a spy in Hart's Elite. He got us

intelligence that Hart was aware of your intentions and planned to have his crossbow guards in place when you got here. If you had walked into this room without us, you would have been turned into a porcupine."

Miranda added, "With you and Jeremy setting off the alarms and distracting the Elite, it was the only chance we'd have to get the Widget and to rescue you from Jeremy. That depended on you—and us—all sticking to our supposed plans. We expected Jeremy to just ditch you, not really hurt you. I'm sorry about that."

Olivia shook her head, straightening. "I see now what Jeremy was talking about with you people."

"I want to know why Hart freaked out when he saw you," Miranda said. "I get him wanting to keep Cora enslaved, and I get him wanting to kill us if he didn't want the circle to form, but why would you scare him so badly? You're not even the one who killed him."

"He spoke of prophets," David mused. "He must have been told you were going to do something important. We'll need to learn more about that, too."

"Beats the hell out of me," Olivia said, bending down to where Hart's blood-spattered Signet had fallen and picking it up.

Before anyone could say a word, all three of them were struck utterly dumb, as Olivia lifted the Signet by its chain . . . and the stone blazed to life.

Twenty-one

"We're on in five minutes," David said. "Are you ready?"

Olivia's voice was tense. "Not really, no."

"You'll do fine," he reassured her. "They're already your allies—you have nothing to prove here."

She took a deep breath. "It's the rest of the Council I have to worry about."

"The ones worth knowing will pay state visits over the next few months. The rest you don't have to worry about for a decade. Relax, Prime."

"Easy for you to say," she said. "You're not a living violation of thousands of years of tradition!"

David smiled. "Yes, I am. They just don't know it yet."

"So am I, for the record," came another voice, as Deven signed on. "My advice is, if you want to get along with everyone, you should probably make other friends besides the deviants and the people who've shagged them."

He could practically hear Olivia's eyebrows shoot up. "Wait, who shagged whom?"

Now David laughed, and said, "Prime Olivia Daniels of

the Northeastern United States, virtually meet Prime Deven
O'Donnell of the Western United States."

"A pleasure," Deven said. "I look forward to watching
you make the Council squirm. Having done it myself, I can
assure you it's great fun."

David frowned listening to him—Deven sounded a little
subdued. "Everything all right over there?" he asked.

"Fine," Deven replied shortly. "Olivia, I'm assuming
before David left New York he hooked you up with all of his
favorite software."

"Yes, Sire," Olivia said. "He was quite thorough."

"None of that 'Sire' nonsense, Olivia. You're one of us
now. We hardly stand on ceremony."

"Sorry, S—um, Deven," she said hesitantly. "This is all
very weird to me."

"Everyone says that," Deven told her. "By the fifth year it
will all be routine. If you need any help, any at all, you need
only ask."

"David has already been very good to me," she said. "I
haven't really thanked him."

"No need . . . my Lady? Hmm . . . we're going to have to
figure out your terms of address. We've always considered
Consorts based on their relationship to Primes, and with one
exception Consorts have always been women—we had a
devil of a time deciding what to call Jonathan. A female
Prime . . . you're something new, in more ways than one."

"Lucky me."

"On the plus side," Jacob said, his icon appearing on the
screen, "the two Primes most likely to raise a fuss about it
are dead now."

"Prime Jacob Janousek of Eastern Europe, meet Prime
Olivia Daniels of the Northeastern United States."

"Welcome aboard," Jacob said, a smile in his voice.

"Have you kept any of Hart's Elite?" Deven asked Olivia.
"I can't imagine many stayed behind."

"Four," Olivia said. "Luckily organizing the Elite is one
thing I have plenty of experience at. With the population
density here I don't think it will take long to fill the ranks,

especially if what I'm hearing about Hart's standing with his people is true."

David smiled; she was already sounding like a Prime. She was going to be fine . . . he would make sure of it. "Let's get started, shall we? First up, I believe Jacob has a report on the situation in Australia . . ."

As the chat program shut down, Deven finally let himself breathe, putting his forehead in his hands, eyes closed.

"I thought you would stay on with David after and tell him what's going on," Jonathan said from where he sat on the bed. He was still in his pajamas and needed a shave, but he had to look a hundred times better than Deven did at the moment.

"Now isn't the time," Deven murmured without looking up. "We needed to present a calm and united front for Olivia. She's under enough stress without thinking one of her new allies is going batshit insane."

Jonathan chuckled; that was a phrase Miranda often used, especially when describing herself as a human. But the concern was still in his voice as he said, "Maybe you should go back to bed, love. You still look exhausted."

"I *am* exhausted."

"Even after sleeping for fourteen hours straight? You practically passed out and fell on the bed without even saying a word to me. I had to undress you and tuck you in, and then you didn't so much as twitch all day."

Deven turned sideways in his chair and leaned his head on the back. "I don't remember. I don't even remember how I got home."

"All I know is, I could feel how upset you were . . . and then it was like you were having some sort of breakdown. Then out of nowhere you went from breaking down to just sleepy, and a little while later you were home. What's the last thing you remember?"

He shut his eyes again and tried to think. "I was up on the Tower Bridge . . . I started to walk home . . . I remember . . .

I remember seeing St. Anthony's, but . . . after that everything fades away."

Jonathan sounded reluctant to ask, but did anyway: "Were you drinking?"

"No. That's just it—if I had been, it would make sense."

"Had you taken anything else? You do keep a wide variety of substances around the house."

"Nothing, Jonathan," he said, exasperated. "I swear. Besides, you can tell when I'm on something—did it feel like anything I've done before?"

Jonathan shook his head.

Deven felt an extremely uncharacteristic urge to curl up in a ball and weep, but resisted . . . barely. "Then I'm going crazy, aren't I," he said. "Just as I thought."

He knew the answer to that. Whatever divine plans David had gotten them into, there was one thing none of them could escape whether mortal or not: time.

Deven, it appeared, was running out. He should have had another fifty years or so, but given the life he'd had, it made sense that he would start to fall apart earlier. It was only a matter of time before he shut down completely—either that or he would pass into a psychotic state and have to be put down like a rabid animal.

"I'm sorry," he said softly. "I wish I knew a way to unbind us so you wouldn't be chained to me for this. You've already dealt with enough because of me."

He felt a hand on his head, moving around to his face, and looked up; Jonathan's eyes were bright, anguished. "Do you really think I would want to live? And would you make me, after what Miranda went through?"

"I just want it over," Deven said. His own eyes were burning, and before he could stop it, a tear ran down his face, onto Jonathan's hand. "If I asked, would you—"

His phone chimed; he didn't even have to look to know it was one of the Elite on Haven duty. "Yes?" he asked, wiping his eyes and sniffing.

"Sire, there's a . . . person . . . here to see you."

Deven and Jonathan exchanged a quizzical look. "Can you be a little more specific, Elite Twelve?"

"I think you'd better see for yourself."

"All right . . . I'm on my way." Deven shook his head, completely nonplussed. "What the hell was that about?"

Jonathan frowned. "We should both go. Give me two minutes to put clothes on."

Moments later they left the suite, headed for the front doors of the Haven. The novelty of the situation momentarily banished the despair from Deven's mind, and about a dozen possible scenarios occurred to him, each one less likely than the last. Very few people in the Shadow World would know how to find the Haven, and even fewer would have the temerity to just show up on the doorstep unannounced.

Elite 12 was waiting for them near the doors. "I showed him into the reception room just over here, my Lords. He's unarmed, as far as I can tell."

"As far as you can tell?" Jonathan asked. "What does that mean?"

Deven reached the door first and pushed it open, readying a firm and commanding interrogation as to what exactly was . . .

He froze with a gasp. A half-step after and at his side, Jonathan halted as well.

"Good evening," came that gentle, accented voice, sending Deven's heart into orbit as suddenly, between one breath and the next, he remembered . . . *everything.*

Rising from a chair, his dark eyes glinting with humor at their expressions, the Elf smiled.

There were certain advantages to being the Signet's pet Witch.

Stella settled happily in the reserved box that would give her a perfect, unobstructed view of the stage; Lark, next to her, was already agog at the first-class treatment they'd received, starting with the limo that had picked them up at

Stella's apartment, and continuing with the concierge who showed them past the people waiting in line around the block and into the posh theater, where they were offered wine, fruit, and adorable tiny pastries while they waited for their seats.

"Do you think we warded your place enough?" Lark asked as they got situated. "You could go back to the Haven, you know—they said any time."

"I don't think those Morningstar people are after me," Stella told her for the tenth time, but she kept any trace of impatience out of her voice. In fact, hearing her friend's worry for her made Stella want to hug her around the middle until she squeaked. "I've got my com, and an emergency signal for my phone, and a patrol team diverted to my neighborhood for the next month to be sure, but I think they've realized they have to change tactics—Miranda and David are just too strong for them."

"But they can still destroy the circle until they find their last member, right?"

"Yeah. But I don't think it's going to be that easy. From what I hear, this Olivia is proving herself to be one tough-ass Prime."

"That is so cool, a girl Prime," Lark said. "Feminism finally hits the vampire world."

The houselights dimmed, announcing it was time for everyone else in the theater to be seated; the Travis Auditorium was part of the university's performing arts complex, and it had seating for about two thousand people. Miranda had chosen it because it was fairly small and had a more intimate feel than a lot of her other options. She wasn't quite ready to get back on a big public stage like the one she'd been shot on only months ago.

A large, hairy guy in a suit came out on stage, and Stella knew immediately who it was—Grizzly Behr, a local music legend, producer of Miranda's first album and head of the Austin Live Music Association. He came out into the spotlight and gave an introduction to tonight's performer, calling her "luminous," "a genuine phenomenon," and "a true survivor."

He had no idea how true that was. Stella shook her head in amazement.

She looked across at the other luxury box and saw a familiar profile: David, sitting alone with two Elite guards standing at the door, his eyes on the stage.

Stella spared a moment of Sight—no one would notice up here—and Looked at him, curious. She'd been right; the transformation that had begun when he came back into his body was complete now, and he was once again part of a whole, energy flowing steadily from him to his Queen and back again. Only now, Stella could also See the other connections—the one to Deven that had formed long ago, and other more tenuous bonds that would connect him to all the others in Persephone's circle of Signets, her chosen children, led by the Thirdborn.

Stella could feel David's love for Miranda reverberating along the bond, and hers for him—they had grown stronger in the broken places, and now that love was like a force of nature all its own. Stella was pretty sure that anyone who tried to Bondbreak them now would get one hell of a surprise.

Apparently what didn't kill them made them damn near invincible.

Behr finished his accolades, saying, "Returning to the stage, back and better than ever, UT Performing Arts presents . . . Miranda Grey!"

Deafening applause followed him off the stage and continued as the curtain lifted.

Stella found herself beaming.

The spotlights fixed and focused on the black-clad, red-haired woman in the center of the stage. Her bright green eyes sparkled with anticipatory mischief, and she stepped forward, slinging her guitar strap over her shoulder, walking up to the mic.

The audience was on its feet. So were Stella and Lark. The love of all those people, their gratitude at having Miranda restored to them, filled the auditorium to bursting, and Miranda drank it all in, grinning from ear to ear.

She struck the first chord, and as her voice began to fill

the theater, weaving its own dark magic in with the lyrics and bringing the entire audience under her thrall, she took in their love and returned it as joy.

"Up here," he said. "One more step."

Miranda peered over the way-too-close edge, and just what she saw from that height was dizzying. "I don't know," she replied. "Are you sure you want me up here? This is your Thoughtful Spot."

He smiled. "I doubt you'll make a habit of it, beloved. But I wanted you to see. Please."

She swallowed hard, trying to push down her terror of heights; this meant so much to him, and she had to admit she was curious about this place where he came to do his brooding. She had been genuinely surprised when he asked her to come with him tonight.

"Okay," she said with a nod.

David offered her his hand. The wall where he was standing was about three feet off the ground, without a step up. She felt his arm muscles engage as he lifted her up off the roof and onto the wall at his side.

"Go on," he murmured in her ear, barely loud enough over the wind. "Take a look."

Miranda took a shaky breath; David's arm moved around her waist, the solidity of his body next to hers comforting. "I won't let you fall, beloved," he told her, kissing the side of her neck. "Ever."

She opened her eyes and gasped.

All of Austin lay before them, from the skyscrapers off Congress Avenue leading up to the Capitol, to the building she recognized as the Travis Auditorium. The city was lit up in golden streetlight and neon red; she could see the marquee of the Paramount Theater.

From this height, everything had order and logic to it; the traffic lights moved the cars along in a pulse like blood through the city's veins, and humans came and went, small enough to be dolls.

This was their city. They had suffered to keep it safe, and who knew where the future would lead, but Miranda couldn't imagine calling any other place home.

"It's beautiful," she said. "Thank you for showing me."

David turned her slowly toward him, careful to keep her feet on solid concrete. A gust of wind caught her hair, unfurling it off to the side like a scarlet cape. David wrapped both sides of his coat around her to keep her warm. She smiled up at him, her heart aching—but this time not with loss or grief, only with happiness.

His hands slid around her hips, drawing her close, and as their lips met, Miranda knew, from some place deep within her that rang with absolute authority, that nothing, mortal or immortal, god or human or vampire, would ever come between them again.

Epilogue

Forgive me. Forgive me.

Jeremy knew he was going to die, and he was grateful.

He woke in chains, so weak he could barely lift his head. The burning pain in his wrists and the sawdust coating his insides told him they had drained his blood . . . nearly all of it. He hung from a wall, shackled, vision fading from color to gray and back again.

Finally he managed to make some sense out of what he was seeing: a stone chamber with an altar facing him. On the altar was a large, leather-bound book with yellowed pages, lying open. There was also a bowl of dark liquid . . . he knew it was his blood.

The sound of a door opening . . . hooded, cloaked figures filed into the room. He couldn't think straight enough to count them. They formed a circle around the altar, but there was enough of a gap that he could see what they were doing.

One figure stepped out before the others and laid something on the altar.

Jeremy's entire body went cold.

His Signet.

Oh God.

He had known they would kill him. He hadn't known they were going to do this.

He deserved to die—he knew that. But whatever they had planned would be far worse than his continued existence.

The lead figure began a chant, which the others took up in call-and-response. He couldn't understand it; the language was unfamiliar. Their voices were hollow, like a cold wind through reeds. Fear crawled up his spine.

Finally, the leader said in English, "We have come tonight to complete the Ritual of the Quickening, in the name of our Lord."

The others answered in unison, "So let his will be done."

The leader reached into his cloak and pulled out a heavy gold chain he wore around his neck . . . on which hung an amulet set with a dark stone. One of the others brought forward a wooden plate . . . holding the artifact stolen from Hart.

The leader picked up the artifact, flipped over his amulet, and snapped one onto the other decisively.

Then he returned to the altar and lifted up the bowl of blood, saying, "Let the sacrifice we make tonight charge this blood, drawn from the veins of the enemy of the Holy, that it may grant our warriors the strength and speed to hunt them down to the last and restore this earth to righteousness."

The stone in the amulet began to glow.

Suddenly, Jeremy panicked—something about what he was seeing overwhelmed what little conscious mind he had, and all he was left with was an atavistic terror. He struggled in his chains, fighting to get free, but it was no use; he was too weak.

I have to warn them . . . they have to know . . .

It's too late.

As he stared at the Signet on the altar, the full weight of his failure fell around his shoulders. He knew what they were about to do, and knew, from watching his own victim, how much it was going to hurt. But on the far side of that torment would be an end at last. He wouldn't have to see the damage he'd caused with his last moments. He wouldn't have to know who else would die because of him.

One of the men brought their leader another object.

A hammer.

Jeremy closed his eyes.

The last thing he heard before hell descended upon him was the sound of a shattering stone.

THE FINAL BOOK IN THE
NEW YORK TIMES BESTSELLING SERIES FROM

CHARLAINE HARRIS

DEAD EVER AFTER
A Sookie Stackhouse Novel

Sookie finds it easy to turn down the request of former barmaid Arlene when she wants her job back at Merlotte's. After all, Arlene tried to have Sookie killed. But her relationship with Eric Northman is not so clear-cut. He and his vampires are keeping their distance…and a cold silence. And when Sookie learns the reason why, she is devastated.

Then a shocking murder rocks Bon Temps, and Sookie is arrested for the crime.

But the evidence against Sookie is weak, and she makes bail. Investigating the killing, she'll learn that what passes for truth in Bon Temps is only a convenient lie. What passes for justice is more spilled blood. And what passes for love is never enough....

Available May 2013!

charlaineharris.com
facebook.com/CharlaineHarris
facebook.com/ProjectParanormalBooks
penguin.com

M1218T1112